WHAT WA... ... ...

"LA native Joseph Schneider shows off his roots once again, leading the reader and quirky detective Tully Jarsdel on a richly detailed, highly nuanced mystery through the City of Angels."

—Joseph Reid, author of the Amazon Charts
bestselling Seth Walker series

"*What Waits for You* is irresistible. I read it in a blur, and it stuck to me like a shadow when I was finished. Joseph Schneider should be on everyone's radar."

—Jonathan Moore, Edgar Award and Hammett Prize finalist

"Schneider's riveting prose, incredibly original protagonist Tully Jarsdel, and brilliant evocation of LA add up to a novel you won't be able to put down. A read that will get under your skin and stay there for a while. I can't wait for the next book!"

—Luca Veste, author of *The Bone Keeper*

"Schneider's pulse-quickening prose and facility at evoking menace elevate this well above many similarly themed books."

—*Publishers Weekly*

ONE DAY YOU'LL BURN

"An auspicious and engaging debut. Mr. Schneider conjures up an original protagonist in LAPD Homicide Detective Tully Jarsdel—and prestidigitates a thoroughly thrilling narrative ride through the mean streets and glittering boulevards of Los Angeles. The reader looks forward to many more Jarsdel mysteries in the coming years."

—Eric Overmyer, executive producer of *Bosch*

"A brilliant first novel. Joseph Schneider's contemporary writing evokes some of Hollywood's most classic crime stories, from *Chinatown* to *LA Confidential*."

—Dick Wolf, creator of *Law & Order*

"*One Day You'll Burn* is much more than just an intriguing Hollywood mystery. It's a captivating character study of a unique academic/historian turned police detective who can't keep his deep intelligence from bubbling out—often to his own embarrassment and the reader's delight. Joseph Schneider has created a very appealing character whom readers will definitely want to see more of."

—Kenneth Johnson, bestselling author of *The Man of Legends*

"Schneider redefines the detective genre while giving us a history lesson of Hollywood, the town of dreams it was, and the nightmare it has become."

—Jim Hayman, executive producing director of *Judging Amy*

"Tully Jarsdel joins the gumshoe greats in this whip-smart riff on sunbaked LA noir."

—David Stenn, TV writer and producer

Also by Joseph Schneider
One Day You'll Burn
What Waits for You

THE
DARKEST
GAME

A NOVEL

JOSEPH
SCHNEIDER

Poisoned Pen
PRESS

Copyright © 2022 by Joseph Schneider
Cover and internal design © 2022 by Sourcebooks
Cover design by Pete Garceau
Cover images © laddio1234/Getty Images

Sourcebooks, Poisoned Pen Press, and the colophon are registered trademarks of Sourcebooks.

Published by Poisoned Pen Press, an imprint of Sourcebooks
P.O. Box 4410, Naperville, Illinois 60567-4410
(630) 961-3900
sourcebooks.com

Library of Congress Cataloging-in-Publication Data

Names: Schneider, Joseph, author.
Title: The darkest game / Joseph Schneider.
Description: Naperville : Poisoned Pen Press, [2022] | Series: An LAPD
   Detective Tully Jarsdel mysteries ; book 3
Identifiers: LCCN 2021037063 (print) | LCCN 2021037064 (ebook) | (trade paperback) | (epub)
Subjects: GSAFD: Mystery fiction.
Classification: LCC PS3619.C446868 D37 2022 (print) | LCC PS3619.C446868
   (ebook) | DDC 813/.6--dc23
LC record available at https://lccn.loc.gov/2021037063
LC ebook record available at https://lccn.loc.gov/2021037064

Printed and bound in the United States of America.
KP 10 9 8 7 6 5 4 3 2 1

For Tenzel and Ahalya. May I live to see the world promised in your smiles.

PART I

A DEATH IN HOLLYWOOD

PROLOGUE

The first bullet would've been enough.

Instead, the hammer falls again, striking the firing pin against the primer of the next .45 ACP cartridge. The jacketed hollow-point bullet rockets down the barrel, topping a thousand feet per second upon its exit. It's followed by another, and another.

The first bullet plows through the man's chest, reducing eons of highly evolved cardiac structures to a smear on the wall. The next two shots take him in the nose and forehead. The fourth and final round would've landed only a couple millimeters to the left, just above the ear, but by then there's no flesh to meet it. The bullet sails through blood-misted air and buries itself in the brickwork fireplace.

Night is always busy in Hollywood, especially in the hills. From Griffith Park to Laurel and Benedict Canyons, the bobcat, coyote, and gray fox prowl and hunt. Insects thrum, owls pluck mice from clumps of thistle and sumac, and possums big as border terriers trundle across the roads, eyes flashing emerald in the wash of headlights.

Gunfire in the hills stops the action, but not for long. The creatures fall silent, predator and prey alike pausing in their deadly game. A gunshot isn't a growl or a snarl or a hiss, but its sheer power commands respect.

Sound travels strangely in the hills, coming from everywhere and nowhere at once, and the night fauna await more data—a scent trail, some movement, a pressure wave stirring an antenna or whisker. But their senses come up blank, and in collective, silent agreement, they resume their business.

For the dark is precious, not to be wasted, and soon the hated sun will roll over the land again.

1

Y ou'll starve."

Detective Tully Jarsdel looked up. "Say again?"

"I said you'll starve." Shana—that was the name on her tag—pointed to Jarsdel's plate, where a cold omelet glistened in the diner's fluorescents.

"Yeah." He shrugged. "Guess I'm not hungry as I thought I was."

"Can I get you something else?"

"Kind of you, no. Just the check."

"You're not married, are you?" It was more an accusation than a question.

Jarsdel reached for his wallet. "Am I in the married-only section?"

"You're so *thin*," said Shana. "Single guys are either too fat or too thin. Mostly too fat, I guess, come to think of it. But you know what I mean. You got that single-guy kinda vibe, like you got no one around to help pick out your clothes. And no ring, obviously. How old're you?"

Jarsdel glanced around. The place was full, being one of the few decent sit-down restaurants in walking distance from the court-house. He looked back at Shana. "I'm flattered, but—"

"Ha. No, not for me. I got a daughter. Twenty-six. She'd like you. Likes cops. And skinny guys."

"Ah." Jarsdel took a twenty out of his billfold and tucked it under his water glass.

"Forget it."

"No, I want to pay."

"You didn't eat anything. And you're a cop. Maybe next time one of those homeless guys comes in and won't leave, you guys'll get here a little faster."

Jarsdel stood and headed for the door. "Thanks again."

"So that's a no on my daughter, huh?"

Jarsdel hadn't worked a fresh homicide in nearly a month, when a woman had run over her boyfriend after he'd stormed out of her car during an argument. He'd been big, over two hundred pounds, but there'd been enough ground clearance for him to go under the bumper. He might've survived, but he snagged on the suspension, painting Melrose for sixty yards before popping out from under the left rear tire. It had been an easy case, a slam-dunk second-degree charge with enough physical evidence to convict a hundred times over. Wisely, the accused had gone for a plea deal.

Crime stats were down. A good thing, a great thing. But that meant sifting through the division's back catalogue of unclaimed, unidentified corpses. Dead in a corner, dead in a bathroom stall, dead in a gutter. Dead in tall grass, in a railway yard, in a dry swimming pool. And so many of them. Piles upon piles of exanimate flesh.

These cold cases—or "open unsolved," as command preferred—were casualties of Hollywood Homicide's initial closure in the early 2000s, chilling as they were traded off to Wilshire or Olympic. As new bodies stacked up, momentum on the cases had first slowed, then stopped altogether.

It probably would've stayed that way if not for the unexpected revival of the Hollywood Homicide table. The brainchild of Deputy Chief Cynthia Comsky, HH2 would pair seasoned homicide detectives with recruits fast-tracked from patrol. With only two positions available, selection was highly competitive. A successful candidate would have to possess both high fluid and crystallized intelligence and demonstrate a diverse range of skills. These included critical thinking, cross-cultural communication, emotional competence, and spatial reasoning.

Out of nearly five hundred applicants, Comsky's review board had conducted fifty interviews. Half of these went on to undergo a battery of aptitude tests, after which ten were polygraphed and given psychiatric evaluations. Following a final round of interviews, the board had chosen Kay Barnhardt, a former clinical psychologist, and Marcus Tullius Jarsdel, who'd cut out halfway through a PhD in ancient history to become a cop.

The "professor detective," the *Times* had called him. It wasn't a compliment. There was the initial sense that HH2 was a gimmick, that the force was being given an intellectual façade to make it more palatable to the Hollywood left. But when HH2 began clearing cases at twenty percentage points above the national average, the mockery dried up.

Jarsdel liked the cold cases. The emotional distance afforded by time allowed him to focus purely on the details. They were contained, in a sense. Black boxes to be analyzed and modeled. Of the ones they were currently working, three interested him the most.

First on the list was Kyle Antoine, who'd died in a house fire—his own arsonous creation—while trying to commit insurance fraud. He'd almost certainly had help from his brother Mitch, who'd been caught on security footage the previous day filling a gas can. No crime there, but he'd driven up to the pump in a working automobile, hadn't put a single drop in the car's tank, and didn't own any gasoline-powered equipment. As for his alibi the night of the fire, Mitch Antoine had married himself to a rickety, overly elaborate story involving a date at Moonlight Rollerway in Glendale, dinner at the Galleria's food court, and caring for his girlfriend's sick chinchilla. Antoine claimed he'd attended to the animal through to the early hours of the next morning and that the poor creature "couldn't keep nothin' down, not even water." It was a phrase he'd repeated so often in his interview that it had become a Hollywood Homicide catchphrase. Morales even printed it on a T-shirt, which he'd given to Jarsdel for his birthday.

Jarsdel sensed Antoine would buckle if further pressed—not least because chinchillas and other rodents are incapable of throwing up, a critical component of the alibi. Jarsdel looked forward to pressing him. A manslaughter charge would stick nicely, along with felony conspiracy.

Next up was Hal Pickett, a seventy-eight-year-old retired worker's comp attorney who'd been found dead by his nephew—a drifter who worked odd jobs and boasted a rich criminal history. The cause of death had been loss of blood due to a deep scalp laceration. Pickett had struck his head on the lip of his clawfoot bathtub after apparently slipping on a bar of soap. He'd been at risk for deep vein thrombosis, and his doctor had put him on a daily 5 mg prophylactic dose of the blood thinner Coumadin. Four times that amount was found in his system at autopsy, and considering the size of the pool of blood at the scene, the medical examiner believed Pickett had been fed increasingly large doses of the drug for weeks. That was certainly interesting, but for Jarsdel the most compelling evidence was the soap—an Ivory knockoff called "Serene." It was sold exclusively at 99 Cents Only stores, where Pickett's nephew liked to shop. There was also no other bar soap in the house, no soap dishes in the bathroom, and no soap residue in the tub. And none, not the merest trace, on the soles of Pickett's feet.

Finally there was Sarah Hoover, the one they called the Lady in Pink—a junkie in salmon-hued rayon pajamas who'd been found aspirated on her own vomit in a Los Feliz apartment. It would've been written off as just another OD, but the now-retired detective who'd originally worked the case determined that the Lady in Pink was left-handed. Despite this, she'd injected the hot dose into her left arm. Junkies didn't usually switch to their subdominant hands—enough trouble keeping the needles steady as it was—but the biggest red flag was that Hoover never used the veins in her arms at all. She was self-conscious about track marks and shot up in the webbing between her toes. It was classic JDLR—cop shorthand for *just doesn't look right.*

But who'd have wanted to kill her, and why? She didn't have money, kept to herself, had no known enemies. Her hobby was fostering injured animals until they could be released back into the wild. And yet someone had entered her living room, administered the lethal dose without incurring a struggle, and left behind not a single piece of physical evidence. Jarsdel had asked Morales his opinion on who might've done it. "Ninjas," his partner replied, giving a grave shake of his head.

What brought Jarsdel to downtown LA on that muggy June morning was the last of his fresh homicides to go to trial and the most important to him personally.

Fiona Rose Huntley. The eight-month-old had been teething, something her nanny would've handled by giving her a frozen strawberry to gnaw on, but she'd left for the day and returned the child to the care of her parents. The young professionals quickly tired of the crying, strapping the baby in her stroller and rolling her out onto the back patio—just a cotton onesie between her twenty-pound body and the coldest night of the year. Mom and Dad then put away three bottles of red wine, had sex, passed out, and woke sometime late the following morning.

Fiona Rose Huntley. That name—he'd heard it and read it and spoken it so many times. And always like that too. Her whole name, never just Fiona. Wavy blond hair, almost white, and in the photographs, her eyes sparkled with something akin to wisdom, like she had all the secrets of the universe ready to tell, needing only the words to express them. Jarsdel had never seen those eyes in life. By the time he looked on them in Ipgreve's autopsy suite, the once vibrant green irises were black with the tache noire of death.

Criminal neglect, child endangerment, involuntary

manslaughter. Whether the parents were responsible wasn't up for debate, but they'd decided to go to trial, angling for a kind of diminished capacity defense without actually saying those forbidden words. The jury hadn't bought it, finding Brett and Liz Huntley guilty on all three counts. Today, the Honorable Judge Kleinfeld would hand down his sentence.

Jarsdel crossed Hill Street and climbed the steps of the Stanley Mosk Courthouse. Morales waited for him at the top, leaning against the railing and gripping a coffee thermos stenciled with *Los Angeles County Department of Medical Examiner-Coroner*. Below this, in lettering faded by countless trips through the dishwasher, was its unofficial motto: "Our day begins when your day ends." His partner wore a gray suit, shiny at the seat and elbows, a paisley tie, and scuffed wingtips. Instead of keeping his gun on his hip like most of the detectives, Morales stored his in a custom leather shoulder holster.

He's put on weight, Jarsdel thought, noticing the way the gun now bulged beneath the man's jacket. Morales had always been heavy, and the cold cases were depriving him of even the meager exercise offered by field interviews.

"You try the omelet?"

Jarsdel nodded. "Delicious."

"Told ya. Best in downtown." He checked his watch. "Got ten minutes. Wanna head in?"

The detectives showed their badges to the deputies working the metal detector and were waved inside. The elevator was probably the slowest in the city, but Jarsdel called it anyway. His partner had once taken a handful of buckshot to the knees and wouldn't have been able to make the three-story climb.

"Talked to Mannone just before you got here," said Morales as they ascended.

"What he say? She decide she's gonna speak?"

"He thinks so, yeah."

Lou Mannone was the DDA assigned to the trial. He was in his late seventies, a jocular, broad-shouldered man who spoke with a sharp Chicago accent, and he'd come out of retirement solely to try the Huntley case. And now it seemed he'd finally been able to convince the dead toddler's maternal grandmother to make a victim impact statement.

The elevator doors shuddered open, and the two men headed down the hallway toward Room 417 of Department 41. They joined the spectators as they filed into the courtroom and took seats as close to the front of the gallery as possible. Morales seized an armrest in each hand and carefully lowered his bulk into the chair, gaze locked on the defense table. The detectives were at enough of an angle that they could see the Huntleys' profiles as they conferred with their attorneys. Brett's daytime-TV looks were at last showing the wear of the trial and its guilty verdict, and he gave tight little nods as his lawyer spoke. Liz, whose shoulder-length auburn hair had the volume and bounce of a salon treatment, could just as easily have been waiting for a table at the Palm. Perhaps sensing his attention, she looked over at Morales. Her expression was blank for a slow five count before blossoming into a smile. It then fell away as suddenly as it had appeared, and she turned back to her lawyer.

"Nice," said Morales. "Dead kid, right? But what's important is mad-doggin' me, white-collar style. Fuckin' reptiles."

"Psych eval said they were competent," said Jarsdel.

"Nothin' to do with it. Can be a competent reptile. I bet we watch 'em eat, we'd see their jaws unhinge so they could swallow those same little frozen mice my kid feeds his ball python. I tell you my new angle on capital punishment?"

"Uh-huh."

"I did?" Morales squinted at him. "No, I didn't. I woulda remembered."

Jarsdel sighed. "Okay, what's your new theory?"

"It's a reptiles-only policy. Someone gets convicted of murder, they only get sent to the wrong side of the grass if they get one of those brain scans shows they got no conscience."

"Interesting."

"I saw they can do that. Parts of the brain don't light up if you're a sociopath. Proven scientifically now, not just with those personality tests and shit. So it's only those people who actually get the death penalty. That's the big liberal concern, right? Wrongful convictions? With my system, it don't matter, because even if we make a mistake and one of those reptiles turns out to be innocent, everybody still wins. Get rid of someone who was only gonna bring misery to the world one way or another. No appeals either. Just *bang*—over and done."

"I see," said Jarsdel. "So assuming there's no danger of false positives with this brain scan you mention, you're saying that socio-paths shouldn't get the same rights to due process as everyone else?"

"Yeah, 'cause they're not full humans. Not full people. Missing that essential bit of hardware. Gotta have a conscience to call yourself a person."

"You're right, Oscar. Airtight reasoning."

"Yeah, fuck off."

"No, it's beautiful. Can't conceive a single reason such a system wouldn't work. Write your congressman."

The door to the judge's chambers opened, and Kleinfeld entered, his robes shapeless on his thin figure and more closely resembling a barber cape.

The bailiff announced his arrival with a flat, rapid-fire delivery. "Remain seated, come to order—Los Angeles Superior Court, Department 41 is now in session. Honorable Judge Barney Kleinfeld presiding."

"Good morning," said the judge, taking his place behind the bench. He adjusted his glasses and scrutinized the paperwork before him. He looked up. "Okay, we'll try that again. Good morning."

"Good morning," came the scattered response.

"Thank you. We're going on the record with People v. Brett Huntley and Elizabeth Huntley, B-CR-874459." He gestured toward the defense table. "Go ahead."

One of the two attorneys, a bearded young man in a navy-blue suit, got to his feet. "Thank you, Your Honor."

"You can stay seated."

The man sat back down. "Sorry, Your—"

"Keep it moving, Mr. Saroyan."

"Yes, Your Honor. Uh, Michael Saroyan for Brett Huntley."

"Jennifer Wachen for Elizabeth Huntley," said the other attorney.

There was a long pause, and Kleinfeld frowned at the prosecutors, who were in the midst of a whispered exchange. "Come on, folks, stay with us."

"Sorry, Your Honor. Lou Mannone for the people."

"Pamela McWilliams for the people."

"All right, everyone," said Kleinfeld. "This is a sentencing hearing. The jury has weighed the evidence, has considered both the people's case and the version put forward by the defense. And the jury has found that the defendants are guilty of the charges listed in the indictment, with count one being a violation of California Penal Code 273a, subsection *a*—abandonment and neglect of a child resulting in great bodily harm or death. Guilty verdicts were additionally rendered on count two, that being a violation of PC 273d, sub *a*—cruel or inhuman corporal punishment resulting in a traumatic condition—and count three, violation of PC 192, sub *b*—manslaughter owing to gross negligence.

"Mr. Saroyan, do you have any legal reason why sentencing shouldn't proceed?"

"No, Your Honor."

"Ms. Wachen, do you?"

"No, Your Honor. Just allocution at the appropriate time."

"So noted. Mr. Mannone, do you wish to be heard further regarding sentencing?"

"Thank you, Your Honor. If it please the court, the child's grandmother has come to say a few words."

"Her name?"

"Dana Lee."

"By the difference in the surnames, I'm presuming this is the maternal grandmother?"

"Yes, Your Honor."

The judge made a note. "Go ahead."

Mannone turned toward the gallery and nodded. A woman emerged from the crowd, making her way past the partition and over to a lectern set up near the prosecutor's table. She looked young, only a few years older than the daughter glaring at her from the defense table, but Jarsdel could see by the taut skin and flared, upturned nose that it was the kind of youth bought with a scalpel.

She unfolded a piece of paper and began to read. "It's been almost a year—"

"Please state your name for the record," said Kleinfeld.

"Dana Lee."

"L-e-e?"

"Yes."

"Thank you."

"Can I speak?"

The judge motioned for her to continue.

"It's been almost a year since my granddaughter died on your patio. Not a day passes that I don't think about her last moments—what she must have been thinking and how those thoughts took form. She didn't have the vocabulary to speak, so I imagine her thoughts were similarly wordless. Instead, they were raw emotion. Sadness. Terror at being abandoned. Needing and wanting only one thing: her mother."

Lee's voice tightened, and she wiped at her eyes. "But her mother did not come. Her mother was, in fact, drinking alcohol and having sex on the living room couch. Her mother...was warm and safe." Lee exhaled shakily, sniffled, and smoothed out the piece of paper against the top of the lectern. "The day Fiona Rose was born was the second happiest day of my life, after the birth of my own daughter. I can't say either of those things anymore. I have now lost both my grandchild and my daughter to the same tragedy. The first to death and the second because she and her husband were responsible for that death. Your incredibly awful decisions have changed my life and the lives of all those who loved Fiona Rose. You've deprived the world of an angel." She refolded the piece of paper and looked at Kleinfeld. "Thank you."

"Thank you," said Kleinfeld, "and I'm very sorry for your loss."

Lee returned to her seat in the gallery.

"Counsel, is there anyone else who wishes to speak before the court imposes sentence?"

"No, Your Honor," said Mannone.

"Very well. Now, Mr. Saroyan and Ms. Wachen, do either of you have anything to say on behalf of your clients?"

"Yes, Your Honor, if it please the court," said Saroyan, getting to his feet. He hesitated somewhere in between. "May I stand, Your Honor?"

"I'm hearing formal address at this time, not taking roll, Mr. Saroyan. You may stand."

Morales grunted. "Like the way he fucks with the defense."

"Your Honor," said Saroyan, "I'd just like to say on behalf of my client that he is absolutely devastated by the loss of his child and regrets very deeply that this incident occurred. He wishes he could go back in time and make that moment right, but of course, there's no way to do that. He has therefore resolved to move forward and do what he can to uplift the community. He's already joined Alcoholics Anonymous and attends daily meetings. He wants to tell his story so that future tragedies like this may be avoided and so that something positive can come out of his daughter's death. To that end, we respectfully ask for a sentence that would allow Mr. Huntley to do the most good, and we don't believe a prison term serves justice or the public interest. This is a man who knows what he did was wrong, he's punished himself more than the state ever can, and he wants to make his life mean something. Thank you."

Kleinfeld's expression was unreadable. "All right. Ms. Wachen?"

Liz Huntley's attorney stood. "Yes, Your Honor."

"You indicated your client wishes to allocute?"

"Yes, Your Honor, thank you." Wachen sat, whispering something to Liz Huntley, who got to her feet.

She dabbed at her eyes with a tissue, took a slow breath, and spoke. "I've been thinking a lot about what I was going to say today—"

"Speak up please," said Kleinfeld.

Huntley sniffled, then began again. "I've been thinking a lot about what I was going to say today. Not just what I was going to say but how. What I would wear, who I should look at while I spoke, whether I should be looking up at all. What right does someone like me have to look up? To have her head held up high? Shame is like a garment, and once you put it on, you can't take it off.

"Those of you who've watched this trial from the beginning are probably thinking to yourselves, 'Shame? What does she know about it? Didn't she plead not guilty? Wouldn't a truly remorseful person have thrown herself to the floor and begged forgiveness?'" Huntley covered her face in her hands. Her shoulders shook.

Morales nudged Jarsdel with his elbow. "Reptile," he mouthed.

Wachen lifted her hand from the table, probably with the intention of rubbing Huntley's back to soothe and comfort her. The angle was wrong, however, and the only thing within reach was Huntley's butt. She lowered her hand.

Huntley blew her nose into the same sodden tissue, pressed a sleeve against one eye, then the other, and collected herself. "My plea had nothing to do with my guilt or innocence. Of that, there's no question. My husband and I are responsible for the fact that Fiona Rose is gone, and it tears us apart. What I could *not* do was plead guilty to an intent to harm. The idea of hurting our girl on purpose is so despicable, so inherently hateful to me, that I could not stand before the world and say that yes, that was my intention.

"On the advice of our attorneys, neither of us testified. I wanted to, though, and I now wish we had. Because I don't think the jury understood exactly what we were pleading not guilty to. Fiona's death? No. Guilty. But cruelty? Corporal punishment? When we were presented with a plea agreement, we would've had to accept responsibility on those counts. The DA's office wouldn't budge. So here we are. Our girl is gone, our lives ruined. And now we're judged guilty on the very charges we worked so hard to prove were not true. I have nowhere else to go. Not in the world, and not within myself. Brett and I are separating. I will never have another child. I've been fired from the dealership."

Huntley's voice squeaked, taking the last word up a register. She worried the tissue in her hands, eyes downcast. Someone in the gallery coughed.

"Is that all?" said Kleinfeld.

Huntley nodded and sat back down.

"Okay, is there—"

"Your Honor?" Wachen stood. "I would also just like to add to that, if it please the court, my client has no criminal history whatever, that she is a dedicated member of the Encino Chamber of Commerce, and that her family has for several years made large donations to the Children's Hospital."

"Thank you, Ms. Wachen."

"I'll add that my mentioning—"

The court reporter held up her hand.

"Apologies," said the judge. "At least once a day I'm reminded how difficult a job it is to keep track of everything said in here. In many ways, Ms. Fine here runs the proceedings. If she tells us to slow down, we—"

The court reporter waved her hand again.

"I'll be silent," said the judge. A low chuckle bubbled in the gallery, then dissipated. The court reporter gave a thumbs-up.

"Ms. Wachen?" said Kleinfeld.

"Yes, Your Honor. My mentioning this is not an attempt to diminish the death of Fiona Rose but merely to illustrate that Mrs. Huntley is a civic-minded individual who puts the concerns of the community before her own. Whatever, uh, mitigation this court might draw from that would be very much appreciated. We do take issue with the jury's ruling and continue to dispute that any child abuse took place and ask that Your Honor also consider our objection in sentencing. Thank you." She retook her seat.

"S'like whack-a-mole," said Morales.

Kleinfeld sighed. "I've reviewed the evidence, and I've taken into consideration everything said before the court. I'm aware emotions are running high, so before I impose sentence, I want to be clear: somebody in here is going to leave unhappy today—that's just the way these things go. So if you don't feel you can control yourself as I read out the sentence, I would rather you left now. If you elect to stay and engage in any outbursts, you have fair warning that I have the power of contempt over you. It's not my goal, and it doesn't make me happy to do that, but this is an orderly court, and I don't tolerate jeers, applause, gasps, or any other of that kind of business— particularly from the gallery."

When no one moved, the judge nodded. "The victim in this case, Fiona Rose Huntley, was eight months old. When her parents decided she was being a *nuisance*"—here Kleinfeld held up his fingers in air quotes—"they strapped the defenseless child into her stroller and put her outside on a frigid night in early February. The defense alleges it was their intention to retrieve her after she'd calmed down and that their failure to do so was not an intentional act of neglect but rather the result of intoxication. The court takes a dim view of this argument. Being under the influence of a mind-altering substance carries no exculpatory power. The drunk driver does not intend to maim or kill, but when such is the result, they are nevertheless held accountable."

Kleinfeld shuffled through his papers. "On the other hand, I can't see the value of compounding tragedy with tragedy. During any sentencing, several factors must be weighed. Does the defendant present a danger to the community? Is recidivism likely? Is there previous criminal activity? Are there any mitigating circumstances? Is rehabilitation possible, and if so, how is that rehabilitation best achieved? What punishment would be commensurate with the severity of the offense? Only when all these questions are answered may we say that justice has been served. My job is to serve that justice and to do so dispassionately."

"The fuck's he going with this?" Morales murmured.

Jarsdel glanced at his partner but said nothing. He too felt something turn in his guts. It was a sensation he was well familiar with. The slipping away of a case, like trying to grip water in a fist. It was bad enough when it happened at trial. Postconviction was worse.

"I don't think there's any concern regarding re-offense. The Huntleys have no other children, and anyone who'd trust either of them to babysit should probably get a CAT scan. As to mitigating factors, both defendants are working professionals and active participants in their community. These are not hardened criminals. Counsel, have your clients stand to receive their sentence."

Saroyan, Wachen, and the Huntleys got to their feet amid the squeaks of chair legs against linoleum.

"For count one, abandonment and neglect of a child resulting in GBH or death, the court sentences the defendants to two years in a state correctional facility. On count two, cruel or inhuman corporal punishment resulting in GBH, the court sentences the defendants to two years in a state correctional facility, set to run concurrent with the penalty outlined in count one. As to count three, manslaughter owing to gross negligence, the court finds that while negligence did occur, it was done in the commission of a lawful act that might produce death—i.e. rolling the child in her stroller onto the patio— rather than during an act of an unlawful or overtly hazardous nature. The court therefore sentences the defendants to two years in a state correctional facility, sentence to run concurrent with the penalties outlined in counts one and two.

"Sentences on all three counts are suspended pending successful completion of forty-eight months of probation. During this period, the defendants are to abstain from drugs and alcohol and will be subject to random urinalysis tests by their probation officer. Defendants are further required to successfully complete no less than one year of a child abuser's treatment counseling program approved by the probation department. The defendants shall produce documentation of program enrollment to this court within thirty days, along with quarterly progress reports.

"Mr. Huntley, do you understand your sentence as I have described it to you?"

Huntley looked dazed. He'd been expecting to go to prison. Instead, he was on his way back home. If he felt like it, he could be on the patio of the Polo Lounge in an hour.

"I do, Your Honor."

"Mrs. Huntley, do you understand your sentence as I have described it to you?"

Liz Huntley was back to quietly sobbing again. Her attorney was finally able to deliver the back rub she'd been preparing for and performed the task with the gravity befitting the moment. Slow, gentle circles with the palm of the hand.

"I...do...Your Honor," the defendant managed.

"Very well. This court is adjourned." Kleinfeld gave a single, sharp rap of his gavel and disappeared into chambers.

Morales practically shot to his feet, knee pain forgotten. "This is some *bullshit*."

Jarsdel stood, and the two of them followed the crowd shuffling out of the courtroom. Reporters pushed past, racing to hammer out the bulletin on their laptops.

The detectives exited the building on the Grand Avenue side. Once on the sidewalk, Morales stopped and faced his partner. "What's with you?"

"What d'you mean?"

"We switch places or something? Used to be I was the flinty, cynical guy and you were the fuzzy-headed idealist. But you just took that on the chin and didn't even blink. Don't it piss you off? Kid froze to death screaming her mommy's name—bitch I might add's busy gettin' her shit pushed in on the living room couch—and all the parents gotta do now is show up to huggy-feely circle time and steer clear of the Two-Buck Chuck."

Bright morning sunlight bounced off the building's ceramic veneer. Jarsdel shielded his gaze and squinted up at the terra-cotta sculptures set above the entrance. Three figures—Moses with the Commandments, an English knight proudly unfurling Magna Carta, and Thomas Jefferson gripping the Declaration of Independence.

"You know—" Jarsdel began.

Morales waved a hand as if to dispel a stench. "Forget it. Not in the mood."

"Hm? Oh. I was just gonna say that the knight's sword should have an octagonal pommel."

Morales narrowed his eyes. "Smelled some sermonizing on its way. Can always smell it."

Jarsdel shook his head.

Morales was right, of course. Jarsdel had been about to retreat into the comfort of lecture. Something about how Plato really would have been a more appropriate counterpart to Jefferson. The Founding Fathers had after all been classicists and drew their inspiration less from Mosaic law than Athenian.

He was glad Morales had stopped him. The unoriginality of the thesis lent it a dull, plodding weight even inside his own head. That it was the most profound thing he could think to say in that moment only frustrated him more. The Huntley case deserved a better send-off, something more meaningful as it went down in postconviction flames. He thought of the child's gray skin and blackened irises, of how the once plump cheeks had sunken like soft clay. Fiona Rose Huntley, who'd known all the secrets of the universe. After nearly a year's worth of investigating, court appearances, and liaising with the DA's office, they'd scored a win against two entitled kids from the Valley and their slick defense attorneys. And now they'd watched the whole thing reduced to a mere four years of probation, as if the Huntleys had landed a first-offense larceny conviction. Thieves who sawed the catalytic converters off parked cars did tougher time.

"We lost," said Morales. "We won, and we lost anyway."

"It's one way to look at it." Jarsdel tried for a smile, but it didn't take. "I like to think we came in second."

2

The moon was still out, fat and pale above the Santa Monica Mountains, as Jarsdel pulled into the lot at Hollywood Station.

It was cold that morning, and he thrust his hands in his pockets as soon as he was out of the car. He headed toward the front of the building, avoiding the station's back door. A recent DUI suspect, a teen in full-sleeve tats screaming about his alleged membership in the Verdaderos Asesinos street gang, had kicked the metal jamb with such force that the door now stuck in its frame. Jarsdel wasn't sure what was more impressive—that the kid had managed the feat with what could only be described as a skeletal physique or that three days had elapsed since the arrest and the city still hadn't repaired the damage. Taxpayers concerned about flagrant police spending would do well to take a tour of Hollywood Station, where the solution for a leaky roof was a wire wastebasket lined with an empty Doritos bag and what the supply closet lacked in essentials like printer toner it made up for in unopened boxes of pristine, blank VHS tapes.

Jarsdel pushed through the Wilcox Street entrance, earning no more than a glance from the desk sergeant, and made his way to the squad room where he dropped into his chair. For the thousandth time, he was surprised at how stiff and uncomfortable it was, not

giving the merest degree to his weight. Jarsdel reminded himself—
again for the thousandth time—to buy something better.

A leg peeked out from under the cover of a manila folder.
Another of the nameless dead clamoring for his attention. The
bloated, purple limb of a suicide by hanging, or maybe an autoerotic
asphyxiation, or maybe some rough play gone wrong. Hard to tell,
even for Ipgreve, the medical examiner. It didn't matter. Either way,
homicide or suicide, if it had the right suffix, it went to Morales and
Jarsdel.

He tried to think of as many other -*cides* as he could. Pesticide,
regicide, fratricide, infanticide, matricide, genocide. He knew he
was missing a few biggies. Ah, right. Parricide, familicide—

"Hey."

Jarsdel looked up and saw Morales. "What're you doing here?"

"Good question." He sat and studied Jarsdel. "Turns out I work
here. Weirdest thing. I come in and solve crimes and stuff and get
paid."

"I mean this early. Why this early?"

"Me—what about you? Heard last couple days you been practically livin' here. Wanted to see for myself." Morales took a sip of
coffee, screwed up his face in displeasure, and took another sip.
"Gavin's not gonna give you any overtime."

"I'm not here for overtime." Jarsdel patted the stack of files. "Lots
to do."

"At five in the morning? You know we start officially in, like,
three hours, right? When you gonna sleep?"

"I just wanna—"

"You know what fatigue does to your reflexes? Get your ass
killed out there, or worse—mine."

"Couldn't sleep anyway. Might as well not be sleeping here."
Jarsdel picked up one of the murder books. "Gordon Marquand.
Wanna give it a look?"

Morales made no move to take the binder. "Dead-end city.
Why're you wasting your time?"

"You're right. Maybe you can show me how to treat these cases with the considered flippancy they deserve."

He tossed the murder book back onto the table, turned the cover, and began to skim the report. It was the usual ingredients of misery, an interchangeable soup of words and phrases—the refrigerator magnet poetry of a homicide detective:

Blunt-force trauma

Subdural hematoma

Stomach and intestinal contents

Slippage

Blood alcohol content

Livor mortis

Intracranial bleed

Brain stem herniation

Images too.

Close-up of a lacerated scalp, skin popped open like a burst sausage casing, curls of subcutaneous fat spilling onto the forehead. Coarse black hair shaved down to stubble to reveal the wound. Harsh overhead light turning already waxy flesh into a strip of yellowed rubber. An angled contact wound to the chest, a tight fan of blackened flesh sprayed with powder tattooing.

"You seeing anybody these days?" Morales asked.

"Just you."

"Well, enjoy the freedom. Got no idea what it's like being married. What's that thing called—like self-pity but designed to piss me off? I never remember the thing it's called."

"Passive-aggressive."

Morales snapped his fingers. "Yeah. Patti does that. Did it to me yesterday—something about why don't I go ahead and hang out with my friends, because it's *definitely* her job to put the kids down and she *loves* doing it so much. Like that, with all that emphasis where I put it just now. And it sounds even bitchier in *español*."

Jarsdel turned a page. Another photograph, this time of the passenger's side floor mat of the victim's vehicle. Among dozens of discarded Starburst wrappers were patches of dried mud, and these bore distinct, diamond-shaped tread marks.

"And the best part is," Morales continued, "the boys are nine and twelve. Shouldn't even need to be put down for bed anymore. Shit, man, when I was nine, I was taking care of myself and my three sisters. Way Patti coddles them... I mean, Ephraim doesn't even know how to run a load of laundry. *Minecraft*, though? Oosh. All I can say is he better make a bundle in software or some other kinda job you don't need real-world skills for." He took another sip from his thermos.

"Kids today," Jarsdel murmured.

"Damn right, kids today. Cliché as shit, but it's true. You can laugh 'cause you don't have any. And I noticed how you changed the subject."

"From what?"

"Why you're here. 'Cause both you and I know that none of this is fucking pressing right now."

Shoe treads, thought Jarsdel. *Shoe treads, mud, plant fibers. Starburst wrappers with saliva on them. Killer sits in the passenger seat, eating Starbursts as the victim drives. He opens the wrappers partway, then uses his teeth to pry the candy the rest of the way off the wax paper. Each individual wrapper carries the same DNA profile, along with scratch marks from the killer's nails. These are easiest to see on the wrappings for orange- and cherry-flavored Starbursts. The killer's nails are long. One of them—probably the thumb—is chipped, leaving a jagged corner sharp enough to penetrate the paper.*

"I think I get it," said Morales. "It's the Huntley thing, right? You were all Mr. Badass leaving the courthouse. All—you know—'It's Chinatown, Jake.' All, 'Suck it up, Morales. We came in second.' The reality though—that shit got to you. Gonna fight the forces of darkness now, right? Batman with a pocket protector."

Jarsdel turned the page. A strand of brown hair taken from the headrest, laid out next to a ruler. Nine and three-sixteenths inches, with a split end. None of the victim's friends or known associates had hair that long.

"Only stats are down," said Morales. "Nothin' fresh comin' through the door, so you gotta get your fix cracking these creaky old sons o' bitches."

Killer's a slob. Doesn't wipe his feet before getting in the car. Picked up funny ways of eating, habits a lover would find repugnant. Hair overgrown and unkempt. Long nails, haphazardly cut. No woman would wanna have his hands on her body. If he gets any sex at all, he's paying for it.

Jarsdel looked up at his partner. "I'd know this guy if I saw him."

Morales leaned in. "Who?"

"The suspect. He walked in here, I'd say, 'Hey, that's him.'"

"Why, 'cause of the hair?" Morales turned a page. "Could be anybody. And you know this was seven years ago, right? Suspect's—"

"Probably either dead or in jail. I know." Jarsdel stood and stretched. There were no windows in the squad room, just in case someone thought it might be fun to toss a brick or a pipe bomb through the glass, so it looked the same in there whether it was noon or midnight. But from where Jarsdel stood, he could spot an angle of the Wilcox entrance, and the street outside had lightened to the gunmetal hues of morning.

"You know who this victim was? Lemme tell you 'bout this guy." Morales said.

Jarsdel saw his partner now had the murder book in his hands, gripping it like a hymnal.

"Gordon Marquand, thirty-five. First arrest, 1999, felonious assault, sexual imposition. Same year, breaking and entering. 2001, receiving stolen property, failing to comply with an officer's lawful order, fleeing the scene. 2002, public intoxication, possession of drug paraphernalia, resisting arrest. 2004, domestic violence, obstructing official business, criminal damaging. 2007, robbery, another B&E, driving a stolen vehicle. Big year with 2008. Criminal mischief, receiving stolen property, fictitious plates, contributing to the delinquency of a minor, passing bad checks, carrying a concealed weapon other than a handgun, assault with a deadly weapon. Finally some hard time. Four years in Solano. LA shoulda had a fuckin' fireworks show to celebrate. Anyway, released after thirty months and right back at it. 2011, several counts of no driver's license, grand theft of a motor vehicle, felonious assault, attempted felonious assault, expired plates, strong-arm robbery, possessing criminal tools. Guy's a one-man crime wave. Back to Solano, out in 2015."

Morales closed the murder book and held it up. "This case cries out for justice." He put it back on the pile. "I see something like this and think wow, eventually the world just got tired of this motherfucker. If you're lookin' for a substitute for the Huntley girl, this ain't it."

Jarsdel put his hand on the stack of royal-blue murder books, the ones toward the bottom so old they were practically gray. "Yeah."

Morales blinked. "Yeah? That's it? Usually you got some life lessons to send my way."

Jarsdel wasn't in the mood to explain. For him, it was only about the murder. Murder set you apart as a traitor to your species, one who preyed on his own. In cases like that of Gordon Marquand, the duty of a homicide detective wasn't to act as karma's watchdog, restoring justice to the universe, but to isolate and remove those who'd crossed such an ancient and terrible boundary. Murder was as base and perverse as cannibalism. The moment you'd broken that taboo, no one would ever again be safe at your table. It didn't matter how nice the linen was or that the silverware was shiny. You'd turned on your kind, and if you'd done it once, you were capable of doing it again.

It was easy to get angry when the victim was sympathetic—an innocent whom chance and circumstance had set in the path of destruction. The single mother beaten to death for her rent money, the high school social studies teacher shot for interfering in a gang fight, the toddler who died of exposure when her parents got tired of her crying. The spotlight shone on these cases brightly, making it easy to ignore the corners. The corners were where the Gordon Marquands of the world went to die. As everyone's attention was

28

locked on the circle of illuminated tragedy, outrages crept by unnoticed, out of sight. What most citizens didn't understand was that evil always began in those corners. It never appeared center stage without first taking nutrients in the dark. That was why you couldn't let anything go, not ever.

"You want the big win, I get it," said Morales. "Big win's nice, but it don't last. Won't carry you through to your retirement party." He gestured at the murder books. "This shit's mostly where it's at. Most of the time, it's a job, Tully. Ain't a calling. It's a job." He nodded at something over Jarsdel's shoulder. "Here comes Curran."

The desk sergeant approached them clutching a torn piece of paper. Jarsdel had been watching Curran for three years now and knew he handled everything that way—in a knotted fist, like it was going to escape. He white-knuckled pens, coffee mugs, forks. When he spoke, he affected the role of the station's éminence grise—sardonic, wise—but it was an act that fell apart the moment he picked something up or got out of his chair. He was a man who moved uneasily through the world.

"Here," he said, bypassing Jarsdel and handing the note to Morales. "Address up in Laurel Canyon. Fresh one."

"Coulda texted it to me," said Morales. "Saved yourself the trip from your desk."

"Nah, needed the exercise."

Morales entered the address into his phone. "Anyone over there now?"

"Katsaros and the FNG."

Morales smirked.

"How many?" asked Jarsdel.

Curran ignored him. "Katsaros—you believe that figure? Shit, I know we're not supposed to say that kinda thing anymore, but *dang*. That's a body made for loving. Supremo cutie on duty."

"You hear Tully's question?" said Morales.

"Huh? What?" Curran glanced at Jarsdel as though he'd just appeared. "What question?"

"How many?" Jarsdel repeated.

"Oh. Just one. Likely the property owner, but we're nowhere near a positive ID."

"Why's that?" said Morales.

Curran smiled. "You'll see."

3

There wasn't much remaining of the man's features. Tully could make out the right eye, the chin, and the bottom lip—which gravity and rigor had shaped into a disapproving frown. The remains of a few teeth sprouted above, crooked and chipped as ancient grave markers. The rest of the face had mushroomed away from the bullet hits, the cavities in the skull unable to snap back into place as they would in softer tissue. The effect was that the head looked much bigger than it would have in life, a mass of hair and bone and macerated flesh that bulged up and over like some ghastly dewlap. A trio of flies swung lazy circles around the erupted head.

The detectives were lucky. The air-conditioning had been running full blast at the time of the man's death; otherwise, the smell would've been considerably worse. A three-day-old corpse wasn't as bad is it could get, but it wasn't lavender potpourri either. Jarsdel's intimate familiarity with the smell of human decomposition had—if anything—made him more sensitive to the odor, not less. Now even after he showered, he could still catch traces of it in his hair, his clothes, even in his shoelaces if he bent close while tying them. Belches were the worst. Decomp coming back at you when you burped told you just how deeply in your body you'd absorbed the cadaver, all those billions of microscopic pieces of it. And it could happen any time, even the next day when you're eating a sandwich and watching *Wheel of Fortune*. Vanna White turns a letter and your stomach discharges a ghost.

"Got a feeling," said Morales, "and I wanna get your thoughts on this as well, but I'm just getting a sense this guy might be deceased. We get a doctor in here, do a quick check of his vitals?"

Jarsdel bent down and planted a knee in the rug's thick pile. "No casings."

"Wheel gun. Pawn-shop special."

"Or he picked them up. Four shots, shooter standing still. Wouldn't be too hard to collect the casings if you had a penlight."

Morales braced his hands on his thighs and leaned near Jarsdel's ear. "Why?"

"Wants to use it again without tagging it to this victim, I'd imagine. Guns aren't cheap."

His partner chuckled. "Guess what? I actually been doing this a while, so you don't gotta assume my question was the dumbest-ass possible thing I could've asked. What I was trying to figure out isn't why *anyone* would pick up their shell casings but why a *home-invasion robber* would go through the trouble. They don't give a shit. Nervous, pressed for time, desperate. Nature of the act."

"Fair point." Jarsdel stood. "Then it's a pretty decent-sized weapon. Not the sort of thing you cram into your waistband. What d'you think—.357?"

"Nah. We still got some of the head left. With a .357 at this range, we'd be lookin' at a stump. Gonna go with a .38."

"What's an FNG?"

"Huh?"

"Curran, back at the station. He called Katsaros's partner an FNG."

"Oh, yeah—fucking new guy. Har-har. Nobody says that anymore. Curran likes his little acronyms. FNG, DFQ—dumb fucking question, IPS—important police shit. Thinks it makes him sound like a badass."

"Initialisms," said Jarsdel.

"What are?"

"You said he liked his acronyms, but those are all initialisms. You can tell because you pronounced them one letter at a time. Acronyms are like AIDS or NASA or FUBAR. You say them—"

"Tully. Just...please. No Rain Man shit. Too early, okay?"

Jarsdel stood. "Some blood on the books, but only on the spines."

Morales thought about that. "He searches the room after he shoots the guy. Otherwise, there'd be spatter all over the covers."

"Yeah. I lifted up *From Bauhaus to Our House* and looked underneath. Plenty of blood on the carpet."

"So he's staging it. Wants us to buy the robbery angle, but it's really an execution."

"Maybe. I mean, you're right. Wallet's gone, and if he was wearing a watch or a ring, they're gone too." Jarsdel pointed at the couch cushions, which had been yanked free of the sofa and tossed on the floor. "Why that? Even if you're faking a robbery, you wouldn't bother with the cushions. Bit of an oversell."

"Could be he was out of parking meter change. Or like you said, an oversell."

"And the car's still in the driveway, which dampens the whole roving, opportunistic crackhead thing. We're two and a half miles up Laurel Canyon. If the killer had come on foot, he would've taken the car."

"So he drove," said Morales. "Makes my point even more. Came up here to kill this guy. Rest is just visual noise."

"Visual noise." Jarsdel nodded. "That's a good way of putting it." He wandered over to a rolltop desk, where a sheet of yellowed paper peeked out from behind a wastebasket. Curious, he nudged the wastebasket aside with the toe of his shoe and saw the paper was in fact a page from an old book. Not torn out, though—no ragged edges. Instead, it looked as if the book's binding had come loose and the page had simply fallen out.

The print was small, and even with his glasses on, he had to bend close to see what it was.

And before we judge of them too harshly, we must remember what ruthless and utter destruction our own species has wrought, not only upon animals, such as the vanished bison and the dodo, but upon its inferior races. The Tasmanians, in spite of their human likeness, were entirely swept out of existence in a war of extermination waged by European immigrants, in the space of fifty years. Are we such apostles of mercy as to complain if the Martians warred in the same spirit?

Ah, thought Jarsdel. H. G. Wells. *The War of the Worlds*. He wondered where the rest of the book was. Not in the wastebasket, which was empty. Surely no one would keep a novel whose pages were falling out. That meant it had either sailed free when the wastebasket had been dumped or it had glanced off the rim and never made it inside to begin with.

"What'd you find?" said Morales.

"Nothing."

He looked around the room. Several plein air oils had hung on the walls, but they'd been ripped down with great force, their frames cracked and the canvases drooping out the backs. Additional casualties included a Lalique vase, a multicolored Tiffany floor lamp, and an entire shelf of pre-Columbian pottery. These, which included a Moche portrait vessel, were smashed beyond repair.

"Thinkin' he's got a temper?" asked Morales.

"I'm thinking when we find this guy, I'd like to explain in great detail and over multiple, lengthy seminars, the artistic value of everything he destroyed. He'll get to know terms like 'historicism,' 'sociocultural anthropology,' and 'macro-level orientation.'"

Morales shook his head. "That'd impinge upon his Eighth-Amendment rights. Cruel and unusual punishment."

Jarsdel took off his glasses and rubbed at a smudge with his necktie, which popped off in his hand. He'd begun wearing clip-ons in patrol, where they were required for the officer's safety. An authentic double Windsor might convey both style and authority, but it wasn't worth a suspect choking the life out of you. The policy didn't extend to the Detectives Bureau, however, where clip-ons were considered gauche. But for Jarsdel, practicality outweighed sartorial prestige. He'd calculated that the average detective spent upwards of twenty hours a year tying and untying conventional ties. That seemed an absurd amount of time to spend on a fashion accessory, so he was unique among his colleagues in his persistent fondness for clip-ons.

Jarsdel replaced his glasses and refastened the tie. Morales gave him a disgusted look. "I know you think people can't tell you're wearing those, but you look like a sixth-grader." Something caught his attention. "Shit, check it out." He crossed the room to a large mahogany cabinet, which consisted of double doors inset with glass on top and three drawers for storage below. On display was a collection of Japanese art, including several X-rated miniatures.

"I saw," said Jarsdel, joining Morales. "Fornicating netsukes," he said, indicating the figurines on exhibit. "Highly collectible."

"*Dude*. I don't give a shit about the little Asian guys plowing away. I'm talking about the drawer."

Jarsdel saw the bottom drawer was open halfway. He approached and looked inside. Napkin rings, coasters, votive candles, and holiday linens. "What about it?"

"The fact that it's open."

"Why's that interesting?"

Morales frowned at him. "I swear, you spend so much time looking for the most complex thing, you miss some seriously obvious shit." He pointed with the toe of his shoe. "*This* drawer's open, but not the other two above. Pros, they always open drawers from the bottom up. Saves time. Nothin' in that one you wanna steal? Open the one above it, and so on. You start from the top, though, you gotta close it before you can see what's in the one underneath. Less efficient."

"Yeah, okay," Jarsdel said. "I do remember reading that somewhere, now that you bring it up."

"Sure you do. Anyway, tells us our guy's not a pro, and he was definitely looking for stuff. Maybe this really ain't staged, or maybe just some of it is to cover up what he was really looking for."

There was a knock behind them, and the front door opened. Katsaros leaned inside. She was thirty, tough and lean, black hair cinched in a regulation bun.

"Hey, don't wanna interrupt you guys, but if we're assuming the dead guy's Dean Burken, the property owner, he didn't have a criminal history. And the car outside's registered to him."

"Okay, thanks," said Morales.

"He's got some takeout or something on the passenger seat. Unopened, but I think it's a sandwich. Wrapped in that white paper they use."

"Really?" said Jarsdel. "There a receipt with it?"

"I didn't see one. Thought we'd leave all that to SID. Didn't wanna touch anything."

"Oh hey," said Morales, "how's your trainee workin' out?"

Katsaros glanced over her shoulder. "Straight-up oxygen thief. No people skills."

"Not like you, huh?"

Katsaros smiled. "We servin' a habeas grab ass yesterday—some old traffic warrant—and the suspect didn't treat him with what I guess he thought should be the proper respect. He escalated and the guy backed off, but it was dumb as shit and totally unnecessary. Boo-hoo, some punk hurts your feelings. Told him he pulls anything like that again I'm gonna wash him out."

"Excuse me, Officer Katsaros," said Jarsdel. "You said when we first came in here that this was called in by an exterminator, right?"

The street cop looked at Morales. "Why's he talking to me like that? All the 'officer' stuff. Am I in trouble or something?"

"No," said Morales. "People skills run dry here too."

"Got it." She nodded, then said to Jarsdel, "This is, like, the third time we've met. You can call me Maria. Yeah, a technician from one of those subscription pest eliminator services you can sign up for. Comes by once a month to spray and sweep out spiderwebs. Looked right through the window on the east side of the house and saw the victim. Said he thought at first he was looking at someone who'd spilled chili all over his face. Which is great, 'cause that was literally what I was gonna make for dinner tonight."

Jarsdel flinched at the misuse of "literally" but congratulated himself on keeping silent. *People skills running dry indeed*, he thought.

"Same guy every month?" he asked.

"Nah. Just whoever's available to do the job."

"When's the last time that particular technician came out to this address?"

"I didn't ask. Why? You think the pest guy was in on it? Like he cased the place or something?"

"I don't think anything yet."

"I mean, 'cause you should have seen his face. He'd already thrown up, like, four times."

"And the door was unlocked when you got here?" said Jarsdel.

"Yup."

"How're we doing with next of kin?"

"Nobody we can find. Deceased was sixty-eight. Unmarried. Had a sister, but she died last year. No kids. DMV doesn't even have him down as an organ donor. Not that that matters—dude's ripe."

"Was he retired?"

"The rookie's trying to figure that out."

"Okay, thanks, Officer—um, Maria."

Katsaros left, closing the door behind her.

"Wonder if our guy found what he was looking for," said Jarsdel.

"You should get her number," said Morales.

"I'd say money, jewels, maybe rare coins. Definitely didn't know what they were looking at in here. That Granville Redmond painting on the floor over there's probably worth close to a hundred grand."

"Or don't get her number," said Morales.

"She's ten years younger than me."

"So?"

"And we work at the same station."

"So?"

Jarsdel bent down and poked at a shard of the Tiffany lamp. It rocked a few times, then stilled. He nudged it again.

Morales sighed. "I told you, man, I told you. Can't keep pulling these early days. S'like hangin' out with my cousin Jorge. Never knows where the fuck he is. You'll be talkin' to him and he's like..."

The front door opened again. Instead of Katsaros, it was Brodeur, her trainee. Stocky and barely five foot four. His uniform appeared old and worn, more gray in places than black. Some recruits did that out of the academy—stressed the cloth so it would look like they'd been on the job for years.

"Sirs? I called around and did a few Google searches. Our victim's employed at a place called the Huntington Gardens and something?"

Jarsdel stood up. "Huntington Library, Art Museum, and Botanical Gardens. What's he do there?"

"I dunno. Just that he works there. What is it, some kinda open space?"

Jarsdel turned to Morales. "You ever been?"

"Yeah, field trip I think, back in the '80s. Bunch of us thought it was the White House."

"Hey," Jarsdel said to Brodeur. "Can you get on the phone to the Huntington and find out which department our victim worked in? Who his supervisor was and everything?"

"Yes, sir," said the rookie. He pulled out his phone and left to make the call.

Morales snorted. "Used to have to be five eight at least. Even if he ends up being a good cop, he's always gonna be Napoleon or Shorty or something. Who's gonna take him serious? And you know that, by the way? That we got rid of all the height and weight requirements? Now nobody can be too fat or too short or too whatever. You could end up with Tyrion Lannister as your partner, and you wouldn't be able to say shit about it."

"I don't know who that is."

"Tellin' you—s'all part of this very special new world where everybody's a winner. Everyone gets a trophy for trying, and nobody gets to be told no anymore. Oh, you're a one-legged ninety-year-old blind dude with an anxiety disorder? Okay, you got a criminal record? No? Here's a gun. Go fight crime. S'fuckin' *bullshit*, man."

The room was getting hotter. The June sun had crested the tree line and now shone fully on the house, stirring up all the room's available aroma compounds. Jarsdel's throat felt slick and greasy, and Morales's harangue wasn't helping him feel any better.

"Gotta get some air," he said, going out the front door. Crossing the driveway, he spotted Brodeur in the patrol car, talking on the phone. The officer gave him a two-finger wave, like a benediction.

A piercing cry overhead. Jarsdel looked up and saw a hawk coasting over the thermals. It soon found a column of air and spiraled higher.

"Do I have to call you Detective, or is Tully okay?"

Jarsdel saw Katsaros come around the side of the house. "Tully's fine."

"Just finished walking the perimeter. Nothing else of interest, but you'll probably wanna take a look yourself." She studied the home—a single-story, 1930s French country farmhouse. "There's a pool in back. No leaves or bugs in it or anything. Really good filter."

The hawk's cry sounded again. When Jarsdel glanced toward the sound, the bird had gone.

Morales stepped outside. "Just got a text. SID team's on the way, but Ipgreve's in the middle of an autopsy, so it'll just be the guys in spacesuits."

Brodeur shut the car door and headed over. "Okay, uh, so the victim—Dean Burken—worked in archives and acquisitions. He was supposed to come in today and hasn't shown up."

"Did you tell them anything?" Jarsdel asked.

"No, definitely not. Just that we were trying to locate him."

"Good. Who'd you talk to?"

Brodeur's brow creased. "Just some...I don't know. Maybe they said but I don't remember. Really sorry, sir."

"Doesn't matter." To Katsaros, he said, "Can you guys hold down the fort for SID? We gotta follow up with the employer."

She hissed and shook her head. "We were already supposed to be off two hours ago, and I know Gavin's gonna give us so much shit about OT that it won't even be worth filling out the paperwork."

"I get it," said Morales. "So call somebody else, but we gotta take off. Banning works day shift now, doesn't she?"

"Uh-uh, no. *You* guys babysit the dead guy. I'm gettin' some sleep."

"I don't have a problem with staying," said Brodeur.

"See?" said Morales. "Quality trainee you got. Besides, this house was in that documentary on Laurel Canyon. Graham Nash and Joni Mitchell used to live here."

Katsaros's eyes narrowed. "Joni lived here?"

"Pretty sure, yeah."

"You're full of shit." But Katsaros gave a thin smile. "Fine. You owe me, though."

"Aquavit, right?"

"Yeah, but I'm thinkin' two bottles this time."

4

Someone had struck a deer on the narrow two-lane climbing up to the Huntington. It was a buck, and its antlers were the first thing that came into view as the detectives crested the hill. Jarsdel wasn't sure right away what he was looking at, wondering why one of the museum staff was standing in the middle of traffic, guarding a pair of road cones that in turn guarded a cluster of branches. Then he saw the animal's sleek figure stretched out diagonally along the road. It was a tight squeeze getting past, and the man assigned to manage the alternating flow of cars looked nervous.

"Maybe we oughta get out and help move it," said Jarsdel.

Morales exhaled through his teeth. "Go ahead if you want. Not goin' near that thing. You want Lyme disease?"

They passed when it was their turn to go, Jarsdel glancing out the passenger window at the fallen animal. Its eyes were open, filmed over and locked on the sky. Flies crawled over the corneas. It looked so uncomfortable that a part of him hoped the deer would blink just once to get rid of them and then go back to being dead.

They turned into the gravel parking lot and stepped out into the baking heat. It was still June, the season's fury nowhere near its peak, and Jarsdel could already sense it was going to be a bad summer. Barely ten in the morning and already the air stung his sinuses when he took a breath. The detectives made their way toward the palatial library building, a Mediterranean revival mansion that had once been the home of Henry and Arabella Huntington. Henry had been the nephew of Collis Potter Huntington, the Gilded-Age Caesar who'd stamped the Transcontinental Railroad onto the American landscape. Young Henry also enjoyed playing with trains, making his fortune owning and operating LA's Red Car system.

Arabella's passion, however, was art, and her enthusiasm rubbed off on her new husband. With her encouragement—and buoyed by an endless stream of cash—Henry had snapped up the finest pieces a weary, post–World War I Europe was willing to sell. Portraiture, drawings, landscapes, ceramics, and sculpture rolled across the sea by the ton, bound for the orange groves of Pasadena. At the time of his death in 1927, the collection had been worth one-point-three billion in today's currency. Now it was priceless, unimaginably vast, with enough material in its archives to fill a thousand museums.

Jarsdel had grown up only a mile and a half away. For long stretches of his childhood, he and Baba and Dad came every weekend with a picnic lunch. Dad would always insist on a pilgrimage to the Ellesmere Chaucer, an illuminated manuscript of *The Canterbury Tales* so beloved by Professor Robert Jarsdel that he referred to it simply as "Elle"—as in, "Gotta go stop by and see Elle." Baba, on the other hand, valued the Huntington more for its sprawling, labyrinthine gardens. If allowed, he'd wander for hours, spending most of his time among the towering cacti and boojum and aloe of the Desert Garden. The Desert Garden had frightened Jarsdel throughout his early childhood. The plants there were far too wild and dangerous looking, not like Earth flora at all but rather sentient Martian stalks—things that could seize you and plunge a thousand envenomed needles through your flesh. And they didn't grow the way trees were supposed to, with stately leaves and branches stretching toward the sun. The inhabitants of the Desert Garden sulked in their arid landscape, leathery appendages inelegantly hooked and twisted. Even their flowers seemed hostile, calling to mind the lures of lantern fish—profane, deadly imitations of beauty. Jarsdel had hated the flowers most of all.

Excepting that lone part of the property, however, he knew the Huntington as if it had been an extension of his own home. Now he led the way without thinking, pulling away from Morales and practically bounding toward the admissions and membership booth. There was a line of people waiting to get in, and he fell in behind them. Morales soon arrived at his side.

"You remember we're here on a homicide, right? No, like, little side trips or anything."

"I know exactly why we're here," said Jarsdel. "Why the not-so-subtle inimicality?"

"Oh, *shit*." Morales grinned. "Man, oh man."

"What? What's so funny?"

"You. Holy *shit*, man. This is a nightmare." Morales shook his head. "*Inimicality*, huh? So we finally found it. This place is, like, where you come to recharge, right? You get close and it fills you with its pompous-ass power."

Jarsdel had already begun to sweat, and he wiped his temples with the sleeve of his shirt. "We didn't go over how we're gonna do this. Should probably talk strategy."

Morales had begun to laugh. "Lemme guess, you basically spent every spare second of your childhood here, right? Just fermenting. Getting weirder and weirder. I can see it. You'd maybe start acting normal, watching Saturday morning cartoons or playing handball with the other kids or some shit, and your mom'd freak out. She'd be like, 'Ooh, Tully! Tully-wiggins! We're off to the Huntington!' Man, oh man...everything finally clicks."

It wasn't too far from the truth, except of course for the part about Jarsdel's mother. And for the first time in three years, he actually considered sharing that with his partner—something along the lines of, "No, didn't have a mom. Two dads. And they think about as highly of us as you do about them." But he didn't say anything, and once the moment passed, relief washed over him. It was the same kind of relief one feels after a near head-on collision. The knowing that your life had almost taken a sudden and terrible turn. He trusted Morales, but only to a point.

"Hello? Excuse me?"

Jarsdel and Morales turned to see a woman heading in their direction from the gift shop. She was about fifty, with straight, shoulder-length hair. She wore a navy-blue suit, dark pantyhose, and a nervous smile. A name tag identifying her as *Lorraine Cinq-Mars, Donor Engagement Director*, was affixed to her lapel.

"Are you gentlemen from the..." She reconsidered her words. "Would you actually mind joining me this way?" Cinq-Mars hurried back into the gift shop without checking to see if the detectives were with her.

"Fuck she goin'?" Morales muttered.

The two of them followed, and both exhaled with relief as they entered the cool of the gift shop. The sort of heat already filling the day normally behaved itself, remaining in those parts of California whose names alone made you want to reach for a glass of water—Dante's View, Furnace Creek, Death Valley. But that steady broil broke free during the summer, cinching Los Angeles in blistering chains so tight it felt like someone was sitting on your chest.

Cinq-Mars was at the back of the store, holding open a door for them. Morales took his time—much more than he needed to, Jarsdel observed—and the already strained smile at Cinq-Mars's mouth grew more taut by the second.

"It's this way," she said, as if the problem were one of comprehension. Morales paused, feigning interest in a rack of postcards featuring some of the Huntington's more famous holdings. He picked up a few, studied them, and put them back, frowning.

Jarsdel glanced at Cinq-Mars, whose smile now more closely resembled the lipless grin of a skull. "It's this way," she repeated.

Stifling a laugh, Jarsdel touched Morales's arm and spoke in a low whisper. "C'mon. She's about to have an aneurysm."

"Promise?" said Morales. But he got moving again, and soon

they were heading down a broad hallway. Cinq-Mars picked an unmarked door and knocked. No answer came, and she hurried them all inside. Only after she shut the door behind her did she appear to relax a little.

It was a meeting room of the sort Jarsdel was intimately familiar with. Despite the tasteful opulence of the rest of the museum, the furnishings in there were dull and utilitarian—half a dozen black swivel chairs arranged around a gray composite table, an ugly triangular conference phone squatting at its center.

"Please," said Cinq-Mars, gesturing vaguely at the chairs. Morales and Jarsdel sat on opposite sides of the long table, while Cinq-Mars took her place at the head. In her effort to maintain some authority over the proceedings, she'd inadvertently positioned herself in the most vulnerable spot for questioning. Once the detectives got going, they could bounce her attention between them like a tennis ball. She'd have nowhere to avert her eyes if she wanted to pause to massage her story a little, nowhere to escape from the probing stare of the investigators.

Cinq-Mars rested her palms on the table, took a breath, and shook her head. "This is terrible."

"What's terrible?" said Morales.

"Well, the *death*. The death—my goodness, what else? Dean's worked here almost as long as I have. It's just tremendously shocking."

"I see," said Jarsdel. "You heard about what happened, then?"

"Well, you guys are the ones who called me! A little over an hour ago. Officer...I don't remember his name. Deep voice."

"Brodeur?"

"That was it. You can't imagine the shock of hearing it like that, over the phone. I'm just very shaken."

Morales and Jarsdel exchanged a look. One of them would have to tell Katsaros about her lying fuckup of a trainee. Reactions could be gold to a homicide investigator. The things people did and the language they used after being told of someone's murder were potentially valuable early clues, and much less so if tainted by advance knowledge of the detective's arrival. If anyone at the museum knew anything about Burken's murder, they would've had an hour to prepare their story.

"We should probably introduce ourselves," said Jarsdel. "I'm Tully Jarsdel, and this is my partner, Oscar Morales. We'll be the ones looking into what happened to your colleague. Now are you meeting with us because you were Mr. Burken's supervisor, or are you here in some other capacity?"

"I don't know," said Cinq-Mars. She touched her name tag. "I'm Lorraine."

The detectives waited for her to elaborate, but she seemed to feel that was enough. "You were close to Mr. Burken?" said Jarsdel.

"No. I mean, yes. Pretty close."

Jarsdel brought out his notepad. "I'm just gonna jot down a few things while we talk, okay?"

Cinq-Mars nodded.

"We understand, it's stressful," said Morales.

She continued to nod.

"Most people don't ever talk to detectives, so it's okay to be nervous. We have some specific questions, but first is there anything you can think of that we should know?"

"Like what?" Cinq-Mars looked alarmed.

"Let's start over," said Jarsdel. "Dean Burken's body was found this morning in his home. And yes, it, uh, looks like foul play."

Morales coughed into his elbow.

"Oh my God," said Cinq-Mars. "What happened?"

"We can't go into details," said Morales. "But it's pretty clear the wounds sustained were inflicted intentionally."

"And again, just to clarify your role here," added Jarsdel, "were you his supervisor?"

"Dean didn't really have a supervisor, per se, unless you count the board," said Cinq-Mars. "His official title was donor engagement director, but he did a lot more than that."

"Okay," said Morales. "So we have a few standard questions we usually like to get through. First is gonna be, can you think of anyone who didn't like him?"

Something interesting happened to Cinq-Mars's features. Jarsdel at first interpreted it as astonishment that anyone could ask such a question. Burken was beloved, her expression seemed to say, and anyone who claimed otherwise couldn't possibly be talking about the same man.

But Jarsdel was wrong. What gave it away was how long it took her to answer. It was a look of surprise, that much was true, but of the opposite kind. Cinq-Mars was struggling to think of anyone who *wouldn't* have wanted to see him in the ground.

Jarsdel waited to see what she'd say.

"You know," she admitted finally, "Dean might not have been the easiest guy to get along with."

The detectives nodded for her to continue. They knew most people were reluctant to speak the least ill of the dead, so when they did, it was safe to assume they had good reason. "Not the easiest guy to get along with" was a bland, ponderous substitute for "asshole." The suspect pool in the Burken case might be large.

"He liked things a certain way," Cinq-Mars continued. "Very regimented, very serious. Didn't like anyone talking to the donors but him. I mean, I don't think any of this could justify anyone wanting to *hurt* him, but..." She searched for what to say next.

"You'd be surprised the kinda stuff gets people hurting each other," said Morales. "Sometimes it ain't much. Mr. Burken was killed on Friday. He have an altercation with anyone preceding that?"

"Not that I'm aware of."

"Anyone in particular he rubbed the wrong way?"

"No. I mean, not in particular."

Another clumsy dodge, thought Jarsdel. *Translation: had problems with everybody.* "How'd you get along with him?" he asked.

Cinq-Mars looked up and to the right, her baseline look of

concern braced for the impact of her own incoming bullshit. "I'd say very civil," she said, regaining eye contact. Apparently she'd forgotten she'd already answered that question. When Jarsdel had first put it to her, albeit with slightly different phrasing, she'd answered "Pretty close." Now she was down to "very civil." Her relationship with the dead man was deteriorating at a remarkable rate.

Her eyes suddenly went wide. "Wait, *I'm* not a suspect or anything, am I?"

"Absolutely not," said Morales, his tone reassuring. "But we'd like to talk to more people. Maybe someone's got an idea how this coulda happened."

Cinq-Mars tightened her mouth. Jarsdel could see the muscles of her face working, especially at her temples, where they fluttered like trapped moths. "When you say *talk to some more people*," she said, "how would you go about doing that?"

"Pretty straightforward," said Morales. "We go around and, you know, talk to some more people. That's basically it."

"What about security footage?"

"What about it?"

"Well, we value our privacy. It's a legal matter too. We won't be able to turn anything over to you without a warrant, and I don't think there's a need to go in that direction. Do you?"

"We're not talking about that yet," said Jarsdel.

"Okay, because you don't *anticipate*... I mean, I'm going to have to tell our security people that the footage—"

"Hey," said Jarsdel, puzzled by her sudden fixation. "We don't need to see any footage. Just wanna talk to some folks."

"I foresee lots of issues with that," said Cinq-Mars.

"Why?"

"I'm not saying it's not possible. Of course you have to do your job and find out what happened, but this isn't just a museum. It's a research institution. We have academics here from more than thirty countries." She cleared her throat. "It's not a matter of one specific thing that would be problematic. The issue has more to do with things like tone—how you'd approach our staff and our researchers."

"You mean reputation," said Morales.

"I *do* mean reputation. I also mean what the atmosphere is like here. The culture. Hundreds of people engaged in serious scholarly pursuits, who've worked tremendously hard to get to this point, and I think it could be very damaging for their progress if they suddenly found themselves mired in a murder investigation." She blinked and shook her head, and the nervous smile was back. "We just had a major fundraiser on Memorial Day. Everyone was here, even the mayor of Pasadena. So this is freakish. Just the idea of it. Very upsetting. I mean would you just go tromping around and stopping people, or..." Her hands came off the table and performed a brief bit of interpretive choreography—rising, fingers wiggling to indicate the escalating uncertainty and chaos brought on by a police visit. When they reached their apogee, the hands dropped back to the tabletop, connecting with a smack.

Cinq-Mars fixed them with a grave look. Morales was unimpressed. "Ma'am, we're gonna need a list of people who worked with Mr. Burken. The more help you give us, the less we'll have to go *tromping around*."

"I'm troubled by this," Cinq-Mars said. "I'm very concerned."

"You should probably be more concerned with the fact that one of your colleagues was murdered. This is no joke."

That silenced her. Jarsdel glanced at his partner, then back at Cinq-Mars. "We need to get started today. All that stuff you hear about the first forty-eight hours after a homicide being the most crucial are true, and they're already way behind us. We're playing catch-up, and every minute that goes by increases the chances of whoever did this getting away."

"And maybe you didn't like him," said Morales, "but you still gotta—"

"I never articulated..." Cinq-Mars cut in, but Morales held up his hand.

"It don't matter. We're gonna sit here, and you send them in, okay? Start with the people closest to him, then work down from there."

Cinq-Mars swallowed, gave a single nod, and closed her eyes. When she opened them again, they were clearer, more focused. "It started out so pretty today," she said, getting to her feet. "Sunlight in the trees just right."

Jarsdel and Morales spoke to three people within the next hour, and they all said basically the same thing: Dean Burken had been respected but not liked. A gruff, unpleasant man who nonetheless— according to both the associate director of major gifts and the senior director of gift planning—had a knack for securing large donations. This talent had made him a favorite of the board.

It wasn't until the first researcher arrived in the early afternoon that the detectives heard anything new. She was just under thirty and exhibited a collection of traits Jarsdel knew well: cracked lips, rumpled, stained clothing, unkempt hair, pasty, sun-starved skin, gray half-moons under the eyes. It was a look shared by the other-wise divergent worlds of crippling heroin addiction and academic overachievement.

"Good afternoon," Jarsdel said.

"Hi," she said, sinking into her chair.

"What's your name, please?"

"I'm Kristin. Beets. Spelled like it sounds." She yawned, covering her mouth with the back of her hand. "Sorry."

"You a researcher?" said Jarsdel.

She nodded and yawned again. "Sorry. Not getting a ton of sleep."

"Doctoral candidate?"

"Yeah."

"What's your dissertation on?"

"Land and wildlife management methods of Native Californian tribes."

Jarsdel brightened. "I'm sure you've read *Tending the Wild*? Picked up a copy last year at Skylight and got through it in two days."

"You read *Tending the Wild*?" Beets didn't try to soften her amazement.

"Excellent book, beautifully researched. What's fascinating is how applicable and relevant—"

"Yeah, definitely," said Morales. "It's good stuff. Anyway, Ms. Beets, you know why we're seeing people here today?"

"Uh-huh."

"Were you close to Mr. Burken?"

"No. Not even a little."

"Okay. What can you tell us about him?"

Beets thought that over a moment. "What we talk about in here, is it confidential?"

"For sure," said Morales.

"Well, provisionally at least," said Jarsdel.

Beets gave a weary smile. "Which is it?"

Morales shot a glance at his partner. "What he means is that something you say could lead us to some new evidence. Unlikely, but if so, it could come out later."

"If it's unlikely, why're you talking to me?"

"Gotta cast a wide net."

She pursed her lips. "I dunno. I mean, can't you guys drag me into court if what I say ends up being important?"

"Okay. Look. Ms. Beets."

"Kristin's fine."

"Kristin, cool." Morales massaged his forehead with the stubby end of a thumb. "We've had a long day. Man's been killed. Whoever did it's not gonna have a problem doing it again. We don't want that. Let's not think six months or a year down the line. We need your help right now. What can you tell us?"

She thought a moment, and Jarsdel could see as her fatigue faded away until it had gone completely. In its place, vivid in the set of her jaw and her now blazing eyes, was anger.

"It doesn't matter, actually, because I'm taking action," she said. "It's hard to prove, and it's the kind of thing that if you complain, everyone says how much they understand and that they'll look into it, but what really happens is you get squeezed out. Blackballed. Replaced by someone who doesn't say anything."

Jarsdel thought he saw where she was headed. "Did Mr. Burken assault you in some way?"

"Um, no." Beets shook her head. "If he'd done that, the crime scene would've been here at the Huntington."

"Then what?"

"I really don't think you'd understand."

"I might," said Jarsdel.

"Really? You have any idea the kind of politics involved with getting a research position at a place like this? How much your work depends on the goodwill of the archivists and the administrators? What the competition's like for every single chair in the library?"

"Some idea, yeah. What'd he do?"

"He invited me to dinner."

"And?"

"And I said no."

The detectives waited, but she didn't add anything else. "And?" said Morales.

"Amazing things began to happen," said Beets. "All of a sudden, the materials I'd requested were unavailable. If they weren't in the library, they'd be in the archives. If they weren't in the archives, they'd be in long-term storage. If they weren't in storage, they'd be lent to some other museum. Some just vanished completely. Then my schedule started to get weird. Things were cancelled or I'd find out something I'd wanted to do was double-booked. My parking pass didn't get renewed, even though I sent in the paperwork and everything. I was hitting walls I didn't even know were there. And you know what's really incredible? It took me weeks to figure out what was going on, because it was just so freakish that it didn't even occur to me. So I finally mention what I suspect to my advisor, and

I'm thinking she's gonna tell me how paranoid I'm being. Instead, she says, 'Oh yeah, that kind of thing happens all the time.' Just like that. Blasé. I felt like such an idiot."

Morales nodded. "Happens all the time in general or with this guy specifically?"

"Both."

"Who else he do this to?" asked Jarsdel.

Beets shrugged. "I wouldn't know. It's not something people advertise. My advisor told me she'd heard stuff about Dean in the past, but it was always this sort of thing. He only asks girls out once. Doesn't nag or make threats or suggestive little comments. Nothing physical, nothing that could get him in trouble. Even the invitation to dinner is put in a way that he can claim it was only about research if anyone ever challenges him. So he asks once. And if you turn him down, he starts picking away at you. But as to how many times he's done this? I'm sure it goes back years."

"You said you're planning on pursing it?"

"Oh yeah. I'm not a wilting flower. I took it to Cinq-Mars, who did fuck all. But I'm not giving up. More's to come. I'm already talking to a lawyer, and I know she'll do some investigating. Get more people. I told Cinq-Mars that too, so it's funny she didn't say anything to you. But I'm not surprised. That's the way it is. Believe me, though, it's gonna come out."

Jarsdel took in what she said and checked in silently with Morales. His partner gave the faintest tilt of his head, and Jarsdel braced himself for the next question he'd have to ask.

"Kristen, we're going to be talking to a lot of people. And if what you're saying was a typical part of this guy's routine, we'll most likely meet others who've had similar experiences. Experiences like that can be potentially inciting, and we need to be able to definitively eliminate—"

"What we mean," said Morales, "is can you tell us where you were Friday night?"

5

Kristin Beets was easily cleared. Even assuming a woman who didn't own a handgun and had no criminal record would decide to commit premeditated murder, the timeline wasn't remotely close. Friday night, she'd been at a poetry reading at an indie bookstore in Westwood that had evolved—or *devolved*, depending on your point of view—into an open mic. This had gone on until the last bottle of red blend and the last wedge of waxy brie had been consumed—just after one in the morning. Beets had taken a Lyft back to her apartment in Los Feliz, arriving at close to two.

Burken, on the other hand, had left the Huntington that evening at seven, crawling across town on the gridlocked 134. The sandwich Katsaros spotted on his passenger seat—a pastrami Reuben—had come from Greenblatt's, the iconic Jewish deli on Sunset just east of Crescent Heights. They'd found the credit card receipt in the dead man's wallet, the timestamp indicating he'd made the purchase at eight thirty. Figure in ten or fifteen minutes for the guys behind the counter to make the sandwich, and Burken would have finally rolled into his driveway around nine. Neither the food nor the moscato he'd bought with it ever left the car, a clear sign the killer had ambushed him as soon as he'd stepped out. Around the time the first hot slug slammed into Burken's chest, Kristin Beets had been listening to a ten-canto poem about the psychosexual and sociopolitical significance of hair. Privately, Jarsdel wondered whether Burken hadn't gotten off more lightly.

So Beets was out, and none of the other women Jarsdel and Morales spoke to so far admitted to having any trouble with Burken—at least not of the particular flavor the young researcher had been subjected to. These included the head of reader services, the curator of Western American history, and the curator for the history of medicine and allied sciences. To them, Burken was simply a condescending prick. Even if they'd wanted him dead, all were able to provide alibis.

These were official, salaried employees, however, and all of them married. Predators—especially the passive, quietly vindictive type—tended toward the path of least resistance. The accounting that took place in the predator's mind was based on a simple balance sheet, one with only two columns: risk and reward. For Burken, bothering married women with established careers would have been out of the question. For his racket to work, he needed to be in a position of power. Minimal risk for maximum reward.

There were a dozen interns who fit Burken's targeted profile, half of whom were tightly alibied. The rest either couldn't be definitively eliminated or hadn't yet been contacted. Of these, three were particularly vulnerable: foreign nationals whose visas were attached to their research positions at the Huntington. It was just the sort of ammunition Burken would have used: spurn him, get sent home. Jarsdel and Morales had ended up dismissing these women from the suspect pool, however, since the likelihood of a resident alien getting her hands on a firearm was very slim.

The men hadn't yielded any promising suspects either. Indeed, male employees and interns who'd worked with Burken either didn't have an opinion about him or, in a few cases, openly admired him. One man in particular, Dr. Ezra Louro, had been a particular fan of the deceased, calling his death an "incalculable loss." He'd sought out the detectives on his own, offering his help. Immediately suspicious of anyone trying to insert themselves into an investigation, Jarsdel and Morales accepted his offer and were set to meet with him the following day.

They were now having lunch in the station's break room, takeout boxes of Thai food stacked atop an abandoned arm-wrestling table that hadn't seen action in over a year. Tacked on the wall beside them was a photograph of muscled convicts in a prison exercise yard. A few threw up gang signs; the rest just stood, arms crossed, glaring at the camera. Someone had torn a piece of copier paper in half and pinned it below the photo. Scrawled on it in thick black Sharpie was, "They worked out today! Did you?"

Morales had just scooped a forkful of beef pad see ew into his mouth when Officer Katsaros entered the room.

"Been looking for you."

Morales raised his eyebrows and pointed at himself.

"You got it, big guy. None other."

He turned the finger around and held it in the air, pleading for patience. He took his time, chewing slowly.

Katsaros put her hands on her hips.

Morales closed his eyes and made little sounds of approval. He finally swallowed. "Sorry. What can I do for you?"

"Couple days back, you—"

"Ooh, one sec. Little dry." He grabbed his soda and took a long pull through the straw, drinking until he reached the bottom, then vacuumed up the last drops as loudly as possible.

"Such a dick," said Katsaros.

Morales dabbed at his mouth with a napkin. "I'm all yours. What's up?"

"Last week, you made me play *Weekend at Bernie's* up in the hills after I told you I was tired as shit and wanted to go home. I said fuck no, and you kept pushin' till I finally said yes, but you'd owe me one."

Morales squinted. "This happened?"

"And now I'm calling it in." She slapped a Post-it onto the table between the detectives. "Code Walter. We've responded to her twice already. I think she's Egyptian or something."

"How d'you know?" said Morales. "She *walk* like an Egyptian?"

"Yeah, we'll see if you keep those jokes coming after you meet her."

"Hey, wait, I thought that nasty-ass liquor you like was gonna cut it. The aquavit."

"I don't see any bottles yet, bitch. Say hi to the Walter for me." Katsaros left the room.

A Code Walter referred to a particular breed of elderly complainant. When responding officers arrived, the original cause of the emergency call—most often a prowler sighting—would magically diminish in urgency. It would instead be replaced by the caller's desire to discuss more pressing needs: the volume of the neighbor's sound system, the homeless man who'd set up camp in the nearby park, the glasspack mufflers used by local teens, and the always popular invective against off-leash dogs.

"Shit," said Morales. "Got better things to do, man."

Jarsdel bent forward and read the Post-it.

Nourangiz Rostami
108 Ambrose, Apt. 7b
Have fun, chucklefuck

"Iranian, not Egyptian," he said.

Morales looked at him, eyes widening in hope. "You speak that stuff, right?"

"Stuff?"

"The language thing they talk there."

Jarsdel cocked his head. "You don't even know what it's called, do you?"

"Iranian."

"Remind me not to recommend you for community outreach in Westwood any time soon. It's Persian, or Farsi."

"Yeah, yeah, fine. I've heard you do it. S'what you talk when you order from that shawarma place. And they always throw in extra garlic sauce for us."

Jarsdel considered that. "Shawarma. Yes. Also, the language is spoken by over a hundred million people and occasionally comes in handy for daffy little trifles like reading Rumi and Hafez and Nizami in the original, but yeah, shawarma—"

"Mea-fuckin'-culpa, okay? Tell you what, you handle this for me, and I'll owe you one."

"You want to go from owing Katsaros to owing me instead?"

"Will you do it? You just said how bad I am with the public. Probably say something offensive."

"Pretty much depend on that," said Jarsdel. "I gotta write a progress report for the LT."

"Perfect, I got it."

Jarsdel hesitated.

"C'mon, I'll buy you a new pair of horn-rimmed glasses with masking tape *already* wrapped around the bridge. Doesn't get any better than that. Even throw in a polka-dot bow tie."

Jarsdel got to his feet. "Fine."

"Just think how happy you'll make that old lady. You guys can nerd out on what's the best brand of pita and stuff."

"I said fine, I'll do it."

Morales peeled the Post-it off the table and held it out.

"Got it memorized," said Jarsdel, heading out of the break room.

"You're my hero—you know that, right?" Morales called after him.

Over half a million Iranian Americans live in Los Angeles, making it home to the largest Persian community outside Iran. Most had come during the post-revolution diaspora, flourishing in business, arts, technology, and politics, making such an indelible mark in such a short time that "Tehrangeles" now stood among the city's many nicknames.

Jarsdel's baba had been in one of the first waves. His life had most certainly depended on it. Back in Iran, he'd already had points against him for coming from a prominent Zoroastrian family. Despite it being the oldest religion in the country, Zoroastrianism had faced brutal suppression since the collapse of the Sassanid Empire. Its dwindling adherents were second-class citizens, haunted by centuries of pogroms whose specter still lurked behind every daily prejudice. Then a thirty-year-old Western history professor, Darius Jahangir had woken up one morning to discover that not only was his job now obsolete, but his fondness for Baroque nudes might get him declared a *mohareb*—one who wages war against God. Once painted with that particular brush, it would be off to Evin Prison, a facility that acted more as an oubliette than a jail and that housed so many of Baba's colleagues it came to be called "Evin University."

As Jarsdel approached the door of apartment 7B, he became acutely aware of the scent of *advieh*—a staple blend of spices that included coriander, cinnamon, turmeric, and cumin. The smell was so familiar to him, so much a part of his sense memory, that he was already in a better mood than when he'd left the station. He pressed the doorbell.

The sound of someone shuffling to the door. "Hello?" The voice was thickly accented, husky, and nervous.

"Hello, Mrs. Rostami, police department."

There was a pause, then, "You don't look right. Where is uniform?"

"I'm a detective." He unclipped his badge, held it to the peephole, then replaced it on his belt.

There was the snap of a dead bolt and the door opened a crack, held in check by a security chain. The smell of *advieh* grew stronger, and a worried face appeared.

"They tell you why I call?"

"No, ma'am. Just that you might need assistance."

The door shut for a moment, there was a rattle as the chain was disengaged, then it reopened. Rostami was his father's age, maybe a couple years younger, with richly dyed black hair, full lips, and a natural beauty that age hadn't diminished. "Quick, come in."

Jarsdel stepped into a studio apartment—kitchenette, bathroom, closet. He wondered where she slept, then noticed the pressure marks on the rug from the pull-out sofa.

Rostami hurried to the kitchen. "Tea?"

He wasn't in the mood. It was in the nineties outside. "No, thank you," he said.

"The tea is very good. You are welcome to it."

"Really, I'm fine, thank you. Very generous of you to offer."

"Don't be polite. Have some tea."

Although he really didn't want any, he was charmed by the exchange. He'd just engaged in classic *taarof*, the Persian ritual of manners that so often included a triplicate back-and-forth of offer and refusal. To take anything when it was first offered was considered rude, since the host might merely be making a pro forma gesture of politeness. Both sides had to make absolutely certain that both the offer and the refusal were genuine before either made a move.

"In that case," said Jarsdel. "Thank you, yes. Some tea would be wonderful."

"Sit, please."

Jarsdel did as asked, picking an ornate ebony armchair. Rostami returned a minute or so later with a teacup and saucer, which she set on the table in front of him.

"Thank you," he said.

Rostami went back into the kitchen to get her own, along with a bowl of rock sugar infused with saffron. "I am very upset," she said, taking her place across from him.

"That's what I've heard." He could immediately tell it was the wrong thing to say. Rostami looked horrified that her private business—whatever it was, he had no idea—was now station gossip. "I only mean that the patrol officers told me you've been having some trouble." She relaxed visibly. Jarsdel popped a lump of sugar into his mouth and took a sip of the tea. It was good, the flavors fresh and bright.

Rostami smiled. "You know how to drink the tea."

"My baba's from Iran," said Jarsdel in Farsi.

Rostami took in a breath of surprise and delight. "Really?" she replied, also in Farsi. "But your features, they're very...ah, of course, your mother must be American."

Jarsdel didn't tell her there was no mother, that both his parents were men and that he himself had been carried to term by a surrogate paid handsomely for the service. He had a feeling their acquaintance wasn't ready yet for a whole lot beyond a shared language and the proper way to drink tea.

"Yes, long story how they met," he said, hoping to head off any further questions. "Can you tell me what's been bothering you?"

"So many things," said Rostami. "Very bad neighbors, the worst. There's these people on the second floor, just above me, and they smoke marijuana all day long. All day."

Jarsdel gave a sympathetic nod. "That can be a nuisance."

"It's *wrong*. What about jail?"

"It's not illegal anymore, I'm sorry."

Rostami snorted in disgust. "Just make everything legal. The *smell*. I go outside to take a walk and there's clouds of it. And they give me dirty looks whenever they see me."

"Do you live alone?"

"Yes."

"No kids to check in on you?"

She'd relaxed since they'd begun speaking in her native tongue, but Jarsdel could tell this question upset her. She tensed, her lips flattening to rigid parallel lines.

"No. No children."

"Well, as long as these neighbors are obeying the law, there really isn't much I can do."

"I'm sure they're selling it too. Drugs."

"You've seen them selling?"

"They have parties. Many people come and go. All hours of the day and night."

"Have you let your landlord know? I'm sure there're bylaws in your building's lease regarding noise."

She made a dismissive gesture. "I don't want to talk about them. What's your name?"

"Marcus Jarsdel."

"Jarsdel? Is that how you say it?"

"I know, it's not a Persian name. It's complicated."

"It isn't your mother's surname, is it?" The prospect seemed to appall her.

"Not exactly. As I say, complicated." He hurried to change the subject. "What province are you from, if you don't mind my asking?"

"Mazandaran," she said, her expression brightening. "In Amol. We could see Mount Damavand from my window."

"I don't doubt it," said Jarsdel. "It's only eighteen thousand feet high after all."

Rostami laughed. "You've been, then?"

"Sadly no."

"No? But you've seen Iran, of course?"

"Not yet."

Her expression clouded. "But you must go! It's partly your homeland. Why hasn't your baba taken you?"

"It just hasn't come up," said Jarsdel. "He's very busy."

"For your whole life, he's been too busy to take you to see your home?"

Jarsdel didn't know how to answer. If Professor Jahangir went back to Iran, there was a better than even chance his cell at Evin University would still be waiting for him.

"It's a long and uninteresting story," said Jarsdel, mispronouncing the last word in an effort to redirect the conversation.

"*Dastan*," Rostami gently corrected. "But your Persian is excellent."

Jarsdel smiled at her.

"So strange to see a man with your features speak our language so beautifully. Your baba must have passed on very few of his attributes."

"On the outside, yes," Jarsdel agreed, then touched his temple. "But there's plenty of him is in here."

That seemed to please her. They sipped their tea in a silence broken only when Jarsdel bit down on his chunk of sugar.

"More tea?" Rostami asked.

"No, thank you."

"*Taarof* aside, would you like more tea?"

"Really, I'm fine. Is there anything you'd like me to do? Take a report, perhaps? Otherwise, I'm afraid I can't stay."

"But you only arrived," she said. "And there's so much crime in the neighborhood."

Jarsdel thought it over. "If you like, I can come back to check on you."

She brightened. "You will?"

"Happy to. Here." He took out one of his business cards and handed it to her. She pinched it delicately between thumb and forefinger, as if it were an old photograph she didn't want to smudge.

"Call anytime," said Jarsdel, standing. "You have a beautiful home. Thank you for your hospitality."

Rostami stood as well. "Thank you for coming, Detective. I feel much better. About everything."

6

J arsdel leaned over the manuscript, amazed.

The Discovery of Witches:

In Answer to severall QUERIES,
LATELY
Delivered to the Judges of Assize for the
County of NORFOLK
And now published
By MATTHEW HOPKINS, Witch-finder,
FOR
The Benefit of the whole KINGDOME

The document was nearly four hundred years old and had sent perhaps as many people to their deaths. Opposite the title page was a woodcut frontispiece, showing the witch-finder himself inter-rogating two of the devil's consorts. The man and woman pointed at their familiars, a collection of both earthbound and fantastical creatures bid to aid the couple in their malefic wizardry. There was a rabbit named Sacke & Sugar, a dog named Jarmara, and a horned, Seussian beast called Vinegar Tom.

Jarsdel had never read the book himself but knew enough about Hopkins to be impressed. The self-styled "witch-finder general" had appeared during the English Civil War, claiming to have been awarded a Parliamentary commission to root out evil. For two years, he prowled East Anglia with his assistant, preying on isolated, war-ravaged villages. During that time, Hopkins racked up thousands of pounds of revenue and sent to the scaffold more accused witches than had been executed the entire previous century.

One of his favorite methods was to search the accused's body for "the Devil's mark," a blemish of flexible description that indicated the spot where Satan had scratched his servants as proof of their fealty. The mark's authenticity was revealed through "pricking," wherein a thick needle was inserted into the suspected area. According to the ad hoc logic employed in witch hunts, if no blood were to flow, the mark was genuine. And since Hopkins's reputation—and therefore the size of his purse—depended on his ability to uncover witches, the needle was most often rigged, retracting into its hilt like a gag knife in a toy store.

The book before Jarsdel was the life's work of a true villain and of the kind who can only come to power when the social order is in crisis, just as certain plants thrive exclusively in ash-nurtured soil. Jarsdel wondered how many had read this very copy as it made its journey through time to arrive on the table in front of him. How many minds had been poisoned against their neighbors, and how many of those had been stretched or burned or broken because of it?

Morales drew up next to him. "Who's that dude?"

"Sociopath. Professional witch-hunter."

Morales pointed at Hopkins. "Looks like one of those construction-paper Pilgrims I had to make for Thanksgiving when I was a kid."

"Careful, your finger."

"What?"

"You almost touched it."

"Who gives a shit?"

"I do."

Morales stared at him.

"I'm not being difficult," said Jarsdel, lowering his voice. "We want these people to cooperate with us. I don't think the first thing they're gonna want is to see us putting our hands all over the exhibits."

The detectives stood in the Book Conservation Laboratory, a division of the ten-thousand-square-foot Avery Conservation Center, which was responsible for the maintenance of the Huntington's collection. The space was wide and airy, dominated by rows of spotlessly clean worktables. A rectangular section of the surface was inset with illuminated panels so that a document could be lit from beneath. Compound microscopes hung suspended from the ceiling on hinged arms. Between the tables were computer stations, scanners, bins of exotic solvents and cleaners. In one corner of the lab was what Jarsdel recognized as a paper conservation table—a slab of stainless steel topped with an airtight dome. Two technicians, working on opposite sides, could insert their hands through specialized sleeves and repair a document under the most protected conditions.

But despite all the advanced technology, most of the tools were distinctly old-world. There were hundreds of knives and cutting tools—most with burnished wood handles—brushes, awls, brayers, punches, hones, and a massive cast-iron press. Block out the electronics, and you could be looking at an eighteenth-century master artisan's workshop.

Morales plainly hated it. His mood had been foul as soon as they'd stepped inside and took a darker turn when they were told the man they were there to meet was running late. They'd only been in there a few minutes and already he looked like he was ready to smash something, staring down each item he encountered with the same venom he directed at career criminals. So far, he'd held back from vocalizing his disgust, but now it appeared the tipping point was going to be *The Discovery of Witches*.

Jarsdel was relieved that the four staff members present were on the other side of the room, gathered around a pile of yellowed letters. "Why're you so agitated?" he asked.

Morales gave a hiss of contempt. "It's incredible, man. All this..." He waved in the direction of the technicians. "All this," he repeated, "all this money and work and everything, all going to save this creepy little book. Strange fuckin' priorities we got."

Jarsdel cast a glance over his shoulder. "First of all, it's not just *this* book. What goes on in here is protecting our shared cultural heritage."

"*Your* cultural heritage."

"No, *ours*. Ours as in the collective—"

"It's a luxury, man. *Cultural heritage.* You know what matters? The basics. Food, clothes, not getting shot at. You tell some of the kids in my neighborhood growing up that we need to spend all this money fixing up a book, and that's why they don't eat. Tell 'em it's for their cultural heritage. That'll make 'em feel better." He shoved his hands in his pants pockets. "And it's cold as shit in here too, by the way. Know what this does to my knees?"

Jarsdel was rattled. "I think," he began, but that was as far as he got. Just then, the pneumatic double doors at the far end of the lab opened with a sigh of their air canisters, and in came Dr. Ezra Louro. He looked to be in his fifties, the oversized lab coat trailing behind him as white as his puff of unkempt hair. He was as tall and lean as Jarsdel, but with a hunched, almost furtive bearing, as if he'd just broken something expensive and wanted to escape unnoticed. The look on his face, however, was cheery—even gleeful—and his eyes beamed behind thick wire-framed glasses.

"Look, Tully," said Morales when Louro was still out of earshot. "It's your dad."

"Gentlemen! I'm Ezra." Louro held out his hand, then let it fall, looking chagrined. "Sorry. I keep forgetting we're in pretty much a post-handshake world. Anyway, I'm glad you came. What should we touch on first?"

"We're—" but that was as far as Jarsdel got.

"I know," Louro cut in, his expression suddenly grave. "Lorraine mentioned you had concerns about Dean's professional life. Something like that anyway. And I just wanted to say that whatever that was, I don't know about it. Never had any problems."

Not that you would've, thought Jarsdel, then said, "You worked closely with him?"

"Well, sure. I work with all the registrars. Except for botany. My talents don't mean much when it comes to plants. Can we talk over here? I need to check on something."

Without waiting for an answer, Louro edged between the detectives and approached one of the worktables. Morales threw Jarsdel a sullen look, and the two of them followed. Louro was bent close over a weathered, hand-drawn map of Southern California, its four corners held down by padded weights. In dozens of spots, the paper was eaten through where the place names had been written, creating gaps in the shapes of the missing letters.

"What a mess," said Louro. "If only more cartographers bothered studying chemistry."

"So, uh," Morales began, "what can you tell us?"

"This was the last piece Dean sent over here." Louro pointed at the holes in the map. "Iron gall ink. Eats right through the cellulose, so that's bad enough. But then you've got that cheapo paper—everything after 1860's a bitch—with this crazy low pH. We call it 'slow fire.' Paper turns brown and falls apart. Put those things together and you end up with something that makes you wonder why you didn't go into glass or ceramics. Had to pick books and ephemera, didn't I?"

He pulled open a drawer and brought out a length of PVC pipe.

"*This* is what it was rolled inside of when it arrived. I'm being completely serious. This is so far from archival tubing that I'm thinking they were actually *trying* to destroy the map." Louro tossed the pipe back into the drawer and swept it shut.

"I'm sorry," said Jarsdel. "But I'm not sure what this has to do with Mr. Burken."

"Because I want you to know that despite what you might hear about him, you need people in a museum who get things done. Know what I call the board of directors? I call 'em the packrat brigade. They'll hang on to a Kleenex if Woodrow Wilson blew his nose with it. You need guys like Dean who can reckon with the hard truths of this business. That just because it's old doesn't mean it's worth keeping. Now this map..." He held his palm a foot over its surface and passed it slowly from left to right. "This map was the *best* preserved piece of paper matter willed to us by the Theodore Smith estate. The *best*, which means everything else we got was in worse condition. Follow me? Which also means if it weren't for Dean Burken, my staff and I'd be sifting through acid-burned paper for another month just so some grad student can scour the private ramblings of one of the most insignificant, peripheral figures of the Gold Rush."

"Huh," said Morales, shooting a pointed look at Jarsdel. "My partner here was saying how important it is to keep stuff because it's part of our heritage."

Louro looked surprised, then offered a sly smile. "Posilutely. Absolutely positively. Everything we handle is part of the public trust." He held up his right hand in a mock oath. "According to both our mission statement and the AAMD Code of Ethics, once we accept an item into our care, its worth surpasses mere pecuniary considerations because it's now officially part of our species-wide cultural wealth." He lowered his hand. "But let me ask you something. What would you rather have? This?" He stabbed a finger toward the map. "Or a latte?"

He exhaled and gave a rueful shake of the head, perhaps sensing he'd gone too far. "Been a long week. Acquisitions are through the roof, so we're under all kinds of pressure down here. With Dean gone, it's only gonna get worse. He and Ellery have been responsible for more deaccessions than anyone else I've worked under, and what that allows us to do is focus our energy on the stuff that really matters. The stuff that deserves our attention."

"Responsible for what?" said Morales. "De-*what*?"

"Hmm?"

"You said he was responsible for more of something than anybody else."

"Deaccessions," said Jarsdel.

"Correct," said Louro.

Morales winced and massaged the bridge of his nose. "Yeah, okay, great. But what is that?"

"It's when the museum gets rid of something," said Jarsdel. "Usually if it doesn't fit with the collection or the cost of maintaining the item is a strain on resources."

Louro was delighted. "You know the business. Excellent. But you forgot to mention that an item can also be deaccessioned if it's damaged beyond repair. And it's situations like that where you run up against the packrat brigade. Dean couldn't stand that kind of mentality, thought the collection was getting too big for its own good. You hang on to everything, and it dampens the impact of the really standout pieces. Dean's philosophy was cut, cut, cut. You know what they called him upstairs? 'The Butcher.'"

"You mentioned another name," said Jarsdel. "You said Dean and...?"

"Ellery." Louro nodded. "She's on the board too, but definitely not one of the packrats. Before you can deaccession something, you need a director's approval, and Dean always went to her. He'd give her these huge inventory lists and say 'Let's eighty-six these,' and she'd sign off. Trusted him to do his job."

Jarsdel brought out his field notebook. "What's her full name, please?"

"Ellery Keating. Been on the board here longer than just about anybody. Used to be you needed a majority vote to get rid of something. You have any idea how long that'd take? We maintain millions of items. That's not hyperbole. Millions. Anyway, she got the policy changed to just one director to approve."

Jarsdel wrote down the name and tucked the book back into

his jacket pocket. "Why do you think that is? I mean her being so relaxed when it came to collections management."

Louro grinned at him. "You're one of them, aren't you? Packrat type?"

Morales snorted, and Jarsdel suppressed a pang of indignation.

"It's not that I don't get it," Louro went on. "Once something's gone, it's gone. The past is erased forever. But you know how that old joke goes—history's the hardest subject to learn because they keep adding to it. Not everything's worth keeping, right? Imagine what this place would be like if we hung on to all our donations. Gotta jettison the ballast."

"Ms. Keating shares that philosophy?"

Louro shrugged. "She's a businesswoman. Practical. Something costs more to house than it's worth in ticket sales or research value, it goes." He went back to scrutinizing the map.

"Anyone around here disagrees with that approach?" said Morales.

"Ha. Plenty."

"Disagrees strongly?" asked Jarsdel.

"Sure," said Louro. "Art arouses something in us. Brings out our passions. Even people who you'd normally look at and think, wow, what a wet noodle. Get 'em going about art, they turn into tigers. Ah! There we go." He plucked a whisker-thin paintbrush from a caddy and used it to point at a spot near what was today downtown Newport Beach. The place name was hard to make out but not impossible.

King Henry's Pride.

"Phantom settlement," said Louro.

"What do you mean?" Jarsdel asked. "Like a ghost town?"

"No, no. It's a cartographer's trick. You put something on a map that doesn't actually exist. It's always small—something that wouldn't cause problems for someone using the map. Kind of a hobby of mine, looking for them."

Morales leaned in, now curious. "What's the point?"

"Guard against copyright infringement. Maps aren't easy to make. If you're the unscrupulous sort after a quick buck, it's sure a whole lot easier to copy an existing map and sell it as your own. Used to be a big problem. So let's say someone decided to do that with this one, they would've copied down the phantom settlement of King Henry's Pride. And because it's entirely the creation of the mapmaker—in this case Ennis P. Smith—you can prove you got ripped off."

Jarsdel nodded. "Like a fictitious entry in a dictionary. Same kinda trap."

"Right." Louro looked at Jarsdel curiously. "Gotta say, wouldn't've pegged a policeman as the sort who'd be familiar with fictitious entry."

"Yeah," said Morales. "He knows all kinds of useful stuff like that. Back to what we were talking about, anyone you can think of specifically that Mr. Burken really pissed off?"

"I told you," said Louro, "there's no shortage of haters when it came to Dean. Ellery too. It's a long list." He finally broke away from the map and faced the detectives. "I'm not being serious, you know."

"What d'you mean?" asked Morales.

"It's just that...yeah, they had lots of enemies. But still, we're talking about the art world here. I can't actually believe anyone would get so worked up over a few deaccessions to commit murder. Their most vocal critic is an eighty-year-old art history professor."

Jarsdel had his notebook out again. "Name?"

"Come on. This is goofy."

"We're not accusing anyone. Only thinking maybe they could help us out."

Louro hesitated. "She's on the board too, so don't say I put you on to her, okay? Margaret Rishkov. She hates—well, I guess I should say hated—Dean Burken more than anybody alive."

Jarsdel put the book away. "Appreciate it."

"Hey," said Louro. "If you guys really think someone killed Dean over all this, you might wanna talk to Ellery. Just to let her know to be careful."

"We'll talk to her."

"She's on the city council down in Newport. Maybe tell the cops there to keep an eye out too."

"Newport, huh?" said Morales. "Where's she live? King Henry's Pride?"

Louro didn't smile. "Really. Let the cops know."

"Are you two friends?" said Jarsdel.

Louro shook his head. "No. But losing Dean was bad enough. Anything happens to Ellery, we'll be up to our eyeballs in slow fire."

7

A few months after his dad was diagnosed, Jarsdel read that cancer was inevitable. Mutations were a constant in the biological forge, and it was only a matter of time before one snuck past cellular quality control and into general population. Cancer was the house edge in a casino. Play long enough, and eventually the math catches up with you. Jarsdel had found this news strangely comforting.

The fallacy of fairness had long been one of his tormentors. He'd always correlated fairness with divinity—visualized them as ordered pairs on a two-coordinate plane. If there was a deficit in one, the other must likewise suffer. He therefore considered even minor injustices as evidence that the cosmic plan was in jeopardy or—much more terrifying—that perhaps there really *wasn't* any such plan.

He also knew his thinking was flawed, his designations of fair and unfair based not on objective criteria but on his own deeply personal notions. This self-awareness, however, made no appreciable difference. Merely knowing it was his own judgments that lay at the root of his gnawing disquiet did nothing to dampen it.

Cancer had long been Jarsdel's heavyweight champion of unfairness. He'd seen it eat people alive, had watched his grandmother lose her long silver hair and in a matter of weeks transform into a wasted, bat-like remnant of her former self. His beloved sociology professor had gone a similar route, shedding his own abundant locks to chemo and dropping weight so fast it was like watching air leave a balloon. Lung carcinoma, even though he'd never smoked. He coped with it as best he could, hiding his sickly dome under an Oakland Raiders baseball cap and passing the bulk of his workload over to his graduate assistants. Dead less than a month later. Jarsdel heard his last days had been hideous—the bleeding in his lungs so severe he'd required multiple cauterizations of the pulmonary tissue. Thus he was spared from the comparatively quick death of choking on his own blood and delivered instead into the jaws of the tumor. Consumed, from the inside.

Last year, cancer had reentered Jarsdel's life, this time swinging its cold finger around to mark his father. It had arrived like a cartoon storm cloud, doggedly pursuing its victim to cast down rain and lightning while everyone else stood in the sun. It was unfair, Jarsdel decided when he learned of the diagnosis. Terribly unfair. Dad had been healthy, hadn't smoked since the early '70s, drank only wine—sure, sometimes a bit much—but only the good stuff. Besides, Dad wasn't just *Dad*, he was *Professor* Robert Jarsdel, the maven of English letters, a man whose annotated *George Bernard Shaw: Collected Works* had for three decades been a standard text in undergraduate seminars from USC to Cambridge. People like that shouldn't die from something as stupid and humdrum as cancer. Of course everyone had to die from something, but death—like life—should have a purpose.

The cancer had rooted in his father's pancreas, a part of the body no one gave much thought to until it stopped working. Only then did you discover that the inelegant, tadpole-shaped organ served more than a few key functions. As it failed, Dad began to fade from the world. His shape changed, contracting as the weight fell off, and his skin took on the sepia hue of a polluted sunset. Searing abdominal pains transformed his confident gait to a tentative shuffle. Besides his bed, he spent more time in the bathroom than anywhere else. And then the chemo came along—dacarbazine, streptozocin, doxorubicin—substances that sounded more like fuel additives than something you'd deliberately put in your body, and they'd torn through him like ground glass. Neoadjuvant therapy, designed to do to the tumor the same thing it had been doing to its host. When it was small enough, they'd be able to get it all out with "surgical debulking," provided it hadn't metastasized.

It was around that time Jarsdel found the article, something in *Los Angeles* magazine about what it was like to grow old in the city. It was an unremarkable piece—a thinly disguised where-are-they-now of famous Angelenos, along with the requisite handwringing about LA's alleged cultural decline. The death of Charles Bukowski was singled out as the defining moment in the city's plunge into artistic bankruptcy. Bukowski had died of leukemia, and tucked amid a summary of his literary contributions was the simple observation that cancer would get you in the end—so long as nothing else got you first. It didn't matter if you lived in a hermetically sealed bubble, shielded from even the most flaccid carcinogens. Cancer was a certainty, an immutable law of biological mechanics.

In just that single sentence, cancer went from Jarsdel's bête noire—the mascot of a corrupt and uncertain world—to a disinterested natural process. It took some of the sting off. Not all of it, but enough so that he no longer saw the battle between Professor Robert Jarsdel and the tumor in quite the same terms. It wasn't good versus evil, he now saw, but rather nature versus itself.

The surgery was a success, at least so far. Dad would have more tests next month to see if the cancer had reappeared anywhere else. Until then, he lived in sanitized purgatory, his world narrowed to the handful of things he could do without risking his life. The days melted together, their monotony broken only by the nuisances and petty humiliations of a post-op existence. Baba changed his surgical dressings, administered the insulin injections, and doled out the Norco tablets. To make sure the painkiller regimen wasn't too high,

Dad had to blow into a three-ball spirometer. If he couldn't get the last ball to rise at least an inch in its cylinder, his next dosage of Norco would be one pill instead of two. So far, that hadn't happened.

"I'm the Big Bad Wolf when it comes to my Norco," Dad joked whenever the subject came up. It was delivered with the forced humor of a prisoner whose only window gave a view of the gallows, and both Jarsdel and Baba had long given up any pretense at finding it funny.

And that, perhaps, was the strangest thing to come out of the cancer's arrival—Jarsdel and Baba on the same side. The two hadn't agreed on anything in years—not since the day Jarsdel announced he was abandoning his doctoral candidacy for six months of police academy training. When he'd told his parents, Dad became dejected, withdrawn, but Baba gave a bitter laugh. "I've always wondered what kind of person tosses a newborn baby in a dumpster," he'd said. "Now I have my answer." Since then, they hadn't so much drifted apart as hurtled away from each other, as if they now shared the same magnetic polarity and it was nothing less than the laws of physics that kept them at a distance.

But it was different now. Dad's sickness had united them in the predictable way such things do. Predictable, maybe, but Jarsdel was still surprised. A year ago, such a thing would've seemed impossible. It had happened slowly, neither he nor Baba commenting on it, probably fearing that to do so would halt or even reverse its progress. It was a fragile thing, their burgeoning renewal as Baba and Tully—an exquisite piece of pottery still firing in the kiln.

A conspicuous feature of their wary alliance was date night. Each week, Jarsdel made the trip out to Pasadena and took his baba out to dinner. Sometimes a movie, if there was anything good playing. The tradition was three months strong, and the only rule that had emerged was that they trade off choosing the restaurant. Tonight was Jarsdel's turn, and he'd selected Nick's over on Lake Avenue, an elegant but unpretentious gastropub specializing in hearty sandwiches, wood-oven pizzas, and fountains of chilled beer.

Jarsdel got out of the car and headed toward the front door, shooting a glance up at the darkened panes of the second floor. Since Dad could no longer climb stairs, his parents had little reason to go up there anymore—half the house surrendered to the disease. It was one of cancer's many pre-deaths, little rehearsals before the big event.

He pressed his thumb against the bell, and the door swung open to reveal Baba. Dark, lean, severe Baba. He was in his midseventies now, and while his once black hair had all but completely frosted over, it was just as coarse and thick as it had been in his youth. Together with his arched, regal nose and smooth, unlined brow, he had assumed the kind of ageless appearance one associated with rigorous spiritual practice. Draped in a tallit, he would've made a convincing Hasid; with white robes and a conical felt hat, he'd be transformed into a Sufi mystic.

But not quite, Jarsdel thought. The sharp cut of Baba's jawline and the small, flat mouth it framed suggested less of the ecstatic than the militant. A Dominican friar presiding over the Galileo affair, perhaps, was more apt.

"I should've called," he said. "Dad's had a rough day. I don't feel right leaving him."

"Oh," said Jarsdel. "That's okay. Want me to pick up some takeout? I can go grab it and be back in twenty."

Baba shook his head. "We got some chicken in the fridge."

"Dary?" someone called from inside. Jarsdel knew it was his dad, but only because no one else in the world referred to Professor Darius Jahangir as "Dary." The voice itself was unrecognizable, stripped of the baritone rumble that had once shaken university auditoriums and made lectures on Dryden or Poe into impassioned sermons. What now drifted out of the house was the reedy, choked speech of a lifelong asthmatic.

"I'll be right there," Baba yelled over his shoulder. He turned back to his son. "Let's reschedule."

"Dary," Dad called again. "Is that Tully? Have him come in."

Baba's near-permanent frown deepened, if such a thing were possible. "He doesn't look good," he said, his voice low and soft. "Prepare yourself."

Jarsdel stepped inside and crossed the wide foyer, knowing he'd find his father in the living room—a place his parents insisted on referring to as "the salon," as though Stein and Hemingway were about to drop by. It was the only room in the house that could comfortably fit Dad's new oversized recliner, a giant leather cloud that could arc back into a sleeping position or, with the touch of a discreetly placed button and the purr of its motor, rise and tilt itself forward, depositing the user gently onto his feet. It also offered heated massages of the head, lumbar, thighs, and calves, with each of these available in three distinct modes—wave, pulse, or press.

Jarsdel turned the corner off the kitchen and stepped into the salon. His father was where he'd expected him to be, wrapped in a wool blanket despite the summer heat, a copy of *House of Leaves* facedown on his lap. Jarsdel had tried to prepare himself as Baba suggested, but it hadn't worked. Dad was a husk of the man he'd been, the arms protruding from his pajamas—once thick with muscle—stripped down to pale matchsticks. Now that he'd backed off the chemo, his neck and jawline were heavily stubbled, though not enough to mask the pruned, papery flesh beneath. His eyes were the most startling. Since the rest of his features had collapsed and retreated, his eyes had appeared to grow larger. They rolled in their orbits to meet Jarsdel's gaze, moist and meerkat-like behind their thick prescription lenses.

"Tully!" he croaked, lifting his arms for an embrace.

Jarsdel hesitated. The man was so frail it seemed a hug might snap him in half. Dad gave a sad smile and lowered his arms.

"I know. I could play Lear."

"Act Five," Jarsdel agreed.

The professor made a sound somewhere between a laugh and a grunt. "You going out with your baba?"

"I think that—"

"No," said Baba, startling them both. For a tall man, he moved with unnerving soundlessness. For the eighteen years Jarsdel had lived at home, he and Dad averaged at least one shriek of terror per week when Baba inadvertently snuck up on them.

"No?" said Dad. "Why not?"

"What if you need to get up for something to eat? Or you need the bathroom?"

"I'll be fine, Dary. You two go off. Have fun."

Baba looked at his son. "He fell yesterday."

"I did *not*," Dad protested.

"His magical chair put him on his feet, then he fell straight down onto the carpet. Sprained his wrist catching himself. If I hadn't been there..." Baba shook his head.

"It wasn't a fall," Dad said. "I just lost my balance a little. And, Dary, I hate that. Don't ever tell anyone ever again that I *fell*. Sounds so pitiful. It's always codgers falling down. 'Ooh, did you hear? Jim fell.' 'Oh no, did he really?' 'He certainly did, and he bruised his hip.' I can't stand it, Dary. Promise me, never again. Pitiful. An old man falling down. I'm not an old man."

"You're seventy-five."

"And you're seventy-six. Are *you* old?"

Baba crossed his arms and leaned against the wall. "I'm not going anywhere. Not unless you get up and push me out the door yourself."

Dad swung his head back in Jarsdel's direction. Atop his wasted neck, it was like a bowling ball balanced on the end of a drinking straw. "Would you please escort your baba out of the house? You're armed, aren't you?"

Jarsdel looked from one man to the other. "I think he's probably right. I don't wanna leave you alone either."

Dad scoffed, but Jarsdel could see he was pleased. The three of them hadn't shared a meal in a long time. "Fine, you ninnies. Stay. There's some chicken in the fridge, I think."

The now-famous fridge chicken consisted of a wing and a few strips of dry flesh clinging to a rib cage. Baba took it from its plastic hot case shell, wrapped it in tinfoil, and put it in the oven. Once it was out, he spent the next several minutes picking apart what little there was to eat.

Seeing where the evening's gastronomic fare was headed, Jarsdel dug a half-eaten bag of pretzels out of the pantry and a tub of hummus from the fridge. He sat at the table and began snacking, then watched as Baba continued to work. After portioning the chicken, he got out a heavy ceramic salad bowl, dumped in a bag of prewashed greens, and tossed in some gloopy vinaigrette.

"Sorry I don't have enough meat, but do you want some salad?"

"No thanks," said Jarsdel.

"Pretzels and hummus isn't much of a dinner."

"I'll grab something after I go. Nothing to worry about, I promise."

"I'm not worried. Nor perturbed, anxious, or apprehensive."

Jarsdel smiled. This was an old game, and the rules were fluid. Sometimes it was about quantity—whoever could name the most synonyms would be the winner—while other times credit went to the one who dredged up the most obscure and unusual choice. On particularly competitive rounds, synonyms from other languages were allowed. On New Year's Eve of 2009, Jarsdel had triumphed with the German *Papierkrieg*—literally "paper war," the overly complex paperwork associated with making a complaint—coming back strong from Dad's *administrivia*.

"Agitated?" Jarsdel asked.

Baba shook his head. "Not alarmed, uneasy, nervous, or even— though it pains me to say it—trepidatious."

"Dammit, I was gonna say *trepidatious*. That would've clinched it for me."

"No, I was just getting it out of the way. It's a stupid, inelegant word. One of those SAT words, the sort you have to memorize but no truly literate person ever uses. Of the same ilk as *loquacious* or *impecunious*. Fat on the English language, ready to be trimmed off."

Baba underlined his pronouncement by balling up the wad of

greasy tinfoil the chicken had been reheated in and hurling it into the trash. Jarsdel glanced into the living room to see that Dad had fallen asleep in his chair.

"How's work, by the way?" said Baba.

"Hmm? Oh. It's good."

"*Good*. A description so vivid, it's like you're right there, slapping the handcuffs on yourself. I take it from your answer you don't wish to discuss it?"

"I'm fine discussing it. What do you want to know?"

Baba took salad bowls down from the cupboard and began filling them. "Anything I would've seen on the news?"

"Maybe. I'm on the thing with the guy from the Huntington. Did you hear about that?"

"The Huntington? No, what happened?"

"One of the employees was shot."

Baba gave him a concerned glance. "Not Timothy, I hope."

"No. Who's that?"

"Gardener. One of the few who could get those terrestrial bromeliads looking healthy. They're very fussy, you know."

Jarsdel didn't care for bromeliads, terrestrial or otherwise. They were down in the Desert Garden, with the other creeping, Lovecraftian flora. "Well, no, it's not him. This guy was in archives and that sort of thing."

"Why're you working on it? Pasadena isn't in your...whatever it's called. Jurisdiction."

"He was killed at home. Laurel Canyon."

"Ah." Baba brought the food to the table and set the plates on a pair of worn, mint-green place mats. He went back into the kitchen and returned with a pill organizer. He unsnapped the lid, took out two large pills, and set them next to Dad's plate. They looked as big as suppositories.

"CREON tablets," said Baba. "Pancreatic enzymes. I have no idea what CREON stands for, but as you can imagine, your dad can't resist constant references to *Antigone*."

"Let me guess," said Jarsdel. "'My part is not an heroic one, but I shall play my part.'"

"Of course. Exclusively at first. When I threatened to reenact the play's conclusion with one of our Wüsthof kitchen knives, he started branching out. I even caught him looking up new lines. He likes to pretend he's got the whole thing memorized. You know how he is."

Jarsdel did. He would have done the same thing.

"Robert, food's ready," Baba called.

"He's asleep, I think," said Jarsdel.

Baba craned his neck to see into the salon. "He really needs to eat."

"Want me to wake him?"

"No, I'll give him a few minutes. We can catch up."

Jarsdel scooped up another dollop of hummus with a pretzel. He ate, watching his father pick at his salad. There was no wine on the table, hadn't been for months. Dad wasn't allowed to have it, and Baba had wordlessly joined the abstention in solidarity.

"I've missed you," Jarsdel said.

Still chewing, his father looked up from his food. After he swallowed, he said, "You have?"

"Yes, of course."

"You see me every week."

"That's not what I mean." Jarsdel picked up a pretzel, decided he didn't really want it, and ate it anyway.

"All right," said Baba, "how do you mean, then?"

Snoring from the other room. Jarsdel glanced into the salon to see Dad, mouth partway open, a look of concern pressed on his features. If he was dreaming, it wasn't of lollipops and unicorns.

"He snores a lot now," said Baba. "It's the meds."

One of Dad's arms had fallen off the chair and now hung down at his side. The sleeve was pulled up a little, and the gaunt, clawlike hand that emerged looked like it belonged to a stranger.

"Tully," said Baba.

Jarsdel looked at him. "Sorry. I was trying to say something. I'm not even really sure what it was, though."

Baba appeared to be waiting for him to go on, but he didn't know what else to add. Finally, his father spoke.

"You'll be okay, you know."

Jarsdel blinked. "What d'you mean?"

"After we're gone. You'll be okay."

"Little dramatic, don't you think?"

"Not really. Something you should start thinking about. I wasn't prepared when my parents died, and it was harder for me than it needed to be."

Jarsdel ate another pretzel. They were stale, almost chewy, but they gave him something to do. He looked at Dad's vacant chair, at the bland meal of chicken and salad, and at the pair of CREON tablets laid neatly next to the plate. His gaze snagged on Dad's spirometer, which one of his parents had left on the kitchen counter. It was transparent plastic, about the size of a book, and consisted of three vertical chambers and a hose to blow into. Each of the chambers housed a single ball. The first was powder blue and the lightest in weight, the third navy blue and the heaviest. That was the ball Dad had to elevate at least an inch for his full dose of Norco.

A year earlier, the spirometer wouldn't have been there. Neither would the Norco nor the CREON nor the magic leather cloud. Conversations were free to flit from the peak of one empty, intellectual construct to the next. It was freedom as they knew it.

Sickness might be invisible, but it moved in with you anyway. It was the world's worst roommate, imposing itself no matter where you turned, appearing in every pill, in each grab bar bolted over a bathtub or beside a toilet, in every new accommodating piece of furniture. It even edged its way into your vocabulary. Your inside became your outside, every hidden, private mechanism laid bare in conversation. Liver enzymes, bilirubin, blood, urine, bowel movements, all now open for discussion. Sickness didn't so much invade your life as replace it.

"It's a lot," said Jarsdel.

Baba swallowed a bite of food. "What's a lot?"

"All this. Dad, the cancer. Just the way everything's different. Kind of incredible how quickly we adapt to all this, you know? I guess I'm surprised at how fast everything can change."

"Things are always changing."

"I know. I understand that intellectually. It's just different when "

"Usually for the worse." Baba shrugged. "You don't get used to it, but you do learn to expect it. I was a decade younger than you when my country was taken away. Each morning, I'd think, well, we've hit the bottom. Can't go on like this. And of course I've told you what happened the day the shah fell. That was the moment my naivete crested." Baba made a single wavelike motion with his hand. "After that, I knew there was no bottom limit."

Baba's younger sister Tahmina had had a beautiful, snow-white Samoyed. He was called Mehrdad—*given by the sun*—and had been beloved by all in their little Zoroastrian enclave. The Avesta, the religion's ancient scripture, decreed that dogs were sacred beings, connected at once with the world of forms and the one that lay beyond. A dog's gaze could banish malefic spirits, and Mehrdad was thought to be particularly powerful in that regard. He'd been brought in to attend the dying on numerous occasions, and it was said that when he slept, he guarded the bridge to heaven.

Tahmina was out walking him when news came that the shah had been deposed. A band of teenagers, giddy with revolutionary fervor and aware of Mehrdad's significance, had seized the dog and, forcing Tahmina to watch, looped an extension cord around his neck and hanged him from a tree.

Baba had first told Jarsdel the story when he was seven years old, far too young to hear it, and it raked troughs of psychic damage that felt so real and so deep, it was as if they'd been made by actual claws. Since then, he'd seen Mehrdad many times in his dreams, turning lazily in the late afternoon sun, blackened tongue forcing itself from between his jaws.

"So you see," his father went on, "I'm a difficult man to surprise."

Jarsdel sighed. "Come on, Baba."

"What do you mean?"

"I mean I think this is all a bit overly dolorous. I hope you're a little more positive around Dad."

"What do you mean, 'positive'? You think we should sit around and read excerpts from *The Secret* to one another?"

"Right, because there's no happy medium."

Baba grunted. "Your dad's a realist, like me."

Jarsdel began to feel frustrated. All he'd wanted was to share a small moment of commiseration, but Baba couldn't even spare him a pat on the arm and a grudging word of comfort. Just a simple "I understand" would have accomplished much. Instead, his father had used the conversation to showcase his ersatz brand of existentialism. Hopelessness masquerading as detached toughness. An excuse not to care, because caring was painful.

He was tempted to say so, to strike at Baba with his words. To somehow penetrate that implacable veneer and make the man do something—anything, so long as it was raw and true.

Jarsdel was startled by a grinding sound that suddenly erupted from somewhere behind him. He jerked around in his seat, expecting to see some sort of rusted engine spitting out twisted, smoking gears. But it was only Dad, asleep in his leather cloud, his mouth an open frown.

"Gets loud," Baba said. "One of the reasons we got the chair in the first place. So he could sleep out here."

Jarsdel turned back to face him. "My God. Does he do that all the time?"

"Even with the door closed and the sound machine on, I can still hear it. Rattles the walls."

"Does it mean anything? Sleep apnea? Does his doctor know?"

Baba dabbed at his mouth with his napkin and crossed his arms. He fixed his son with an expression of fatherly sternness. There was some sympathy in it, but not much.

"Tully," he said. "He's an old man. *I'm* an old man." The hint of sympathy dropped away, leaving only the unforgiving gaze of the Dominican inquisitor. "Pretty soon," he said, "you're going to have to get really cozy with the concept of impermanence."

8

A cloud of gnats ambushed Jarsdel as he made his way up Ellery Keating's walkway. It was a hot blue July day, and the Keating place was far enough inland for the insects to frolic unmolested by the ocean breeze.

It was one of those Spanish revival houses that sprang up following the Great War, a construct of a more romantic, chivalrous age—however fictional. Old California, as seen through the eyes of white boosterism. A place where sleepy Mexicans snoozed under giant sombreros and corrupt alcaldes fell to Zorro's blade. It was the California of stuccoed walls and patches of artfully exposed brickwork, of desperados yipping and firing their guns at the sky, of cacti and burros and rattlesnakes, of serenading troubadours and swooning señoritas. It was the California that eventually gave birth to Speedy Gonzales, to the Frito Bandito, to chain restaurants with serapes and candied skulls on the walls.

Morales had decided to wait in the car with the windows rolled down. He was expecting a call from a friend of his who worked bunco in the Commercial Crimes Division and didn't want to risk interrupting the Keating interview.

"You'd like this dude," he'd said to Jarsdel. "Imagine you, but angrier and a little better looking. Mike's thing is numbers. When

CCD wants somebody put away, they put him on it. Someone steals a fuckin' thumbtack, he'll track it down. So all I told him is the name Ellery Keating. Go crazy, see what comes up."

Jarsdel pressed the doorbell, kicking off two bars of chimes and the deep, wheezy bark of an old dog.

"Presley! Quiet!" A bullwhip of a voice. The animal went on barking. "Shut up. *No.*"

The door opened partway, revealing a woman somewhere in her sixties. Her hair was the bright red of cheap strawberry preserves, and she wore baggy jeans and a Tommy Trojan T-shirt pocked with bleach stains. But she was old money, Jarsdel could tell, and it wasn't just because of the fat sapphire on her finger. She had that kind of casual wealth that defined Orange County elite, the easy confidence of someone in the top tier of the steak-of-the-month club. An overweight Lab mix strained to get free of her grip on its collar.

"Who're you? You a cop?"

"Ms. Keating, I'm—" Jarsdel began.

"This about Dean?" She yanked up on the collar, but it didn't stop the dog's barking. Only added a little jazzy grit.

"Can we talk inside?"

"Shit. Hang on." She nudged the door shut. More barks, more reprimands, and finally the unmistakable whispering sound of the dog being dragged along the floor. Somewhere a door slammed, and the barking grew fainter.

The front door reopened, this time all the way. "Okay, you can come in. He doesn't like men."

Jarsdel went in, enjoying the chill of the air as it met his skin.

"Hot out there?" Keating asked.

"A little."

"Weather says it's gonna get to a hundred and eleven on the Fourth."

"I saw that."

"Get you anything?"

"No thanks."

Keating pointed to a living room with bone-white stuccoed walls and high, timbered ceilings. "We'll go in here. Presley's not allowed on the sofas, so you won't get dog hair all over your pants."

It could've been the showroom of an antiques dealer. A portion of a Gothic choir stall abutted the far end, archangels carved into its varnished misericords. Nineteenth-century oils in gilded frames crowded the walls, and a UN of statuary occupied practically every square foot of available floor space. There was Guanyin, Kali, Hildegard of Bingen, the Marquis de Lafayette, a Shinto dragon. A portrait bust of Vespasian—missing a nose but otherwise in good condition—sat on a glass pedestal above a Persian carpet. The multiple medallion and sickle-leaf designs told Jarsdel it was from Kerman province—probably late Qajar dynasty, considering the vibrancy of the dyes.

As valuable as the collection was, Keating had put no thought into its display. Rather, the haphazard jumble and discordant clash of styles called to mind a rodent's hoard. Accumulation for accumulation's sake, the shiny paper clip and platinum cuff link held in equal esteem.

"Beautiful home," said Jarsdel.

"Belonged to Vernon McManus," said Keating. "Bootlegger. First wife's supposedly buried in the foundation."

Mounted above the fireplace was the largest TV Jarsdel had ever seen. On the screen was a still image of a Colonial mansion, fronted by Corinthian columns and a pair of stone lions guarding the steps.

No—not a still image. The branches of a tall, leafy tree swayed as they were stirred by a breeze.

"That's Graceland Cam," said Keating. "Live feed. I like it. Always keep it on when I'm not watching anything else."

She dropped into a restored Louis XIV armchair and gestured to the facing sofa. This was upholstered in royal-blue raw silk, and Jarsdel didn't so much sit as sink into it. The dog continued to bark from wherever Keating had locked it away.

"Comfortable?" she asked.

"Very soft, yes."

"Hundred-percent duck down."

"Sorry?"

"The cushions. *Duck* down, not goose. From Muscovy ducks farmed along the Rio Grande. A good, big duck like a Muscovy can give you the same fill power as goose, but I think they're even softer. And raised right here in the USA."

"Guess it's something I never thought about," said Jarsdel.

Keating frowned. "Here." She leaned forward, retrieving a pillow that had been supporting her lower back, and held it out. "*Squeeze.*"

Jarsdel did as he was asked. "Okay."

"That's *goose* down. Feel the difference?"

"Wow."

With a satisfied set to her jaw, Keating replaced the pillow behind her back. "It's the plumules. How much air they can trap. For back support, you want some firmness, so I use goose for that. Goose for support, duck for comfort."

"Huh. Anyway, I'm wondering if we could discuss the case I'm working on," said Jarsdel.

"It's why I'm sittin' here. Though you really should've called first." She crossed her legs, and something on the bottom of her shoe blinked green in the light.

Jarsdel brought out his field interview notebook. "How long was Mr. Burken with the Huntington?"

Keating cocked her head in thought. "Long time. Maybe twelve, fifteen years? Dunno exactly."

"The two of you close?"

"More'n he was with anyone else. Want anything to drink?"

"No. Thanks. How would you describe him? Personality wise."

"I wouldn't'a called him a little sunbeam, that's for sure, but he was punctual, fastidious. Guess you'd say *anal*, which is a word I never liked, but it's probably accurate." She put her palm at an angle near her mouth, as if to deliver a stage whisper. "More ways than one."

"I don't understand."

Keating pursed her lips and fanned herself with a fluttering of the hand. Jarsdel supposed the gesture was meant to convey genteel shock.

"I'm sorry, I don't... Are you saying he was gay?"

Keating shrugged. "That's the rumor. Doesn't matter to *me*, you understand. I've had lots of gay friends over the years. Didn't vote for Prop 8 even though our pastor told us to. It is funny, though, if you think about all the stereotypes. So many of them *do* go for things like hair styling and antiques and haute couture and gourmet cooking and what not. More so than women even, as a whole. So it's not like they're women in men's *bodies*. And how many straight florists have you met? And those others—what're they? Not aromatherapists, the other—right, perfumers. I was thinking of the French word, *parfumiers*, but that woulda sounded a bit on the chichi side."

"Ms. Keating." Jarsdel held up a hand.

"Ellery." Her expression hardened. The muscles at her temples twitched. She folded her hands in her lap and sat up straighter.

"Ellery, then. I wanna keep us on track. Mr. Burken was murdered in his home. It was pretty brutal. He have any enemies? Maybe someone was after something?"

"He had money. Probably one of his dates—what do they call them? Hustlers? Those boys on Sunset. Either them or one of their friends."

"But no one specifically you know who was nursing a grudge?"

"From where, the Huntington?" A squawk of laughter. "These're PhD students and artsy-fartsy board members. Definitely didn't all love him, but you're lookin' at a crowd's never been in a schoolyard fight, let alone own a gun or know what to do with one if they did."

It was a nervous, rapid-fire delivery, and her foot bobbed as she spoke. Again, something wedged in the treads of her sneakers caught the sunlight. Too brilliant to be ordinary glass—a precious stone of some kind, maybe an emerald.

"I think you stepped on one of your earrings."

"What?"

He pointed at her shoe. "Looks expensive. You've probably been wondering where it is."

Plainly confused, Keating bent forward and examined her shoe. "Oh. I see it. Thanks." She got up and left the room. There was the sound of Keating rummaging through a junk drawer, probably as she searched for something to pry it free. Jarsdel wondered what it was like to be so wealthy you dug emeralds out of the soles of your shoes.

When she returned, he asked, "When you say they didn't love him, what'd you mean by that?"

Keating dropped back into her chair and resumed bobbing her foot. The jewel was gone. "Remind me, what are we talking about?"

"You said people around the museum—employees, students— that they didn't love him."

Keating shrugged. "He had his ways of doing things. Didn't suffer fools."

Jarsdel scribbled a series of wavy lines in his field interview notebook. It served no other purpose than to break up the pace of the interview and give him time to think of his next question. His notebook had more curlicues, spirals, and fleurs-de-lis than it did actual words. It also provided a period of silence that could last as long as it needed to, one that most people felt the need to fill with more dialogue. Keating soon obliged.

"He could yell. Corner someone and yell. Really unpopular with the interns. Most of the board too."

Jarsdel glanced up. "Anyone he offended in particular?"

"Take your pick."

"But you got along with him."

"Sure. Birds of a feather. We understood each other. An appreciation for the finer things. Dislike of what's common and ugly."

Jarsdel drew more squiggles. "And did that dislike affect how he managed the collection?"

"Don't know what you mean."

"How he handled deaccessions."

A flicker of alarm crossed Keating's features. She tried to turn it into irritation but was too slow. "That's the kind of question makes me think you already know the answer. 'Deaccessions' isn't a word just anybody throws around. Who've you been talking to? Mousy Miss Cinq-Mars or Margaret Rishkov, the queen bitch?"

Another squiggle. "Been talking to lots of people," said Jarsdel. "Whether they approved of him or not, everyone agrees Mr. Burken liked to cull the collection."

"So?"

"And you approved his decisions."

Keating put her hands on her knees and leaned forward. "Somebody had to. Our operating expenses went down one and a half percent because of that. Now that might not sound like much, but considering the size of our endowment, one and a half percent ain't licorice money."

Jarsdel had pushed as far as he wanted to in that direction. He'd triggered self-righteousness, the wrong kind of resistance. He decided to apply pressure elsewhere and indicated their surroundings. "Was he a collector too?"

"Saw his place, didn't you?"

Jarsdel nodded. "Impressive, but I think you got him beat. That Vespasian over there is pretty special on its own. Where'd you get it?"

"Hmm?" Keating turned to look. "Which?"

"The Vespasian bust."

"I don't..."

"*Emperor Vespasian*. Right over there." Jarsdel couldn't stop a flicker of contempt from clouding his expression, but luckily Keating wasn't looking his way.

"Oh, right." She turned back. "Always thought that was Julius Caesar. All those emperors looked pretty much the same."

"Julius Caesar wasn't an emperor," said Jarsdel.

Keating looked amused. "Pretty sure he was, darlin'."

"No, I promise you. His adopted son Octavian became the first Roman emperor, Augustus. Julius Caesar, on the other hand, was named *dictator perpetuo*—dictator for life."

Keating pursed her lips and sucked in a breath. "*Well*. My goodness, if you say so."

Jarsdel smiled. "Was it a gift?"

"No, I bought it."

"Seems strange."

"Why's that?"

Jarsdel chose his words carefully. "Just find it odd you'd spend so much on something without knowing more about it."

A crease formed on Keating's brow. "Thought you wanted to talk about Dean."

"It's why I'm sittin' here."

Keating smiled sourly at her own line being tossed back at her. "Let's get to it, then."

"Sure. What I have so far is..." He checked his notes. "Mr. Burken wasn't well liked but had no standout enemies, and you believe he was murdered by a male prostitute."

"I never said it straight out like that. I mean, I don't know for hundred percent *sure*."

"What puzzles me," said Jarsdel, "is no one else I spoke to shares your theory. Mr. Burken had a reputation for making life difficult for *female* interns if they snubbed him. Gaslighting, that sort of thing. Also numerous complaints about his behavior went unanswered by the board."

Keating shook her head. "All news to me."

"Is it?"

"You don't think I *ignored* that sort of thing, do you? This day and age?"

"I have a grad student who claims otherwise. She's bringing a lawsuit."

Keating affected a look of horror and shock. As acting jobs went, it was a D minus at best.

"Sorry," said Jarsdel, getting to his feet. He gestured at the bust of Vespasian. "Could I take a look? Ancient history's kind of a hobby of mine."

Keating flicked her hand at him. "Suit yourself."

Jarsdel approached the statue and bent close. His eyes met a cold marble gaze. "Great condition. You can actually still see tiny bits of pigment in the creases between the hairs."

"Pigment. You mean paint?"

"Come over and see."

"Not supposed to be any paint on it." Keating came over and squinted at where Jarsdel was pointing. "You mean I gotta get it cleaned?"

"Not at all. Most people think of Roman statues as dead-eyed, stark, and lifeless, but in their day, they would've been painted as realistically as possible. That was the whole point. Must have been truly terrifying."

"What d'you mean 'terrifying'?" said Keating.

Jarsdel glanced at her. "The Jews had strict laws against creating graven images, so you can imagine the effect of something like this showing up in Jerusalem. Great, staring, frozen men. Indestructible, implacable, always watchful. What were these things? Just statues, or maybe something more? Remote conduits to the emperor's consciousness? Perhaps he could see out of their eyes. Perhaps even animate the stone into sudden, murderous life. Gotta wonder how many rebellions were quashed by nothing more than the unblinking glare of a stone Caligula. Was gonna be my dissertation, actually. 'Shock and Awe: Roman Art as a Tool of Colonial Expansion during the Early Principate.'"

Keating grunted. "Sounds like quite the beach read."

He reached out, paused, and turned to Keating. "May I? I'll only touch with the back of my hand. Not as many oils."

"If you want."

Jarsdel touched the emperor's forehead for a few seconds, then took his hand away. "It's not reverence," he said, still studying the bust.

"'Scuse me?"

"I think of these sorts of things as little time machines. You're touching the work of someone who's been completely tilled under—their matter scattered and recycled. So I'm not paying tribute to the man Vespasian but rather asking myself, who was the first person who touched this? I'm the last, but who was the first? Because neither of us can see each other, but we touched a common object across a two-thousand-year gap. It's exhilarating."

"Whatever does it for you."

She began tapping her foot, probably to encourage Jarsdel to hurry up and leave. The sound excited Presley, wherever he was, and he started up again. The barking was close, and Jarsdel could hear scratching coming from the other side of the wall to his left. He faced Keating.

"It's interesting. All the Roman statues you could've had in here, you ended up with Vespasian. Did you know he put a tax on urine?"

Keating snorted. "Ha."

"It's true—was a legitimate commodity. Used in leather tanning, also good for whitening togas. So Vespasian's trying to find new ways of boosting tax revenue, and it occurs to him he should start charging the laundries and the tanners and the fullers for the countless gallons of plebeian piss sprayed in municipal toilets every day. Son Titus complains, says Dad, this is a pretty ignoble way to make a buck. Vespasian holds up an aureus—a gold piece—and asks him if the smell bothers him. Titus says no, 'course not. Vespasian says *Atqui ex lotio est.* 'And yet it comes from urine.' To this day, public urinals in Italy are called *vespasiani.*"

Keating looked bored. "Are we gonna be talking any more about Dean? If not, I'd like to let Presley out and get my day moving again."

"Thing is," said Jarsdel, "Vespasian was wrong. I'd say the exact opposite is true. Money carries a stink better than just about anything—something the Spartans understood well. Know what they did to discourage bribery? Currency had a built-in anticorruption feature. Instead of coins, they used iron bars. Clever, right? The solution to the greatest of all civic ills was simply to make money inherently cumbersome."

"All right," said Keating, leaving Jarsdel's side and heading toward the foyer. "Appreciate you coming by. I'd offer you a water for the road but I'm fresh out."

Jarsdel made no move to go. "A corrupt Spartan was easy to spot. He's the guy with the team of draft animals lugging around thousands of iron bars. These days, money weighs nothing—can move it around the world at the speed of light, keep billions of dollars in a thumb drive. Can't help thinking that's probably not a good thing for us. Makes theft easier to commit and harder to prove. But not in all cases."

Keating stopped. She turned around, crossing her arms and leaning against the wide arch of the entrance to the living room. "You tryin' to say something, Detective?"

Jarsdel looked at the bust of Vespasian, then at Keating.

She began shaking her head. "No." She held out a single flat palm. "You just stop right there. This is my house, okay?"

"Okay."

"Well—*ha*—you can't come into my house and accuse me—accuse me of what, exactly? I'm in shock. I acquired every single piece in this room legally and transparently."

"You have the paperwork to back that up?"

"I do *not*," she scoffed. "That's not my responsibility."

"Who then? Your attorney?"

"Dean had all that stuff. At least he should."

"So Dean sold it to you? How'd he get it?"

"I'm in total shock. You've shocked me. Are you saying I *stole* this stuff? Ha—that I, what, like just *barreled* into the Huntington and cleaned the place out?"

"Not exactly."

"Okay, I'm gonna *explain* something to you. Gonna explain all the dark, behind-the-scenes stuff goes on at a museum. If your precious heart can take it."

Jarsdel nodded at her to continue.

"Hope you braced yourself. This is some lurid material."

"Uh-huh."

"We get far, far more donations every year than we can keep. The cost of housing those items in many cases exceeds their value. Following me so far?"

Jarsdel didn't answer. Keating was puffing up her language to buy time to get her story straight. It was fascinating to watch, but he wasn't going to participate. Eventually she gave up and went on.

"Disposing of thousands of surplus items in a cost-effective manner is a burden on time and resources. Talkin' about things like appraisers and sales agents and printed literature and holy *smokes*, we are certainly talking about packing materials. You got *any* idea how much it costs to pack an eighty-pound hunk of marble? Or what about a Chihuly? All those bits of glass and such? *Well*." She leaned her shoulder against the archway, grimacing and pinching the bridge of her nose. She held up her free hand to ward off any questions.

Very dramatic. Jarsdel made it all the way to thirty before she lowered her hand and opened her eyes. She took several audible breaths before speaking, making a little *O* with her mouth for every exhale.

"Cluster headaches," she said. "You never had one, I tell ya they're no Sunday picnic."

"You were saying about packing materials?" Jarsdel reminded her.

"Yes, but even if none of the stuff I mentioned was an issue, there's a whole other aspect to running a museum that folks don't think about, and that's *theme*. Just like a movie—what's the theme? Now you have enough of a kind of thing, like let's say gamblers' pistols, then you do an exhibit. If it's super popular, you make it permanent. But if you only got one or two, then you can't just shove 'em in anywhere you want. Our curators' entire job is putting together those exhibits in ways that make sense and look good. So what do you do with those random pieces?"

"Dunno," said Jarsdel. "Maybe donate them to another museum?"

"*Well.*" Keating grinned. It was the look of a schoolteacher who'd tried her best to educate a moron, failed, and was amused at the absurdity of her own efforts. "Did you even *hear* me about the packing issue? Excelsior," she said, counting on her fingers. "That's *aspen* excelsior, which doesn't exactly grow on grape arbors. Bubble wrap. Packing peanuts—ooh, not the Styrofoam kind, holy smokes no, not for these tree huggers, so you gotta spring for the starch kind. Air pillows. Crinkle paper. I'd keep going but I'd run outta fingers. This all coming together for you?"

"Ms. Keating. Are you telling me that you purchase the museum's surplus items?"

She lifted her arms. "Hallelujah. And there it is, the dark underbelly of managing a major collection. Let me know when your pulse stops racing. You go to any museum in America—heck, the world—and you'll find the same thing. There's a reason board members are of a certain *zip* code. Helps settle issues like this if you've got some folks with ready cash on hand."

"Do the other board members know?"

"Everyone knows. And there's nothing illegal about it. Now, we don't shout it from the mountaintops because no one wants to make a donation if there's a chance it won't end up on display. You got no *idea* the kick folks get when they see that little brass tag with, you know, 'Courtesy of the Blaumensteen, Shlumenshtoon, Ooglepoogle, Woogle-*noodle* family.' You go into a museum sometime and see how many of those tags say 'Courtesy of Anonymous Donor.' You get back to me and tell me how many."

"So to make sure I understand this correctly," said Jarsdel, "Mr. Burken would allow you to peruse donations to see if there was anything you wanted. If there was, you'd pay him and he'd pocket the money?"

Keating slapped her thighs. "Ha. Wow. Absolutely *not*. Money always went straight to the museum. Of *course* it went to the museum. As soon as they were donated, those pieces became Huntington property. I can't—I'm just in total *shock*. Dean didn't keep a penny from those sales. Woulda been stealing."

"True," Jarsdel agreed. "Assuming everything you told me is—"

"I'm not *lying*."

"All right, but if what you told me is accurate, how'd you ensure you were paying a fair price for the artwork? Especially since, by your own account, there were no appraisers involved?"

"Well—*ha*—this might surprise you," said Keating, "but I don't mind if I pay a little extra and that money goes to a place I love."

"You misunderstand. I'm not concerned you were overly generous. If indeed there were only you and Mr. Burken involved with these transactions, how can we know you didn't undercut the market value?"

Keating swallowed. "What?"

"That you weren't paying the—"

"Oh, no, I heard what you said. Just having trouble believing someone actually came into my home accusing me of being a thief. I offered you a *water*."

Mental exhaustion was one of the more interesting phenomena to observe, thought Jarsdel. It made him think of a bird looking for a place to land and finding no rest anywhere. Every time it began to fold its wings and settle onto a branch, jaws would snap and claws would swipe. The bird had to take off again, circling, searching, ever more desperate as its muscles burned hotter with fatigue.

He offered a taste of relief. "Listen. End of the day, I don't care about the details of whatever arrangement you and Mr. Burken enjoyed. What I *am* trying to do is figure out why a man was killed." His tone cooled. "To do that, I have to look at anything that's the least abnormal. A board member offended by Mr. Burken's methods or a resentful grad student—certainly, but less obvious places too. A donor who didn't get his name on one of those brass tags you were talking about." He shrugged, then pushed hard. "Maybe a criminal associate. Someone he conspired with to defraud a museum.

Someone who didn't want to be identified if the scheme came crashing down around her ears."

Keating blinked. "Ha—you…" She blinked again, sucking air in through her nose. "I want you out."

"Too close to home?"

She smiled sweetly, holding up a middle finger. "Climb it, Tarzan. Now outta my goddamn house."

Jarsdel had screwed up. Instead of steering Keating toward new information, he'd made her shut down. The anxiety he'd been seeding in her mind, along with the escape hatch he'd labeled so carefully, had completely lost their power. A few words too many, and he'd armed her with one of the most powerful defensive weapons a suspect could wield against the police—righteous anger. Interviews and interrogations depended on flexibility, and he'd locked himself into a strategy that he should've abandoned at the first sign it wasn't paying off.

He took out his wallet, removed a business card, and set it atop Vespasian's head. "I have no social life to speak of, so I've got plenty of time to devote to my work. There's anything to find in all this, I promise you I'll find it."

Keating used the same extended finger to gesture toward the front door. Presley let out a few barks, and there were more scratches from the other side of the wall.

"Body buried in the foundation, huh?" Jarsdel said, making his way into the foyer. "Don't it give you nightmares?"

He stepped outside and Keating shut the door, hard, leaving Jarsdel alone with the gnats and the heat. The temperature had risen, and the air seemed to close around him as he headed back to the car.

Morales was on the phone when Jarsdel got in. He'd rolled down the windows and reclined his seat as far as it would go, and now that his partner had arrived, thumbed the switch to return himself to a sitting position. Jarsdel started up the engine and had just pulled away from the curb when Morales ended the call.

"Don't wait for me to put on my seat belt or anything," he said, snapping the buckle in place.

"So?" Jarsdel asked.

"She's got what they call a healthy and diverse investment portfolio. Got an LLC registered in Nevada, something like McCormick & Associates or McCormick Partners or some shit. But it's all made up. There's no McCormick and no partners. Just her." His stomach growled and he made a face. "Let's grab a bite."

"How's the LLC make money?"

"Real estate. Most of the developments right here in Newport. Handful in other places. Where you wanna stop for lunch?"

"I dunno. Longer we wait with the traffic..." Jarsdel turned onto Pacific Coast Highway in the direction of Huntington Beach, checking the car's GPS for the quickest way back to LA. On their left, azure slices of the Pacific shimmered between hotels, restaurants, and art galleries.

"Fuck traffic, I'm hungry," said Morales. He brought out his phone and began typing with his thumb. "Gonna find us a place."

An idea occurred to Jarsdel. "Keating—how's she with her taxes?"

"Forget it. Not gonna get her on any of that Al Capone stuff. Pays every year, never been audited. Why, learn something good on your end?"

"I think she and Dean Burken were embezzling donations from the museum. You should've seen the inside of her house. Stuff just crammed into every available space. Wouldn't've been surprised if she'd been using the Rosetta Stone as a coffee table."

"Dude," said Morales, thumbing the screen of his iPhone. "Keep going about another mile, then hang a right on Walnut."

"Why?"

"You'll see."

"Seriously, why? We'll make good time if we hit the freeway now."

"Patience, grasshopper." Morales squinted ahead at the street signs. "Comin' up pretty soon."

"You at least tell me how this place is on Yelp?"

"Just up ahead. Make a right."

Jarsdel exited the highway at Walnut. "Now what?"

"Left at the first light. Dude, left—get in the *left* lane."

"I'm *doing* it." As he waited for oncoming traffic to thin out, he added, "Just so you know, because of this, we're listening to an audiobook on the way back. Gonna be about a two-hour drive by the time we leave." They made the turn, preceding along a narrow commercial street. "What now?"

"Grab a meter."

Jarsdel pulled over and cut the engine. "Tell you what. I'll give you a choice, and you can pick which one interests you most. I just downloaded Foucault's *Discipline and Punish*, so—"

"Hey." Morales rapped his knuckles on the dash, then pointed out the windshield. Jarsdel looked, then his eyes too twinkled in fascination.

"Huh. Okay."

They were parked in front of a Western-themed bar, its façade of horizontal lap siding weathered to suggest the rugged spirit and hardscrabble living of the frontier. A sandwich board planted on the sidewalk advertised "Hot food and cold beer."

Above the pair of batwing doors, in the wide, Victorian cursive of a Deadwood saloon, were the words "King Henry's."

The detectives were seated at a booth with a view of a televised golf tournament. The sound was down, and Jarsdel didn't care a whit for the game, but he nevertheless found himself drawn to the flickering images. He glanced at Morales, whose gaze was also fixed on the screen.

"You know the first written reference to golf was a royal edict prohibiting it," said Jarsdel. "James II said it was a distraction from archery practice."

"I just don't get it, man," said Morales. "Know who loves golf?

The LT. That should tell you something." He shook his head. "So you're saying back in medieval times, there were enough dudes who'd rather do *this* than shoot arrows into things? That it was enough of a problem that the king had to be like, 'Hey, shit's off-limits. Stop dickin' around with the plaid pants and get back to being useful.'"

"Something like that."

"Scottish, right? Golf?" said Morales.

"Game as we know it today, yeah. Shepherds whacking rocks into rabbit holes with their crooks."

"Doesn't fit. Scottish dudes are all about, like, blue face paint and organ meats and chuckin' boulders at each other for fun. Tough hombres. So badass they can wear those skirts without feeling self-conscious."

Their server arrived. She was college aged, skinny, blond hair in a ponytail. Despite her youth, the expression she wore was guarded, even sullen. Jarsdel noted with interest that she wore a T-shirt with the command *Save King Henry!* printed across the chest in bolded letters. Beneath was a website, savekinghenry.com.

"What can I getcha?" The smile she offered was brief and didn't reach her eyes.

The detectives looked down at their menus—long one-sheets of thick, sepia card stock. The lighting in the bar was low, but Jarsdel could still make out several stains and even bits of crusted sauce on the paper.

"I should get something healthy," said Morales.

"Want me to come back?" said the server.

"No, lemme have that bacon cheeseburger."

"Wheat or brioche?"

"Wheat's healthier. Let's do wheat. And everything but whatever the house sauce is. None of that. And gimme Swiss."

"We do the burgers medium. That work for you?"

"Yup."

The server turned to Jarsdel. "You?"

"May I please have the wedge salad?"

She scribbled down the order. "We're short-staffed in the kitchen today, so it'll be about twenty minutes."

"Oh, can I ask you something? Says scallions. Do they do, like, a lot of scallions, or is it—"

"You want me to ask them to hold the scallions?"

"No, actually I was wondering if I could get extra scallions."

She sighed and made a note on her pad. "Anything to drink? Our signature drink is the King's Tonic, and we've also got Guinness on tap."

"Arnold Palmer would be great," said Jarsdel, "but would you mind filling it mostly with tea, like about three-quarters, then the rest with lemonade?"

"Water's fine for me," said Morales.

"Aquafina or Smart Water?" said the server.

"Tap."

She sighed again and left.

Morales glared at Jarsdel. "Extra scallions? I'm stuck in a car with you the rest of the afternoon. Kind of a dick move." He shook his head, then brought out his phone and began scrolling through emails.

Jarsdel hardly registered the complaint. His attention was on the room's décor—typical paraphernalia of the Disneyfied Old West. The walls were hung with mining equipment—pickaxes, pans, and shovels—along with dozens of horseshoes, a coiled lasso, painted saws, and several wanted posters, though Jarsdel couldn't tell from where he sat whether they were genuine. There were a few framed oils, which included a bland panorama of a wagon train and a hideous portrait of John Wayne, his trademark laconic gaze rendered here as the unfocused stare of a corpse. Considering the proximity to Hollywood, there were surprisingly few references to movie cowboys. The only others Jarsdel could see were a gray Stetson that a placard identified as having belonged to Tom Mix, and a replica of Roy Rogers's six-string.

The most notable piece was a life-size wooden cigar-store Indian standing to the left of the hostess station. The wall adjacent was decorated with dozens of photographs—arranged in a grid—of people posing with the sculpture. The first few along the top row were in black-and-white, but the rest were all in color. Each picture was labeled below with a plastic tag identifying the year it was taken; these began in the upper left with 1952 and finished in the bottom right with 2021.

Their server returned with the drinks, tossing two worn coasters onto their table before setting down the tumblers. "Pardon me," said Jarsdel, "About your shirt—who's King Henry?"

"That thing," she said, pointing to the wooden Indian.

"Really?" Jarsdel looked at it with renewed interest. "Why 'save' him? Does he have termites?"

"It's a long story. Gotta get back to the kitchen."

Once she'd gone, Jarsdel got up and went over to the statue. Even with just a cursory examination, he spotted several errors. The Indian wore the bone hair-pipe chest plate and feather war bonnet of a Sioux but the arm tattoos and brass earrings of a mid-Atlantic tribe. His skin—painted a tomato red—was bare beneath the chest plate, but he was clad below the waist in heavy leather leggings, something he would've only worn during the winter. Further complicating the ensemble was the knife protruding from the waistband, with its distinctly southwest Apache deer antler grip and obsidian blade, and the war paint, which included the signature black handprint across the cheek of an Iowa warrior. Most puzzling of all was a belt of wampum—the shell tapestry used as currency among the Pequot of Massachusetts—slung over his shoulder. It was clear whoever had carved the sculpture had selected the most obvious Native American tropes and simply slapped them together.

Jarsdel studied the wall of photographs. Now that he was close enough, he could see it was the same two people, a man and a woman, in all the pictures spanning 1952 to 1991. They looked happy in all but the last one, in which half the man's face drooped from a stroke and the woman leaned heavily on her walker. The next thirty years of photographs were of another, initially much younger couple. The final 2021 picture showed only the man, arm around King Henry's shoulders, his smile so muted it was hardly there at all.

Below the photographs, in a lighted display cabinet, were more of the *Save King Henry!* T-shirts, along with a myriad of gimcrack merchandise—beer cozies, buttons, baseball caps, even mousepads all printed with the same slogan.

"First time in?"

Jarsdel turned his head and found himself face to face with the man from the 2021 photograph. He too wore one of the *Save King Henry!* shirts.

"Yeah, quite a place. This in particular"—he indicated the King Henry sculpture—"is really something."

"Yup," the man agreed. "Been in our family more'n a hundred years."

"You're the owner?"

"Sure am." He removed his hand from his pants pocket and stuck it out. "Lance Hocker."

Reluctantly, Jarsdel took it in his own. COVID might be gone, but touching a stranger still felt unnecessarily risky. Hocker's hand was warm and a little damp from being in his pocket. Jarsdel forced a smile.

"Tully," he said.

Hocker let him go and stood arms akimbo, admiring the Indian. "Hand-carved from a single piece of wood. Granddad got it in trade from the artist. He was a mechanic. Fixed up the guy's Model T, but the guy couldn't pay. Granddad pointed at this and said, 'That'll do right there.' Probably worth about twenty grand today." He looked at Jarsdel, who nodded in appreciation.

"Our server said something about his name being King Henry?"

"That's right."

"What's the origin of it?"

"Some local Indian guy, way back. Might've been a chief, I

think? Kind of a folk hero. Helped some of our settlers get, you know, settled." Hocker chuckled.

"And this was what he looked like? King Henry?"

"Nah, it's just some random Indian. But knowing the local stories, that's what Granddad decided to name him. Then he gave it as a gift to my pop when he bought this place in '52." Hocker nodded at the wall of photographs. "At first, he couldn't think what to call it, then he gets this guy here, and it just clicks. 'I'll call it *King Henry's*.' Rest is history."

"What's wrong with him?" said Jarsdel.

The man's eyes narrowed. "What d'you mean?"

"I mean the shirts and the buttons. Does he need restoration work?"

"No, he's in great shape. It's that they're tryin' to make us get rid of him."

"Who are?"

"Idiots." Hocker chewed his bottom lip. "Apparently he offended some people. Not Indians, mind you. These are rich white kids. Anyway, King Henry made it so they didn't feel *safe*. God forbid, right? Then because they got nothing better to do, they went after our Yelp page and got a bunch of their snowflake buddies to flood us with one-star reviews. Wanna ruin my business over this. Compared King Henry to those lawn jockeys down South, said we're all in the Klan. Now they got a petition going to try to convince the Better Business Bureau to revoke our accreditation unless we remove the statue." His frown lines deepened. "Just bonkers. So depending on how far this goes, we might have to go to court with the BBB. All this merch is basically for his legal fund."

He noticed the badge on Jarsdel's belt. "LAPD? Something goin' on I should know about?"

"No, routine business. Stopped off here for lunch. Actually, one of the things that brought us to your restaurant was the name. I didn't know about this whole story with the petition, but I'd actually come across that name recently. King Henry."

Hocker raised his eyebrows. "No kidding?"

"It was on a map. Old map of Newport, done about a hundred fifty years ago. Cartographer labeled part of the town 'King Henry's Pride.' You ever hear of a place like that?"

"No, sure haven't. Interesting though. Love to see that map if you got it handy."

"It was up at the Huntington Museum in Pasadena."

Hocker looked thoughtful. "Wouldn't be a bad idea for me to get in touch with them. Might help with the BBB if we can talk about this whole thing in terms of local history. Preservation and stuff." His expression brightened, and he reached behind the display cabinet and brought out a pair of *Save King Henry!* buttons the size of tea saucers. "Here," he said, holding them out. "Couldn't hurt to have a cop wearing one of these. You can take the other one to your partner over there."

"Oh," said Jarsdel. "We're not allowed to wear anything that takes a position on an issue."

"What about drunk driving? I see those bumper stickers on your cars. Wife beating too."

Jarsdel shot a longing glance at their table, where Morales was still bent over his phone. "Those're, you know, more about concrete legal issues."

"Well, take 'em anyway," said Hocker, thrusting them into Jarsdel's hands. "Give 'em to your kids. Get the word out. We're being bullied."

Jarsdel accepted the buttons. "Thanks. Good meeting you."

"Back atcha."

When he returned to the table, Jarsdel slid the buttons across to his partner.

Morales didn't look up. "What's this?"

"Souvenirs. We'll always have Newport."

Morales brushed them away. One glanced off a ketchup bottle. "Anything interesting?"

"About King Henry? Supposedly a real guy. Local Indian leader.

Though he wouldn't have looked at all like that statue. Well, no one did. That's some kind of fantasy amalgamation. There're about ten different tribes represented, and from wildly divergent cultural modes."

"Gonna tell you something honestly," said Morales. "Some of the words you say—I dunno, maybe it's more like the *way* you say them—actually make me tune out as soon as they hit the air."

Their server returned and set down the burger and the salad. "Here's another water," she said, replacing Morales's empty glass with a fresh one. "Don't want you to get thirsty."

He gave her an admiring smile as she left. "Spicy." He looked at Jarsdel. "She's spicy, man."

They tucked into their food. The blue cheese dressing was heavy with thickeners and light on flavor, the bacon freeze dried, and the lettuce was too cold. He could even feel ice crystals fracturing as he bit through the leaves. "How's your burger?" he asked his partner.

Morales swallowed with some effort and took a long swig of water. "Doesn't make me wanna save King Henry."

9

She hardly moves, Jarsdel thought.

Margaret Rishkov was a short, round woman with close-cropped silver hair and unruly eyebrows. And the shapeless, ankle-length brown dress she wore could have been mistaken for clerical. But the most striking difference between her and fellow board member Ellery Keating was her stillness. Whereas Keating had been in near-constant, nervous motion, Rishkov only troubled to move if performing a discrete task—reaching for a glass, asking a question, even blinking her eyes, which she hardly ever seemed to do. Once the action was completed, she'd return to her state of uncanny dormancy. She was like a portrait that came to sporadic life, and then only at the periphery of your vision, so you weren't sure whether it had moved at all.

Not quite, Jarsdel considered. Rishkov's intelligence was obvious. One need only meet her gaze to sense the tremendous power behind it, but this was a power set apart from the mere sum of her accumulated knowledge. The mind that quickened before him was of a kind Jarsdel knew well. Baba had it too, and there was only one word that got close to describing it: *fierce*. This wasn't a living portrait, Jarsdel decided, but rather a cat—muscles coiled, watching from the tall grass.

He hadn't wanted Morales there, had thought his partner would only get in the way and shut Rishkov down with his open hostility toward academics. Now he realized he could've used the company. Something about the elderly professor, a rocks glass in one veined fist and the handle of her Alpacca wolf head cane in the other, made him uneasy.

"Care for another?" she asked.

Jarsdel looked down into his tumbler. A faint glimmer of gold at the bottom. Treaty Oak Ghost Hill Texas bourbon, and it was almost gone.

"Thought bourbon had to come from Kentucky," he said.

"Common misconception," said Rishkov. "Would you? Like another, I mean."

Jarsdel gave a reluctant shake of his head. "Thanks, no."

"Served its purpose."

"Sorry?"

"You're not allowed to drink on duty, I'm sure, but you accepted my initial offer of a drink to build rapport. Now that's done, so you don't require a second glass." She reached for the bottle, poured herself three fingers, and slipped back into stillness.

Jarsdel finished the last teaspoon of spirit, enjoying the sensation of the liquid ember as it slid down his throat. "Why would I need to build rapport?"

"Aren't you here to ask me if I killed Dean Burken?" Rishkov asked.

That caught him off guard. It shouldn't have; those gifted with fierce brilliance tended to venture in unexpected directions, and it was wise to be ready for anything they might say. But the question was so bold that Jarsdel had to scramble to catch up with her.

"Is that a question I should ask?"

A smile appeared, then dissipated. "Let's play a game. You approach me through a series of pointlessly meandering questions. I respond in an equally evasive manner, trying at the same time to learn as much as I can about your investigation. We spar like this for a half hour, neither of us gaining ground, until one or the other of us breaks from the routine and says something useful. Or we could just start there and skip the preshow event. Any preferences on your end?"

Jarsdel tried to look directly back into her eyes but found he was unable to do so. It was like staring into the sun. You sense you're doing damage to yourself, and it would be best to turn away.

He gave a single nod.

"Good. No, it isn't a question you should ask. I didn't kill Dean, and should someone send Ellery to join him, it won't be me either. Now am I glad of the former and hoping for the latter? Yes and yes. Dean was a blustering windbag who used his position as registrar as a means of propping up his own ego."

"He had good taste in art."

"So did Göring." Rishkov took a long sip of bourbon. "I'm also convinced he derived sadistic pleasure in his role as resident spoliator. A few years ago, I got word we received a collection of ephemera that included a handwritten letter from Nellie Bly to Jules Verne. It had just arrived, so it was still in quarantine."

"Sorry," Jarsdel broke in. "New acquisitions go into quarantine?"

"Of course. We often have no idea what condition a piece is in before we receive it. It could be sick, so to speak. Mold and pests— silverfish, for example—could contaminate our existing collection. Bronze disease may not be bacterial, but it's just as contagious. A single Roman coin coated in those corrosive chlorides can destroy any copper alloy it touches."

"All right," said Jarsdel. "You were saying about the letter?"

"Our quarantine facility isn't adjacent to the main building— another safeguard—and only a few people are allowed in. Dean was one of them, of course, since registrars are responsible for overseeing the entire accession process from evaluation to display." She paused, and her expression clouded. "I couldn't wait to see that letter. It's my area—the Gilded Age—and I made the mistake of asking him when he thought it would be released to archives. He assured me it wouldn't take long. A few weeks passed, and none of the curators had seen it, so I asked Dean again. 'Oh, very sorry,' he said. 'I'm afraid we found book lice eggs. It had to be destroyed.' He actually smiled as he told me that."

Rishkov sipped her bourbon and became very still once again.

"And Ellery?" said Jarsdel. "How does she fit in?"

"Ellery Keating is the face of the modern American museum. She's a symptom of the times, like type two diabetes or communication addiction disorder."

"Can you elaborate?"

"It all goes back to the '80s. Withdrawal of government support for the arts. Boards of directors were once exclusively populated with artists, historians, conservation specialists. People like me, in other words. Our work was seen as a public service. By the time the '90s rolled around, we discovered that was no longer the case. Suddenly we needed money, and where were we going to get it?"

With a single, measured motion of her cane, she gestured at their surroundings. The difference between her living room and Keating's was striking. Rishkov's felt much freer and open. There was no sense of the flea market stall, no piles of loot. The walls were mostly bare; only a few pieces adorned them, thoughtfully displayed and illuminated in the soft glow of picture lights. But Jarsdel understood her point, and it had nothing to do with design sense. Her house, tucked amid the low hills above Eagle Rock Boulevard, was a quarter the size of Keating's mansion.

Rishkov lowered the cane, planting it on the floor with the authority of Judge Kleinfeld's gavel. "*Give or get.* That became the new motto. Sure, there're still a few token experts kept around to lend credibility to the operation, but in general, you're on the board because you've got plenty to donate, or you have the connections to raise funds. Ideally both."

Keating herself had said as much, Jarsdel remembered. He considered his next words carefully. "Isn't that the whole point of philanthropy? I mean, don't museums depend on the wealthy?

Artists are friends with other artists, which is fine, but millionaires are friends with other millionaires. If I were in your position—and forgive me if this sounds ill informed—I'd wish for a dozen Ellery Keatings. I just don't see the downside."

Rishkov gave no sign that his words had affected her, just looked out at him from the camouflage of her unnerving stillness.

"Detective," she said finally, "none of this interests me. I'll be eighty next month, and my doctor tells me I've two or three good years before the hypertension either kills me or casts me into the same fog of vascular dementia that took my mother. By then, I won't be able to tell a Hopper from a Lichtenstein, much less care who Ellery Keating was. I won't have to worry about Dixiecrat senators slashing the National Endowment for the Humanities, and it will no longer bother me that the petty and the shockingly idiotic will eventually triumph in their aim to suck as much beauty out of the world as they can. I've done all I'm able to save you and your solipsistic little generation, and I sincerely hope the last headline I read before my brains turn to stump water is that suicide is at an all-time high."

Jarsdel allowed a brief silence, then said, "You used the past tense."

"Really?" said Rishkov. "I count simple present and simple future."

"You said you won't care who Ellery Keating *was*. Expecting something to happen to her?"

Rishkov smiled. "Wishful thinking."

Jarsdel nodded. "Are you familiar with the most recent acquisition? I'm referring to the..." He checked his field notebook even though he didn't need to. "The Theodore Smith estate."

"Certainly," said Rishkov. "Astonishing any of it made it out of quarantine."

"What can you tell me about it?"

"How could that possibly be of interest?"

"Goes along with my *firsts and lasts* rule," said Jarsdel. "In my job, you pay attention when someone does something for the first time, no matter what it is. Could be calling in sick, forgetting a birthday, getting into a public argument. And you pay attention to the last thing. Processing the Theodore Smith estate was one of the last things Mr. Burken did before he was murdered."

Rishkov twisted her cane back and forth between thumb and forefinger, the silver wolf's head catching the light each time it faced Jarsdel. "Theodore Smith was the last of a long line of dullards dating all the way back to Jamestown. No relation to *John* Smith, incidentally, though the family encouraged speculation. At any rate, Theodore's great-grandfather, Ennis P. Smith, was a mediocre Boston attorney and amateur cartographer who ditched his family for a new life as a California treasure seeker."

"He find anything?" Jarsdel asked.

"Gold? Rumors aside, very unlikely. This was 1851, after the smart ones had already flooded the hills. But he had everything else going for him—boring, racist—so he fared well enough. Served as one of our first state representatives."

"Then what was so special about his family's bequest to the Huntington?"

Rishkov sighed. "I never said there *was* anything special about it. No unity at all. A scattering of ceramics, maybe three of which are actually worth anything, some wood carvings, a few Indian artifacts, and a mountain of paper matter."

"Memoirs? Legal correspondence?"

"Both, certainly. And stacks of piano rolls. Mostly Welte & Sons, which makes them collectors' items, but what on earth we're going to do with them, I have no idea."

Jarsdel wasn't sure, but he guessed that piano rolls were the spools of perforated paper sheets used in old player pianos. "So if you've still got the piano rolls and the ceramics," he said, "then the map wasn't the only thing Mr. Burken held on to."

"I didn't say that either. I said it's the only thing that made it out of quarantine before he was killed. Under Dean, most things didn't."

Her eyes narrowed only a little, but it was a striking change on a face that gave so little away. "You don't know how museums work. When you give us something, we first have to choose to accept it. It's a substantial responsibility. We're assuming stewardship, but the item still technically belongs to the public. If an item is accepted, it's issued a unique accession number. It's then appraised for insurance purposes and evaluated by a conservator. Then it goes into quarantine. Quarantine is where the Butcher liked to do his work. He had complete control over what came out of there. And he'd initially accept far more items than a reputable registrar. He'd take virtually any donation just in case it could suit him in some way. Or to deprive another museum from having it."

"Did you ever suspect," Jarsdel ventured, "that he might have been running a business on the side?"

"When it came to Dean, I suspected everything. Do I believe he allowed Ellery to use quarantine as her personal Aladdin's cave? Certainly. But here we run into the grayest areas of collections management ethics. If we ever want to sell or trade a single part of it, we must only do so if such a transaction is in line with our mission, not—and I can't emphasize this enough—*not* to make a profit. Would it be a conflict of interest for Ellery Keating to purchase a piece from the same museum whose board she sits on? Absolutely. Is it actionable? No. And she's far too valuable. Her Memorial Day fundraiser just netted one-point-two-five million, costs of patriotic bunting aside."

The room was warm enough that Jarsdel was beginning to sweat, and his glasses kept sliding down his nose. "Earlier, when I asked about Ennis Smith finding gold, you said no, but there'd been rumors."

Rishkov swirled the bourbon in her glass and took a long sip, eyes closed to focus her sense of smell. "Absurd," she said, setting down the tumbler. "Probably ginned up to get him into the state legislature. Establish him as a gentleman adventurer and not just another failed Yankee prospector." Her gaze flitted to her mantel clock, then settled back on Jarsdel. "Afraid I'm going to have to kick you out, Detective."

"Of course." Jarsdel got to his feet. "Plans this evening?"

Rishkov made no move to stand. "No, but I make it a rule not to see homicide detectives after five. Feel free to show yourself out."

As Jarsdel headed for the door, she called after him. "By the way, I don't have an alibi for the night Dean was shot."

He paused, hand on the door handle, and looked back at her.

"Just in case you were curious," Rishkov added. "And don't forget, I'm in my twilight years. First-degree murder cases are complex. By the time I actually made it to trial, I'd be as crazy as a dog in a hubcap factory."

"Okay," said Jarsdel. "All that's very interesting. Own a gun?"

Rishkov only stared at him.

Jarsdel shrugged. "Easy enough for me to check. We'll be in touch."

"Oh, I certainly hope so," said Rishkov. "You probably can't tell from my expression, but this has all been very stimulating."

After the previous date night, which had terminated in stale pretzels and Baba's icy philosophizing—all against the soundtrack of Dad's chainsaw snores—Jarsdel had assumed the nascent tradition was dead. He was surprised, then, when Dad called just a few days later to tell him Baba wanted to try again, and could he be there by six?

"I promise he'll be good," he said.

Jarsdel arrived on the hour, and a moment later, Baba slunk out of the house and got in the car.

"Okay," he said, crossing his arms.

As Jarsdel drove, he reconstructed how he imagined his parents' day had unfolded. They'd begun arguing early—probably during breakfast—about whether Dad should be left alone. This continued into the afternoon, pausing for an occasional break, all the way through to early evening until their son arrived. Baba had obviously lost, and Jarsdel wasn't surprised. Despite his steel hide, Baba could be cowed by his husband. Dad was a gentle and soft-spoken man, but not during arguments, which he approached with the skill of a master craftsman. If he was failing on logos, he'd retreat to ethos. If that didn't work, he'd bounce to pathos. His opponents were ever off-balance, reeling from direct hits and then finding their counterattacks landing at abandoned positions. Jarsdel had never seen him lose an argument against anyone, regardless of the subject. He'd rail just as passionately against moral relativism as he would for the superiority of the bassoon over the other woodwinds.

Baba hardly said anything as they drove, still nursing whatever wounds he'd sustained back at the house. He spent most of the time looking out the window, commenting only occasionally on a new construction project or the ubiquity of LA traffic. When he saw they were heading toward Los Feliz, he grumbled, "Hope you made reservations. I'm starving."

They got off the freeway near Griffith Park. Jarsdel turned left, crawled through half a mile of gridlock, then swung up into the hills to avoid the worst stretches of the boulevard. He and Baba winced as the setting sun lit up the windshield, and both men flipped down their visors to cut the glare.

Jarsdel's phone buzzed. He unclipped it from his belt and held it out to Baba.

"Can you see who it is?"

"What do I do?"

"Just take it and look."

Baba took the phone. "It's dark."

"You waited too long. Just hit the button, and the screen'll light up again."

"What button?"

"The main button. The big button. Right there on the side."

"This one?"

"I can't look. I'm driving." Jarsdel let out an annoyed breath. "Never mind. Just put it in the cupholder."

"It lit up again."

"What's it say?"

"*Very sorry to have bothered you.*"

"That's what it says? The whole thing?"

"It went dark again."

Jarsdel pulled over. "Give it to me, please." He took the phone. It was a two-part text from an unknown local number.

This is Mrs. Rostami. Can you help please?

Very sorry to have bothered you.

She lived on Ambrose, only a few blocks from where they were now parked. He swept the dial icon and put the phone to his ear.

"Who're you calling?" Baba said.

Jarsdel held up his hand.

Rostami answered on the first ring. "Hello?"

"Hello," said Jarsdel, speaking in Farsi. "This is Detective Jarsdel. Everything all right?"

Baba perked up at hearing his native language.

"No," said Rostami. "I've been robbed. Can you come?"

"Robbed?" Jarsdel repeated. "What was stolen?"

"My samovar. It was my grandmother's."

Jarsdel understood. Samovars—the ornate water boilers beloved by so many European and Asian tea drinkers—were often family heirlooms. "Did you call 911?" he asked.

She didn't answer.

"Mrs. Rostami?"

"Sorry," she said. "I'm just embarrassed a little. I wanted to call you first. I feel more comfortable because I know you. The other police...I don't think they'd understand the way you do."

"That's fine. I'm in the area now. Would you like me to come by?"

"You would do that?"

"Of course. I can be there in a few minutes."

After he hung up, he turned to Baba, who looked annoyed. Something else too, though Jarsdel couldn't make out what it was.

He tried to put him at ease. "This'll only take a sec."

"Who was that?" Baba asked.

"Just a citizen. I think she's lonely, and I'm the only one in Hollywood Station who speaks Persian."

"I told you, I'm starving."

Jarsdel reflected on how his main purpose in life now seemed to be playing chauffeur to hungry, demanding men. "Baba, I promise it'll be quick. Someone stole her samovar."

His father grunted. "Ridiculous things. Get an electric kettle."

"That's good," said Jarsdel, driving again. "Exactly the kind of cultural sensitivity stuff they teach in the academy."

Baba was looking out the window as they made a left onto Hillhurst and crossed Los Feliz Boulevard. "Welcome to the twenty-first century," he muttered. "Cost of admission: one samovar. You give me the samovar, I hand you an electric kettle, and everyone's friends now."

Jarsdel turned onto Ambrose and double-parked in front of Rostami's building. "I know she'd like meeting someone else from Iran. Wanna say hi?"

"To whom? Your samovar damsel? No. And don't be long. I'm starving."

"Huh, had no idea. Wish you'd mentioned that earlier." Jarsdel pointed at the door to Rostami's apartment. "I'll be right there. Five minutes, tops. I'll leave the engine on in case you need to move the car."

He got out and jogged across the small courtyard, then up the steps to the second floor. There was the smell of *advieh* again, and his stomach grumbled.

Rostami opened the door before he could knock. The first thing she said was, "I feel terrible for bothering you."

"Not at all," said Jarsdel. "I should've contacted you sooner like I said I would."

"It's fine, it's fine. I know how busy you must be. Please come in."

"I can't, sorry. Only have a couple minutes." Her disappointment was immediate and apparent, so he tried to redirect her attention to the reason she'd called him. "You say you were robbed?"

She nodded. "It's a Borujerd samovar, with German silver. Very expensive, of course, but the value to me is so much more."

"Did you get a look at the assailant?"

"No. It happened when I was at the store."

Jarsdel frowned. "Oh, then you mean you were burgled, not robbed."

"Isn't that the same thing?"

"Not exactly, so I'm glad you weren't robbed. That can be very traumatic."

"This *is* traumatic," she said. "The feeling of violation. It's…" She shook her head.

He examined the doorframe and noticed there were no tool marks. "Do you ever leave your door unlocked when you're out?"

"Never."

He bent forward, squinted at the dead bolt. It bore the scratches of daily wear, but nothing stood out. The thieves must have used a lock-picking gun. The days when only licensed locksmiths could get their hands on one were long gone. Still, you had to work at least a little to acquire them, so that meant the burglars were pros—or at least dedicated wannabes. He brought out the field interview notebook and readied his pen. "Can you tell me what the samovar looked like?"

"Gold. In color, I mean. I already mentioned it's a Borujerd. Hundred fifty years old. Oil heated."

As she went on, Jarsdel realized how absurd this all was. He was asking her to describe the samovar as if there were a database of stolen Iranian water-boiling vessels, and he could put a BOLO on it. Most likely the samovar had been taken by one of Rostami's neighbors and traded for a dime bag. By now, it was probably in a Panorama City pawn shop.

When she finished, he put away his notebook and offered a reassuring smile. "I'll make a report soon as I get back to the station, then pass it on to Burglary. You don't by any chance have a picture, do you?"

She shook her head. "Only black-and-white. They won't help."

"Well, I'll certainly let you know if anything turns up. Wish I could stay longer but I'm going to dinner with my baba."

Rostami's eyes brightened. "Such a good son. How wonderful you're so close."

Yes, thought Jarsdel, *so close*. "Well, have a lovely evening. If you..."

Rostami put a hand on his arm, and he trailed off. It was so unusual for an Iranian woman to touch a man outside her family that whatever she wanted to tell him, it must be important.

But all she said was, "Have dinner here. I can cook for the three of us."

"I'm sorry," said Jarsdel. "This isn't the best night. My baba and I haven't had an evening in a while."

Rostami was already nodding. "Of course. Such a good son. Please, wait here just a moment. I have something for you."

She released his arm and disappeared into the apartment. Jarsdel drummed his fingers against the doorjamb, hoping she'd hurry up. He wasn't interested in more complaints from Baba.

Rostami returned about a minute later, thrusting a hammered copper bowl into his arms. It was filled to the brim with saffron pudding and sealed in with a taut film of plastic wrap.

"What's this?" Jarsdel asked.

"For you and your baba to share. My own recipe."

"Oh, Mrs. Rostami—"

"No *taarof*." She gave a quick but forceful wag of her finger.

"But the bowl."

"Bring it back when you can. No rush. Regards to your baba." Without further conversation, she shut the door.

Hefting the bowl of pudding, Jarsdel descended the steps to the ground level. Along the way back to his car, he caught the whiff of pot smoke and decided Rostami's suspicions were probably correct. Her neighbors would easily know when she left the apartment, and a lock-picking gun would have gained them entry in seconds.

Baba had turned the engine off for some reason, but the car was where Jarsdel had left it. He opened the back door and set the bowl carefully on the floor mat, wedging it between a copy of the *DSM-5* and a forgotten twelve-pack of Kona Brewing Longboard Island Lager. That done, he went around to the front, got inside, and twisted the key in the ignition. "Okay, thanks for your patience, so to speak. You ready to…"

The words died in his throat. He'd been about to back up and had just turned his head so he could see out the rear window when he caught a glimpse of his father's face. The man's skin had taken on a grayish cast, and the eyes that stared out were wide and vacant.

"Baba!" Jarsdel seized his shoulders.

His father closed and opened his eyes in long, slow blinks.

"What's going on? You need a doctor?" He reached for the dashboard radio only to have his hand close on nothing but air. This was his personal car, not his unmarked Crown Vic. He grabbed his cell out of the cupholder.

"Hang on, I'll call—"

Baba put his hand over Jarsdel's. "No."

"Well, what is it?" Realization dawned, and it settled in his gut like an icy fist. "Something happened to Dad."

But Baba shook his head. He took a deep breath, then let it out in ragged exhales. Jarsdel tried to be patient, to let the man explain whatever was going on when he was ready, but it was impossible. Never could he recall him looking like this. The only word he could think to describe him was *destroyed*.

He tried to speak as calmly as he could. "Baba. You really have to tell me what's going on, okay? If we need to get to the ER, let's go now."

No answer.

"I'm just gonna start heading toward the hospital unless you tell me otherwise. All right?"

Baba closed his eyes again. Jarsdel backed up, threw the car into drive, and was looking for an opening in the passing traffic when his father finally spoke.

"Stop."

Jarsdel put the car back into park. "What d'you mean?"

"No hospital."

"Then what's happening? Tell me what to do."

"Take us to dinner."

"*What?* You look like you're dying." A terrible thought occurred to him. "You're not sick too, are you?"

"I'm fine," said Baba.

"Then *tell* me. I'm not going anywhere until you explain what's happening."

Baba opened his eyes. They still stared straight ahead, but they were clearer now, more his father's eyes than those of a terrified stranger.

"Panic attack," he said.

Jarsdel was baffled. "Since when do you get panic attacks?"

"Since your dad got sick."

"Why didn't you tell me?"

"Please, Tully. Let's go."

"I'm not dropping this, Baba. How serious is it? Are you getting treatment?"

"Shut your mouth and drive!"

It was the first time Jarsdel could remember Baba ever raising his voice at him. Above the man's desk at USC was a framed quotation, rendered in Persian calligraphy by his own hand. He'd written it down during the worst days of the revolution, translating it from the English of William Gladstone.

The heated mind resents the chill touch and relentless scrutiny of logic.

As a boy, Jarsdel had been forced to copy the line again and again. It was how he'd learned the Persian alphabet. It also became, by repetition if nothing else, the unofficial family motto. "If your opponent yells and shouts, you've won," Baba had told him. "No matter what they say in that moment, how much they curse and stamp, don't take it personally. Instead you should thank them, because they've just shown you their necks and their bellies. Their softest parts. They've told you they have nothing further to contribute to the conversation apart from an increase in volume."

Jarsdel thought of those words now, trying to reconcile them to the stricken man beside him.

They were sitting on the patio at All Time, a café on Hillhurst specializing in gourmet comfort food. Jarsdel was working his way through Grandma's focaccia, a toasted slab of the herbed bread heaped with homemade burrata and Sun Gold tomatoes, and Baba had settled on something called "the Good Ass Salad," though he refused to order it by name.

He'd only picked at it since their food arrived, and though his color had returned somewhat, he remained silent and withdrawn. Jarsdel had by now gone from concerned to annoyed.

"This isn't exactly what I pictured when Dad told me you were gonna be on your best behavior."

Baba stabbed a cherry tomato, turned it in the low light of the patio, then scraped it against the edge of the bowl. It fell back into the salad, deflated and oozing juice. Jarsdel felt a flush of anger.

"You know what? Why don't we just take off. I've pretty much lost my appetite anyway. We can throw our stuff into takeout containers."

He was about to signal the waiter when Baba spoke. "I have a problem."

Jarsdel waited for him to continue, but after an appropriate interval passed in silence, he said, "That's pretty clear."

A souped-up Firebird roared by, making the diners jump. The driver of a Highlander it had nearly sideswiped screamed out, "Hope you die slow, motherfucker!" as he accelerated up the hill after him. The Doppler effect distorted the last word, rolling it out and deepening it into the tormented lowing of a steer at slaughter.

A man at a nearby table laughed nervously. "Jeez," someone else commented. "I love LA," added another.

Baba gave no sign he noticed. "Can I ask you something?" he said.

Jarsdel nodded. "Sure."

"What was it that made you decide to become a policeman?"

"Christ, Baba. How many times are we—"

His father gave a dismissive flutter of his hand. "That's not what I mean. I'm not asking why you left behind academics, none of that old conversation. I'm asking sincerely. What motivated you? What was the one thing that changed for you? You never expressed any fascination in this kind of work when you were a boy. So what changed?"

Jarsdel was suspicious. Whatever the man was going through, he had no idea, but he wasn't about to endure another browbeating over his career. "I've told you," he said.

"No."

"I have. About five thousand times."

"Yes, you've said you wanted to be among those who renew the world. Very lofty. Zoroaster would be delighted. But it's abstract, Tully."

Jarsdel began to protest, but again Baba waved him off. "I'm not suggesting you're being dishonest, either with me or with yourself. It's a fine goal to better the world. But no one does what you did, sloughing off everything, sacrificing security for uncertainty, without there being some kind of push. What your dad would've called the 'inciting incident' in one of his English classes. What moved you?"

Jarsdel stared at Baba, realizing he was right. He'd never told anyone what that push had been, and no one had ever asked. All anyone wanted to know was how he could leave his old life behind to do something so radically different, so obviously strange and foreign considering his background. But none had ever asked him *why*.

He could tell it was suddenly important to Baba, that the man was searching for something. And he loved his father and wanted to help him. Then he thought of the years they could have shared that Baba had wasted through bitterness and obstinacy and of how much affection he'd denied his son purely on principle. And how now, after seven years, he suddenly wanted access to Jarsdel's innermost drives.

Baba appeared to register his son's reluctance. He reached out to touch his arm but stopped when he saw him stiffen.

"I don't blame you," he said, letting his hand fall into his lap. "It's a family tradition. My father passed it to me, and now I see I've passed it to you. The Jahangir curse, you could call it. The urge to grasp so tightly that our children flee from us. If you're ever lucky enough to have a family, I hope you'll follow a different course."

His eyes seemed to fix themselves on a point past his son, somewhere in the far distance. He murmured something, but a burst of laughter from a nearby table drowned it out.

"I can't hear you, Baba."

"I said horror is a rotting thing."

"A rotten thing?"

Baba shook his head. "A rotting thing. A cancer. As bad as what your dad's fighting, only I'd rather have that than..." He focused his gaze on his son. "You know what I mean, don't you? About horror?"

Jarsdel wondered what time it was. He still had to get Baba all the way back to Pasadena, then cross town again in the other direction to his apartment in the Fairfax District. If they left now, he might get home before it was too late to watch that new Netflix thing—the one about Pompeii where the characters actually spoke Classical Latin. He was curious if the actors rolled their *r*'s properly. *Littera canina*, the Romans had called it. "The dog letter," because of its growl.

"I know you must have seen it," said Baba.

For one strange moment, Jarsdel thought his father was somehow talking about the Netflix show. "Seen what?"

"The thing I'm talking about. You've experienced it. Real horror."

He had, of course. But again, Baba was too late to the party to commiserate. Jarsdel shrugged, something he knew his father hated.

The man offered a weak smile. "A rotting thing. I know you don't think I have a right to give you much advice, but please listen. Watch for the rot, Tully. Watch for the rot, and don't let it take hold."

11

No, Rishkov didn't own a gun—or at least didn't have one registered. Morales had laughed when Jarsdel asked him to run a background check on her and laughed harder now that he held the printout.

"Holy shit," he managed, dabbing at his streaming eyes. "Public Enemy Number One over here." Jarsdel snatched the pages out of his hands. Undergrad in French from Chapel Hill, PhD in history of art and architecture from Brown. Taught at Amherst '68 to '82, then moved to California to work as a curator-restorer at the Huntington. Began serving on the board of directors the following year. Jarsdel wasn't sure exactly what he'd been hoping to find—maybe a long-buried criminal history or, better yet, a sealed juvenile record. He'd get a warrant to have it opened, whereupon a veritable resume of psychopathy would spill forth. Pet disappearances, fires, the mysterious death of a handyman. Margaret Rishkov as Rhoda Penmark.

Morales clapped a hand on his shoulder. "You know," he said, still grinning, "she may look like my *abuelita*, but fuck with her tea cozies and she'll ventilate you, man. Stashes her piece under her muumuu." That set him off again, his body shaking with laughter.

The two of them decided to split up again, Morales to stay at his desk, digging further into Ellery Keating's financials with his friend in Commercial Crimes. It would be a day of phone calls, public records searches, and credit checks. Meanwhile, Jarsdel was on his way back to the Huntington to compare Dean Burken's accession numbers with the items in quarantine.

"Why?" Morales asked.

"A hunch. The Smith estate was the last donation he processed. I want to get a good look at it." What he didn't say was that his hunch was based on something Rishkov mentioned during their meeting two days before. It had since stuck in his mind, as persistent and irritating as a hair on the tongue.

"You're just hopin' for another excuse to hang out over there."

"Ah, you got me," said Jarsdel. "Nothing like spending a couple hours in a storage facility. I'll bring you back a used air filter if you like."

Dr. Louro was waiting for him when he arrived at the Steven S. Koblik Education and Visitor Center. The museum wouldn't open for another half hour, and aside from a few elderly docents, they had the place to themselves.

"Appreciate your meeting me," said Jarsdel.

Louro wasn't as ebullient as he'd been last time. Even his spray of white hair, previously as full and frothy as the head on a pint of beer, sagged in lopsided clots. He pushed open the door to the building, giving a muttered "After you" as Jarsdel went inside.

Jarsdel remembered from his previous visit that the paper preservation lab was to their left, through a heavy fire door marked with a *Staff Only* sign. But instead of leading them in that direction, Louro had them cross through the visitor center toward a lone elevator. Without anyone else in the vast lobby, their footsteps echoed like hammer falls.

Louro pushed the button to call the elevator. "It's underground," he said.

Considering it was only a one-story building, Jarsdel had easily deduced this. All the same, he gave a mild sound of approval.

Inside the elevator, Louro inserted a key into the panel and pressed the only available button—*B*—which now glowed orange. The descent was brief—a hum of a few seconds, and they were there. But it was enough time for him to study Louro's profile and confirm his earlier observation. Something was bothering the curator, and if he was making any efforts to conceal his feelings, they weren't working.

The two stepped out into a stark white corridor. The ceiling was inset with powerful LED cans, their glare illuminating the lacquered walls to create a kind of sterile, alabaster umbilicus. The effect was heightened by the wide spacing of the doors along the sides of the hallway, and these too were white, with only a small inset window to engage the eye.

The only one that stood out in any way was at the very end. It was the same as the others, but affixed at its center was a red placard.

RESTRICTED
AUTHORIZED PERSONNEL ONLY
PROTECTIVE GEAR REQUIRED

Louro made it to the door first and made a show of blocking the security keypad with his body. He punched in a flurry of numbers, and there was the snap of the magnetic lock disengaging.

"Gotta suit up," he said as they stepped through. There was a sanitizing station just inside, and the men put on gloves and masks as the door behind them sucked itself shut.

Despite the immense size of the quarantine room, Jarsdel could see they were alone. Aisles of heavy chrome wire shelving stretched across five thousand square feet of gleaming white. Stacked on and around the shelves was Monte Cristo's treasure hoard—statues, paintings, furniture, lamps, rugs—all things Jarsdel had expected to see, though their sheer quantity was still astonishing. What he hadn't expected were the excised portions of architecture, entire portions of homes that had been selected for preservation and surgically removed. There were fireplaces—he counted three—along with doors, window casings, a painted ceiling leaning on its side and secured by thick straps, even a mahogany staircase terminating against one of the pristine walls. It was alone, resting along the east end of the facility. The effect wasn't so much that the staircase had been transported but rather that the house around it had been carefully erased.

Shades of Magritte, he thought, then shivered. The mercury had already been topping ninety when he arrived at the museum, but in here, it felt like it was in the fifties.

Louro led him down an aisle and stopped, pointing at the top shelf. "From here," he said, then swept his finger down to the bottom shelf. "To here. The entirety of the Smith estate. Go nuts." He retreated a few feet and brought out his phone, then appeared to remember there was no reception underground. He shoved the phone back in his lab coat and crossed his arms sullenly.

Jarsdel produced a folded sheet of paper—Burken's catalogue of the donation, laid out in order of accession number. Morales had retrieved it from the deceased's computer with the aid of an officer from Forensic Science Division.

Jarsdel studied the first item, 21-355-001, a rawhide chair. Looking up, he spotted it on the bottom row, then made a check mark to the left of the number. Next up was 21-355-002, a U.S. cavalry saber. Jarsdel saw it on the shelf, set against purple velvet in an art display case, which had also been labeled with the accession number. He noted it on his list, then moved on to the third item, a box of original photographs taken by Ennis P. Smith.

After checking it off, he tapped the sheet with his pen. "How do these numbers work?"

"In numerical order," Louro said, punctuating the riposte with a little sniff.

Jarsdel looked at him, unsmiling.

Louro relented. "It's NPS standards. Algorithm standardized by the National Park Service. First two numbers represent the year. Second three indicate where in the sequence of that year's acquisitions the piece came into our care. In this case, 355 acts like a batch number, so the final three digits on the right tell you when the item was processed within that batch number. Some places use American Alliance of Museums standards, or American Association for State and Local History, but we like this one. If for some reason we get more than 999 batches of donations, we simply shift to an alphanumeric system. 21–355A, et cetera. It's a good, simple system." Then he added, "One almost anyone can understand."

"Okay," said Jarsdel, flicking the tip of his pen to the bottom of the sheet. "So our final number on here, 21-355-039, that tells us there are thirty-nine items in total in the Smith estate's donation?"

"If that's what it says."

Jarsdel looked down at the sheet, then back at the collection, frowning. "Who comes up with the names of the items? I'm talking about the descriptive names here, things like 'Nineteenth-century land survey equipment' and 'Handwritten draft, Indian Protection and Inclusion Act.' Does the donor do this or does the registrar determine it?"

"The donor. They tell us what they're giving us, and we assign the number. For tax purposes, ours and theirs, our lists need to match. Also of course our appraiser and our insurer are part of the process. We don't want to pay to insure something that isn't authentic. If we need to change the description of an item, we'll do so and notify the donor."

"I see," said Jarsdel. "Pretty airtight."

Louro didn't comment. The thin metal ribs embedded in the mask, one on either side of the nose, gave a vaguely duck-like cast to his appearance. A pair of teardrop-shaped nostril holes, marked with a Sharpie, would have completed the effect.

Jarsdel leaned to get a closer look at the middle shelf. He examined a label, then found the matching accession number on his sheet. "There's something missing."

"No, there isn't," said Louro.

"Actually, there is."

"*No*, there isn't," Louro repeated. "It's not missing at all. Map's already been released. Remember the phantom settlement? You saw it in my lab. Last thing Dean approved before he died." He waved at the shelves. "All these could be released by now. We just need to get a new registrar in here to sign the paperwork. Yet another pain in the ass."

"I'm not talking about the map," said Jarsdel. He pointed at a black, leather-bound book. "Label there reads 21-355-033, which on my form here is described as 'Private journal of Ennis P. Smith.'"

"Yeah. Terrific," said Louro.

"Didn't Smith die in 1878?"

"I dunno. Sounds right."

"Then the journal is missing. See for yourself."

Louro uncrossed his arms and approached. His movements were wary, as if he feared a trap. He bent close and read the book's spine.

"*The Irrational Knot*," said Jarsdel. "Shaw's pretty big in my family. Anyway, would have been a challenge for Smith to have picked up a copy. Wasn't published until 1905."

Louro didn't comment.

"Mean anything to you?"

"It's just a mistake." Louro straightened up. "Doesn't happen often, but even the best registrarial practices..." He shrugged.

"Seems odd," said Jarsdel. "Especially considering what you just told me—that it's the donors who draw up the inventory. And that afterward, Mr. Burken would have evaluated it and entered it into the system with an accession number. And what about the appraiser and the insurer? No one in that whole chain happened to notice this was a novel and not a diary?"

Louro pointed at the inventory sheet in Jarsdel's hand. "Lemme see that."

Jarsdel gave it over and watched Louro study the words. He looked at the novel, at the list, then back at the book. "There's an explanation."

"Okay," said Jarsdel. "What's the explanation?"

"Just a stupid mistake."

Jarsdel's jaw tightened. "That's the same thing you said before. Human error."

"Yeah, but now I really see it—how it could've happened. The book must have been switched out for another at some point during the quarantine process. Or maybe the journal's inside those two covers. You think of that?"

"Take a peek," said Jarsdel.

Louro carefully removed the book from the shelf and opened to the faceplate. He frowned at the yellowed paper. "Slow fire," he muttered. "Embrittlement and loss of fiber strength." He quickly ran the pages off his thumb.

"Anything?"

Louro put the book back and lifted his palms. "I got no definite idea. Only thing makes sense is either Burken screwed up, which is unlikely, or some jackass switched them by mistake."

"I see," said Jarsdel. "How many jackasses do you have on staff?"

Louro's expression turned hard. "I hardly see why this is so important."

"How many have access to this room?"

"Not many."

"How many?"

Louro exhaled between his teeth. "Regular access? Two dozen, maybe."

"Any board members?"

"Only if they're currently licensed curator-restorers or registrars. Otherwise, no."

Jarsdel picked up *The Irrational Knot* and turned to the frontispiece. Wasn't signed, wasn't even a first edition. He'd tried reading it once, many years earlier, and found it a crashing bore. "What about Margaret Rishkov?" he asked.

"No," said Louro. "She let her license lapse."

"May I?" Without waiting for his response, Jarsdel plucked the inventory from Louro's hands. He tapped the upper right corner. "Says this was all logged in on May twenty-eighth. Any way of finding who accessed this area between then and now?"

"Yeah, but it won't do you much good." Louro pointed to a security camera mounted near the door. "That'll tell you who came in and out, but it won't show you what they did once they were inside. And the people you're talking about would all have very good reason for being here. Catching them on camera wouldn't prove anything."

Jarsdel cocked his head, curious about Louro's wording. *Wouldn't prove anything.* That sounded a little defensive.

"Because you will find all those people on the security tape," Louro went on. "All of them. Me and Dean and everyone else who has access. This is a busy room. Everyone's checking on their pet projects, looking for mold or bronze disease and hoping it isn't there." He reached out his finger and tapped *The Irrational Knot.* "This is a mistake. Doesn't mean anything. I understand you're looking for evidence, but I'm telling you this is silly."

"Silly," Jarsdel repeated.

"Look around," said Louro. "Thousands of items move in and out of here all the time. Bound to be the occasional error."

"Any idea what was in that journal?" he asked. "You maybe get a look at it?"

"No. Why would I?" Louro scoffed. "Wasn't out of quarantine yet. I mean, no more than a cursory inspection. If it'd been released, I woulda done a full scan, then had one of the interns type up a transcript."

Jarsdel had mostly tuned him out. He thought of what Rishkov had said about the rumors surrounding Ennis P. Smith and his alleged gold strike. *Probably ginned up to get him into the state legislature.*

That was the alluring idea that had brought him to the Huntington that morning. Just that one word—

Gold.

Why not? Millions upon millions had died for gold, either in its desperate pursuit or in defending land rich with its veins. Maybe Ennis P. Smith really had struck a major claim and socked the treasure away like a storybook pirate. Maybe he hadn't. But whether it was true or not ultimately didn't matter. It was the belief that was important. The belief that Smith had disclosed the gold's location in his diary. For many, Jarsdel knew, it was a belief worth killing for.

He wondered if the shooter had found it, then remembered that whoever had murdered Dean Burken also yanked out the couch cushions. At the time, he and Morales speculated it had been a ham-fisted misdirection, a ploy to reinforce the robbery scenario. But now it fit perfectly. A diary was small and compact enough that someone searching for it might check there if they'd exhausted more likely options.

Then he realized he'd answered his own question. Burken would never have stored something so valuable as that book under a couch cushion, and the killer had probably known that. Which meant searching there had been an act of desperation before fleeing the scene.

No, the killer hadn't found the diary. Couldn't have.

Who, though? Who'd have even been aware of its contents? One of the appraisers or insurers? Probably not, since they wouldn't have needed to read the book to make their estimates. Rishkov? Possible but unlikely. Why would she suddenly take an interest in what was, on the face of it, such a bland acquisition? Besides, she didn't have access to the quarantine room.

What about Keating? No, for the same two reasons. She also didn't need the money, so why kill for it? That left the two dozen or so conservator-restorers who did have access, including, of course, Dr. Louro.

Jarsdel locked eyes with him and was interested to discover he didn't try to look away. "Speaking hypothetically, what do you think happened to the diary?"

"Nothing," said Louro. "At this point, I'm doubting whether it even existed. In all likelihood, what we've got is a mistake on the donation form that gets perpetuated by the appearance of this other book here."

Jarsdel thought that a ridiculous explanation and decided to say so. "That doesn't make a lot of sense to me."

Louro didn't flinch. "If you have any better ideas, then by all means. Otherwise, I've got more than forty documents to treat with paper keeper. That's what you do with a doctorate these days, in case you're interested. Spray acidic wood-pulp paper until it gets a minimal two-percent alkali reserve." He gave the spine of *The Irrational Knot* a contemptuous flick with his finger. "At least I don't have to worry about this one, right?"

Two dozen people with regular access, Jarsdel considered. He had to agree with Louro's assessment of the evidentiary value of the security footage. The camera was facing the wrong direction, set at such an angle that it only showed who came in and out. And it wasn't as if the diary would've been difficult to smuggle from the room. It could've been thrown in with a cartload of Burken's deaccessions or simply tucked in someone's armpit. He didn't for one minute believe Louro's explanation but had no way of refuting it—at least for now.

Instead of bringing clarity, his trip to the Huntington only raised more questions. Had Burken actually taken the diary? If so, how did his killer know he had it? And most importantly, where was the diary now?

Jarsdel felt an ache settle into his mandibular nerve, just above his ear. It always began that way, at the spot he'd been cut by a murder suspect years before, and if he got to some aspirin in time, he could usually keep it there. Otherwise, the pain radiated outward from the root, passing down into the muscles used for chewing. On bad days, each beat of his heart felt like a punch to the right side of his face.

He looked again at the curator. Was this the man? He tried to imagine him training the muzzle of a handgun at someone's heart, then squeezing the trigger—not once but four times.

Louro appeared to read the direction of his thoughts, and even though he wore a mask, it was easy to imagine a smirk forming at his lips. That was one of the things living with COVID had done, Jarsdel reflected. Deprived of half a person's face, you got very, very good at reading what was left.

"Okay, Detective," said Louro. "I think I've given you about all the help I'm inclined to provide. You want anything else, even if it's to ask how my day was, you'll have to go through museum counsel." He glanced at his watch. "Gift shop's open by now. Recommend you pick up one of the scented candles. Local artisan, and they're soy, no parabens. Chinese character on the front reads 'Harmony.' Might soften your tense disposition."

Morales was at his desk reviewing paperwork, a pen clutched between his stubby fingers, when Jarsdel returned to Hollywood Station.

As he approached, he noticed something and frowned.

Their two desks abutted, facing each other, the seam where the two battered slabs of wood met acting as a kind of demilitarized zone. Morales, however, appeared to have taken advantage of his partner's absence to allow for unauthorized troop movement. A *Far Side* desk calendar and a copy of *1001 Films You Must See Before You Die* had drifted across to Jarsdel's territory, and he pushed both items back to where they'd come from. This caused some problems on Morales's side, which didn't have a square inch of free space. A box of paper clips and the squad room's entire stack of communal takeout menus tumbled over the opposite side. They hit the ground, fanning out like a deck of cards.

"*Dude.*" Morales drew the single word out into a grave pronouncement. "I swear..."

Jarsdel took his seat across from his partner. "Got the motive. Gonna require a little faith on your part, at least when I first explain it. But anyone who reads *1001 Films You Must See Before You Die* must have a lot of practice with suspension of disbelief."

"You got the motive, huh?"

"I do."

"And that motive would be…?"

"Buried treasure."

Morales looked up, puzzled at first, then a delighted smile spread across his face. "Yeah?"

"I told you," said Jarsdel, "you'll have to let me explain."

"You mean, like, actual treasure? Like One-Eyed Willie's gold?"

"I don't know who that is, but yes, actual treasure. And it *is* gold, though I don't know what form it's in. Could be ingots, coins. Could even be unrefined."

Morales leaned back in his chair, the box of paper clips and the takeout menus apparently forgotten. "I'm hooked. Keep goin'. How'd you put it all together?"

Jarsdel knew his partner was mocking him, but he didn't care. It felt good to lay it out, to begin dispersing the fog of mystery that hung around a lonely, violent death in the Hollywood Hills. He related what he'd learned from Rishkov about Ennis P. Smith's alleged gold strike, then how he'd uncovered the discrepancy in the quarantine room. He concluded with Louro's caginess but without going so far as to suggest he might be a suspect.

Morales pursed his lips. "Cool, cool. So lay it out for me. Who killed Dean Burken?"

"That's not important right now."

"No? Aren't we, uh, homicide detectives?"

"Well, of course it's *important*, ultimately. But what this information does is help winnow down our suspect list. Cross some people off and focus our investigation."

"Sounds good. Who can we get rid of?"

"Ellery Keating, for one. I know you've been looking at her. We both have. And I know a lot of that initial push came from me over the art at her house. So yes, she's almost certainly crooked, but she's got plenty of money. Doesn't make sense she'd shoot Burken for the diary."

Morales grinned, and that gave Jarsdel pause. His partner wasn't known for his megawatt smiles, and he reserved them only for those moments of purest delight.

"What is it?" said Jarsdel.

"Ellery Keating. That's just a whole lotta funny."

"Why?"

"No, go ahead. Keep goin'."

"Oscar, I'm not interested in entertaining you. If there's something that frustrates my theory, please share."

"Okay," said Morales. "Then let me tell you a little about the last couple days, okay? While you been gettin' out, driving' around in the sun and shit, I been in here—phone, email, Zoom, the excitement doesn't stop. You know Art Theft Detail folded?"

"I did."

"Well, see, I didn't know that. So one of the fun things I got to do was track down all the detectives who used to be in Art Theft, finding out they'd been reassigned to just about every other branch of Commercial Crimes Division. There's the guy I told you about, my buddy Mike, but I needed to talk to anybody who knew about the kinda shit Keating was into. Turns out nothing she was doing was strictly illegal."

"I could've told you that," said Jarsdel. "Unethical, but not illegal."

"Would you listen? That's not the whole thing. I was checking our options, seeing where we could squeeze. That maybe we could get her on embezzlement or even conspiracy if Burken was up to some funky shit and she knew about it or was helping him out somehow. I also wanted to know if maybe she was some kinda high-end fence. You were the one told me the inside of her house was packed to the nuts."

Jarsdel nodded.

"So I'm dancin' around, trying to make stuff fit. Even spent two hours reading transcripts of Newport Beach city council meetings, just hopin' for somethin' to click. That lady likes to talk, dude. She's all over those meetings. Anyway, Mike finally gets back to me. Gone as deep as you can go without a warrant. And he tells me Ellery Keating's in serious trouble."

"What do you mean? How?"

"Remember McCormick & Associates? Her LLC outta Nevada? The info he had from before was from lists of shareholders in real estate developments. Her company's name popped up all over the place. But those were dated at the end of the previous fiscal year. It's like the Academy Awards. *Casablanca* won 1943's best picture, but it actually hit theaters in '42. Make sense? So to double-check, Mike calls up those developments individually to see if McCormick's still a shareholder. Guess what?"

Jarsdel stared blankly at him, and this seemed to please Morales even more.

"Gone. Turns out McCormick divested most of its holdings, funneling more than ninety percent of its total portfolio—and we're talking about fifteen million here—into a single project."

Morales searched his desk and found the corner of the document he was looking for peeking from beneath a stack of papers. He tugged it free and handed it across.

It was a color mockup of a proposed development. A forty-five-degree downward-angled panorama of something called "the Strand at Newport." Acres of shops, fountains, cafés, parking garages, an arcade, and even a scaled-down amusement park, Keiki Cove.

The text below read, "A bold new project from Pruitt Equities Group, a private, family-owned, full-service real estate investment and development company."

Unclear about whatever revelation he was building to, Jarsdel held the sheet out to his partner.

"Keep it," said Morales. "Anyway, what you're looking at there is one of the biggest real estate developments in OC. Three-quarter bil. Lot of very rich people gonna get even richer once this thing opens up."

"Okay," said Jarsdel. "I'm with you. So the bulk of Keating's funds are tied up in this thing. Why's that so interesting?"

"Were you, like, paying even a little attention about the city council stuff I was just talking about? District 4. Here." Another sheet of paper, this one featuring a color-coded map of Newport Beach divided into its seven districts. District 4 was rendered mint green, contrasting with the blue of 3 to the northwest and the yellow of 5 to the south.

Morales sat back again. "You'll never guess where they wanna build the Strand at Newport."

Now Jarsdel understood. "She's invested anonymously through the LLC, and meanwhile, she pushes for the development in committee."

"Took you long enough," said Morales. "Thing is, this is a controversial project. Lots of variances to the original land-use plan. Talking about things like height restrictions, residential versus commercial zoning, noise ordinances. Dealing with the California Coastal Commission, which is basically like the Mafia if they used time and paperwork as weapons instead of guns and car bombs. Keating basically shoved the project down everybody's throats. Supposed to break ground next month, but now it's on the skids, getting sued by, like, three different homeowners associations—used to be twice that but some got thrown out due to lack of standing—and a couple environmental groups. Some lizard in there's endangered or something. Now she might get it all sorted out, but it's gonna take time, and until then, she's cash poor. Worse comes to worst and the thing stalls out indefinitely? Pretty much ruined. 'Cause who's gonna wanna buy her out if the project's dead?"

Jarsdel picked up the mockup of the Strand and held it side by side with the district map of Newport. "This thing's a monster."

"And that's just phase one. You read the brochure on the website, and later on they gonna add a resort and an eighteen-hole golf course."

"You know," said Jarsdel, "if anything, this reinforces my theory.

If Keating's in danger of losing her fortune, she might kill for a chest of gold."

Morales's grin returned. "Corrupt Newport councilwoman guns down sleazy museum dude so she can keep the buried treasure all to herself. Big story, big drama. And a big win for Tully J, super cop." Then he affected a theatrical expression of puzzlement worthy of a dell'arte player. "But wait. What do you mean this reinforces your theory? Thought you said Ellery Keating was the first person we eliminate."

"That was only based on my understanding that she was wealthy. With this information—"

"*My* information," Morales cut in.

"Fair, yes, *your* information—I think that puts her at the top." For the first time, he wondered what Morales had been working on when he came in. From his vantage point, it was upside down, so he leaned forward to get a better look. "That for a warrant?"

Morales tossed the packet across the desk. "Wanted to get her specifics so we could start building a case. Don't know if I buy your gold angle yet, but she was definitely workin' through some big stressors. Maybe Burken had finally gone too far with one of his interns, like physically too far, and Keating can't protect him. So he says he's gonna expose her whole conflict of interest thing with the Newport city council. That would really run her into some problems."

Jarsdel picked up the affidavit and scanned the request. He could tell right away his partner had tailored the writing for Judge Lori Monson, who preferred the use of the more formal third-person in her warrant affidavits. It opened with the standard "hero sheet"—essentially a short bio of the applicant, with an emphasis placed on experience and credibility.

```
Your affiant is Detective II Oscar Morales with the
Los Angeles Police Department, Homicide, Hollywood
Division. Det. Morales is a twenty-six-year veteran
```

of the department and has investigated hundreds of
homicides. He holds an associate degree in criminal
justice from Saddleback Community College and has
completed additional training in forensic science,
narcotics, cybercrime, gangs, WMDs, ballistics,
forgery, and conflict resolution. Det. Morales
is a fluent Spanish speaker and is known for his
community relations work in traditionally Latino
neighborhoods.

"You're supposed to say Latinx now, not Latino," said Jarsdel.
"Huh?"
"If you say 'Latino,' you're excluding Latinas and those who
don't gender identify. Latinx covers everybody."
"Dude, shut the fuck up." It was said dismissively, not angrily, as
if Jarsdel had been recounting tall tales of undersea kingdoms and
hundred-foot lumberjacks.
Jarsdel turned the page.

Based on your affiant's training, experience, and
conversations with other law enforcement officers,
along with public reports that your affiant has
read, your affiant knows that banks maintain
records that can be obtained by a search warrant.
Aforementioned records may be maintained at corpo-
rate offices, central processing, and data centers.
Your affiant seeks all account information in the
name of KEATING, ELLERY, D.O.B. 8/22/53, and any
account in which Ms. Keating is an authorized signer
thereof, including those in the name of MCCORMICK &
ASSOCIATES, LLC. This information is to cover the
period—

"Hey," said Morales. "Gotta sign that shit. You done?"

Jarsdel handed over the affidavit. "Looks good."

"Thanks. Was really hoping you'd like it. My Latinx ass feels all validated."

Jarsdel got to his feet, stretched, and yawned. "Gonna get that over to Judge Monson today?"

"It's the Fourth of July, man. Federal holiday."

"You could call her."

Morales looked at him as if he'd lost his mind. He held up the warrant. "This ain't Bin Laden here. Don't need to bother the judge on no holiday. And me too, you know. This isn't how I wanna spend the rest of the afternoon."

"Ridiculous anyway," said Jarsdel. "Everyone's got the day wrong."

"What d'you mean, everyone's got the day wrong?"

"Continental Congress voted on Richard Lee's resolution, officially declaring independence on July second. The fourth was only the day they approved the final draft of Jefferson's document. And if you read what John Adams—"

"Stop. I don't care. Like"—Morales held up his thumb and forefinger pinched together—"not even this much."

Most of the Hollywood Station personnel had already left for the day to be with their families, and Jarsdel began thinking of the screened-in patio of his apartment and how nice it would be to sit out there with a perfectly chilled glass of Nicolas Feuillatte and a Jeff Peterson album. *Maui on My Mind* or maybe *Slack Key Travels*.

Once Morales had gone and Jarsdel knew he wouldn't be needed, he made the drive back home. It was only a few miles, but it took nearly an hour. The streets were strangled with sun-beaten cars, drivers seething as they crawled through the city. AC on full and still fighting to keep the heat at bay.

It was nearly five when he finally pulled into the Park La Brea complex. The small parks and playgrounds scattered throughout the grounds were crowded with celebrants, the air hazy with barbecue smoke. Jarsdel didn't have an assigned parking spot and had to circle for another fifteen minutes before a space opened up. By the time he entered his two-story, prewar apartment, he was hot and irritated, and he knocked the cover of the thermostat loose when he turned on the air.

Throwing off his clothes, he showered and shaved, then fulfilled his promise to himself and put on some Jeff Peterson. No Nicolas Feuillatte though. *Right*, he now remembered. He'd popped it on impulse a couple weeks ago while watching a documentary on Gino Bartali. He settled for some bargain chardonnay and dropped into his wingback chair.

Jarsdel took a drink of the wine and let the music play, hoping that together they'd massage his thoughts a little, which felt tight and jumbled. Something was bothering him, *had* been bothering him ever since his meeting with Keating, but whatever it was danced just out of reach.

He closed his eyes, willing his mind to focus, searching his memories and replaying the last few days of interviews as best he could. He didn't know exactly what he was looking for, but he'd recognize it when he found it—his old friend, the golden thread. That one little fibril of electrochemical perfection that, when teased apart from the rest and given a firm pull, could unspool the densest knots of confused thinking.

He started at the beginning, with Lorraine Cinq-Mars and her wide, nervous eyes. He tugged at the memory, but nothing gave. From her over to Kristin Beets, the research fellow whom Burken had tried to freeze out when she'd spurned him. She'd been clean, though. No gun, and solidly alibied at that terrible poetry reading. He tugged anyway—nothing.

Dr. Ezra Louro, who'd championed Burken's slash-and-burn style of collections management. Louro, who'd gone out of his way to contact the police and asked to speak with detectives.

He thought of Louro's jauntiness when they'd met in the paper restoration lab. How he'd cooed over the map and the phantom settlement of King Henry's Pride. Jarsdel contrasted that with

Louro's naked annoyance the morning they toured the quarantine room. Why? He'd been so eager to talk a couple days before, so what changed? Jarsdel turned the question around in his mind, looking for anything that accounted for it. Nothing did.

On to Ellery Keating herself. That strange interview in her house, with the dog locked away somewhere the whole time, barking and scratching to be let out. Keating, with her threadbare Tommy Trojan T-shirt and the hoard of pilfered treasure, which she'd arranged as artfully as a sale bin at Dollar General. Keating, who thought her Vespasian was a Caesar.

Bet she also thinks he's famous for his advances in salad dressing.

She'd been nervous from the outset and only grew more so when he began questioning her about the statue and her arrangement with Burken. Then he'd screwed up, pushing her into self-righteous indignation. Had she been about to reveal anything? If so, what?

Come to think of it, what did he actually think had happened? Did he even have a theory? For the moment, he shoved the question away, putting in its place the image of Margaret Rishkov. She'd actually taunted him, encouraging speculation that she might've been responsible for Burken's death. It had been an obvious ploy to hamper the investigation, to get the police to waste time on a dead-end lead. Jarsdel understood why, of course. She'd hated Burken with a rare and brilliant passion, so why not drop coy hints about being the murderer and give the real killer a little more time to get away?

Or I could be seeing it wrong, thought Jarsdel. It would also make for a paradoxically clever ruse if she'd been the one who'd actually done it. By overtly pretending to be guilty, she might be hoping to be dismissed as a serious suspect.

Jarsdel's scar sent out a warning pulse, so he took a couple more long sips of wine to quiet the damaged nerve.

So what do you actually think happened? he asked himself again. *You really believe there's a cache of gold somewhere?*

He thought of the scene in Burken's house and the way the blood had painted half the living room. High-velocity spatter on the walls and the spines of his books. Thick drops on the carpet, their directional trails pointing toward Burken as he staggered backward away from the gunfire. Then the killer had ransacked the place, ripping down artwork and dumping books from the shelves. No spatter on their covers, just the spines, because the killer had shot Burken prior to his search. And then there was the mahogany display cabinet with the half-open bottom drawer. Morales had pointed out—astutely, Jarsdel admitted—that the killer hadn't been an experienced burglar.

What had been the killer's true objective? Murder or theft?

Both, he reasoned. It had to be both. The killer ambushed Burken as soon as he'd stepped out of his car. They knew that because both the sandwich and the bottle of moscato were still on the passenger seat when the police arrived on Monday. The killer had led his victim into the house at gunpoint, then probably demanded to know where the diary was. Burken must have either refused to tell him or he'd decided to lie. Either way, whoever pulled the trigger that night left empty-handed. The couch cushions proved that. Searching under those cushions had been the killer's final, desperate act before fleeing the scene.

Jarsdel remembered the Tiffany floor lamp, shattered beyond repair, shards of blue, red, yellow, and shimmering opalescent spread across the floor. He frowned at the thought and took another drink of wine. It would have been reasonable to search behind the paintings, where a small, compact diary could conceivably be hidden. But smashing the lamp and the pre-Columbian pottery served no discernible purpose. It was simply a tantrum, a final *fuck you* on the way out the door.

The lamp, something about the lamp.

What about the lamp? His deeper, intuitive mind had made a connection somewhere, but it was eluding him. He reached within himself—could practically feel his conscious self probing the poorly lit corners of his thoughts. When that didn't work, Jarsdel cocked his head, as if perhaps gravity could dislodge the answer and roll it out into the light where he could study it.

He waited, eyes closed, but nothing came to him.

Jarsdel finished his glass of wine and poured himself another.

Someone had launched a firework just outside Park La Brea's Fairfax gate. It hadn't gone far—only thirty feet up before planting itself in the top of a dying palm tree. It had caught fire immediately, and the neighborhood was now illuminated in the rippling light of a giant torch.

Inside his bedroom, Jarsdel pulled down the blinds to shut out the unsettling yellow glow, but still it crept in around the edges. It didn't matter anyway. Soon the fire trucks arrived with pealing sirens and that terrible grating horn, and he might as well have been trying to sleep on top of an active volcano.

Jarsdel got up and went to the kitchen, grabbed a tumbler off the counter, and pressed it against the button inset in his fridge door. Cold water jetted into his glass, and he filled it to the top. He drank it all, refilled the glass, then drank that too.

It was hot in his place, despite the whooshing air conditioner, so he took off his T-shirt and returned to bed in his boxers. To block out the light from the fire, he propped a spare pillow over his eyes, leaving his nose and mouth clear. The pressure and coolness of the fabric was nice, too. The sirens outside had stopped, and he felt himself finally begin to respond to his body's demands for sleep. Ideas, images, and the logic of dreams began to edge their way into his thoughts, and those thoughts were of Keating.

She had her routine down cold. Folksy vernacular and brassy twang—the woman of the people. She got to have it both ways, a pretty good trick for a politician. The emerald caught in the tread of her sneaker was a perfect metaphor.

Jarsdel tore the pillow away from his eyes and sat up.

Because it hadn't been a precious stone on the bottom of Keating's sneaker but a fragment of green Tiffany glass.

Ellery Keating had been the one who'd shot Dean Burken.

He reached for the phone on his nightstand to call Morales, then stopped himself. It wasn't as if the two of them could just drive down to Newport Beach in the middle of the night to arrest a councilwoman on suspicion of murder, and all because of a shard of glass that *might* have come from Burken's lamp. It wasn't even their jurisdiction. No, if Keating was going to rise to the top of their suspect list, they'd have to proceed very, very carefully.

Proceed carefully. I can do that. And that'll begin with not waking up my partner over this.

Jarsdel lay back down and replaced the pillow over his eyes. He didn't expect to sleep, not after just having found the golden thread. It would be too tempting to begin tugging at it to see what came loose.

But he was wrong. The initial surge of enthusiasm settled into a warm contentment, which first embraced him, then pulled him into sleep.

Aside from the standard work schedule, sworn LAPD personnel usually have the option of organizing their week as four days of ten-hour shifts. Jarsdel had been on the four-day plan but had been lately been starting work so early in the morning that Lieutenant Gavin had cut him down to three. That meant that whether he wanted it or not, Monday the fifth was a day off.

He slept in, then called Morales around eight to tell him about the Tiffany glass. When his partner didn't answer, he composed a text.

Call when you can. I have an idea.

He almost hit send, then changed his mind.

Ellery Keating's our shooter. Call for details.

That would get his attention.

Satisfied, he hit send, then watched the dialogue box for the telltale ellipsis that meant the recipient was typing a reply. Thirty seconds passed, and Jarsdel put the phone away. He did it reluctantly, hoping it would buzz in his hand. It didn't.

It had been so long since he'd had a win—even a relatively small one like this   that he just wanted to share it with someone. For a brief moment, he even considered calling Baba and somehow working it into the conversation.

Restless, Jarsdel prowled his apartment. He glanced at the growing pile of dishes in the sink, gave serious thought to cleaning them, and decided it could wait until later. It had been a few minutes since he'd checked his phone, so he checked again. Still no word from Morales.

Reading would pass the time. Back in the living room, he examined the books threatening to spill from his overstocked shelves, moving his finger along their spines. He hesitated over Umberto Eco's *On Ugliness*, which he'd bought but hadn't yet read, then moved on to *Learn Nahuatl: Language of the Aztecs and Modern Nahuas*. A month ago, he'd finished Gary Jennings's *Aztec* and decided on Nahuatl as the next language he'd study. Aside from his native English, he already had Farsi, Latin, and Ancient Greek. He was capable enough with Demotic Greek to count it as well, so that technically brought him up to five. One more and he'd be considered a hyperpolyglot. It would also happen to put him ahead of Baba, which—he assured himself—scarcely counted among his motivations.

Nahuatl excited him—a language of extraordinary beauty that shared absolutely no cognates with English, which made it a challenge. He took the book out, frowned, decided he really *wasn't* in the mood for a challenge—not now anyway—and put it back.

All he could think about was Ellery Keating. He tried to imagine Burken's face—something he'd only seen whole in photographs—as she leveled that weapon at him in his living room. Could he tell that she really meant to do it? Had he seen the change in her expression as she moved from the threat of violence to the act itself?

Not for the first time, Jarsdel wondered what it would be like in that moment when your own impending murder became a certainty. To see the intent to kill in the eyes of a fellow human and to find it was you—*you*, out of everyone else drawing a breath on our pale-blue dot—who'd been selected to die. The homicide lottery was played less and less often in the twenty-first century, but somehow, bucking the odds, you'd drawn the black stone.

He himself had looked into the eyes of a would-be killer, but he'd never actually reached true certainty of death, had never been totally helpless. Very few could, he supposed. You'd have to be brought to the very edge, consciously, and still somehow survive.

More than anything, he thought, you'd feel a crushing, all-consuming grief. Truly all-consuming, one that eclipsed fear in its own far darker shadow. Some of the grief would come from mourning the end of your existence, but most of it—he was certain—would consist of a deep and terrible feeling of rejection. The knowledge that someone hated you enough to want to kill you. No, even if hate didn't enter into it, someone had judged your continued being as undesirable. You'd been weighed like a mass on a scale, on one side dead, on the other alive. The world, at least according to one person, was better off without you.

"Keating's dead."

Jarsdel had never been a fan of slapstick comedy, particularly that old standby, the double take. Real people simply didn't behave that way, so it was impossible for him to find it funny. But when Morales spoke those two words, he felt himself perform that very same hackneyed, bewildered headshake of the cheap vaudevillian.

He was in the Original Farmers Market, the collection of shops and food stands across the street from his apartment. He'd been sipping a Virgil's root beer and spooning his way through a bread bowl of clam chowder when he got the call. Seeing it was Morales, he quickly rehearsed how he'd tell him about the piece of Tiffany glass. Once he decided on what would produce the maximum effect, he answered. And then Morales's opening line changed everything.

Jarsdel plugged his left ear to block out some of the ambient chatter. "Wait—did you say *dead*? Ellery Keating?"

"Yup. Last night on Catalina Island. They're county over there, so it's Sheriff's Department, not us. Deputy on the Island calls it in to their own homicide guys, and they're out there right now."

"Catalina?" Jarsdel didn't understand. "What was she doing over there?"

"Hell do I know? Celebrating the Fourth, I guess."

"By herself?"

"Tully, pay the fuck attention. *I don't know*. Only reason I even found out is 'cause I'm on the phone with Commercial Crimes to see what our options are in building a case. While I'm talking to them, *they* do a search on her to see if they've got any files, and up pops a notice from Critical Reach. Guy I'm talkin' to is like, hey, no worries about building a case, 'cause the lady's dead in Avalon."

Critical Reach—formerly TRAK—was a software program that allowed separate law enforcement agencies to communicate with each other. Appeals for information on serious crimes like armed robberies, sexual assaults, and homicides could be e-blasted to multiple jurisdictions.

"We sure it's the same Ellery Keating?" said Jarsdel.

Morales exhaled. "You seriously asking if I didn't match up the address and DOB?"

"Sorry, you're right."

"What—you think I don't know, like, *basic* police procedure?"

A man at a nearby table was on the phone and giving an animated harangue on the dismal spec scripts flooding his office. He gestured wildly, swatting his wineglass with the back of his hand. It tipped over with a musical *clink* and sent a crimson waterfall over the side. "Aw *shit*," he said, trying to catch as much as he could with a dinner napkin. Jarsdel noted the bottle was a Pahlmeyer red blend. An *expensive* crimson waterfall.

"How'd she die?" said Jarsdel.

"Shot at a party, only no one saw or heard the shooter—something like that. I actually didn't even get to read the bulletin yet. This is all just secondhand."

"When can we get over there?"

"I'm calling the LT soon as we get off the phone. He'll have to get in touch with the Sheriff's and tell 'em we've been working Keating and we'd like to come out and do some interviews."

"Gavin'll drag his feet. He's not gonna want to deal with any interagency stuff."

"Yeah, 'course not. 'Cause deep down, he knows his people skills are worse than yours. But I'll stay on him. Kinda excited, actually. Never been to Catalina."

Jarsdel thought about Keating and how convenient it was that now no one would be able to ask her about her arrangement with Dean Burken or whatever role she'd played in his death.

He tried for another spoonful of chowder, but it had cooled enough that a skin had formed over the top, and it tasted slimy. He pushed it aside.

"Still there?" Morales asked.

"Yes. Would it offend you if I suggested we get the names of everyone who bought a ticket on the Catalina ferry within forty-eight hours on either side of Keating's arrival?"

"I don't get *offended*. Piss me off a little, though, obvious as it is. Besides, already looked into it, and it's pointless. Thousands of people coming and going every day, with terminals in San Pedro, Long Beach, and Dana Point. And it's not like these are passport checkpoints. No security, no need to present an ID. Lotsa customers pay cash. And that's just the ferries. Not even talkin' about charters or guys who got their own boats. Huge waste of time to even—"

"Okay, okay. Got it. Forget investigating the passenger manifests." He exhaled, then decided he might be able to salvage at least a portion of his triumph. "By the way, Ellery Keating was our shooter.

Well, one of them anyway. It's pretty clear now she must've had an accomplice."

Now it was Morales's turn to be caught off guard. "What d'you mean?"

Jarsdel explained how he'd noticed the piece of glass in her shoe and assumed it had been an earring. Then he recounted his revelation of the night before. "You remember that lamp in Burken's living room? One that got smashed during the homicide? That's Tiffany glass. Refraction analysis will confirm it, but I'm sure. It's a distinct recipe, as damning as a fingerprint." *Well, not quite*, he thought. But it sounded good.

"Okay," said Morales. "But it's not like that's gonna help us too much. Even if you could prove it, there's no way she hung on to that tiny piece of glass."

Jarsdel finished the last of the Virgil's, which had warmed and flattened out during the call. "I know. But at least we can proceed from the assumption..." He trailed off, defeated. If anything, his partner was being generous. It didn't get them anywhere new. She'd already been a suspect. Now she was a dead suspect.

"I'm still listening, believe it or not," said Morales.

"Never mind. Let's get to Catalina in the morning. Meantime, I think we should try to get Keating's body over to Ipgreve."

"Already done. Got airlifted to county coroner's last night."

"Good. I'll talk to him, see if he can—"

"Did that too," said Morales. "He can't do it today or tomorrow. Maybe Thursday."

"Look," said Jarsdel, suddenly irritated. "I didn't *want* to take the day off. The LT made me. And if you were so busy, you could have called. I'd have been happy to take on this stuff from home."

"Dude, whoa. I didn't say shit. Chill out."

"Sorry."

"Yeah..."

"I said sorry."

"And I said *yeah*. Maybe this is good timing for both of us.

Couple days of sun, sand, and mai tais. They probably got a library over there you can check out. Could be pretty rockin'."

After they hung up, Jarsdel threw out the rest of his congealed chowder and went back across the street to pack. He hadn't been to Catalina since an eighth-grade class trip, but that had been on a remote part of the island. He and his partner would be going to Avalon, the glittering beach town once known as Hollywood's playground. A shorts and sandals kind of town. But Jarsdel wasn't a shorts and sandals kind of guy. Bring a swimsuit, maybe? Might be fun to get in the water. He reached for a pair of modest blue shorts, then hesitated. If Morales caught one look at his long, fish-belly-white legs, the jokes would never stop. His partner was a prolific giver of nicknames, and Jarsdel could too easily imagine a few new ones—"Egret Boy," "Officer Giraffe," or perhaps simply "Chopsticks."

He decided against the swimsuit. Thirsty, he went into the kitchen for a drink of water. As he filled his glass, he noticed Mrs. Rostami's copper bowl, the one she'd loaned him for the pudding. He went over and picked it up, studying the intricate patterns worked into the metal. It was a beautiful piece, certainly an antique. Not the sort of thing most people would risk lending out. So why had she?

Because she's lonely, you idiot. She obviously wants you to return it so she can see you again.

He thought of the way she'd asked him to stay for dinner, which she'd probably had ready in case Jarsdel said yes. Had there even been a samovar, he wondered.

It didn't matter, and he pushed the thought away. She was a good, kind person and deserved understanding. He tucked the bowl under his arm, left the apartment, and got in his car. As every Angeleno does, he automatically performed the rudimentary traffic equation as he pulled out of his spot. Distance, time of day, day of the week go in one end, intuition is applied, travel time comes out the other. According to his estimate, he'd be at Rostami's in a half hour.

Unscientific as his calculations might have been, they were usually correct, and he arrived just two minutes shy of his target time. It wasn't until he was out of the car, bowl in hand, that it occurred to him he probably should've called first. Mrs. Rostami didn't strike him as the sort who liked surprises. He glanced up at the door of her apartment and brought out his cellphone. He was scrolling through his contacts when he caught some faint snatches of conversation.

Jarsdel looked up again, and this time Rostami's door was open. He could hear her voice, but she was otherwise blocked from view. A man stood there, his back to the street, as they made their farewells. He couldn't make out all the words, but the ones he did hear were formal, even deferential. He didn't call her Nourangiz or Mrs. Rostami, but Bânu Nourangiz—a term equivalent to "Lady," and one that implied she was his social better.

Under normal circumstances, he reflected later on, he'd have known who the visitor was long before he turned around, familiar as he was with the man's ascetic build and iron bearing. But his presence was so unexpected and far removed from its usual context that while a part of Jarsdel recognized him, he didn't quite accept it as fact until he saw his face.

Baba gave a cheery wave as Rostami closed the door. Once he was alone, he simply stood there in profile, unmoving. Jarsdel almost called out to him then but quickly changed his mind. Something was obviously wrong. Baba's posture sagged and he hurried away from her apartment. He stopped when he came to the top of the second-floor landing, seizing the railing on either side of the stairway like a gymnast about to perform. He clamped his eyes shut, and Jarsdel could see his thin chest rise and fall. This went on for nearly a minute, then Baba opened his eyes, straightened up, and descended the stairs.

Jarsdel moved back, ducking behind a clump of overgrown bougainvillea. But he still had enough visibility through the branches to make out Baba as he headed down the sidewalk to his car. He slumped again, gripping the wheel, and Jarsdel again considered whether he should reveal himself and see what was going on. But Baba soon raised his head, started the engine, and pulled into traffic. Jarsdel turned away as he passed by and listened for the car to slow down or for his father to call out, but neither occurred.

He took the stairs two at a time, reaching the apartment just a few minutes after Baba had left. He knocked, and Rostami's voice sounded from inside.

"Ah, Professor! Did you forget something?"

The door swung open, and Rostami blinked in surprise. "Detective. What are you doing here? Where's your father? You must have just passed him. You weren't waiting in the car this whole time, were you?"

Jarsdel realized he hadn't given any thought to what he was going to say. He held out the copper bowl. "I wanted to thank you for lending me this."

"Did you enjoy the pudding?" Rostami took the bowl and regarded him with concern. "Are you all right?"

"Yes, it's just..."

Just what? He didn't know.

"You didn't come together?" Rostami asked.

"No, I saw him drive off. Didn't know you two knew each other." He felt dirty, certain he was prodding at something personal to his father, but his curiosity was overpowering.

Rostami smiled, and in that smile, Jarsdel saw a much younger, stronger woman. Gone was any hint of the anxious Code Walter that Officer Katsaros had been so eager to dump onto Morales. "You should come in."

She guided him to the chair he'd sat in the first time he came over but didn't go through the tea-or-no-tea routine. Instead, she brought over a photo album, opened it toward the middle, and set it on the table in front of him. She tapped one of the photographs with her fingernail.

"See for yourself." She sat across from him and waited as he studied the picture.

It was Baba—there was no mistaking the piercing eyes and wiry, marathon runner's physique—but then again, it wasn't Baba. The face was all wrong, completely absent the troughs that years of frowning would work into his flesh, and the lips were full, even sensual. He was much younger, so of course that accounted for most of the outward changes, but there was something deeper. The very substance behind his expression seemed to come from a different man. There was no scarcity of heart, no smirking upturn at the edge of his mouth, the one that said the world was mad and oh, how few saw that as clearly as he.

Baba had his arm around a teenaged boy with wide, kind eyes and a shy smile. In contrast to Baba's lean intensity, the youth's features were soft and rounded. Together they stood in front of a bust of Shams of Tabriz, whom Jarsdel knew to be Baba's most beloved Sufi master. He doubted he'd ever seen his father look so genuinely happy.

"That's Izad," said Rostami. "One of the last pictures I took of him."

"I don't understand," said Jarsdel. He pushed the album away as he looked up to meet her eyes. It bothered him to see his father that way, almost like encountering a ghost. "Izad's your son? I thought you said..."

"What, that I didn't have children? I don't, not anymore. That was a long time ago. Your father was Izad's professor. All he ever did was talk about him and his classes. You must understand, almost everyone else who taught at Tehran University were old men. But Professor Jahangir, he was full of energy and passion. And absolutely brilliant. He could quote Dante, William Blake, John Donne."

"Mrs. Rostami, I apologize if I'm ignorant of all this, but I didn't know any of it until now. He doesn't talk much about his life back then. During the revolution, I mean."

"I don't blame him. Many of us would like to forget. But that's not something I can do." She leaned forward and patted the photograph through the protective plastic film. "My Izad was just like any other young man. Proud and fierce and excited about life. For him, there was no higher calling than the pursuit of truth. Over and over again, one of your father's mantras: 'The least initial deviation from the truth—'"

"'—is multiplied later a thousandfold,'" Jarsdel finished.

Rostami beamed. "You know it."

"I lived it. Every lie I tried to get away with when I was a kid, out trotted Aristotle."

"Then you know the effect your baba had on Izad. Until he began taking his classes, he was an apathetic student. Education was simply a nuisance. He wanted to do something, to change the world with his heart and his hands. And your baba told him, look, you can do all that. You can do anything, but only if you study. Your mind is a weapon. He would say that, your baba. He'd say your mind is a weapon."

That sounds more like the man I know, thought Jarsdel. Then he looked at the picture again and felt a tightening in his throat. He knew at that moment that if he dug out every photo of Baba and him together, not a single one would show his father the way he looked here.

"I don't want to bring up anything painful," he said, "but could you share with me what happened?"

Rostami appeared conflicted. Someone downstairs turned on some techno music with the bass cranked up high. A porcelain cup resting on the dining room table rattled against the wood. She got up, put a napkin under the cup, and returned to her seat.

"I don't know if it's for me to tell you everything," she said at last. "If your father has kept this part of his life to himself, I can't see what right I have to violate that privacy."

Jarsdel didn't comment, sensing she hadn't yet finished.

"Then again," Rostami went on, "this was more than forty years ago. And he was my son after all. How much do you know about the revolution?"

"Only what I've read in the history books," said Jarsdel. When Rostami looked doubtful, he added, "Documentaries too."

"You haven't spoken about it with anyone who was there?"

"No. Baba won't talk about it, and his sister—my aunt—she won't either." Then he blurted out, "They killed her dog. I think that's why."

Rostami nodded. "Mehrdad. I remember. My husband helped to cut him down."

"You knew them? My family?"

"Of course. They were very well respected, especially for Zoroastrians." She paused to collect her thoughts. The music from downstairs quit. There was a burst of muffled laughter, then it started up again, louder. Jarsdel was about to offer to go tell them to turn it down, but Rostami didn't seem to notice the noise.

"It's almost impossible to explain," she said. "The sudden knowledge that enormous decisions are being made every day that will upend your world. Of course this is always true, but most of the time, the change is gradual, and we don't notice. And then at some points in history—like that one—those things condense. Speed up. So you have this certainty, every day you feel it, that big things are happening all around you, and there's nothing you can do. And you soon realize you have three choices. Pardon me a moment."

She went to the kitchen and came back with a glass of water for herself. "My throat gets dry," she said, then took a breath, refocusing her thoughts. "Three choices. The most obvious is you do nothing. You stay where you are, keep to your routine, and hope everything goes back to normal. That's the first choice. The second is you flee. You go somewhere that seems better or safer. You become willing to sacrifice your home for a strange place far away. The third option, as I'm sure you've guessed, is that you stay and try to push back against the change. And that's what Izad did."

She took a sip of water and wrinkled her nose. "I still can't get used to the water here, even after forty years. There's no life in it." She took another sip and set down the glass. "Your baba was pushing back too. He supported Shariatmadari. You know about the MPRP?"

Jarsdel nodded. The Muslim People's Republic Party, led by the Grand Ayatollah Mohammed Shariatmadari, had opposed Khomeini's regime and tried in vain to convert Iran to a democracy. When his efforts failed, his family was tortured, his followers jailed or killed. As further punishment and to avert more bloodshed, he went on national television to apologize for defying the new Islamic Republic. It was a bitter, ironic twist. It had been Shariatmadari himself who'd saved Khomeini in the early '60s, when the shah had wanted the firebrand cleric executed. In a move he must have later regretted, Shariatmadari gave Khomeini the title of grand ayatollah, conferring upon him immunity from the death penalty.

"He'd been against the shah, your baba, but Khomeini really worried him. He organized protests with the MPRP. Almost seemed like they had a chance too. There were moments when I thought it could really happen, that we would go from the shah, through the blood and flames of that year after he was gone, and then experience rebirth. There was hope and talk among the students that the suffering was critical, that it would propel us forward. Iran would see the shah wasn't the answer and that Khomeini's theocracy wasn't an answer, and we would achieve balance. Your father believed that very strongly. And Izad was his most dedicated disciple."

To be among those who renew the world, Jarsdel thought.

"There was a big march planned, timed to support the protests in Tabriz. I told Izad not to go, that the Hezbollahi would be watching. But he was fearless. He said that as long as Professor Jahangir was going, he must be there." She shook her head. "He didn't understand that the rules had changed. I don't think even I understood completely, not then. The shift had already taken place. Any opposition at that point was meaningless."

She drank from her glass. "They were arrested. Izad, your father, I don't know how many others. They let your baba go, probably because he was already so well known in the West. A kind of cultural ambassador, and Khomeini still wasn't sure himself if he'd need him and others like him. That all changed very soon afterward, and your whole family had to emigrate if they wanted to stay alive. But for Izad, no. To them, he was merely an upstart, a troublemaker. And he vanished. When your baba saw me, the night you came by, he felt he had to help. Such a generous man. I tell him it's not necessary, that I have no trouble with the rent, but he's very insistent."

Jarsdel stared at her. He didn't know what to do with everything she'd just said, didn't know where to put it within himself. It was as if any information about Baba had to pass along established grooves, and what Rostami told him didn't fit in those grooves. To force himself to accept his father as a once-jailed freedom fighter, one who'd lost a student to an unspeakable fate, would be to shatter those grooves. He would have to remake and rebuild his father as he knew him.

Rostami seemed to understand—if not the particulars of Jarsdel's struggle, then at least the substance. She leaned toward him. "Your father's a brave man. I don't blame him for this. My son had to follow the commands of his heart, just as your father did." She wiped at her eyes with her thumb. "And maybe I'm wrong, you know? Maybe it wasn't meaningless. Maybe no true sacrifice goes unheard. I'd like to believe that."

PART II

THE GREAT TEMPLE

12

The cloud cover broke early, seared off by a July sun that already had the back of Jarsdel's neck prickling with heat. They'd only just left Long Beach Harbor, the Catalina Island ferry finally reaching speed, and he wanted to stay on deck and enjoy the wind kicking off the waves. But he also knew if he didn't get back inside soon, the fair skin of his cheeks would take on an embarrassing scarlet flush that could last as long as a week. He thought of what Mrs. Rostami had said, about how little he must have inherited of his baba's features. She'd been right about that, especially when it came to his vulnerability to sunburn. He and Dad shared what Baba referred to as "the pallor of a Borstal hooligan weaned on neeps and tatties."

The boat hit a swell, misting the air with bow spray. Jarsdel tasted salt on his tongue. It had been years since he'd been out on the water, and he'd forgotten how good it felt.

A few more minutes, he thought, then reminded himself what it would mean. A week of Morales and jokes about whether Jarsdel was wearing rouge. He went back inside, sparing a curious glance at the upper deck and the enclosed Commodore Lounge, the Catalina Express's version of a first-class cabin. Lieutenant Gavin had ensured the department paid only for general seating, and Jarsdel had suggested to his partner that they kick in the extra thirty bucks for the lounge. Morales refused, calling it a rip-off. But it looked quieter up there, and you got a free drink.

Morales was having a Bloody Mary and reading something called *Chain Saw Confidential*.

"Pretty bright out there," said Jarsdel as he sat across from him. "Forgot to put on sunscreen."

Morales raised his eyes, grunted, then went back to his book. "Yeah, wouldn't want any color. Gotta stay lookin' like a Tim Burton character."

The boat hit another swell, and Jarsdel's stomach turned. "I didn't take any Dramamine. You have any?"

"No."

"What if you get seasick?"

"I don't."

"Maybe the server will have some." Jarsdel looked out the window. San Pedro Bay was to the north, the enormous container cranes of the Port of Los Angeles hooking out over the water like giant steel fingers. Jarsdel checked the time on his phone. They had almost an hour before they'd arrive in Avalon. He returned his gaze to the rolling blue surf, smiling when he spotted a pod of dolphins playing in the waves.

"I've been thinking about something. The nature of a homicide in a contained space like the one we're going to. Can't drive in and out, obviously. Access is limited. You've got ferries like this and the helicopter, right?"

"Who're you talking to?" Morales said. "Are you actually talking to me?"

Jarsdel was puzzled. "Who else?"

"Then can you actually look in my direction when you're conversating? Starin' out the window, givin' me that Jorge routine again. Like you been smacked in the head with a Wiffle bat, talkin' to yourself."

Jarsdel pulled his attention away from the scenery. "Okay, I'm looking at you."

"That's great, but I don't wanna talk about this shit right now," said Morales.

"You just told me to look at you."

"Yeah, if you're gonna talk to me, look at me. That's what grown-ups do. But right now, I just wanna sit and relax and read this fucking thing. All day every day, I either gotta deal with you or I'm at home and got the wife and kids all over my ass. Never a second to myself. So I don't think an hour's a lot to ask."

Jarsdel spotted an open bag of pretzels at a nearby table, then considered Morales's drink. "Any good?"

Morales shrugged. Jarsdel got up and went to the bar. A minute later, he had his own Bloody Mary. "No celery stick," he said, sitting back down. He frowned, stirring it with its pair of skinny black cocktail straws, and finally took a sip. "Mix is a bit on the sweet side, isn't it? Wonder if they're better in the Commodore Lounge." He thought about that. "At least it would be free."

Morales clapped his book shut and set it on the small table between them. "I just wanted an hour. Just one. Know what? Gonna call you Needles, 'cause that's what you do. Like little needles pokin' away. I bet that's why you got such a high closure rate too. Make a dude fall apart with your buggy-ass questions. Confess just so long as you'll leave 'em alone. You should write your own interrogation textbook. Somethin' like *Annoy Your Way to a Conviction* or some shit."

Jarsdel stirred his drink again, hoping that would improve it, and took another sip. "Well, now that you're available, it wouldn't be a bad idea to go over our schedule. We're meeting the deputy after check-in, right?"

"No, man, already told you. Check-in's not till four. Cheap fuckin' hotel. We just drop off our luggage and shoot him a text. He'll come by and take us over to the scene, which I'm sure the locals have been stomping through since it happened."

Jarsdel checked his phone but didn't see any new messages. "Hear anything from County yet?"

Morales shook his head. "I looked before we got on the boat."

Until Dr. Ipgreve got to work on Keating's body, all they had were the bare circumstances of her death. According to the Sheriff's Department, EMTs had been summoned to the Avalon Yacht & Fish Club following the annual Catalina Island fireworks show. Keating had been drinking champagne and had fallen asleep in a deck chair, and when fellow members were unable to revive her, they'd called 911. After she was rushed to Avalon's small emergency department, the nurse discovered blood in her hair. A portion of her scalp was shaved, revealing a medium-caliber bullet hole—what Ipgreve called a "copper migraine." Eyewitnesses who were questioned that night and throughout the following day claimed they hadn't heard any gunfire, but considering Keating had probably been shot during the fireworks show, that didn't mean a whole lot.

"We should talk about how we're gonna divide up the work," Jarsdel said now to Morales. "Two days isn't a lot of time. We'll need to check out anyone she interacted with while she was on the island. I especially want to talk to the deputies stationed in Avalon. Find out anything unusual going on, any suspicious characters."

"Absolutely not," said Morales.

"What do you mean?"

"I'll do the talking when it comes to any LEOs."

"Why?"

"It's goofy you're even asking me that. Further proof I'm the one should talk to the cops." Seeing Jarsdel's baffled expression, he went on. "Look. You're Rain Man. You know it and I know it. Nothin' to be ashamed of, but you make a shitty diplomat. You never had to splash around in anybody else's pond before, right? So you don't know how this works. Second we get off that boat, we're in that dude's territory. And I know that guy, okay?"

"You do?"

"I know the *type*. Met him a thousand times, and it's always the same. Small towns like this are the worst. These departments, you got a couple assholes here..." Morales held his palm parallel to the table, then raised it higher. "And big, king, dick-fuck asshole up here. And they run their little substation like a clubhouse. Anything happens in their jurisdiction, and it's always 'My town *this*,' and 'My town *that*.' Like, 'Those perps made a big mistake causin' trouble in *my town*.' They actually say that too—'perp,' like it's a fuckin' *Kojak* episode. Real badasses, and now they got the LAPD comin' around and needing their help, and boy oh boy, just watch the ego parade. Next forty-eight hours gonna be us tryin' to kiss as much ass as we can without throwing up."

Jarsdel opened his mouth to speak, but Morales put up a hand. "Look, you're the smartest guy I know, okay? But on this one, you gonna be the strong, silent type. Cool?"

From the mainland just under thirty miles away, Catalina Island is most often visible as a long, low smudge on the horizon. On clear days, a keen-eyed observer might pick out some details of its topography. A canyon or a cove, or even the spot where Mount Ada slopes downward to the island's narrowest point—its pinched, half-mile-wide isthmus.

But even the best pair of eyes would have trouble making out the city of Avalon. It occupies hardly more than two square miles—a city in the loosest possible sense, at least in terms an Angeleno would understand—and lies tucked away in the island's southeast pocket of coarse, cream-colored sand.

Most LA natives live their entire lives without setting foot there, a surprising number of whom see Catalina's gray silhouette daily from choked freeway overpasses and downtown skyscrapers. It's probably for this reason more than any other that those who do make the trip are astonished to discover Avalon has more in common with Capri than Los Angeles. Stuccoed homes with low-pitched, red-tiled roofs cling to the rugged mountains flanking the town center, itself a cluster of pastel bungalows, gelato shops, spas, restaurants, and hotels. A walk of perhaps thirty feet will take you from Steve's Steakhouse into the pure sapphire waters of Avalon Bay, the waves licking its leeward shore the most docile in what's technically still the state of California.

The ferry docked, and Jarsdel and Morales picked up their overnight bags and joined the throng of tourists streaming over the gangway.

"Remember," said Morales. "After we get to the hotel and meet this sheriff guy, I do the talking. Any historical tidbits or grammar correction stuff, feel free to keep to yourself. Okay?"

Jarsdel didn't respond. The two began to weave their way through the dense crowd of the open-air boat terminal.

"Okay?" Morales repeated.

"Oh, I'm allowed to speak?"

"Ah, c'mon. Don't get like that."

"Like what?"

"Like overly sensitive. I'm not saying you can't talk. Just, if you're gonna say something, have it be about how nice and pretty everything is here and what a stand-up job the local cops are doing."

"I see. Maybe it would be safest if I sent you a list of comments you could preapprove."

Morales blew an audible stream of air from his nose. Something to their right caught his interest. "Hey, what's that thing? The big building?"

Jarsdel looked to see he was pointing at the Catalina Casino, the crown jewel of Avalon—an enormous Mediterranean revival and art deco wonder. At its ground level was the island's sole movie theater, a grand palace of cinema's golden age. The second story housed the world's largest circular dance floor. The building's title—simply "gathering place" in Italian—was a source of constant confusion to visitors, as it had been named before the term came to be associated with gaming.

"Casino," said Jarsdel.

"Yeah?" Morales brightened. "That's awesome. You know what table games they got?"

Jarsdel was thinking up a response when someone called out, "Ahoy! Detectives!"

They stopped, having made it to the broad walkway leading into town. To their left was a small parking lot, its few available spaces occupied by taxis. A sheriff's squad car was parked in the white zone. Leaning against its side, arms crossed, was a grinning deputy, the double gold bars on his lapels identifying him as a captain. He was in his forties, his face freckled and deeply lined, rising to a sharply receding hairline of vivid red. Pinned to the right breast pocket of his shirt was an ID tag reading *Oria*.

Morales stepped forward and extended his hand, which Oria gave a vigorous, two-handed shake.

"I'm Ken. Welcome to Avalon. Figured you guys might not know where your hotel was—maybe could use a ride. You're at the Dew Drop Inn, right?"

"Yeah," said Morales. "That's cool of you, thanks. I'm Oscar, and this is Tully. Appreciate your hospitality."

"Nah, my pleasure. Glad to help LAPD however we can. Imagine you gentlemen'll want to get to work right away. Figure we'll drop your stuff off and hit Yacht & Fish straight after. Besides, sooner you're done, sooner you can join me and the guys at Topsides for happy hour." He moved to the back of the car and popped the trunk. "Go ahead and toss in your bags."

Soon they were on their way, Morales up front with Oria and Jarsdel crammed in the back, knees pressed against the security partition. And despite the outwardly clean appearance of Jarsdel's seat, there was still the faintest whiff of vomit. He guessed a large portion of Oria's duties involved corralling intoxicated tourists.

"Been to Catalina before?" asked the captain.

"First time," said Morales.

"Well, I wish you were here under different circumstances, but I still think you'll enjoy yourself. Couldn't be a nicer summer.

And about ten degrees cooler than overtown, which doesn't always happen." He glanced in the rearview at Jarsdel. "How 'bout you? First time?"

"Actually my dads—I mean, my dad used to take me here when I was a kid. But it's been about thirty years."

"Lotta new stuff since then. Got a zip line goin' all the way down the canyon now. An obstacle course up in the trees—it's safe, you wear a harness, but it's a heck of a lot of fun. But I guess most stuff's stayed the same, which is why we all love it here so much. Can't beat the vibe. You must've done the glass-bottom boat here when you were a kid, right?"

"A few times, yeah," said Jarsdel.

"Still got those. And now we also got the submarines—well, partially submersibles, to be fair. Pretty cool all the same. Lemme think what else. Couple new eco tours, safari-type deal where you get in this big open-air bus and go way up into the mountains, see some buffalo."

"Got buffalo?" said Morales.

"That we do. Bunch escaped from an old silent movie shoot and they flourished. You see bison on the menu in town, that's from right here on the island. Ship 'em overtown alive, get processed, then sent back here for food."

They reached Crescent Avenue, the main pedestrian thorough-fare running between the beachfront businesses and the sand itself. Oria made a left at the vehicle barrier, heading inland. They passed row upon row of tightly packed, candy-colored houses.

"Lotta golf carts," said Morales.

"Yup." Oria swung right, now running parallel to the beach. "We keep it that way on purpose. Very few actual cars besides emergency vehicles. Small town, so space is a premium. We actually got one for you to use."

"For real?"

"It's got the sheriff's logo on the side, so you can park it anywhere you want." He reached into the cupholder, plucked out a rubber mermaid fob with a single key dangling from it, and handed it to Morales. There were normally no cupholders in squad cars. If you were drinking coffee when you got a call, you'd have to dump the liquid out before you drove off or you'd end up with it all over your lap. The presence of the cupholder in Oria's car told Jarsdel two things—first, that it had been converted for law enforcement use later in its existence, and second, that the sheriff's budget in Avalon wasn't too robust.

Morales pocketed the key.

"It's about a block over from your hotel, right in back next to the service entrance of Topsides. Owner lets us park there. You'll meet him later."

Oria spotted something and came to a stop, rolling down his window. "Hey!" he called. "Can I get your autograph?"

A man who'd been strolling along the opposite sidewalk stopped, saw Oria, and gave a sly smile. Wiry gray hair poked out from under his Dodgers baseball cap, and he wore dark sunglasses. He ambled in their direction.

"Careful there," said Oria. "Lookin' at a jaywalking ticket."

"Shucks," said the man, planting a hand on the cruiser's roof. "Sure am sorry, officer."

"That's okay. I always let celebrities off with a warning."

The older man chuckled. "Warned you, didn't I? Never moon a werewolf."

Oria let loose with a high-pitched laugh. "I like the getup. Too many people stoppin' you on the street, you gotta go 'round incognito?"

"Oh, you bet. Got girls tossin' their panties at me."

Another explosion of laughter from Oria. When he recovered, he said to the detectives, "This here's Tom Ledbetter. Used to be my boss."

"Still am," said Ledbetter. "Pay your salary, don't I?"

Oria's laugh this time was more perfunctory. He crooked a thumb toward Morales. "Honored guests. LAPD."

Ledbetter's sly smile disappeared. "Yeah, been expecting that." He gave a somber nod. "Anyway, plan on hittin' the Top tonight?"

"You know it."

Ledbetter gave the roof of the car two quick slaps. "Catch you fellas later."

"Tom's a great guy," Oria said once they were underway again. "I was razzing him 'cause he won our club's last shooting match, along with a hundred bucks of my money."

"You usually win?" said Morales.

"Well, I'm no Wild Bill, but I guess I win more'n I lose. You shoot? I mean, other than your qualification cycles."

"Used to, before the kids came along."

"I hear ya, man."

"Be kinda fun to get back into it maybe."

"Open invitation," said Oria. "We meet second Saturday of the month."

"Where? Long Beach?"

Jarsdel began to feel like the kid who gets to tag along with his big brother so long as he behaves himself, and was glad when they stopped at their hotel. They'd probably driven no more than half a mile since they'd left the Catalina Island Express parking lot. He wasn't sure if that made Oria's gesture to pick them up charming or absurd.

The detectives got out and stared up at the Dew Drop Inn—three stories of columns, gables, oriel windows, balconies, and overhanging eaves. Virtually every trick in the Queen Anne playbook. It also sported a fresh coat of pink paint and a glossy, royal-blue trim.

Morales frowned. "It's really pink."

"I'd say this is my first recommendation for a value stay in Avalon," said Oria.

Once they were in the lobby, Jarsdel understood what the captain had meant by "value." The hotel's stately exterior promised delights within—wainscoted walls, grained woodwork, a lush parlor, and a dining room dominated by an exquisite matched sideboard and cellarette.

But the interior of the Dew Drop Inn was purely functional—almost institutional. The lobby was cramped and spare. There was a Formica reception desk sitting across from a humming vending machine, some retired and badly frayed office furniture, and a rack of brochures advertising local attractions.

"This is more what I expected from the LT," said Morales, sounding somewhat relieved.

"By the way," said Jarsdel, "what happened to all your doomsaying about what petty tyrants the local law was gonna be?"

"Okay, maybe I was wrong. But it's definitely helping that you been quiet."

They dropped off their bags and went outside to rejoin Oria, who'd parked the cruiser up the street. "Easier to walk from here. Yacht & Fish's just around the corner, 'bout five hundred yards."

The three men set off in the rising heat. Morales undid his tie and stuffed it in his pocket. Despite the sweat gathering in Jarsdel's collar, he kept his own tie on. He didn't need Morales and Oria sharing a joke about the clip-on.

The captain pointed ahead. "Gonna make a left up here, then go under that arch that says Via Casino."

Hundreds of tourists swarmed downtown Avalon, surging up and down Crescent Avenue, across the beach, into restaurants. Many wore woven grass hats that Jarsdel was quickly able to trace back to a tiki bar called Luau Larry's, where a dozen customers milled out front, singing "Sometimes Love Just Ain't Enough."

Jarsdel noted it was just before noon. Oria glanced his way and laughed. "Vacationland, my friend."

"I'm not judging," said Jarsdel. "Looks like fun."

"It is. Hell of a karaoke selection in there."

They turned down Via Casino, the shorefront pathway that led from Avalon Bay to Casino Point. Back in LA, the summer sun was relentless, despotic, taking much more than it gave. It baked the trees and the grass, drained the cheer from the city's inhabitants so they were sluggish and mean, even split the concrete underfoot.

But here on Catalina, it lit up the palm trees and the red clay roofs and brought out the quiet, ancient beauty of the rocky cliffside. It splashed over the boats at anchor and the greased backs of the swimmers and turned the water the dazzling blue of a gas flame. Shimmering below the surface, fat orange fish swam lazy, meandering paths.

Morales pointed at one. "Those're cool. What're they called?"

"Garibaldi," said Oria. "They're protected. California state marine fish. Catch one and you better toss it back. Five-hundred-dollar fine."

Morales whistled. "That's some expensive sushi. Taste any good?"

"You're asking me, a sworn law enforcement officer?" Oria gave him a conspiratorial grin. "Not worth no five hundred dollars, that's for sure."

The two shared a laugh over that. Jarsdel rolled his eyes.

"I'ma take a picture for my wife," said Morales. "She loves fish and stuff." He took out his phone, snapped off a few pictures, then forwarded them. "What're they called again?"

"Garibaldi," said Oria. "Don't ask me why."

"General Giuseppe Garibaldi," said Jarsdel. "1807 to 1882. His military campaigns led to the unification of Italy in 1861."

Morales shot him a warning glare, but Jarsdel happily ignored it.

"Those loyal to him wore striking reddish-orange woolen shirts. Similar enough to the color of the fish, hence the name."

"Huh," said Oria. "Been stationed here five years and didn't know that. By the way, anyone gonna tell me why exactly the LAPD's so interested in all this? I mean, this is probably nothing more than some asshole randomly firing a gun on the Fourth."

"Nobody told you?" said Morales.

"Nope. Just some cryptic message from your lieutenant about how he'd appreciate our cooperation. Very mysterious. Is it some big secret?"

Bruce Gavin, master statesman, Jarsdel thought. To Oria, he said, "It's no secret. Ellery Keating was a person of interest in a shooting."

"You're kidding."

"And I have good reason to believe she pulled the trigger."

Morales grunted with amusement. "Pet theory."

"Seriously?" said Oria. "Talkin' about the same Ellery Keating? When was this?"

"Little over a week before she died. June twenty-fifth."

"Who's the victim?"

Jarsdel gave him the basic outline of the Burken homicide, emphasizing the connection between the broken Tiffany lamp and the shard wedged in Keating's shoe tread.

"Opalescent glass is particularly distinct," he added. "Silver nitrate coating. And if we could've matched it up, woulda been as good as a fingerprint."

"I been hearing about this glass all week," said Morales. "He won't let it go."

He halted in front of a long, two-story craftsman bungalow, outfitted with its own private dock. It was late nineteenth century but sturdy and maintained with meticulous attention to detail. To the right of the door was mounted a polished historic marker, stark against the building's bone-white paint.

> NO. 997 TUNA CLUB OF AVALON—The Tuna Club
> of Avalon marks the birthplace of modern big game
> sportfishing in 1898. Led by Dr. Charles Frederick
> Holder, the club's founding members adopted the
> rules of conduct stressing conservationist ethics and
> sporting behavior. Today, their work remains the basis
> for the sport's internationally accepted principles.

"Holy shit," said Morales.

Both Jarsdel and Oria turned to him, drawn by the awe in the man's voice.

"This is the actual place. From *Chinatown*. In that movie it was the—uh, the Albacore Club. Yeah! Wow. This pretty much makes the whole trip worth it. I mean, this is somethin' else. John Huston and Jack Nicholson right here, man."

Oria took a step back and studied the building, looking it up and down. "Huh. Good to know. We should put it on the website if it isn't already." He cleared his throat. "We good to keep going? Yacht & Fish's actually gonna be over there." Oria pointed at another craftsman bungalow farther along Via Casino, this one painted sea green.

"You a member?" said Morales as they got moving again.

"Ha. Hell no, not in my tax bracket. Pretty exclusive too. All these clubs on the waterfront are. Rules at Yacht & Fish are strict." He ticked off the points on his fingers as he spoke. "Gotta bag a tuna at least fifty pounds, I think with a nine-ounce rod, and I forget the gauge of line. Can't be super heavy, though. And this is in addition obviously to all the high society stuff that goes along with this kinda place."

They stopped in front of the building, and Oria brought out his phone. "Gimme a sec. Gonna check in with the guy we're meeting."

He fired off a text. After a moment, there was a responding buzz.

"He'll be right over," said Oria, putting his phone away. "Club's not open yet, but he—" He broke off, shielding his eyes. "Here he comes."

Approaching from the same direction they'd traveled was a lean man of about sixty, muscled and heavily tanned, but with the smooth, unblemished skin that suggested spa treatments rather than sunlight.

Not totally unblemished, Jarsdel corrected himself. Patches of skin were under assault by something that could've been psoriasis, most of it concentrated around his neck and jawline. It looked painful. But aside from that, he was well-groomed, a heavy gold watch cinched around his wrist, and he cut through the crowd with a lithe, confident gait. He could have been Keating's Vespasian bust, come to life for a stroll in Avalon.

Oria raised a hand in greeting. "Appreciate you comin' out, Dell. Thanks." To the detectives, he said, "He's the club president."

The man had been twirling a set of keys around his index finger but stopped once he was within speaking distance, snapping his fist closed to muffle them. "Afternoon," he said, passing them to unlock and open a side gate. "Hope you weren't waiting long. I'm—"

His introduction was interrupted by the melodious tolling of bells. He and the others looked up to where a lone bell tower sat nestled against the hillside, about fifty yards inland. Once it had finished striking noon, the man resumed.

"Anyway," he said, holding open the gate. "Let me know what you need. I'm Larry Pruitt, but call me Dell. Everyone does."

"You were here when it happened?" said Morales.

Pruitt nodded, his dark and deep-set brown eyes full of emotion. "It's unbelievable. Ellery and I go back forever."

"Pruitt?" said Jarsdel. "Any connection by chance to Pruitt Equities Group?"

The man nodded. "That's right."

"You and Ms. Keating were in business together."

Pruitt seemed surprised. "Uh, yeah."

Well, that's interesting, thought Jarsdel. So if this guy and Keating went back "forever," he had to know she was on the Newport Beach City Council. Obviously he didn't possess too many scruples about her conflict of interest.

"You see what happened?" said Morales.

"No one did, far as I know. We were watching the fireworks."

"Everyone was watching?"

"Sure. It's a big deal here. Every Fourth, right over the bay. Yacht & Fish's about as close as you can get to the action without actually being in the water."

"Guessing that's why none of you heard a shot," said Morales.

"Safe to assume. Some of those bangs can be as loud as artillery fire. And a bunch of us got earplugs in to boot. The rest just turn down their hearing aids." He gave a self-effacing smile. "We're not exactly the youngest crowd. I'm sixty-two, and a few of the members still call me 'kid.'"

"Could you come with us?" asked Jarsdel. "Give us an idea of where everybody was?"

"Sure, but there were maybe thirty or forty people."

Pruitt closed the gate, then got in front of the small party to lead the way. Instead of going inside the clubhouse, they went around directly to the dock, where there was a kind of wide, shaded porch. Rattan chairs were arranged for members to enjoy the view of the sea, along with a scattering of small tables where they could rest their cocktails. The dock side of the clubhouse had its own entrance, and Pruitt pointed to the heavily lacquered, salt-encrusted door.

"This was standing open, people coming and going, so it's difficult to say for sure where a specific person was at any given time. But I guess during the show, most of us were outside. Ellery was right here." He patted one of the chairs.

"Did she cry out or make any kind of sound?" said Jarsdel.

"No idea. She might've, but I didn't hear anything and haven't talked to anyone who did."

"When did you realize something was wrong?"

"Not till the show was over. Our eyes are readjusting to the natural light, and we're watching the smoke clear. You know how you're like a kid when you watch a fireworks show. Always wanna keep looking just in case they set off another one. But when it was obvious that was it, everyone clapped and turned back toward this direction, toward the club. And like I said, Ellery was right here. Kinda slumped forward, with her chin on her chest, and we all just assumed she'd fallen asleep. You know, maybe had a little too much champagne and conked out for a while. We've all been there." He rubbed his mouth with the knuckles of his right hand. "I don't think we realized something was wrong for maybe twenty or thirty minutes. It was only because she hadn't moved or anything. Even if you get really soused, you usually move at least a little, right? And once we had the lights back on—we had them off during the show—we saw a line of drool going down her chin."

Morales went over and joined Pruitt at the armchair. "Was it facing like this? Same angle as now?"

"Pretty much, yeah."

"And she got hit right here." Morales tapped the back of his own head. He turned to see where the bullet could have come from. There was only one possibility, obvious even from where Jarsdel stood, and that was the hill overlooking the club. The bell tower would have made for an excellent sniper's nest, situated at about a sixty-degree upward angle.

"I thought about that too," said Pruitt. "I mean, once I heard she'd been shot."

"Anyone been up there?" Jarsdel asked Oria.

The captain blushed. "Well, no. Not yet. Been a crazy couple days. We don't get a lot of deceased persons here, and I can't even tell you when the last homicide was. But hang on..." He stepped away from the group and touched his shoulder mic. "Hey, Sean? I need you to get up to Chimes Tower and have a look around. Whole area. Could be that's where our shooter was, so keep an eye out for shell casings."

Jarsdel went over to where Morales had retraced the bullet's path. As he passed him, his partner whispered, "*Crazy couple days. He serious? Doesn't look for fucking shell casings?*"

Jarsdel gave a nod, then got his own look at the possible trajectory. The angle was right, but it was a hell of a shot. Fifty yards from Chimes Tower, passing between a roof-mounted nautical flag and the porch's weathered awning, a window of about ten feet from side to side. It would've been dark too—Pruitt had just said so. Not only would Keating have had her back to the shooter, but apart from the occasional flashes from the fireworks, she would have been practically impossible to see.

Not if the guy had a night-vision scope.

Jarsdel frowned at his own thought. The idea of someone hiring a highly trained, Jackal-like assassin to erase a minor, corrupt politician seemed ridiculous.

While Oria was occupied, Morales turned his attention back to Pruitt. "Gonna ask you something, and I want you to be honest, okay?"

"I'm always honest." His smile returned. "And I'm twice as honest with the police."

"This is probably a dumb question, but you know if any of the club's members brought a firearm to the party?"

The question visibly surprised Pruitt. "No. Never seen anyone do that. Not on the Fourth or any other time."

"You sure? Nothin' like, 'Hey, guys, it's a holiday. Let's shoot this off for fun'?"

"Absolutely not."

"Didn't even have to be like that. Maybe just went off accidentally. I'm sure there's plenty of guns around here someone coulda gotten hold of. Never know who you're gonna run into on the open ocean, right?"

Pruitt shrugged. "Okay, yeah, but nobody's packing on land."

Oria drifted over. "Got a guy headed up there now."

"Thanks," said Morales. "So now for the most obvious question."

"Who, if anyone, wished her ill?"

"Yup. Any enemies?"

Both Oria and Pruitt thought it over, and both shook their heads. "Everyone loved her here," said the captain. "Spent a lot of money in town, tipped good—'specially if the waiter was a good-lookin' guy. Knew everybody. Didn't have a place on the island but came over all the time. Regular at the Pavilion."

Jarsdel had glimpsed the upscale Pavilion Hotel as they'd driven toward town, hoping in vain that was where the LT had put them up.

"It really could've been an accident," said Pruitt. "It's stupid, but it happens. Some idiot fires his gun in the air, and bam. Isn't it statistically the deadliest holiday after New Year's?"

"That's what I was saying," Oria agreed.

"Okay, anyone around here come to mind as a candidate?" said Jarsdel. "As far as idiots go?"

Oria and Pruitt glanced at each other. It was a brief, silent conversation, one that conveyed a kind of weary understanding—two men who'd traveled a long and difficult road. When Oria turned back to the detectives, he gave a slight nod. "Yeah, we might have one or two guys like that."

13

What King Henry's was to the American frontier, Topsides was to life at sea, trading the hodgepodge of Old West clichés for the maritime variety. It began out front, with a huge cast-iron anchor fitted into the concrete. Inside, tattered netting hung from the walls, joined by sand dollars and plastic starfish and a restored ship's wheel. Pelicans and gulls—some in flight, others perched atop weather-beaten posts—were painted against a glossy blue background. Between oversized black and white photographs of caught fish, LEDs flickered inside hurricane lamps. *Nautical vomit*, Jarsdel thought. Looking up, he saw even the ceiling fans hadn't escaped the design scheme, their blades shaped like sculling oars. He doubted, however, that their caking of dust, so heavy in places that tendrils of the stuff drooped from their edges, was part of the overall motif.

Jarsdel and Morales had arrived as guests of Captain Oria, but it quickly became clear Pruitt was their real host. The servers and bartenders snapped to attention when he strode in, and a pair of busboys scrambled to prepare a table in a quiet back corner. It soon came out that the outsized attention shown their party wasn't due to Pruitt's position as president of the Yacht & Fish.

"This new?" Oria asked, pointing at something on the drink menu.

Pruitt looked to see what he meant. "Yeah, few others too, all on tap. New liquor supplier."

"This your place?" said Morales.

"It is, yeah."

"Which means everything's on the house," said Oria. "So drink up."

"You're dreamin'." To Morales, Pruitt said, "Puts my beer away like he's got a hollow leg."

Jarsdel surveyed the room with fresh interest, noticing it was, in fact, Pruitt himself in all the fish trophy photographs, face framed in the cowl of his wetsuit. In the bottom righthand corner, a filigreed label indicated the weight of the catch and the day it was caught. The photos were placed strategically so that wherever you looked, you saw some evidence of the man's angling prowess.

"Speargun," said Pruitt, though no one had asked. "I dive at least once a week."

"I actually took that most recent one," said Oria, pointing to one of the pictures, this one dated June 24. It was a close-up shot, probably to compensate for the relatively small size of the catch on display—a sea bass, mouth agape, a bloody gash in its side. Jarsdel could see that Pruitt's wetsuit, naturally, was monogrammed.

"Got that sucker with my new Cressi Apache," said Pruitt. "Shoulda seen that spear fly. *Fwoosh.* Thing's a powerhouse."

"Here we go," said Oria turning to the detectives. "Talks about his gear like it's his girlfriend. Custom everything. Should hear him go on about his buoyancy compensator, whatever the fuck that is."

"Gotta do it right."

Oria began plucking at a rubber band he was wearing like a bracelet on his left wrist. At first a little tentatively, but then he gave it a real snap.

"Quitting smoking?" said Morales.

Oria smiled. "You try this too?"

"Yup."

"Did it work?"

"Nope, but maybe you'll have more luck."

The men were nearing the end of their first round of Murphy's Stout when Morales began prodding about persons of interest in the Keating case. The search for shell casings at Chimes Tower had turned up nothing, and the detectives didn't want to lose momentum. Again, Pruitt and Oria exchanged a resigned, knowing look.

"Every town's got its bad eggs," said the captain, "and Avalon's no exception."

"Sure we are," said Pruitt. "In that our bad eggs are exceptionally ridiculous."

"Yeah, well, that may be. But anything funky happens around here, and these are the first guys I look at."

"Who is it?" said Morales. "What's their deal?"

Oria took in a slow breath of air, looking to Jarsdel like someone bracing himself to deliver a confession. "They're a gang. Small, only five guys. I guess you'd say they're...basically...*pirates*."

The detectives, failing to see what was so strange about that, exchanged a look of their own. "All right," said Morales. "So they do what, like rob boats and stuff? Shake down the occasional tourist?"

Oria nodded.

"Isn't that a pretty common problem around harbors and marinas?" said Jarsdel.

Oria nodded again.

"Okay," said Morales, then laughed. "Way you guys were leading up to it made us think it was gonna be somethin' weird. I know a couple guys patrol the delta up in Contra Costa County, and they gotta deal with those kinda assholes all the time."

"Not like these," said Pruitt, with a wry smile. "These guys are actual pirates. Or maybe it's better to say they *think* they're actual pirates." He thought that over, then added, "Which I suppose in the end does make them actual pirates. Amusing recursion."

Recursion, thought Jarsdel. *Fancy*. Aloud, he asked, "I'm sorry. By 'actual pirates,' are you referring to the yo-ho-ho variety?"

Oria looked down into his beer, but Pruitt held Jarsdel's gaze.

"That's what we're saying. As you can see, Ken's kinda embarrassed by the whole thing. He—"

"I'm not embarrassed," said Oria.

"You're a little embarrassed. *I'm* embarrassed. We've got pirates."

"I'm not embarrassed," Oria repeated. "It's just a huge pain in the ass. These fuckin' douchenozzles...can't get rid of 'em."

"Whoa, wait," said Morales. "Hang on. I'm just tryin' to wrap my mind around this. You've got dudes actually do the whole Jack Sparrow routine, but for real?"

"Yup."

"Like, legit criminals, dressed for Halloween?"

"Yup."

"And it goes beyond that," added Pruitt. "They're committed to the lifestyle, in a big way. They don't have that *Treasure Island* accent, but they've embraced just about everything else. Eschew society, live off the land—as much as they reasonably can, I suppose."

"And they sing," muttered Oria.

"Ah, that's right. They do sing. That's all from Boaz. He played in that band in Newport, back in the '90s. Still loves to perform."

"Sing?" Jarsdel leaned forward. He wasn't sure he'd heard correctly over the music. "What d'you mean, they sing?"

"Sing," said Oria, more forcefully. "Every now and then, they come through town singing one of those..." He turned to Pruitt. "What do you call those sea songs?"

"Shanties."

"Shanties, yeah. It's their way of waving their dicks around. Throwing it in my goddamned face that they're here and can do what they want. Tourists think it's all just a big show and take pictures with them and stuff. Got no idea these guys are scumbag criminals. You see anybody smoking a joint on Catalina, guarantee you it comes from one of their hidden little grows. And it's not like I really give a shit. I know the battle's over with cannabis. But you know how scarce the water is here, right? That's why all the toilets use salt water. And he's out there wasting our fresh water on his goddamned weed."

Morales was delighted. "This is wild, you guys. Too much, man. Givin' us LA guys a run for our money in the weirdo contingent."

"Why're they so hard to catch?" said Jarsdel and immediately regretted the question.

Oria's expression turned cold. When he spoke, his voice was low, soft, and angry. "You know what it's like to run a small-town police department? Lemme tell you. I got five deputies under my command. Less when we're off peak season. And you probably think we just sit around drinking beer and shooting the shit with the locals, but you'd be wrong. It doesn't stop. I want you to understand that. It doesn't stop. Twenty-four hours a day—parking problems, public intox, skateboarders on Crescent, *rollerbladers* on Crescent, dogs on the beach, open container violations, guys lighting up joints in the middle of town, check fraud, littering, shoplifting, spitting, theft, B&E—"

"You're right," Jarsdel cut in. "I didn't mean to suggest—"

"Oh, I wasn't done. Let's keep goin'. Assaults, noise complaints, heart attacks, diabetic comas, trespassing, vandalism, curfew violation. It...never...fucking...stops. So you take all that and then you expect me to do what, exactly? Lead a raid at Pebbly Beach? We got 'em cited I don't know how many dozens of times. They pay on time and they stay outta jail. But we don't have the resources to do a whole lot else, and even if we did, we don't have any proof. So when a custom stereo system goes missing off a yacht or a drunk tourist gets rolled in the dark—yeah, we know it's them. Everybody knows it's them. Whole other thing to prove it."

"Who's Boaz?" said Morales, trying to steer the conversation away from Jarsdel's blunder. "Earlier you said Boaz was a musician. He one of the pirate dudes?"

Still smoldering, Oria didn't answer, so Pruitt jumped in. "Boaz Nilsen. He's the main guy. Holds absolute thrall over these jackasses. Imagine the world's smallest cult, and you're about there. Paranoid too, so it fits. Thinks everybody's after him. Kind of a self-fulfilling prophecy, though, 'cause of course then he acts in ways that make people take notice."

Morales grunted. "Too crazy."

Silence followed. Another round of beers arrived. Oria settled down some, becoming fascinated with the bubbles rising to the head of his stout. Morales downed half of his in one long quaff, taking advantage of the cover to level a chastising glare at his partner. Pruitt's attention wandered to the bartender, a buxom girl in her midtwenties. She wore her black hair in a vintage flick-up bob, topping it off with a Minnie Mouse bow. Intricate tattoos coiled up her pale arms, and when she noticed Pruitt watching her, she grinned and flicked out her tongue, revealing a gleaming chrome stud. A kind of amused, dreamy curiosity played at Pruitt's eyes, but he didn't smile.

Suddenly energized, Oria sat up and swatted the table in triumph. "Hey. Hang on a sec," he said to Pruitt. When the other man didn't respond, Oria touched him on the arm. "Hey."

Pruitt's eyes blazed at the interruption. It was quick, but Jarsdel caught it. Oria didn't seem to notice, and by the time Pruitt faced him, his expression was mild and solicitous.

"They got you. Like just a few weeks ago, right?"

Pruitt blinked. "Hmm? Who got me?"

"The Natty Lads." To the detectives, Oria added, "That's their stupid-ass name. The Natty Lads." Back to Pruitt, "They got on your boat while you were overtown."

Realization dawned on Pruitt's features. "Yeah. I mean, someone did. Probably them."

"You *know* it's them. Gotta be."

"I said probably. Yeah."

"What happened?" said Morales.

Oria leaned forward, excited. "So few weeks back, Dell was overtown for some business thing."

"I dunno that term," said Jarsdel. "You guys keep saying overtown."

"S'what we call the mainland. Anyway, while he's gone, his boat gets burgled. Ripped off his fish finder, some poles, buncha stuff. And you know what else they got? Tell 'em, Dell."

Pruitt stared down into his beer. He looked miserable. "One Ruger Redhawk, double-action revolver, convertible. Stainless steel with a satin finish. Adjustable rear notch, ramp front with red insert, four-point-two-inch barrel. Absolute beauty."

"Shit," said Morales. "They got your Redhawk? Man, I'd be pissed. I got the Super Redhawk, the—"

"The .44." Pruitt nodded. "Gorgeous weapon. You got the nine-and-a-half-inch barrel? Or the—"

Morales laughed. "Dude. What am I, hunting elk? No man, got the seven and a half."

Pruitt joined in the laughter. "Well, how do I know? Crazy stuff goes on in LA these days. Anyway, you like it?"

"Hell yes. I mean, you're talkin' about large bore wheel guns like that, and then you take into account—you know—the structure and the mass of the weapon, way it dampens recoil. And the accuracy, right?"

"That's the one..." ventured Oria, "that's the one's got the, uh, that Hogue Monogrip, right?"

Jarsdel, bored by the gun porn, allowed his attention to wander back to the bartender. She worked fast, her hands moving with the slick coordination of pistons as she pulled bottles out of the well, two-fisted the pours, and threw in the mixes and garnish. Spills and condensation rings wiped clean with a towel, coasters tossed with unerring precision in front of new arrivals. Rims of margarita glasses, first moistened on a black sponge soaked with lime juice, then tapped in a tray of pink Himalayan salt. Turning, balletic, to pop the caps from a trio of Fat Tire bottles, then pausing to give a slow, sweet smile to a customer as she slid him his check. The short sleeve of her Topsides T-shirt pulled back as she did so, revealing more tattoos: a skeleton, an hourglass, and a red heart impaled with a spear.

"You know, I like that gun too," Oria droned on. "But there's something about that classic, round-butt grip. I mean I like the feel of the Hogue, but I'm talking looks."

"'Cause he thinks he's Frank Hamer." It was Ledbetter, the former captain.

"Hey, man of the hour." Oria stood to greet his mentor, and they pulled up another chair to the now crowded table.

"Looks is all it is," said Ledbetter, still on the subject of the grip. "You've got it in your mind that thing is hand-hewn by some sorta master gunsmith, Hank Williams playin' in the background. Those panels're laser-checkered these days."

"Chief, whoa, Ruger's a *great* company. Their customer service—"

"I'm not sayin' they're not a great company. Just your romantic notions..."

Jarsdel tuned him out. He was watching the bartender again as she plucked used glasses from the bar top, cleaned them in her electric glass washer, and set them in the drying rack. That done, she retrieved the check she'd handed over before, along with its cash payment, and stuffed it all in the pocket of her apron.

Pruitt called to her. "Kayla!" He held up five fingers. "Change it up too."

She nodded and brought out fresh chilled tumblers from the fridge. Once she'd filled them with Sculpin IPA, she put them on the pass for the server.

"We were just talking about the Natty Lads," Oria told Ledbetter.

"Ach. Damn ginks. An embarrassment."

"More than that," said Pruitt, his mood darkening. "They're just lucky I wasn't on the boat when they boarded." He raised his hand in the shape of a pistol, cupping the heel of his palm with the other hand—a shooter's grip. "I'd just..." He lowered his hands. "You know I wish I *had* been there when they'd boarded."

"Maybe with some luck you'll see one of 'em underwater on your next dive," said Oria. "Nail the sucker with your speargun. Can always say you thought it was a fish."

Pruitt smiled. "Bagged a beautiful sheepshead last night. By the way, that new scuba rental place near the pier? Worst regulator I've ever used. Could get someone killed."

"Yeah? That's no good. I'll go by and check it out."

"Speargun," Ledbetter mused. "Definitely have less problems on Catalina."

Fewer, thought Jarsdel.

"Fewer," Pruitt murmured, too low for anyone to notice. Anyone except for Jarsdel. He snatched the word out of the din of Topsides with the same fine-tuned sensitivity that allows for someone to hear their own name spoken in a raucous crowd.

Jarsdel regarded the man with fresh interest. He was a puzzle—the consummate yacht club bachelor, probably with a background in finance, and obviously well educated. But it took a certain personality to correct another's usage and an even narrower personality profile to correct another's usage *without letting them know about it*. This peculiarity—and Jarsdel could speak from experience—had the air of magical thinking about it. The feeling was that a grammatical misstep was in some ways like a destructive particle let loose in the cosmos. It would cause harm to the language, which in turn would cause harm to thought, which would culminate in some far graver, unforeseen consequence. The particle could be neutralized, however, by articulating the correct usage.

Jarsdel experienced a powerful surge of dislike for Dell Pruitt, and one so swift his rational mind had to scramble to make sense of it. It took a minute or so of introspective lavage, but soon the cause of the sudden animosity bobbed, stinking, to the surface.

Pruitt, with his dancer's physique, hundred-dollar haircut, bronzed skin, apparent sexual prowess, and easy camaraderie, meant nothing to Jarsdel.

Pruitt, with his use of the word *recursion* in casual conversation, with his understanding of the difference between mass nouns and count nouns—along with their proper modifiers—meant nothing to Jarsdel.

But at their crossroads existed the educated millionaire yachter, the Vespasian of Avalon, who went from demonstrating his mastery of modern weaponry to quietly neutralizing grammatical gaffs, all in the comfort of his throne room. And *this* Pruitt meant very much indeed.

He can pick one or the other. The sleek, well-oiled playboy or the linguistic purist. He can't have both.

Jarsdel had enough self-awareness to see his reaction for the naked envy it was, but it made no difference. The man sitting just a few feet away enjoyed a lifestyle as foreign to Jarsdel as that of an Ottoman sultan. That there was even a hint he might also possess a comparable level of intellectual horsepower to the detective that, according to *LA Weekly*, "regularly demonstrates investigative brilliance," was grossly unfair.

Pruitt smiled and thrust his chin in the direction of Jarsdel's beer. "Get you another?"

"Sure, thanks."

Kayla was hailed again and returned with another round of Sculpin. A pocket of warmth, small at first, began to expand at the back of Jarsdel's neck and spread along his shoulders. He felt good. More than that, he felt strong. The talk around the table crescendoed as the drinks took effect.

"This is great," said Oria. "It's just a good life." He clapped Pruitt on the shoulder. "And you're the best."

"You just want me for my beer."

Oria snorted with laughter. "You're one to talk. You got majorly hammered that night—what, like, couple weeks back?"

Ledbetter grinned. "He sure did."

"Yeah, yeah," said Pruitt. "It happens."

"What's this?" said Morales.

"He must've got started early," said Ledbetter. "Sun wasn't even down and he was already on his way back to his boat. Swayin'. Barely stand up. Belting out that REO Speedwagon song. I don't remember which."

"'Out of Season,'" Pruitt murmured.

"That's the one." Ledbetter jabbed him in the shoulder, punctuating each word with another poke. "Normally Mister Heavyweight. Mister Always-in-Control."

"Thanks, that's good with the finger," said Pruitt.

Jarsdel took a swig of the cold, tan ale. He hadn't eaten, and it was hitting him hard. He didn't mind. "This is delicious," he said to no one in particular.

"Glad to hear it," said Pruitt.

Jarsdel looked over the man's shoulder at another action shot of his host on his fishing boat. He was aiming an unusual weapon— some sort of wrist-mounted crossbow—at a group of flying fish that'd just broken the surface.

Pruitt glanced at the picture. "Slingbow," he said. "Great with the flying fish. Works just like a slingshot, but with an arrow attached to fishing line, so you can reel 'em in."

"They taste good?"

"Not unless you're in a pinch. More the satisfaction of it. And if anyone's watching, makes for quite the sprezzatura."

Jarsdel eyed him with a contempt he hoped didn't show on face. "Got a little logic puzzle for you."

"What?"

"I said I've got a little logic puzzle for you."

Pruitt, who'd been lounging in his chair, sat up straighter. "Okay."

"This tumbler here." Jarsdel tapped the rim with a fingernail. "I bet you that the circumference of the base is greater than the height of the glass."

"Say again?"

"I'm betting you that the circumference—the overall perimeter of the base"—Jarsdel traced it with his finger—"that it's greater than the height of the glass."

Pruitt pursed his lips. He picked up his own glass and examined it. "I don't know. Could be, I guess. Don't think I'll take that bet."

Pleased, Jarsdel said, "Okay, how about this." He took out his field interview notebook and set the tumbler on top. "That's about three-quarters of an inch higher. Same bet—still the circumference of the base—only now that it's greater than the distance between the table and the top of the glass. That whole distance."

Pruitt studied the setup carefully, then shook his head. "Nah. I'll pass."

Jarsdel took out his black leather wallet, smooth and rubbed to a shine from all the years in his pocket. He lifted the tumbler long enough to slip the wallet beneath it.

"How about now?"

Pruitt hesitated, but his eyes were alive with curiosity. Before he could answer, Jarsdel turned to Morales, who'd been sharing war stories with Ledbetter and Oria.

"Man, I'll take getting tased over that Jesus juice any day. Back when I was on patrol, I got just maybe a drop of that shit in my eye when my partner pepper sprayed some dude. Felt like a fuckin' A-bomb went off inside my head."

"Hey," said Jarsdel.

"What?"

"Lemme borrow your wallet a sec."

"No. Why?"

"Just for this—"

"Your partner's trying to fleece me," said Pruitt with a disarming smile.

Morales gave Jarsdel a pointed look. "You bein' cool?"

"What d'you mean? I'm fine."

Sighing, Morales brought out his wallet and slapped it onto the table. Along with the cash and credit cards, the brown leather billfold was stuffed with so many frayed receipts and coupons that it resembled a dinner roll. Jarsdel flattened it out by tugging out a wad of the debris, then stuck it under the glass to join his own wallet and notebook. The precarious sculpture was now nearly four inches higher than the tumbler had been on its own.

"All right," he said. "What are your thoughts?"

Pruitt nodded in appreciation. "So just to clarify, you're saying that the circumference of the base of the glass is going to be greater than the total height you got now? From the tabletop to the rim?"

"That's what I'm saying."

Pruitt bent close, fascinated, trying to gauge the distance. "What are we betting?"

"Nothing really, just... I don't know. More of a conceptual..." Jarsdel shrugged. "Just some logic fun."

"Ah, c'mon. Gotta have some stakes. Otherwise, where's the excitement?"

"Okay. What were you thinking?"

"How about the tab? Plus a nice tip for Kayla, of course."

Jarsdel thought that over. "I don't really gamble."

"I do."

"Yeah, I don't know. Doesn't feel right."

"Afraid of losing?"

"No."

"Why not?" said Pruitt, his smile vanishing. "This a sucker bet?"

Jarsdel looked at his glass—half-full of Sculpin, perched absurdly atop the wallets—then back at Pruitt. "Not sure what you mean."

"I mean a sucker bet. A bet you know you're gonna win. You should always be a little afraid you're going to lose a bet, right? Otherwise, it's not much of a bet. So when you say you're not afraid, I gotta wonder."

"Forget it. It was just for fun. Wasn't my idea to bring money into it."

Pruitt held out his palms. "Hey, calm. Just wanna make sure the action's square, that's all." The smile was back. "Let's do it. What do we measure with?"

Jarsdel unbuckled his belt and pulled it free.

"Oh dear," said Pruitt.

"It's perfectly clean," said Jarsdel, handing it over.

With a sour expression on his face, Pruitt held the end tip against the base of the glass and wrapped the belt around its circumference. He pinched the spot where it began to overlap, then held the measured length of leather vertically, parallel to the tumbler. It easily cleared the top of the glass with inches to spare.

Pruitt laughed, handing back the belt. "Pretty smooth. I'm okay with that one. Had a certain elegance about it. It *was* a sucker bet, though. You realize that."

"Gimme my wallet," said Morales, taking it himself and stuffing the receipts back inside.

"I was gonna cover the drinks anyway," said Pruitt. "So no worries."

But Jarsdel didn't hear him. He'd been watching Kayla again when she'd done something very interesting. There was an old man at the end of the bar with a shaggy gray beard and rheumy eyes. When Kayla dropped off his drink earlier, Jarsdel noticed how she'd touched his wrist and how the man smiled in return. Now that he'd signaled for the check, she touched his wrist again and with her free hand dipped into her apron and brought out a drink ticket. It was wrinkled and dog-eared from being in the pocket, but the man didn't notice its condition as she slid it toward him. Once Kayla left to serve another customer, the man squinted down at the bill, dug out some money, and set his empty Collins glass on top of it.

"Kayla," he called, getting off the bar stool and waving.

The bartender blew him a kiss and gave a coquettish little curtsy. The old man left the bar, probably walking a little taller than when he'd come in. As soon as he was gone, Kayla scooped up the money and the drink ticket and stuck them all in her apron. When she looked up and caught Jarsdel staring at her, she froze a moment, then relaxed and offered a wink. When he didn't respond as she'd hoped, she went back to work, a faint crease of worry at her forehead.

"She's cute, ain't she?"

Jarsdel broke his attention away from the bartender and looked at Pruitt. "Hmm?"

"Kayla. She's quite a number."

"Is she?"

"Know what *hanabira* is? Scarring of the mons pubis. It's Japanese, very decorative." He shook his head. "Firecracker."

Jarsdel felt the alcohol turn on him, tripping some unknown switch and setting off his headache. He had about ten minutes to get back to the hotel and into his aspirin if he wanted to stave off the worst of it.

"Well, in my opinion, anyway," said Pruitt. "What'd Shakespeare say? 'Beauty is bought by judgment of the eye.' I think that's it."

Head thumping, Jarsdel leveled his gaze at the man. Had Pruitt really just dragged the bard of Avon into Topsides with them? He'd felt threatened by him before—he admitted that—even envious, but was certain his contempt now stood on more righteous ground. Recruiting Shakespeare for some unearned literary luster was too boldly unoriginal to go unpunished. What was next? Churchill's "courage to continue" line or FDR's "fear itself"? Maybe that all-time Einstein favorite, "Imagination is more important than knowledge"—which, Jarsdel had observed, was so often invoked by those possessing very little of either.

"She's stealing from you," he said.

Pruitt blinked. "What?"

"Your bartender. The recycled check move. They reuse a previous bill without entering a new purchase in the system. Then they just keep the cash payment on the reused bill. Thought you'd like to know."

Pruitt swiveled in his chair to get a look at Kayla and fixed her with that oddly curious expression of lofty amusement. He turned back to Jarsdel. "Not that big a deal. I know all about it, actually."

Whether true or not, Jarsdel wasn't sure. But it wasn't the response he'd been hoping for. "She's pocketing your money. Probably does it all the time, considering how slick she is. Could be costing you hundreds every week."

Pruitt shrugged. "I can afford it. Besides, gotta spend money to make money. Kayla's popular. Lots of folks come in here because of her. And I'll tell you something else. Believe me when I tell you, she's worth it."

The nerve above Jarsdel's ear thrummed a deeper, more

penetrating note that felt like it could rattle his back teeth. Gathering his things, he got to his feet.

"Hey," he said to Morales. His partner barked with laughter at something Ledbetter said.

"Hey," Jarsdel repeated.

Morales turned, irritated. "What?"

"I'm gonna hit the sack."

"Have lotsa fun."

"You need me for anything, I'll have my phone."

Morales was already back with the conversation. Pruitt too had moved on, scooting his chair closer to the others.

On his way out of the bar, Jarsdel met Kayla's eyes. She gave him another wink, which he ignored.

"Come back soon," she called after him.

The night had cooled, the air now a delicious SoCal caress. Hungry, Jarsdel wandered down Crescent, past the beachfront shops. Music and conversation spilled from restaurants and bars, commingling somehow with the sharp smell of saltwater and making him feel at once invigorated and relaxed. He noticed a low-slung food stand up Sumner Avenue on the left-hand side, set back from the street in a wide plaza, a group of customers gathered at the tables out front. He made the turn, the buzz from Pruitt's beers causing him to reel a bit into the path of oncoming pedestrians, but he steadied himself and offered an apologetic smile.

The place was called Pete's, and the food smelled good and greasy. He ordered a bean and cheese burrito, but his stomach growled and he added some chips and guacamole. Foolishly but unable to stop himself, he gestured at the margarita machine, where lime-green slush churned away behind a plastic window. "One of those too, thanks. A large."

After he got his food, he found an empty table and began to eat. He bolted most of it, then slowed down to drink some of the margarita. He licked the rim, but there wasn't any salt, so he picked the shaker off the table and tapped some grains into the palm of his hand. Not enough. He checked the saltshaker and saw some of the holes were plugged with old hot sauce. He picked these off with a fingernail and tried again. Better. He pinched some of it between his fingers and began distributing it around the rim of the flimsy, waxed paper cup. Most of it fell into the drink, but that was okay. It occurred to him he was pretty drunk, and for some reason, he found that funny. Chuckling, he rubbed the rest of the salt off on his pants.

"Look like you're havin' fun."

Jarsdel glanced in the direction of the voice. Two men sat at a table to his right, identical blue-and-white-striped cotton pants, almost like pajamas. One of them was big, heavyset, with a protruding brow. He had a dainty, rosebud mouth framed by a thick black beard. The other was younger, early thirties, with a wispy blond goatee and sun-damaged skin. By the tone and youth of the voice, he assumed he'd been the one who'd spoken.

"Yeah," said Jarsdel. He took another drink of the margarita. For one that came ready-made out of a machine, it wasn't bad at all.

"You're a cop," the blond one said.

Jarsdel ignored him.

"Got a reason for being here?"

Jarsdel put down his cup, his beer buzz retreating as awareness dawned. "Oh. You guys. I've actually heard of you guys."

"Asked you a question," said the blond, his expression flat and mirthless. "Oughta listen up when people talk to you."

Pruitt was right, Jarsdel thought. *They don't put on an accent.* Just the plain old, slightly nasal inflection of Orange County. It made for a strange contrast with their pirate costumes.

Jarsdel stacked his nearly empty plate of chips atop his other one and pushed them aside. "Glad I ran into you. Saves me the trouble."

The blond's eyes narrowed to slits. If he was going for menacing, he'd missed the mark.

"I was curious about how you feel about the Fourth of July. Does it get your patriotic juices flowing? Or do you guys sit that one out?"

Neither of the men answered.

"Bet January twenty-fourth's a big day, though."

"What's that?" said the blond. "First time you and your friends ran train on your whore of a mother?"

Jarsdel grunted with laughter. He couldn't help it. "Sorry. Just not used to the whole routine yet. 'Whore of a mother'—priceless. You guys serious about all this?"

Neither of the Natty Lads answered.

"Well, no, that'd be Henry Morgan's birthday. Never mind. Back to the Fourth, though. Do anything special? Watch the fireworks?"

No answer.

"See the parade?"

For the first time, the bearded one spoke. Looking at him, Jarsdel had expected a rumbling baritone. But the voice was light and breathy, like wind through a knothole. "How'd you get here?"

"How'd I get here?" said Jarsdel. "Not sure I understand."

"It's really pretty simple," said the blond, tapping the side of his head with his index finger. "My mate here's asking how you made it to our island."

"By...boat? I'm sorry, this a trick question?"

The blond gave the heavyset Lad a slow, meaningful nod.

"I must be missing something," said Jarsdel.

"Count on it," said the bearded one.

The corners, Jarsdel thought. *Evil always starts in the corners.*

He got to his feet and collected his plates and napkins. "I'm sure I'll run into you again before we're done here. You're out at Pebbly Beach right?"

No answer.

"Shouldn't be too hard to find. And I'll definitely want to be talking to your supreme leader. Captain Long John Blackbeard himself. You can tell him the LAPD wants a word." He dumped his trash. "Fair winds and following seas, gentlemen."

14

Jarsdel woke early and headed down to the hotel lobby, hoping for a copy of the *LA Times* and the continental breakfast promised at check-in. Instead, there were stacks of the *Catalina Islander* going back three weeks and a basket of hard-boiled eggs. And since wheat had been introduced to the Americas by European colonists, he supposed the "continental" part of the meal was the loaf of sliced bread pressed up against the gummy toaster oven.

Jarsdel poured himself a cup of weak coffee, stirred in as much nondairy creamer as he could stomach, and picked up the Friday, July 1 issue of the *Islander*. The headline announced that the deer population surrounding Avalon had reached a new high and that efforts might be made to cull its numbers. Opposition was anticipated. On a related note, the numbers of yellow-jacket stings had markedly declined this summer, the likely cause being the proliferation of traps. The article emphasized that traps were a controversial issue: The Catalina Island Conservancy had a long-standing ban on yellow-jacket traps for all businesses serving the public, but those same businesses suffered if customers were stung on their premises. It was difficult not to conclude—the story ventured with mounting excitement—that certain businesses must have illicitly installed traps *despite* the ban.

The elevator doors opened, and Morales stepped into the lobby. He went straight to the coffee, decided against the eggs and toast, and surveyed the periodicals.

"This is it? Where's the *Times*?"

Jarsdel glanced up, then went back to the article about yellow jackets.

Morales picked up a copy of the *Islander* and sat across from Jarsdel. He took a sip of the coffee and grimaced. "Hey. What's in this?"

Jarsdel ignored him.

"The coffee," said Morales.

"I didn't make it," said Jarsdel. "Why're you talking to me like I made it?"

Morales opened his paper. "Okay, wanna hear something?"

"No."

"So this is from the night Burken was killed. I want you to pay special attention to this, because I'm seriously thinking of moving here. While our vic was getting his eye shot out up in the hills, you know what was going on here? I'm lookin' at the sheriff's log right now. Right here." He tapped the page. "This is the extent of the madness that's going on here. Ready? Gonna read this shit out loud."

"No need. I already know where this is headed. The island paradise and the charnel house that is Los Angeles."

Morales pushed on anyway. "This is a direct quote. Ready? 'Several visitors experienced nuisance symptoms related to the algae bloom, including itching, swelling, irritation of the mucous membranes, rash'—and on and on it goes. These are unhappy folks here. They got rashes, okay? Now take a kinda little *Reading Rainbow* journey with me toward where *we* are that same night. LA, man. Up in the hills, guy gets his face blown apart by some random dude. Eight lines on the back page of the local. Eight lines—counted 'em. Why even bother reporting it, right? But people over here got rashes, folks, and that's on the front page. Little nausea, right? Perish the thought you get a tummy ache. That's headline material."

"You should go for a walk," said Jarsdel, not looking up.

"Why?"

"Beautiful morning. You can make another pilgrimage to that other fishing club up the road, gush some more over that movie you like. Don't think I'd ever seen you so excited."

"Um, it's amazing, that's why. You seriously have no idea, so you're the one comes off ignorant when you act all aloof about film. Besides, you're missin' out—been tellin' you for years. Like, there's a whole other realm of snobbery and dipshittery you haven't even begun to explore yet with movies. Fit right in."

"You could walk to the casino and back," Jarsdel suggested. "Maybe grab us a couple decent coffees."

Morales thought about that. "The casino—think it's open?"

"I have no idea."

"I mean, they're always open twenty-four hours, but maybe here they got different standards or local ordinances or something."

"They might."

Morales brought out his wallet and flipped through the bills. "Used to be pretty good at blackjack. I mean, beyond basic strategy. Not like those MIT guys or whatever, just a knack of feeling out when the shoe was about to heat up."

Jarsdel folded up the *Islander* and set it back on the stack. "You might be disappointed."

"Why? They don't have table games?"

"I doubt it. This casino's a little more on the traditional side."

"What d'you mean?"

"You'll see."

"Like just a ton of slot machines?"

"You'll see."

"Figures." Morales stood. "Roulette's for suckers, and I never learned the James Bond game."

"Baccarat."

"I know what it's called, Rain Man. *Jesus*. Well, I'm gonna check it out anyway. What time's our thing at the thing later on? Ten?"

"Yup."

"Glad they ain't in a hurry over here. I mean, with algae blooms and stuff, what's a bullet to the back of the head? Shit, man. Shoulda joined the Sheriff's Department. This coulda been my beat."

Morales left and Jarsdel waited a couple minutes to make sure he was well on his way. Then he too left the hotel, turning onto Metropole and making a right on Crescent, away from Via Casino, where Morales was headed.

City workers hosed down the street with saltwater, flushing away the previous day's residue of spilled drinks, melted ice cream, and any number of other bits of human detritus and mystery stains.

He liked Catalina. Not just the way the air had felt the night before but the smells and the colors and the shapes of the buildings. Even the angle of the sunlight as it struck the trees and the craggy hills around Avalon.

The land, he knew, most recently belonged to the Tongva Indians and had been inhabited by humans for much longer. The island was littered with middens—ancient dump sites packed with bones and cactus thorns and abalone shells, the ground blackened with fish oil—some dating back thirty thousand years. It must have been an Edenic wonderland—isolated, fertile, waters bursting with fish, and a beach naturally sheltered from the worst of the Pacific's fury. At one time, it had even been an island nation of giants, evidenced by the unusual number of uncovered skeletons topping seven feet in length.

By the time the first Spanish arrived in 1542, the Tongva on Catalina—a place they called Pimungna—had gained a fearsome reputation on the mainland as powerful sorcerers. This was likely due to their cavernous temple and the rituals performed inside, most notably those involving jimsonweed. Young men first underwent several days of fasting, then drank a tea of concentrated, powdered jimsonweed. If it didn't kill them, it threw them into a state of temporary psychosis during which their visions were considered pure, spiritual transmissions.

The temple itself was gone, with only hard-packed earth to suggest where it might have stood. The Tongva of Catalina were gone too, driven from their island by the ravages of otter hunters, colonists, and smugglers. Absorbed into the Spanish mission system, they either assimilated or, much more frequently, died of disease, abuse, and overwork. Others were hunted for sport. Now there were only a handful left, and Jarsdel doubted any of them were staying at the Pavilion Hotel or throwing back shots at Topsides.

It felt good to get out by himself, away from Morales, and just have some time to think. He still hadn't answered the question he'd asked himself a couple days earlier, and he realized he'd been actively avoiding it.

So what's your theory, exactly?

All right, no more dodging it. Time to work it through.

Ellery Keating had murdered Dean Burken on June 25.

Okay, why?

That was easy. Keating was desperate. All her money was tied up in the Strand at Newport. Burken was going to be forced out, and he wouldn't go quietly. If Keating didn't protect him, he'd expose her conflict of interest with the Newport Beach City Council. She'd be ruined. Financially, socially, professionally.

So who killed Ellery Keating?

Maybe no one. Maybe it was a freak accident, like Pruitt had said. An asshole shooting at the moon. Bullets fell at four hundred feet per second, and that was certainly good enough to punch through a skull if the angle was right.

Then it's a coincidence that your lead suspect in a homicide was killed just as you were zeroing in on her?

No. Then the Natty Lads had done it, just like Captain Oria had suggested. Fired off a couple random shots at the Tuna Club.

And not a single bullet hole anywhere else.

Not that we've found. Could've missed and hit the water.

But one happened to strike Ellery Keating, dead center in the back of the skull. Sounds like you're back at coincidence again.

212

Well, why not? People got killed all the time. The odds of a person dying by misadventure were rare, and therefore the odds of that same person also being wanted in connection with a homicide were vanishingly slim. But to discount the possibility solely on those grounds was a classic cognitive illusion. Sometimes extraordinary things *do* happen. In a field of infinite possibilities and countless trillions of discrete events taking place on earth, a man can win the lottery, get struck by lightning, and be bitten by a shark all in the same day. When you looked at it like that, Keating's death as coincidental didn't seem so freakishly strange after all.

But do you believe it?

He knew which way he was leaning, but to answer the question with greater certainty, Jarsdel brought out his phone, opened a browser, and typed the following:

Catalina Island shooting death

This brought him to Islapedia, a website dedicated to archiving news and events affecting the Channel and Baja Islands. The page in question was simply called "Deaths: Catalina Island" and listed every single fatality of unnatural means occurring there since 1856. The most recent—Ellery Keating's—hadn't been uploaded yet, so he scrolled up.

- March 10, 2021—Bryce Thomasson (49) drowned while diving near Casino Point.
- February 18, 2020—Candy Wilson (56) killed after falling out of a golf cart.

Jarsdel continued scrolling, looking for any deaths involving firearms. There was a murder in 2006 that had taken place somewhere offshore, another in 1927, body unidentified, and a card shark who'd been gunned down in 1902. He found four that had been self-inflicted. Three were accidental—Edwin W. Rogers in 1931, Dr. Clayton E. Wheeler in 1935, Edward Abrahamson in 1950. One was intentional, William Daley, 1935. The only accidental shooting death of one person by another had happened in 1889, when seventeen-year-old Laura E. Pock had been shot at a rifle range. What Jarsdel didn't find was a single instance—let alone a pattern—of reckless firearm discharge during a holiday, Fourth of July or otherwise.

So? Was it a coincidence?

No. Ellery Keating had been eliminated with cunning and precision. The very fact that her death had occurred during the fireworks show highlighted its deliberate, premeditated nature. The killing was too clever for its own good.

It was also, as he'd noted the day before, a hell of a shot. With his phone still out, he went to windfinder.com and looked up weather conditions for Avalon on the night of July 4. Intermittent winds west to northeast at 13 miles per hour recorded at 4:00 p.m. By seven o'clock, the direction had shifted from northwest to southeast. They'd also picked up speed and intensity, from 13 to 17 miles per hour and steady. When they were measured again at ten o'clock, the speed had dropped to 15, but the direction remained the same. The fireworks show had taken place from 9:00 to 9:15.

A bullet traveling fifty yards had a long time to be affected by wind, unless it was a high-velocity round. He knew, however, that it hadn't been a high-velocity round that had killed Ellery Keating. If it had been, it would've passed right through her head and into the deck a few feet in front of her. A high-velocity nonperforating round—some kind of souped-up JHP—would've blown the back of her head off and turned her brains to soup. Blood would've poured out her nose, maybe even her ears and her eyes. No one would've thought she was merely asleep.

Using conventional ammo, the shooter would've had to aim slightly to the left of the target and count on the windspeed to carry the round home. To accomplish that with a single shot, at night, took considerable skill.

Jarsdel found he'd made a large loop and was now heading back toward the hotel. He passed the Catalina Island Museum, the Shops at the Atwater, and finally the Dew Drop Inn. He kept going in the direction of the water and made a left on Via Casino. He was risking running into Morales, but he felt like he'd made enough internal progress for now.

As he approached the Yacht & Fish Club, he saw Pruitt sweeping the deck alongside the building. He'd moved the rattan chairs out of the way and was making repeated, rhythmic passes with a push broom—three short forward strokes, followed by two sharp taps of the bristles. Certainly a dedicated club president.

There was a snapping sound above, and Jarsdel looked up to see the club's nautical flag stirring in the breeze. Unfurling, drooping, then coming to sudden life again. He slowed, then stopped.

"'Scuse me," said a tourist coming up behind him.

Jarsdel stepped off the main footpath and stared at the flag. He watched it dance for perhaps a minute, then called out, "Mr. Pruitt."

Pruitt saw Jarsdel, leaned the broom against the wall, and came over. "Seriously, call me Dell."

"Sure, okay."

"Probably department policy or something, with all the misters and misses, but Dell works just fine. I promise."

"Dell it is. You get here pretty early, huh?"

Pruitt laughed. "No, I basically live here. My boat's moored right alongside. *Sweet Caroline.*"

"You sleep on the boat?"

"Every chance I get. I got a house overtown, but I don't sleep nearly as peacefully as when I got water under me."

"Huh." Jarsdel pointed. "Is that flag always there, or do you take it down at night?"

Pruitt looked. "What flag? Oh." He turned back to Jarsdel. "That's a burgee. Yacht club insignia. Yeah, we keep it up at all times. Old Glory, on the other hand..." He indicated a freestanding pole. "She comes down every night. It's not an all-weather flag."

"Anyone taken it down recently, even just for a little bit? Or maybe traded it out for a new one?"

Pruitt chuckled. "No, sir. This may be a yacht club, but we're pretty tight with our budget. We don't replace things unless they really need replacing. That one's only a year old."

"Can I step inside for a moment?" said Jarsdel.

"Yeah, 'course."

Pruitt stepped aside, and Jarsdel headed straight for the deck where the club members had watched the fireworks. He stood about where Keating's chair had been and looked up at Chimes Tower.

The pennant snapped open—blocking Jarsdel's view—wilted, then flapped noisily. The tower appeared only in brief flashes before immediately disappearing behind the flag.

Burgee, he corrected himself.

"Kinda insane, isn't it?" said Pruitt.

"How so?"

"Just one dilly of a shot. Least I can console myself with the fact that she couldn't'a known what hit her." He scratched at the rash along his jawline.

"Yeah," said Jarsdel. "Only it doesn't work."

"What doesn't work?"

"The shot. I don't care how deadly someone's aim is or whether they were using night vision, but the wind was blowing northwest to southeast, just like now. Only stronger. That burgee would've been blocking the view from Chimes Tower. And even if someone was firing randomly, no specific target in mind, I don't see a bullet hole in the fabric."

Pruitt squinted at the burgee. "I see what you mean. Only you can't know if the wind was constant, can you? I mean like...like right *there*. Just now. It dropped. I'm sure it did the same thing a couple times on the Fourth, even if the wind was stronger."

Jarsdel shook his head. "Doesn't matter. The whole conceit, that someone was waiting for this fireworks show to kill Ellery, it all falls apart with that flag—burgee, I mean. Because in order for that to be true, someone would've had to go up that cliffside and stake out a position. They would've seen right away how risky it would be to pick that spot. It doesn't hold up."

Pruitt thought about that. "A good marksman could pull it off. Patient, calculating."

"It's far-fetched."

"And yet," Pruitt said and shrugged, "here we are. How else you explain it?"

"I'm thinking the shooter was closer. Much closer. This side of the burgee."

"Huh? How?" Pruitt gestured to the path the bullet would've had to take. "She got hit on the top of her head near the back. So if someone was on this side, he would've had to be floating somewhere over there, like fifteen feet off the ground. I think we woulda noticed a levitating swami."

"Or standing right behind her," said Jarsdel. He pointed the first and second fingers of his right hand like the barrel of a pistol, the thumb acting as a cocked hammer. He approached one of the rattan chairs and leveled the finger gun at an imaginary head. "Poosh. Just like that."

"Whoa, whoa," said Pruitt. "That's bonkers. There were two dozen of us here."

"Looking at a fireworks show," said Jarsdel. "You yourself were saying how fixated you were on the finale."

"Yeah, but look, Detective. I don't wanna give you a whole lecture on firearms or anything—I'm sure it's something you know a lot about. But a gun going off ten, twelve feet behind you is gonna be loud. I don't care if you got a suppressor on that thing or you taped a soda bottle to the muzzle or any of that other spy shit. All us woulda jumped, even during the show."

That was all true, of course, and Jarsdel knew it. Still, the shot from Chimes Tower seemed somehow even less plausible.

"By the way," he said, "ran into your local pirates last night."

Pruitt chuckled. "Terrific. Enjoy yourself?"

"They seemed a little edgy."

"Always like that. Paranoid. Which ones?"

"There was a skinny blond one, scraggly goatee, and a big guy—"

"Yeah, yeah," Pruitt cut in. "Always the two of them together. Ricky Caldwell, and the husky one's Leonard Busk. Go by Popinjay and Sad Dog, respectively."

"Wow."

"Uh-huh."

"Thing is, they didn't really strike me as the cool-headed, sniper type, you know?"

Pruitt took the broom from where he'd leaned it and began working at a clot of dried mud on the decking. "So you don't think the Natty Lads are behind this, huh?"

"No. I also don't think it was someone taking potshots at the club or randomly firing in the air to celebrate the Fourth."

"Wrong day anyway," Pruitt murmured.

"Say again?"

"Oh, nothing. Sorry. Just that the Second should really be the holiday, not the Fourth. Long story. Forget it." He knocked the dirt loose and swept it over the side into the water.

Jarsdel nodded, feeling his chest tighten a little. *I don't like this man*, he decided. *I don't like him at all.* Then, because he considered introspection a virtue, he asked himself why.

The answer came easily, startling in its neon-bright clarity. *Because he's handsome, smart, and wealthy, so he's got you beat two out of three.* Jarsdel shoved the thought aside.

"Anyway," he said, checking his watch, "we'll all know more in about an hour."

"Right," said Pruitt. "Ken said you'd be over at the station. Hope you get some answers." He picked up his broom and gestured at the deck. "El Presidente's gotta get back to work. Keep me in the loop if you guys find out anything useful." He nodded in the direction of Chimes Tower. "Not too keen on having to run serpentine every time I pass that thing."

15

When they entered Oria's office, Jarsdel realized he'd been expecting something out of a TV show. The model small-town police station—fishing pole in the corner, shelf of football trophies, an award from the chamber of commerce. There'd be the standard assortment of gewgaws littering the desk: a hula girl on a spring, a Magic 8-Ball, a mug that said something like *It takes a lot of balls to golf the way I do!* or *My wife ran off with my best friend and boy do I miss him!*

But the Avalon sheriff's station was as tidy, functional, and free of those palsied stabs at personality as the lobby of an actuarial firm. The sole indication that the desk Oria sat at belonged to him was a trifold picture frame, he and his wife as newlyweds in the center, school portraits of their children at either side.

That made the only other piece of decoration in the room stand out all the more starkly. Tacked on the wall to the right of the desk were three shot-up paper range targets, each of which Oria had signed and dated along the bottom. An unusually aggressive and unwelcoming display for a rural cop. A novelty mug would've been a better choice. Hackneyed, but comforting.

Morales opened up his iPad and folded back the cover to act as a stand. While he logged on and brought up the Zoom link Ipgreve had sent, Oria caught Jarsdel looking at the range targets.

"You see this one here?" He pointed to a reprint of a vintage target design. Simply known as "the Thug" in law enforcement, the image was a line drawing of a scowling, hairy-knuckled man pointing a revolver straight at the viewer. Oria had shot out both eyes and punched a series of holes at the mouth to give it a bullet-riddled smile.

"Mm," said Jarsdel.

"You know, been thinking about something. Remember I was saying how a few weeks back, Dell's boat got broken into?" He snapped the rubber band against his wrist—one, two, three times.

"Who's Dell?" said Morales.

"Dell Pruitt. Prez of the Yacht & Fish. Dell. You met him yesterday."

"Right. Guy with the rash on his neck."

Oria looked momentarily confused. "Does he?"

"Yeah," said Jarsdel. "'Round his face?" He gestured to his own jawline.

"Oh. Oh yeah, that's true. Bad allergies he said. Anyway, so Dell's boat got robbed. We were talking about it last night. Took his Ruger."

"I remember."

"How much you wanna bet that ends up being the murder weapon here?"

Jarsdel wasn't sure what he meant. "You're saying the Natty Lads stole Mr. Pruitt's gun and shot Ellery Keating?"

"Why not?" Oria shrugged. "Probably didn't do it on purpose. I mean, not on purpose to kill Ellery specifically. But I bet they thought hey, let's pop off a couple rounds at the club. Fireworks are going, perfect cover."

"They have something against the club?"

"Sure. Definitely. Members are rich and successful. High-society types. Exactly the kind of people the Natty Lads hate. Establishment, you know? They've definitely had conflicts in the past."

Jarsdel wasn't sure what he thought of that theory and was glad when his partner spoke up.

"Okay, we're live," said Morales. The three men gathered around the screen as the app cycled, and the dour face of the chief medical examiner-coroner appeared. Morales clicked to maximize the screen and turned the volume up.

"Am I heard?" said Dr. Ipgreve. "Can you all hear me?"

"We got you," said Morales. "You hear us okay?"

"I got ya."

"Joining us here's Captain Oria with Avalon Sheriff's. He's leading the investigation on the island and helping us out."

Ipgreve nodded at the pro forma diplomatic noise. "Okay. My time's short, so I can't stay on long. Obviously I'll be giving you all a full report when I can. This is gonna be just a summary of my findings." He checked his notes, turned a page, then another. "Actually one of the least complex GSWs I've ever looked at. Shooter was nowhere near her."

Dismayed, Jarsdel leaned forward. Nowhere near her? Since his brief meeting with Pruitt that morning, he'd begun thinking about the shooting in a whole new way. Not as a long-range shot from a military-trained sniper but staged—up close, the muzzle perhaps two feet from the skull. Of course he couldn't yet account for why no one had heard the shot, but he'd been working on it.

Ipgreve held up to the camera the unisex template of the human body printed on all autopsy forms. There was a front view, where nothing had been marked, and a back view. Ipgreve used the tip of a pencil to indicate the X he'd drawn just shy of the top of her head. "The projectile entered at the juncture of the lambdoidal and sagittal sutures, breaching the meninges and penetrating the brain case, then continued on one point eight centimeters into the parietal lobe. The resulting mushrooming and cavitation transferred substantial crushing force throughout the neural tissue. Then things really start to go downhill."

He picked up an X-ray. "Got a nice fat epidural hematoma, which anyone'll tell you isn't a blast, a contiguous subdural hematoma, and multiple subarachnoid hemorrhages. Any single one of these could've killed her, so as far as cause of death, I'm just gonna go ahead with a penetrating head injury resulting in TBI. You want it a little sexier, the projectile triggered profound intraparenchymal hemorrhage and subsequent uncal herniation that led to immediate cessation of brain stem function." He shrugged. "Simple as it gets. Only one small thing I'm unsure about—any of the witnesses say she hit her head? Beforehand, I mean."

Oria looked puzzled. "Don't think so. Why?"

"She's got a pretty mean contusion about two centimeters north of the entry wound. Probably nothing. Not uncommon to bang your head and not even realize it, and she might be the kind to bruise easily. Her drinking certainly would account for that. Should see her liver—looks like a charbroiled patty. And she was pretty well blasted on Oxy too."

"Downers, huh?" said Morales. He turned to Oria. "You know anything about that?"

The captain shook his head.

"Dr. Ipgreve," said Jarsdel, "you said the shooter was nowhere near her. I'm assuming you mean no powder stippling." He still held out hope for his new theory about a close-up shooter, but Ipgreve burned it down immediately.

"Obviously, yes. No stippling, but also no GSR of any kind. If that gun had been fired within three feet of her, there'd be something in all that hair. Hair collects GSR like it was made to do it."

"We're thinking across the street," said Morales.

"Have to be up high. No one could've pulled off a shot like that unless they were elevated."

"We got a spot that works," said Oria.

"What's that?"

"I say we got a good spot where that coulda happened. We checked it for casings, of course, but we didn't find any."

"Well, don't rule it out," said Ipgreve. "You wouldn't find any casings for this one anyway."

Morales tilted the screen to eliminate some glare. "Why not?"

"She wasn't shot with a bullet." He reached off camera and came back with a stainless-steel Griffin beaker. Something clinked as it rolled around inside. With his free hand, he produced a pair of forceps, reached into the beaker, and came out with what looked like a lopsided, dull gray marble.

"Hell's that?" said Morales.

"This," said Ipgreve, turning it in the light, "is a first for me. And at this point in my career?" He shook his head. "Those firsts come less and less often. Not since I was in emergency medicine, actually. Jumper landed on some exposed rebar. Perforating head injury, Phineas Gage style. Chunk of brain matter perched on the end of the steel spike like a pom-pom. And apparently that was the bad chunk, because not only did he survive, he was cured. No more suicidal ideation."

"C'mon, Doc," said Morales. "Let's get back to the thing. The thing you got there."

"Ah, right." He set down the beaker so that all the focus was on the strange wad of metal. He took his time, building the moment.

Could've sworn you said you were in a hurry, thought Jarsdel. He reminded himself that actors in Hollywood weren't merely confined to film and TV production. They could be found anywhere.

"You probably can't see it," said Ipgreve, pointing with the tip of his index finger, "but if you look closely right here, there's a little seam where the two halves of the gang mold met. It's an imperfect seal, though, and just a bit of excess lead seeped into the gap, creating that minute ridge."

"Lead?" said Jarsdel.

Ipgreve nodded. "That's right, folks. You got any minutemen hanging around Avalon, go ahead and move 'em to the top of your list, because your victim was shot with a musket ball."

After the Zoom call was over, Morales turned his chair to face Oria, who looked both angry and depressed.

"So I'm guessing this musket ball thing is part of the pirate club, huh?"

The captain nodded, jaw muscles flexing. "They make their own ammo. Just like your ME said. They buy these lead ingots on eBay—pretty cheap, actually—then melt 'em down in this special kettle. Pour the molten lead into these molds. It's another thing they put on for the tourists. Even sell 'em. *Buy your own genuine musket ball, made by a genuine pirate.*"

"Wait," said Jarsdel, "do they actually have a means of firing these things off?"

"Oh yeah. For sure. I seriously doubt any of 'em are originals, but they're definitely functional replicas. Flintlocks, long muskets, blunderbusses. And these knuckleheads go for full authenticity. They could use smokeless powder, but they won't, 'cause that's not what real pirates had. Black powder only."

"And yet they order their lead on the internet."

Oria raised his palms in exasperation, then let them fall at his sides. For a ginger-haired sheriff's deputy, he delivered a pretty mean borscht-belt shrug.

"Can we go talk to 'em?" said Morales.

"You can, but there'd be no point to it. They'll just fuck around with you and waste your time, and if you get close to anything real, they'll lawyer up."

"They have a lawyer?" said Jarsdel.

"Not on retainer or anything like that. These guys are small time. What they've done in the past is call the ACLU, try to make it seem like we're shitting on their civil rights. It's just a big joke to them." He deliberated something, snapping the rubber band against his wrist until the already ruddy skin turned even redder. He appeared to make up his mind, bringing out his phone. "You know what? No. We're gonna do this."

"Who're you calling?" asked Morales.

Oria held up a finger, then spoke into the receiver. "Tom, it's me. We got a serious situation. Guess what the ME just dug out of Ellery Keating's head?"

They'd left downtown behind and were now following a narrow road hewn into the stony coast southeast of Avalon. To their left, sun-dappled waves broke against the rocks, kicking plumes of spray into the air. Morales drove the golf cart, following Oria as he led the way in his squad car. The former captain, Ledbetter, sat in the passenger seat. Before they'd left the station, Oria had explained that he was the only man the Natty Lads truly feared.

"He's a little on the Dirty Harry side. Suspects tended to fall down a lot when he'd go to question them. He'll add the right vibe. Little scenery to get them to behave."

"I don't like it," said Jarsdel, once he and his partner were on their way.

"Not our call," said Morales.

"It's unprofessional."

There were signs for the desalinization plant, and they passed a restaurant called the Buffalo Nickel and the single-pump Catalina Gas Station. The road soon widened, and they drove under a light canopy of trees. Oria slowed and turned right up Pebbly Beach Village Road, which rose at a gentle grade before dead-ending a hundred yards ahead. Bungalows lined either side, built for the pottery workers a hundred years before.

They had to park almost immediately. A scattering of people milled about up ahead, most of them gathered near a grill that sent up clouds of gray smoke, commingling with the exhaust from a dozen blunts to create a pungent haze. The group was made up of working-class whites—hard-looking men and a few harder-looking women, faces sullen and distrustful. A couple naked children darted between the adults.

The three Natty Lads stood out easily. They had on ill-fitting clothes that were nevertheless bright and colorful, including the blue-and white-striped pajama pants Jarsdel had seen the night before. The one tending the grill was tall and broad-shouldered, midforties, wearing a distinct, tomato-red vest of a thick, textured fabric. His auburn beard and mustache were waxed to sharp points.

"He looks like an asshole," said Morales, easing himself out of the golf cart.

Jarsdel got out too, then went around to join his partner. They met up with Oria and Ledbetter, and the four of them made their way up the block. The small crowd immediately thinned out—children scolded, swatted, and scooped under the arms of their mothers—leaving two Natty Lads flanking the one doing the cooking. Jarsdel didn't recognize them, which meant Sad Dog and Popinjay were somewhere else.

The one in the red vest worked a grouping of wide, thin strips of meat with a long fork. Plainly visible on his bare left arm were the tattoos of a skeleton, an hourglass, and an impaled heart. He glanced up, noted the new arrivals approaching, and went back to tending the meat.

"That's Boaz in the middle," murmured Oria. As they drew closer, he waved and called out. "How you boys doin'? Makin' some lunch?"

The makeshift barbecue consisted of a cubic well of cinder blocks topped by a blackened wooden frame. There was a chink at the base to allow air inside, and the fire was low and steady. Some grease spilled onto the charcoal, and there was a fierce hiss. Jarsdel's eyes began to water from the smoke, and he took a step back.

"Don't mind us dropping by, do you?" said Oria.

Nilsen used the fork to indicate Jarsdel and Morales. "Who're these two?"

"We're from LA," said Jarsdel. "Homicide."

Nilsen whistled. "Shit, murder police." He sized up Morales. "Hey, *que pasa.*"

Morales cocked his head.

"Maybe we should go somewhere private to talk?" Oria asked Nilsen.

"I'm good," said Nilsen. "Like it better out here in the open. Safer." He winked at Ledbetter.

"If you like, okay. We're out here canvassing about that thing the other night. Ellery Keating. Sure you heard about it."

Nilsen prodded at the meat. "Funny as shit, yeah."

"Know anything about that?"

Nilsen lifted the strips one by one off the grill and onto a sheet of tinfoil. He then laid down a new bed of raw meat on the wooden frame. Another hiss as some of the marinade dripped off.

"Bible oath, I do not," said Nilsen. "And anyone curious where I was can ask either my messmates."

"Right," said Ledbetter. "As if these knuckle draggers wouldn't alibi your ass if you told 'em to."

The older man wore a light-blue jacket, despite the heat, and from where he stood, Jarsdel could see the black shadow of the pistol in the shoulder holster.

"Bless your rusty heart," said Nilsen, meeting Ledbetter's glare. "But if I wanted anyone dead on this island, I woulda started with somebody else."

"C'mon, Boaz, cut the shit," said Oria. "Lady's been killed, and we just wanna get some answers. These guys came all the way from LA." His tone was calm, even good-natured, one that said he wasn't there to reopen old wounds. Jarsdel appreciated the effort the man was making to hide his animosity toward the Natty Lads. But bringing Ledbetter was a mistake. He guessed Oria was making a ham-handed play for a Mutt and Jeff routine, but it was only going to sabotage their efforts.

Before the conversation could continue to circle, Jarsdel nodded at the barbecue. "Quite a setup you've got here. Build it yourself?"

Nilsen squinted at him. "Aye."

"Looks like a boucan."

The man's expression lit up. "That's right."

Oria was puzzled. "What is?"

"The grill," said Jarsdel. "Old Arawak word—*boucan*. Outcasts from Hispaniola used to live in the woods and roast meat on them—came to be called 'boucaniers,' which eventually became 'buccaneers.'"

Nilsen stared, as if struck with an epiphany. "Huh. Was wondering how you got here. Now it makes sense."

"Yeah, I have no idea what you mean. Couple of your friends last night were asking me how I got here. Can you explain?"

"We'll see. What do you call yourself?"

God, he was tiresome. "Detective Jarsdel. This is my partner, Detective Morales."

"Your amigo?"

"What's up?" said Morales, cupping his ear.

"I said you're his amigo." Nilsen offered a saccharine smile and batted his eyelashes. "Open your lug holes, you papistical, mud-skinned, half Spaniard."

"The fuck..." Morales took a step toward him. Jarsdel moved too, without thinking, getting close to his partner while keeping an eye out for weapons. Fast—the men flanking Nilsen readied themselves for a fight, puffing out their chests and shifting their weight onto the balls of their feet. The tensing of will and muscle so deeply implanted in the habitual lover of conflict. Their eyes gleamed expectantly. Neither noticed Ledbetter's right hand hovering near the opening of his jacket.

"Hey, whoa, whoa," said Oria, getting between Morales and the Natty Lads.

"I'm on fuckin' Mars," said Morales. He looked from Oria to Nilsen, then to Jarsdel. "We really talking to these guys?"

Oria turned to Nilsen. "There's no reason for that kinda thing. Those kinda words."

The leader of the Natty Lads shrugged. "Shows how little it takes to get 'em worked up."

"I'm on Mars," Morales repeated. "You wanna waste your time with these clowns, go ahead. I'm gonna sit down." He went back to the golf cart.

"No sense of humor neither," Nilsen said to Morales's departing back.

Oria's face had flushed almost as red as his hair. He pointed at Nilsen. "Way outta line, man. And frankly, it's embarrassing. I'll tell you—and I want you to listen really good, okay?—I've heard some other shit recently along those lines. Family downtown, something about you calling the dad a fine specimen or a fine example of his kind. And you know what? Nobody wants you spouting that kinda shit. This is a small town, okay? You fuck around like that, talking to tourists like that, and you're making it about Catalina. You're making the—"

"Bit sensitive—"

"*No*. No, Boaz. It's not sensitive. It's not about *being* sensitive. You've got your own little fantasy world you wanna play in, fine, but you bring your bullshit into town and you make money off it, with the stuff you guys sell and the photo ops—and I've looked the other way when you guys ask for tips, okay? I've been cool with you and I've been straight with you, and I expect a little courtesy in return. What you just did is embarrassing. When you call some dad a fine genetic specimen, bred for work or whatever, you're giving this whole place a bad name." His finger, aimed at Nilsen's heart, punctuated his words with little stabs in the air.

The Natty Lad to Nilsen's left, a stocky man of perhaps thirty with a shaved head and a double chin, held up his palm. "Keep your tongue behind your teeth."

Astonished, Oria stared at him.

Nilsen chuckled. "Beef and blood. Notch here's a man of beef and blood. Plenty of rough and tumble courage here in Pebbly Beach. Right, Scupper?"

"Oh, I dunno," said the other Lad, the one called Scupper. He was taller, with shaggy brown hair, his most prominent feature a bulbous Adam's apple, as if a walnut had become lodged in his throat. It twitched up and down as he spoke. "Don't see it takes all that much courage. Just a couple weak-kneed intruders. Look— practically see 'em shakin'. Especially the old man. Itchin' to use that piece, 'cause it's all he got."

Ledbetter's expression was blank. Jarsdel kept his eye on his hands. There were so many things that could go wrong right then, and he had a feeling they'd all start with Ledbetter's hands.

Scupper plowed on. "Wanna go, you creaky fuck?"

"This is really dumb, Boaz," said Oria. "Really, super dumb."

Scupper jutted his chin at Jarsdel. "Or what about you? The whey-faced intruder. How'd you get here? *How'd you even get here?* C'mon, stir your fuckin' hand. I'll cut your ass down to bark."

"Calm down," said Jarsdel. *I'm in the corners*, he thought. *These are those little corners where it always starts.* He kept his voice mild, but he was ready to fight if he had to. He looked once more at Ledbetter's hands.

Oria gestured at Scupper. "And your boy here's getting pretty close to some charges. You wanna have him back off, or someone might go to jail today."

"Can say whatever we *want*," said the one called Notch. "It's our property. You bunch are trespassing. How'd you get here?"

"We're not—"

"We can have you out the second we say so. You refuse to go, we have the constitutional right to remove you by force."

"There's a reason we're here," Jarsdel broke in, hoping to redirect the interview. He brought out his phone and opened the file Ipgreve had sent. He held up the picture of the musket ball.

"What's that?" said Nilsen.

"Normally, I'd say, 'You tell me.' But it's obvious you already know."

"I'm asking why you're showing it to me."

"Is it yours?"

"Who cares?"

"Because this was found wedged in Ellery Keating's brain."

Genuine surprise crossed Nilsen's face, which then blossomed with delight. "Most people, that'd be a problem. Her case probably made an improvement."

The Natty Lads laughed. Jarsdel wasn't sure, but even Ledbetter seemed to find that funny. He'd relaxed somewhat, and the hint of a smile tugged at the corners of his mouth.

Oria was less amused. "You realize that not a lot of people make musket balls anymore, right? So as far as murder weapons go, this one's a rarity."

"No, it isn't," said Nilsen. "Probably sold a thousand of those this year. Some guys use 'em as sinkers. Anyone could've gotten hold of one."

"Yeah, and how many of those people also happened to hate the Yacht & Fish?"

Nilsen set down the fork and pinched a strip of meat between his fingers. He leaned his head back and lowered it into his mouth, chewing lustily. Once it was down, he wiped his lips with the back of his hand.

"Help yourself if you're hungry."

When no one moved, Nilsen gathered up the doubled-over sheet of tinfoil, piled high with dripping meat, and handed it to the one called Notch. "Bowse about and see who's hungry."

"Aye, sir," said Notch, taking the food and hurrying off.

"And you," Nilsen said to Scupper. "Fetch aft the book."

After his own "Aye, sir," the lackey departed for one of the bungalows and disappeared inside.

"What's this now?" said Oria.

"You'll see," said Nilsen.

"He comes back with anything interesting," said Ledbetter, "and I'll drop the two of you."

Nilsen clicked his tongue. "Nah, come on. You only fuck people up when there's no one watching, right?"

"You resisted arrest. Shouldn't resist arrest. Even a waste of humanity like you oughta figured that one out."

"All right guys," said Oria, "Let's..." He trailed off as Scupper returned with a large book bound in imitation leather and fixed with artificially aged iron clasps. He was about to hand it to Nilsen, but the leader of the Natty Lads shook his head.

"Take it to the table." To Jarsdel, Oria, and Ledbetter, he said, "Bear away with me." He led the group over to a picnic table of warped, sun-bleached slats. But the surface was otherwise clean, and Scupper set down the book before taking a step back.

"There's a reason I'm showing you this," said Nilsen, holding his palm over the book.

"Okay," said Oria. "What's the reason?"

"Musket ball or no musket ball, I got no reason to kill Ellery Keating. And this proves it."

Jarsdel looked from Nilsen's fiercely earnest expression to the book in front of them. It was the sort of thing peddled as an objet d'art at big-box home furnishings stores, along with such standbys as enormous sepia-toned globes, fezzed monkey bookends, and Toulouse-Lautrec prints. Off-the-shelf culture, stamped out by the millions to add a little spark to the otherwise anonymous cells of sprawling, planned development hives.

"No one but my boys have seen this." Nilsen opened to the flyleaf. Written there in laborious cursive were the words *Whatsoever May Be Granted*. The author was given as Commodore Boaz Nilsen. "You can think of this as a Talmud for a dawning age. What the Hebrews did with the Torah, I've done with the works of Frank Rudolph Young. Laws of the mind. Refined it, codified it." He raised his gaze to meet his baffled audience. "I been accused of being anti-Jew, but I'm a Maccabee at heart. Woulda fought right alongside 'em. Those were the *real* Jews."

"Commodore?" sneered Ledbetter.

Nilsen turned the page and read the chapter heading aloud. "'Cyclomancy and the New Becoming.' This is the true nature of will as laid out by Frank Rudolph Young. From there I go deeper, following the original text step by step. 'The Composition of the Primitive Autoconscious.' 'The Dynamite Concealed in Your Protoplasmic Irritability.' 'How Your Psychic Arc Controls Your Final Common Pathway.' And here for the first time, I give a true explanation of 'How to Acquire Abnormal Physical Endurance with the Stooping Zembla and the Horizontal Ozona.'"

"Boaz," said Oria. "I don't know what any of this has to do with Ellery Keating."

"Frank Rudolph Young told us how to make a bomb. But he left out some key steps. You do that so not just anyone can come along and build your bomb. They need to work for it, prove they can handle the power. This is that big."

"Again, I don't—"

Nilsen cut him off with a raised finger. "It's pointless, because you won't even believe me when I explain it. Say I'm a kook, and that's just fine. That's what I want you to do. A man tells you he's a vampire, you dismiss him. And you're right to dismiss him. Until the real vampire comes along, of course, and when you don't believe him, there's a consequence."

"Amen," said Scupper.

"You're saying you're a vampire?" said Ledbetter.

Nilsen let out a disgusted sigh. "This"—he turned back to the flyleaf—"is called *Whatsoever May Be Granted*. What's that mean to you?" When neither Oria nor Ledbetter replied, he turned to Jarsdel. "What's it mean? Hazard a guess?"

Jarsdel shook his head.

"No guess? How 'bout this? Ever heard the scientific fact that we form our own realities? It's true, but not in the way most folks suppose. Frank Rudolph Young teaches us it's not multiple realities. It's just one. One reality. But who dominates it? Who decides its course?" He patted the book. "A will of *conscious making*. Conscious. As in *deliberate*. As in *the* man or *those* men who seize upon the dominating strain of thought and press it upon the world. Reality is clay, but you must mold it." He began speaking faster. "One man may dent the reality, as a lump of clay is dented by a thumb. Imagine a hundred men, a thousand, united, conscious, organized, and deliberate will with a single cause in mind. If you're on the wrong side of that, well, I wouldn't wanna be in your shoes."

"Amen," Scupper said again. Notch, who had just rejoined their group after distributing the meat, agreed with a soft "Fuck, yes."

Oria straightened up. "Ellery Keating, Boaz. What's the connection? What's any of this have to do with her?"

Nilsen looked amazed. "Don't you listen? We're gonna remake

the world. What do I give a shit about some rich-ass bitch at the Yacht & Fish?"

"I can't tell if you actually believe your own bullshit," said Ledbetter, "or if you've gone as crazy as everyone says."

"Remake the world," Nilsen repeated.

Without warning, Ledbetter waded in and slammed his knobby fist into Scupper's jaw. His teeth smacked together, sounding to Jarsdel like two billiard balls colliding. He went down on one knee, cracking it against the asphalt, and braced himself against the ground with his palms. If not for the sluggish side-to-side wagging of his head and the strange, low purring sound he was making, he could have been a sprinter about to launch from the starting blocks.

"Shit," said Oria. "Goddammit."

Nobody moved.

Ledbetter fixed his gaze on Nilsen. "Some education for you. That's how it is. And that's how it'll go every time." He turned his hand, showcasing its now-reddened knuckles. "I hit you. I hit you when I *want* to hit you. And when I do, I promise there'll be no body cams."

"Shit," Oria repeated.

Notch hooked his arm under his fallen comrade's bicep and helped him to his feet. Scupper wiped his mouth, and Jarsdel could see bits of enamel on the back of his hand. His eyes were dim and unfocused, but he managed to stay upright.

"You think about that when you're out remaking the world," said Ledbetter.

Nilsen nodded. "Oh, I will. I certainly will. And you'll be there when it happens."

16

The detectives followed Oria back to town, waited while he dropped Ledbetter at his home on Descanso Avenue, then continued on to the station so the three of them could discuss what had just happened in Pebbly Beach.

"I'm not gonna pretend I don't think it's funny as shit," said Morales once they were inside Oria's office.

The captain hung his head. "No, it's not good. Kinda disastrous, actually."

"Nah."

"It's a problem. I'm really questioning my judgment bringing him along. Not one of my better decisions. I guess I just thought... I don't even know at this point. Stupid."

Jarsdel agreed with him but didn't say so aloud. He wasn't sure what the aftermath would be for Ledbetter or Captain Oria and didn't care. It was his own career he was concerned about.

He'd been witness to an assault and hadn't made any move to arrest the guilty party. He also knew that if he so much as floated the idea that Ledbetter might have to face legal consequences, it would sink the Catalina investigation and turn his own partner against him. On the other hand, if he remained silent and the Natty Lads decided to press charges—unlikely, but not outside the realm of possibility—it would come out immediately that he'd been there and done nothing. In fact, every minute that passed between the incident and his own inaction made him increasingly guilty of breaching LAPD's code of ethics. If he waited too much longer, it wouldn't matter whether he reported the assault or not. He'd be complicit, and Lieutenant Gavin would gleefully offer him up as a sacrifice to the Professional Standards Bureau.

What then? Suspension, pending an investigation, and probably without pay. Then the agonized waiting while the PSB conducted its interviews. He could just hear Nilsen laying it out for them. "Arrgh, and after me hearty took the clout on the chin, the skinny pale one there did fuck all." Yo-ho-ho and a career-ending decision.

Jarsdel was thinking of what he should do next. Call his union rep? Or maybe preempt the whole thing and contact PSB himself? That might work. Get ahead of it. But how to do that without throwing everyone else under the bus?

"Hey," said Morales.

Jarsdel started. "What?"

"Why're you so quiet? You're not stressing about this, are you?"

"No."

Morales just looked at him.

"I'm fine," said Jarsdel.

"Yeah, you're stressed." Morales turned to Oria. "Probably wondering how this is gonna bite him in the ass."

The captain didn't seem to hear him. He stared at the wall, brow furrowed. "I guess the guy *did* threaten him," he murmured. "Goaded him a couple minutes before." He gestured to Jarsdel. "And he threatened you too. Something about cutting you down like a tree, right? Shit, what a dumbass move. I really dunno what I was thinking. I guess that he was just gonna add a little oomph to the whole thing, but he ends up popping the guy. Jesus." He pressed his palm against his forehead and moved it in slow circles. "Well, what are you guys gonna do with the rest of your time here?"

"Not much," said Morales. "We checked out the scene, talked to you guys. Got some statements. Might need to come back at some point if we can link this up to our thing back in LA, but I don't see a connection."

"Right," said Oria. He looked thoughtful, then asked, "And you said before that this was only a week before she died? The shooting up in Laurel Canyon?"

"The twenty-fifth," said Jarsdel. "Why? Please don't tell me you suddenly remember she was here on the island."

"Hmm? No, I don't think so. I just remember that day. Things were kinda nuts here in town. Had to close the beach 'cause we had this goddamned algae bloom in the water, so we had about a thousand pissed-off tourists who'd come here to swim and then couldn't. Conservancy says we can expect more and more of those as the ocean heats up. But Dell had a good night. Made a fortune with all the drinking up at Topsides as a result." He gave a wry smile. "Put him in a celebratory mood, 'cause that's the night he overdid it. Never actually saw him drunk before." Oria shrugged. "Anyway. If Ellery really did do it, she's beyond the reach of the law at this point. Death's the great equalizer."

A truly meaningless observation, Jarsdel thought.

"Definitely owe you guys an apology," said the captain. "I'm hoping of course that the bullshit that went down today won't affect your investigation. I mean, I don't think those fuckwhistles would've given you the time of day anyway, but now they're for sure not gonna be any help."

"Don't matter," said Morales. "Seriously doubt they had anything to do with it. Those guys couldn't even run a decent barbecue, so I got a tough time believing they took out Keating with a single shot from fifty yards. And with a musket ball? There's no way."

"Then it really might've been an accident," said Oria. "Freak accident. They fire off one of their weapons, like the subhuman numbzees they are, and pow. But good luck tying them to it. Boaz was right about that—those musket balls being everywhere."

The detectives got to their feet, Morales grimacing as the ache in his knees sharpened under the strain of his weight. "Not for us to prove anyway. Your island, man. Sheriff's case."

Oria drummed his fingers on his desk but said nothing.

"I'll forward you Dr. Ipgreve's report as soon as I get it," said Jarsdel. When Oria didn't respond to that either, he added, "Probably won't have a whole lot that's new, maybe just exact angle of entry. And he'll pass the slug on to forensics, so..."

The captain flapped his hand. "Not gonna hold my breath. I'm sure it won't change anything." He looked up, his expression now oddly amused. "You ever notice how hard we work in our jobs? Every death becomes this challenge to the natural order that's gotta be balanced out. No one gets to just die in peace. Need to drag their body around and stir up an answer, a reason, someone to blame. But you know, every now and then, the universe just erases somebody. No reason. Just gone. Why's that so bad?"

"You think that's what happened here?" said Jarsdel.

"Why not? How many billions of people ever lived, and you're telling me every single one has to have a reason for dying? Not every death needs a story or some grand purpose. Like..." Oria searched for the right words but couldn't locate them. "Forget it. Don't even know what I'm saying. Frankly I think you guys came out here for nothing. Don't get me wrong. I'm part of the reason it's nothing, but it's still just...a whole lotta nothin'. I can connect the Natty Lads to Ellery Keating, but I can't connect them to that murder you had in LA. So even if they had something to do with shooting off that musket ball, I don't see how that could have any bearing on what you guys are working on."

"Nah, neither can we," said Morales. "We'll make sure to say bye before we take off. Appreciate your hospitality. Definitely coming back with the wife and kids."

"Hey," said Oria. "Wait a second. Your LA shooting, the one you you've got Keating as a person of interest—what was the weapon?"

"Never recovered," said Jarsdel. "But the slugs were .38 hollow points. No matches in NIST or NIBIN."

"Remember Dell's stolen .38?"

"The Redhawk," said Morales. "You think the pirates took it from his boat, right?"

Oria nodded. "Yeah. Exactly their kinda thing. Got the Redhawk, 'long with a bunch of other stuff. I'm the one took the report. Look, I know I was wrong earlier today when I told you I thought the Natty Lads had used it to shoot Keating at the Yacht & Fish, but what if it's a match for your case?"

Jarsdel was dubious. "You think it's the same weapon? All the way up in LA?"

"I dunno, but it's weird how it clusters with the theft."

"Lotta .38s out there, though," said Morales.

"I *know* that," said Oria.

"And if it is the same gun, how'd it get into Ellery Keating's hands?" said Jarsdel.

"No idea. Interesting to consider. They steal the gun, she gets it somehow, shoots the guy in LA, then they take her out for...some reason. Maybe to cover up that they sold it to her. It kinda works."

No, it doesn't, thought Jarsdel. It was a god-of-the-gaps argument, requiring tremendous leaps in logic to get past the blurry parts.

"Something to think about anyway," Oria concluded when neither detective endorsed his theory. "Hope you guys enjoy the rest of your stay. Sorry this whole thing was basically a boondoggle."

"Gonna crash for an hour or two," said Morales when they got back to the Dew Drop Inn. "We're planning on meeting up at Topsides for happy hour." Then he added grudgingly, "You can come if you want."

"No thanks," said Jarsdel. Another round of playing fifth wheel to Morales and his new gun buddies was about as dull an evening as he could conceive. "Think I'll just wander around, check out the island."

"Suit yourself."

Jarsdel could tell he was relieved.

They took the elevator up to the third floor and headed down the hallway toward their adjoining rooms. When they got to Morales's door, Jarsdel decided it was time to speak up.

"Oscar, what are we gonna do about what happened today?"

"What d'you mean?"

"The assault. Don't think we can just let that go."

"Guy say he wanted to press charges?"

"No..."

"There ya go." Morales held his key card next to the reader and there was the whirr of the lock disengaging. He pushed the door open, then hesitated. "You're not gonna make a big deal about it, right?"

"I don't know what a big deal would be."

"Like mentioning it at all past this point."

Jarsdel wasn't sure how to answer that. "I don't want it to come back on me."

"Never will. Those pirate dudes're cowards. Even they somehow carry a grudge about it, they'll take it out on Ledbetter. And maybe Oria."

"That's not what I mean."

"Tully, how to explain it to you? This idea you got, that somehow you can get through a career dealing with shitbags all day every day, decade after decade, and not get your hands dirty a little—it's nuts. I mean, that what you really thought when you signed up? Tell you something. If the worst thing you do in your career is you *don't* go running to your LT when you see one citizen sucker punch another, you're the cleanest cop in the history of the department."

Jarsdel wasn't satisfied, but he realized it wasn't about Ledbetter or the Natty Lads or his job.

"We didn't solve this."

Morales shrugged. "We will eventually. Or not. That really bother you? Ellery Keating wasn't exactly saving the rainforest and running an orphanage for crack babies."

No, thought Jarsdel. And that wasn't the point. It wasn't that the Ellery Keatings and Dean Burkens and Gordon Marquands of the world deserved justice. They lived and died in the corners. But whatever killed them rarely stayed there. It would come out, like a troll from under a bridge, and seize an innocent.

He thought about Fiona Rose Huntley, who'd known all the secrets of the universe. No one had been there for her. Far back, somewhere, there'd been the right corner to shine a light on. Something that, once exposed, could have saved her.

But no one had, and the girl was dead.

"Hey," said Morales. "Time's our ferry tomorrow?"

"Ten."

"Cool." Something occurred to him, and his eyes twinkled with amusement. "By the way, never got to thank you for sending me on that wild goose chase to the casino. Table games my ass."

Jarsdel smiled. "Told you it was more on the traditional side."

"Uh-huh. Very traditional. 'Gathering place,' the tour guide said. Looked at me like I was an idiot." He shrugged. "Actually had a good time. You know that was the first movie theater fitted for sound in the world? In the *world*, man. So it's all good. Anyway, 'case I don't run into you later, I'll meet you on the boat."

When Jarsdel got back inside his room, he kicked off his shoes and lay down. His collar felt tight, so he yanked off his tie and undid the top button.

How had Oria referred to their visit? Right—a boondoggle. As good a descriptor as any, he supposed. A waste of time and taxpayer money, all so he and Morales could spend a couple days groping their way around Avalon. What had they actually learned?

That Keating had been shot with a musket ball. For that, they could have stayed on the mainland. Okay, they also found out that Catalina Island had its own brand of homegrown crazy—a small band of lunatic pirate enthusiasts led by a man who believed a determined willpower could shape the very fabric of space-time. Somehow Jarsdel didn't think that was going to help them discover who'd shot Dean Burken or Ellery Keating.

Morales's voice: *Most of the time, it's a job, Tully. Ain't a calling. It's a job.*

His partner was right, of course. It *was* a job, and right now he felt that more keenly than ever. He also realized that up until now, his fuel had been fear.

Not altruism, as he'd told himself time and again, but fear.

Injustice unanswered scared him. Scared him enough to thrust him out of his decadent, meaningless, but so very comfortable existence and into the police academy as the oldest member of his class. That had canceled his engagement and nearly got him disowned, so he supposed injustice scared him more than being alone. Even scared him more than the prospect of being unloved.

It scared him for the same reason cancer did. The fallacy of fairness. Fairness equaled divinity and purpose. A fair world was an ordered world. A world where Fiona Rose Huntley was still alive.

Justice gave the world meaning. As long as he was stacking up at least a few meager wins on the side of good, he was part of that meaning. *He* had meaning. He had worth.

But if injustice reigned, that meant there *was* no meaning. Just void.

What a great word that was—*void*. A single, devastating syllable. Perhaps the most frightening syllable in the English language.

He got the sense then, simply lying there in a drab hotel room in Avalon, that his thoughts were cresting a very, very steep hill and that any moment now, they would go plunging downward, dragging him helplessly along.

Movement was what was needed. He got up, put his shoes back on, and grabbed his wallet. Taking the stairs, he was soon back outside. He walked as fast as propriety would allow on a busy sidewalk and picked up his pace as soon as the crowds thinned out. He was heading inland, up Metropole. No destination in mind, just away from that hotel room where he'd come so close, so dangerously close to thinking—

—*that you're more lost now than you've ever been.*

And there it was. He could slow down now. It was out.

He leaned against a bike rack in front of the Catalina Island Museum, his heart racing.

You did this to yourself. You know that, right? Went all in, thinking you were gonna be some warrior for the cause of righteousness and that somehow that would prove to you that it isn't all just void. You know something? You're as deluded as Boaz Nilsen. He thinks he can remake the world by playing pirate, and you think you can do it by playing police-man. The only real difference between the two of you is that he's more dedicated to his narrative. Not plagued by self-doubt and uncertainty. And he's got a nice burgundy vest.

Before he could stop himself, he'd brought out his phone and was calling Baba. His father answered on the second ring.

"Tully."

"Baba, do you have a minute? Can I talk to you about something?"

"Okay."

"I know this probably isn't something you're ready to discuss. The night we were gonna go to dinner, it clearly brought back some hard memories. But I know about it now. I went to Mrs. Rostami's the other day, and I saw you leaving."

Baba remained silent, so Jarsdel went on. "She told me about what happened in Tehran. The protest and how you were there with your students and went to jail. I guess...I guess I'm just wondering how you knew. I mean, how you knew to commit yourself like that. To something that could—"

"This is none of your business." Baba's voice was as hard and featureless as a block of steel.

"Why?"

"Don't ever mention this to me again."

"But what you did, I need—"

"You know nothing about what I did. I have to go. Your father."

The line went dead. Jarsdel stared at his phone in amazement.

"Hey, you're that cop, right?"

Startled, Jarsdel straightened up. Standing next to him was the bartender from Topsides. She hadn't done her hair yet—no flick-up bob and Minnie Mouse bow—but she was easy to recognize by her tattoos.

"Something I can help you with?" Jarsdel asked, trying to gather his reeling emotions.

She glanced right and left, then shot a look over her shoulder before answering. "I need to talk to you. You and your partner guy."

"Okay."

"It's super important."

"I'm listening."

"Not here. Too many people."

Jarsdel sighed. "Your name's Kayla, right?" That seemed to alarm her, so he added, "Mr. Pruitt—Dell—told me."

She relaxed, but only a little. "Yeah."

"If you've got something serious to discuss, like a police matter, you should probably report it to your local department. Captain Oria's a—"

"*No.*"

The ferocity of her response gave Jarsdel pause. "Why not?"

"He's in on it. It has to do with Ellery Keating. I know what happened."

The words had a remarkable effect on Jarsdel, sharpening his mind and hushing any introspective chatter.

There's the hunt at least, he thought. *If nothing else, you do love the hunt.*

"Tell me," he said.

Kayla backed away from him. "I'm off at midnight. I'll meet you at the playground across from the golf course. Purple slides."

"I don't know—"

"Top of Eucalyptus, where it becomes Avalon Canyon. I gotta run." She hurried across the street and disappeared into a narrow alley.

Yes, Jarsdel thought. *The hunt is good.*

244

17

Jarsdel had dinner on the patio of the Avalon Grille, just on the other side of Crescent Avenue from the beach. He ate well, putting away an appetizer of flash-fried Brussels sprouts tossed with cubes of glazed pork belly and a Wagyu burger with red onion, tomato jam, and avocado. No wine, though. He wanted his wits about him, so it was bottomless Arnold Palmers while he waited for the sky to darken.

He checked his phone. Eight o'clock. Four more hours until he needed to be at the playground with the purple slides. He'd reconned the location after Kayla had spoken with him and decided she'd picked a good spot. It was isolated, far enough from town that they'd be able to see if anyone approached while they met. He still hadn't told Morales, however, and wasn't sure why.

Yeah, you are.

All right, apparently it was a day for some hard truths. Yes, he did know why. Envy. Morales was at Topsides carousing with the boys, and he wished he had even a fraction of the man's ability to get along with other cops. Morales was part of the kind of blue culture Jarsdel had read about in Joseph Wambaugh's *The Choirboys* and in nonfiction books like Miles Corwin's *Homicide Special*. These were men who, when they told you what they did for a living, people didn't say "Really?" with that note of incredulity Jarsdel now knew so well.

I'm a homicide detective, he thought. *As much a cop as any of those guys.*

Yes and no.

I'm a homicide detective. What a knockout line, especially in LA.

The homicide detective. The man of leather and iron. The man who can tell a joke with a moldering corpse only a few feet away, who buys the next round, who's got informants all over the city, who kicks open doors on the first try and tells those bastards inside they better get on the floor and *right fucking now*.

They teach your cases at Quantico. You're so good even the bad guys respect you. A respected character actor plays you in the TV movie. Or, if you're really lucky, a big star takes on the project, ditching the makeup and the personal trainer to look more authentic, and he gets an Oscar for putting on a performance that's so off-type, so not leading man. And the actor thanks you in his acceptance speech, and they cut to you in the audience, smiling humbly as the guy goes on about what a hero is and the difference between *playing* a hero and actually *being* one. Like you. And at the after-party at the Standard, an actress asks if you'd have some champagne with her or are you on duty, and you say no, I'm not on duty. It feels good to use that word—*duty*—and you like the way her eyes light up when she hears you say it. She then asks if you're carrying your weapon, and you say of course. She asks if she can see it, so you pop out the clip and eject the round from the chamber. She points it at the LA skyline and makes a shooting noise, then hands it back to you, her face flushed and excited, and says that guns make her nervous. You say you understand, and before you know it, the two of you are in her room, and on the nightstand is your gun and badge and a tumbler of Laphroaig, the ice cubes melting slowly in the amber potion.

Jarsdel paid the bill and texted Morales.

Need to tell you something. Step outside a sec?

While he waited for a response, he made the short walk to Topsides. He was there in only a few minutes, but Morales was already waiting for him, leaning against the rust-caked anchor out in front. He saw Jarsdel coming and frowned.

"There you are. Was just about to text you. What's up?"

"Kayla wants to meet with us."

"Who?"

Jarsdel nodded toward the building. "The bartender. Says she knows who killed Keating."

"Serious?"

"That's what she said. We're on for just after midnight. Can you get away from your new friends by then?"

"I don't get it. She just went up to you and said she knows what's up with the homicide?"

"Basically, yeah."

Morales wiped his mouth. His eyes were glassy from drinking. "We were gonna play some poker in back."

"I can go alone."

Morales waved that off. "I was just saying. It's no big deal. Shit. Thought we were done. I was just enjoyin' the break."

Jarsdel didn't comment.

Morales stood up easily, his pain receptors well-dampened. "I'm gonna go back in. Meet you out here at like—I dunno—like a quarter till. That okay?"

Jarsdel thought of the range targets in Oria's office—especially the one with the blasted-out eyes and bullet-hole smile. Then he thought of that impossible shot from Chimes Tower. "She said the captain's in on it."

Morales squinted. "Oria? No way. Why?"

"Didn't say. Maybe don't mention it to him, all the same."

"That's weird, man."

"He's also the best shot in Avalon."

Morales thought about that. "Yeah, okay." He headed back toward the door.

"Oscar."

Morales paused, smiled. "Yeah, I know. Be careful, right?"

Jarsdel shook his head. "Slow down in there, okay?"

Jarsdel spent the next three hours reading a paperback copy of *The Captive Mind* he'd brought on the trip, then returned to Topsides at quarter to midnight. Morales emerged ten minutes later.

Jarsdel pointed to his wrist.

"Whatever, man," said Morales. "Why would some random bartender know all this top secret shit? She's probably fucking with you."

The bar was on the other end of town from the golf course and the playground with the purple slides, so they decided to cross through Island Tour Plaza. The streets were empty, the night was cool, and they could hear waves breaking against Avalon Bay.

"What'd you tell your new buddies?" said Jarsdel.

"The truth. I'm tired. Goin' to bed." Morales paused, then added, "I like it here. Definitely one of the better places I've had to go for a case. Ever tell you 'bout the time I had to go out to Barstow?"

"You did," said Jarsdel.

"We were out there looking for this dude who'd shot his girlfriend and kidnapped the kid he had with her. A boy—I dunno, maybe four years old. So we track him to this trailer park, and it's hot that day. And we find the trailer and—you know—we got no idea what the situation's like in there. What's he gonna do if we knock? Kill the kid and set the thing on fire? I mean, you never know, right? So we're trying to think what to do when we see this little boy playing with some Transformers in front of a trailer a couple rows down. And I say, hey, that looks a hell of a lot like the picture we got in our pockets. So my partner goes and checks it out and yeah, that's the kid. Turns out he's been staying with this random old lady for, like, a week now because his dad's been sick. That's what she tells us. That Mr. Dominguez is sick."

They passed a parked khaki-painted tour bus, the words "Catalina Buffalo Tours" stenciled along its side, and turned left up Sumner Avenue. Jarsdel heard a whistle. This was followed by a hooting sound, somewhat farther away. He ignored it and they walked on.

"And she said it like, 'Do-min-gwez,' like that flat way of saying it that only old white ladies can do. 'Do-min-gwez.' Anyway, so now that we know the kid's okay, we go and start pounding on this door. My partner's checking the windows, making sure he's not gonna rabbit out one of 'em, and meanwhile I'm up in front by the door with Barstow PD. People are comin' out their trailers, hoping for some *Cops* shit. So we go for it, bust in the door, and we get inside and pow, the smell. You know the smell. Yeah, Mr. Do-min-gwez is sick all right. Dead sick. Face has that nice purple sheen to it, when it's all puffed up with gas. Hands too. He's in the bathroom, and the dude somehow managed—I don't know if you've seen these trailer bathrooms, but they're tiny as shit—he managed to get, like, wedged between the wall and the toilet. Like, the guy would've had to have actively tried to cram himself in at that angle. I don't know, maybe he was like thinkin', 'I'm about to die, so I'm gonna make it a real pain in the ass for the guys who're gonna have to drag me outta here.'"

As they turned onto Eucalyptus, there was another whistle, followed by another hoot. *The Avalon tipsy*, Jarsdel thought, *Catalina's local bird.* He snorted.

"Yeah, you laugh now," said Morales, "but now we gotta get that muthafucka from out the goddamn toilet. And my partner keeps yellin', 'Stinks in here! Stinks in here!' And I gotta agree, it's pretty bad. Guy still had the bottle of pills in his hand, fifth of vodka on the floor next to him. Puke just caked all over the his chin and upper chest area, probably shat his pants too. I mean, yeah, this isn't a basket of petunias in there. But you gotta be a professional, keep your head in the game. Anyway, coroner shows up, and I'm fascinated as to how they're gonna get the guy out. And here it comes, okay? Coroner grabs the guy's ankles, but the body's too jammed in there with the swelling and doesn't budge. So the coroner plants his foot right on the deceased's chest and tries to get him on his back so he can drag him free. Couple things happen at the same time. The body burps. I hear it happen. All this gas comes out the lungs, smells like the end of days in there, and then come the maggots. Soon as the body tips over, I'm guessing fifty thousand maggots spill out the guy's lap. You can actually hear them when there's that many and they're agitated. Like Rice Krispies. My partner? Forget it. Never seen anyone throw up like that."

The playground was in sight up ahead, dark except for a lone sodium light casting a sickly orange glow. Beyond, in a smaller, separate park, was a scattered collection of public exercise equipment.

"Don't see nobody," said Morales.

"Was she still in the restaurant when you left?" said Jarsdel. "If so, she might be..."

A man stepped out from behind one of the purple slides and began heading in their direction. He kept his head down, hands stuffed in his pockets, then pretended to notice Jarsdel and Morales. It was Popinjay, the Natty Lad from the night before. He held his hands out wide. "Gambrinous gents!"

"Yeah, you enjoy yourself," Morales called back.

"That's one of them," said Jarsdel, slowing.

Popinjay pointed at him. "You I know, but"—he swung his finger at Morales—"haven't met your boss yet."

"Dude," said Morales, making sure the badge on his belt was visible. "Let's call it a night, huh?"

Popinjay stopped in front of them, blocking their way. "How'd you get here?"

Morales put out a palm. "Ren fair's canceled. Go home."

"You don't tell me what the fuck to do, half Spaniard."

Jarsdel's attention had been on Popinjay, but the tensing of his partner's shoulders as the insult landed made him glance in Morales's direction. As soon as his attention was divided, Popinjay moved.

"Shit," Jarsdel began to say, when there was a whooping from behind them. He and Morales spun, hands going to their weapons. It was Sad Dog, bare-chested and wearing tattered, cutoff shorts. He ran at them, twirling something that gleamed in the light—maybe a length of pipe. But before either detective could draw, Popinjay leaped onto Morales's back, jamming a forearm under his chin. His other hand came up and around, gripping a bejeweled, double-bladed dagger.

Jarsdel pulled his Glock 40 from its holster just as something flashed by his nose. He sidestepped, seizing Sad Dog's triceps with his free hand and yanking. He dug in his fingers as he did it, deep into the muscle, trying to separate it from the bone as his attacker's momentum did the rest of the work. Sad Dog's triumphant whoop turned sour as the pain set in. His feet caught on the curb and he bit the sidewalk, hard. The thing he'd been holding spilled from his grip and clattered across the ground. Jarsdel saw it was a cutlass, perhaps eighteen inches of heavy steel sprouting from a basket hilt.

A fucking cutlass.

He turned toward Morales to see him struggling to dislodge Popinjay, who was trying to get enough leverage to bring the knife down in a killing blow. Jarsdel hesitated, keeping the muzzle of the Glock at a downward angle. Even if they'd been holding still, it would've been a risky shot. As it was now, he didn't dare open fire. He decided he'd have to peel Popinjay off his partner manually, which would probably send all three of them sprawling. He holstered his weapon and charged in just as Popinjay went for Morales's neck.

It was his partner's bad knees that saved his life. Struggling to prop up their owner's weight under the best of circumstances, they couldn't withstand the extra buck fifty Popinjay brought to the party. Morales went down just as Jarsdel reached them, turning onto his side as he went and dumping his attacker to the concrete. He gave a shout as his leg became pinned under Morales's bulk.

Movement off to Jarsdel's right—Sad Dog gathering up the cutlass. He hefted it, gave a couple whistling practice swipes, and turned to see Jarsdel's Glock leveled at his face. Blood streamed out of his mouth and from a gash below his eye. He stared dumbly at the weapon, then somehow managed to look annoyed, as if the detective weren't playing fair.

"Hey," he said.

"Drop it," said Jarsdel. He spared a quick glance at Morales, who now had both his hands on Popinjay's knife arm. The Natty Lad showed no sign of giving up, even though his leg was twisted at such an angle that it was almost certainly broken. Popinjay wrapped his arm around Morales's neck for leverage and began guiding the dagger toward his throat.

Jarsdel took aim at the man's head. It didn't look like he'd have a choice—if he didn't take the shot, Morales would be dead.

But in the end, it wasn't necessary. His partner posted on his forearm, raising his hip off Popinjay's leg, then dropped his weight down again. Popinjay howled, abandoning the attack, and Morales slammed the man's hand against the pavement again and again until the knuckles snapped. The absurd dagger, its gold-plated hilt glittering with fake stones, tumbled harmlessly from the shattered fingers.

Jarsdel redirected his Glock to point again at Sad Dog. "Playtime's over."

18

Jarsdel opened the fifth mini cup of half-and-half, poured it into his coffee, and gave it a brisk stir just as Oria reentered the office.

"Sorry that took so long," said the captain. "Just got off the phone with your lieutenant. Not really a people person, is he?"

Jarsdel shook his head. "How's my partner?"

"You kiddin'? Guy's hard-core. Couple bruises, no big deal. But we're playing it safe, don't worry. Doc's looking him over, making sure he didn't whack his head or anything. The other guys—different story. Definitely not a great day to be a Natty Lad."

"Any idea why they did it?" said Jarsdel.

"Revenge for earlier today, I guess. And you know the craziest thing? They don't have any idea what a serious situation they're in. Think it's some kinda game. Almost like another reality. Like we're gonna let 'em out in the morning and everyone's gonna go back to their corners and get ready for another round." He chuckled. "You know Leonard, the big guy? He complained to me that you pointed a gun at him. I'm serious. Said you weren't no gentleman fighter and should have matched him steel for steel. He actually said that."

"Did they lawyer up?"

"Not yet. But they will when we Mirandize them. Ricky will for sure, anyway. Don't know about Leonard. He's all messed up right now. Confused. Don't think he even knows what day it is, and it's got nothin' to do with the knock on the head. I know I keep saying it, but it's nuts. I mean it's just not sticking. Attempted murder of a police officer. *Attempted murder*. These guys're going away forever.'"

"What about Nilsen?" Jarsdel asked. "Any indication the order came from him?"

"Not yet, no. Normally we'd be all over their phones, checking texts and all that, but they don't have any. Part of the whole mystique. No cell phones. Boaz has a computer socked away somewhere, so we'll try to get a warrant on that. But it might not matter. There's a strong possibility we can get Leonard to flip. I think once all this really lands and he realizes the kind of situation he's in, he won't have the stomach for it." Oria grunted. "I'm sure sorry you guys had to go through all this, but if it's any consolation, you did us a big favor. Mighta pretty much solved our problem here with these assholes. What were the two of you doing up there anyway?"

Jarsdel took a sip of his coffee. That was a very good question indeed. He'd have to ask Kayla the next time he saw her. "Just enjoying the evening. Reviewing our notes on the case."

"Really?" Oria looked doubtful. "Seemed like they ambushed you guys."

"They were tracking us, probably since Oscar left Topsides. Heard hoots and whistles and stuff just before they attacked."

That appeared to satisfy him. "Yup. Sounds like their brand of horse shit. Boaz probably read that in some old pirate book and thought it would be cool. Anyway, your LT wants you back in Hollywood tomorrow."

Jarsdel shrugged. "That was the plan." He examined Oria carefully. "I think we pretty much exhausted the investigative potential of the trip."

"Boondoggle," said the captain. "Except of course for getting assaulted. I guess all that's basically my fault."

"Not at all," said Jarsdel, thinking of what Kayla had told him that afternoon—

He's in on it.

"Yeah, well, that's nice of you, but I won't blame you if you don't feel like coming back to Catalina any time soon."

I'm sure you'd like that, thought Jarsdel.

Oria's desk phone rang, and he gave an apologetic smile before answering. "Avalon Sheriff's Department. Oh, hey, Carl. You..."

Whatever Carl said next, it got Oria on his feet. "Yeah. Just now? Okay. I'm on my way." He hung up and headed for the door.

"Got a body. You better come along."

It was about a two-hundred-foot drop from the top of Twisselman Lane to Wrigley Road—one of the few sheer cliffs in Avalon.

Kayla lay perpendicular across the narrow road. She had landed facedown, head tucked to the side, right arm extended out in front, almost as if she were swimming. But the similarity ended there. Falls did extraordinary things to the human body, and Kayla's head was an exploded mass of hair, bone, and blood. When Jarsdel had first approached the body, he'd stepped on what he thought was a pebble. Using the toe of one shoe to scrape the bottom of the other, he discovered it was in fact a molar.

Oria massaged his brow. "I don't even know what to say. Christ." He stepped back and shone the beam of his flashlight up the cliffside. Blue and red flickers indicated the presence of deputies conducting a search of the area above. "The hell was she doing up there?"

"Where's the road go?" said Jarsdel.

"Few of the more expensive houses. But it's not like she hung out with anybody on that street, far as I know. Not exactly the crowd she ran with."

Jarsdel took out his flashlight and squatted down next to the body, or at least as close as he could get without stepping in blood. Kayla had on a knee-high black-on-white polka dot dress and a pair of pristine, cream-colored pantyhose. Her shoes were missing. "How far's the edge of the cliff from the road up there?"

"Uh, I dunno. Maybe twenty feet or so."

Jarsdel stood and scanned the area, illuminating the ground in wider and wider sweeps. "Your men find anything at the top?"

"I'll check." The captain touched the shoulder mic of his ROVER. "Sean, how're we doin' up there?"

A pause and the radio spat back an answer. As Oria asked more questions, Jarsdel's phone vibrated. It was from Morales.

Where are you?

Jarsdel texted back, Wrigley Road. Kayla's dead. Ninety-nine percent sure it's homicide. You okay?

Knees busted to shit, got jumped by a ducking pirate. Yeah, I'm flying, man.

*Ducking. Goddamn autocorrect. JUMPED BY A DUCKING PIRATE. Whatever. Lemme know what's up.

"Well, nothing so far," said Oria.

"No shoes?" said Jarsdel.

The captain shook his head.

Change that to 100% sure it's homicide, Jarsdel texted.

"You think it's foul play?"

Jarsdel put his phone away, irritated the captain had been reading over his shoulder. "You have any doubts?"

"I mean, it's possible of course. We'll definitely need to consider that. But how're you gonna prove it? Even if she was hit or punched or something, there's no way we'll be able to tell."

"It's murder."

"Could be, for sure. Or, hate to tell ya, she definitely enjoyed her own craftsmanship at the bar. Liked to party. Entirely possible she got wasted and went wandering around Avalon. There's a guardrail up there, but she could've easily stepped over it and just tumbled right on down."

If Oria was pretending to be thick, he was doing an excellent job. "Uh-huh," said Jarsdel. "Or she was picked up and dropped off the mountain. Which is what happened."

Oria squinted at him. "That's a lot of assuming. Who'd want to hurt Kayla?"

You, for one. Since she warned me about you. "No, it's not assuming," Jarsdel said, angling his light to point at the soles of the dead woman's stockings. "You said maybe twenty feet between the road and the drop-off. I'm presuming the land in between is dirt, scrub grass, probably those burrs I see everywhere. Right?"

"I guess," said Oria.

"Then how'd she get here?" His phone buzzed, but he ignored it. "Since we didn't find her shoes anywhere, that means she would've had to walk up that entire hill and off the road without getting a single fleck of dirt or oil or plant matter on her nylons. No. Someone drove her up there, lifted her out of the vehicle, carried her to the edge of the cliff, and dropped her over the side. I'm guessing the labs will show she was heavily intoxicated."

Oria gave a subtle flinch as Jarsdel's reasoning settled in. "It's possible," he allowed. "So where are her shoes?"

Jarsdel studied Oria's face. The reluctance of the admission more resembled wounded pride than calculated evasiveness. "Probably with whoever killed her. Someone she felt comfortable enough with to take them off. She have a boyfriend?"

"She was, uh. Well, you know, she wasn't with any one particular guy. Kind of a free spirit. Hung with Boaz on occasion."

Jarsdel nodded. He'd guessed as much from their shared tattoo. "Was she a true believer? All that stuff about the Natty Lads and reshaping the cosmos?"

"Dunno."

"Okay, but I'm assuming you're gonna talk to him, right?"

"Oh yeah, we'll talk to him. I'll have one of my guys bring him in for questioning." He sighed. "Not that it'll do anything. Guy won't say shit."

Jarsdel checked the time on his phone—almost three a.m.—and saw Morales's text.

Doc's letting me go back to hotel to get some sleep. Codeine's a beautiful thing. Leave the body for local cops. Not our problem.

He clipped his phone back onto his belt, thinking of how

annoyed his partner would be in a few hours. He suspected very much that Kayla's death *was* their problem, and he wasn't about to leave that possibility unexplored.

"Let's do it," said Jarsdel.

"Wait, what?" said Oria. "You're not coming, are you?"

"Why not?"

"Well...hey, look, man. I don't want to play those dumbass jurisdictional games, but this definitely isn't an LAPD matter. No relevance whatsoever to your investigation. These are local guys, and you'll just end up antagonizing them."

Jarsdel mulled that over. "Probably not as much as Mr. Ledbetter, though. Right?"

Oria bristled, but he went on before the man could reply. "I can get him to talk."

"Really. How're you so sure?"

Jarsdel looked down at Kayla's outstretched arm and the tattoo of the skeleton, hourglass, and speared heart. "Because I know what he needs."

There was one small interview room at the Avalon Sheriff's Station. Standard setup—one-way mirror, camera in the corner, stainless-steel handcuff bar bolted to a table.

Boaz Nilsen—currently uncuffed—sat with his legs up on the table, arms crossed behind his head. He hadn't been waiting long but had already begun singing to himself to pass the time. The song was "All for Me Grog," whose lyrics he interspersed with a stew of quotations, ramblings, and affirmations.

He fell silent as soon as Jarsdel entered, watching him with the kind of derisive amusement particular to the career criminal.

"Appreciate your patience," said the detective. "Has it been explained to you why you're here?"

No answer.

"Would you like me to tell you?"

No answer.

"It's not about what happened earlier. You probably guessed by now your assassination attempt didn't come off as expected."

"Where's your boss?" said Nilsen.

"My boss?"

"He behind the glass?"

"Who?"

"The fat-ass Mexican, you fucking traitor."

Jarsdel tried to keep his voice even as he answered. "If you mean Detective Morales, no, he's recovering."

"*Detective*." Nilsen made a hissing sound. "Uh, okay."

"You don't think we're real police?"

Nilsen shrugged.

"How'd you come to that conclusion?"

No answer.

"Okay, we'll leave that for the time being. I have some troubling news. We found Kayla tonight."

This time, there was a flicker of uncertainty in the other man's eyes.

Jarsdel continued, "She's passed away."

Nilsen grunted.

"That's funny?"

"This is so cheap," said the pirate. "Who came up with it? Oria? Or was it the Mexican's idea?"

"There's no idea, Mr. Nilsen. She's dead."

"Aft there!" Nilsen shouted at the glass. "Fuckin' traitors! You know who you guys're in bed with?" He slammed the table with a fist. "Anyone else comes into Pebbly Beach better bring some serious fuckin' artillery. Pass that on to Bedwetter."

"Here. I'll show you something." Jarsdel brought up the picture of Kayla's body on his phone and slid it over to Nilsen.

"There's more," said Jarsdel. "Can swipe through them if you want."

Nilsen did so, and Jarsdel noted his familiarity with the

functioning of a cell phone. Not the Luddite he pretended to be. Probably had a phone stashed away somewhere his men wouldn't see it.

He ended on a close-up profile view of Kayla's ruined face. "Fakes?" A question, not an accusation, and one colored by more than a little hope.

Jarsdel shook his head, taking back the phone. "I don't think you did this. But you might know who did."

When Nilsen didn't answer, Jarsdel went on.

"She came to see me. That I'm sure you know. Told me she knew who killed Ellery Keating and wanted to meet me and my partner around midnight. I'm assuming she was acting on your orders."

Nilsen just stared at him.

"I have a proposal for you. Imagine I'm not whoever or whatever you think I am, that it was all some strange misunderstanding or maybe deliberate misinformation. That my partner and I are in fact LAPD homicide detectives."

Nilsen began to sing again.

> Well, I'm sick in the head, and I haven't been to bed.
> Since first I came ashore with me plunder.
> I've seen centipedes and snakes, and I'm full of pains and—

"The musicians shall have rest on the Sabbath Day," said Jarsdel.

Nilsen paused, regarding him with curiosity. "What'd you say?"

"The musicians shall have rest on the Sabbath Day only by right. On all other days by favor only."

"It's not the Sabbath Day," said Nilsen.

"Not yet, no. But I hoped quoting the code would get your attention. I see it has."

Nilsen gave a genuine smile. "The code. Bartholomew Roberts. Brethren of the Coast. 'He that shall desert the ship or his quarters in time of battle shall be punished by death or...'?"

"Marooning," Jarsdel finished.

"Marooning, aye." Nilsen's smile became wistful. "Better time. Men agreed to that code, bound their fates to each other. Strong." Here he clenched his fists side by side, as if working to bend an iron bar. "Who do you know today who'd take up an oath like that? Bind himself, in blood and before God, to death by marooning? Not one."

"No," Jarsdel agreed. "Those days are long gone. But you know what really bothers me? I wouldn't normally mention it, but I think you might actually get it more than anyone else."

"What bothers you?" said Nilsen.

"Pointlessness."

The pirate waited for him to elaborate. When he didn't, Nilsen ventured, "In terms of life?"

"Yes. In terms of life. In terms of the fact that we don't really matter as much anymore, do we? Individually, one person's about the same as another. Especially men. Don't you think?"

Nilsen considered a moment, then gave a single nod.

"Or think of it this way," said Jarsdel. "Maybe it's not that men's lives are more pointless than women's but that it's our basic drives that make us feel our pointlessness more acutely. Women have their own stuff to deal with, but for us—for men—it's a deep, twisting anguish. There's no adventure anymore. Everything's safe. Gotta go out of your way to risk your life these days, and when you do, you have to sign a hundred forms. So we can't help but wonder what it must've been like in a time when we had real purpose. To ally our hands with our spirits. To hurl ourselves into battle with our brothers. It almost didn't matter what the cause was. It gained its righteousness when we attached our honor to it. And our willingness to die."

"Do you have that?" Nilsen asked.

"No. Not most of the time. Most of the time, it's a job."

"But sometimes?"

Jarsdel thought that over. "Sometimes." He laughed. "Had a little of it when your men attacked us earlier."

Nilsen grinned. "You did?"

"That one guy, Sad Dog, threw him face-first onto the pavement. Guess that's something most men these days never get to experience. Either on the giving or receiving end." He saw he wasn't quite getting the reaction he was looking for, so he added, "And in that moment, I felt connected, deeply connected, to every man who came before me. It was like I was honoring my great-great—you know, however far back—great-grandfather. No, it was more like we were all one being. Together."

"So you felt it," said Nilsen, leaning forward. "You actually felt it. The mission." There was a touch of hopeful wonder in his voice. The conquistador finally glimpsing El Dorado through a break in the jungle foliage.

"The mission," said Jarsdel. "What's that mean to you?"

"Sacred purpose. That connection you said. Be like, 'You know what, world? I'm right here, so fuckin' take notice.' You know?"

"'Course."

"Yeah." Nilsen smiled. "I figured it was something. How you got here and everything."

"How I got here. You guys have said that a few times. Can you explain?"

"It's like... Okay, remember what I was talking about in Pebbly Beach? With the book? This"—he rapped the table with his knuckles—"this is a construct, okay? We can shape it. It's just my vision versus yours. Not like you *personally*, but—"

"I get it, sure," said Jarsdel. "Go on."

"We're basically at war all the time. Whose vision's gonna dominate? I'm at war with you, you're at war with the Mexican guy. Not consciously—I mean most people not consciously, but if you *can* get conscious, if you know how it works, you can shift it so you're actually the one who makes the rules."

Jarsdel searched for the right response. "That's pretty mind-blowing."

Nilsen's smile broadened. "Right? But it makes sense scientifically, if you think about it. Most people don't think about it, so for lots of the time, reality is just kinda rolling along, like a ship with no captain. Rudder just goes with the waves. Someone grabs the wheel, though, look out."

"Huh."

"So that's why we were all surprised at you guys getting here, 'cause I was like, nah, I don't accept threats or a threatening presence in Avalon. I've set, like, a boundary. But now I see that you—like with the boucan and how you understand Bartholomew's code—you're actually pretty high up there, mentally, in your directed reality. So you were able to slip on in."

"Oh, I get it," said Jarsdel. "Also it probably helped that we weren't here to threaten you. Weren't after you at all."

Nilsen nodded vigorously. "I see that now, yeah. Shitty misunderstanding."

"No, it's not," said Jarsdel. "It's an abuse of the mission. If evil men know how much the mission means to us, they can use it."

Nilsen was suddenly wary. "Evil men?"

"An evil man can twist the mission for his own aims. Find out what's critical to us and direct us like spears at each other. No honor of their own. No bravery, no code, no sacred purpose. Just void. So all they can do is convince other men to corrupt their own natures."

Just like you and the Natty Lads, he thought. *I wonder how long it'll take them to realize they threw away their lives for your empty bullshit.*

"Like what? Like how?" said Nilsen.

"Like tonight. Tonight someone got you to do something you wouldn't normally have done. Took your mission and they spit on it. Disrespected you. You get it, right? Because they're cowards. Couldn't do the job themselves."

"So it's not, like, the fault of the guy who got tricked?" Nilsen asked. "Because the person who did it was evil?"

"Exactly," said Jarsdel. "You and me now, we can get 'em back for what they did. What was it they told you?"

Nilsen let out a deep breath. "That you were cartel guys. Not real cops."

Jarsdel blinked. "Cartel guys?"

"Yeah."

"Why would the cartel be after you?"

"Business reasons." Nilsen shrugged, but not without some pride. "They ain't exactly into negotiating."

Jarsdel's first assumed he was talking about the homemade musket balls and thought Nilsen must have truly plunged into full-blown psychosis. Then he remembered Oria's complaints about the marijuana grows.

"You mean the pot?"

Nilsen put a finger in front of his lips, then winked. He spoke in a hushed, conspiratorial tone. "Legalization didn't kill drug trade. Just made it more competitive. Soon as the cartel gets word of an independent operator, they start sending in spies to gather intelligence. They deem it's enough of a threat, in come the hitters."

"Wow."

"And it's not like they're gonna show up on Catalina dressed like vatos from East Los, right? Nah, they'll wanna blend in. Better yet, pretend to be cops. Makes sense?"

"For sure," said Jarsdel. "Pretty scary when you think about it."

"Yup. Anyway, that was the word. You were here to mess us up, knock us out of the picture."

"Huh. I think I understand. So when you sent Popinjay and Sad Dog after us, you were just defending yourselves."

Nilsen gave a vigorous nod. "Absolutely self-defense."

"Were they supposed to..." Jarsdel drew a finger across his throat. "Slit our weasands? Bring bloody death upon us?"

Nilsen laughed. "Yeah, pretty much. Good trial run, though, 'case those guys ever do show up. When you gonna let 'em out? My boys, I mean."

"Pretty soon. I think we're almost there. Just need to find out who went to you with that info. About us being cartel hitmen." He saw the smile on Nilsen's face fade, and then he understood. "Was it Kayla?"

"Yeah."

"Any thoughts as to how she came up with that idea?"

Nilsen squinted and looked up to the left, trying to remember. "Heard it at work."

"At Topsides?"

"Yeah."

"Who?"

"Dunno. I think she overheard someone talking about it. You know, how you guys weren't really cops and that the whole murder investigation thing was just cover and how you were gonna blow us away if you got us alone."

"Who?" Jarsdel repeated.

"She didn't say."

"She didn't say, or you don't remember?"

Nilsen yawned. "Sorry, I'm fading."

"Try to focus. This couldn't have been that long ago. Did you actually get a name?"

Nilsen shook his head. "No. It was a rumor, like more than one person. I think Dell said he heard about it too."

"Pruitt? The owner?"

"That's the guy, yeah."

Jarsdel nodded. "Good. That's good. Thank you." He got to his feet. His clothes felt gummy with the accumulated sweat of nearly a full day on his body.

"This was wild," said Nilsen, also standing.

"Going somewhere?"

"I think I'll just head back to Pebbly Beach. Get some sleep."

The door to the interview room opened and a deputy entered, trailed by Captain Oria. "Hey, Boaz. Do me a favor and turn around and put your hands behind your back."

"What d'you mean?"

Oria nodded at the deputy, who gently but firmly helped Nilsen face the wall.

"What do you mean?" Nilsen said again. "Why're we doing this?"

The deputy brought out his cuffs and had the pirate bound in under two seconds.

"It was self-defense!" Nilsen's voice had climbed an octave. "I was acting in self-defense! I don't recognize this arrest. I *do not* recognize this arrest."

The deputy grabbed the handcuff chain, then pressed his other hand against Nilsen's back and marched him from the room. The pirate continued his quavering monologue as he was led away.

"Why're we doing this? You take your hand off me. False arrest, hello? Why're we doing this, though? Ever heard of self-defense? Huh? Stand your ground?"

It was just the two of them left in the room then, Oria and Jarsdel.

"Well," said the captain. "Gotta say I'm a little miffed you held back about that stuff with Kayla and the setup. Thought we were kind of a team here."

"Wasn't personal," Jarsdel lied. "Wanted to keep it quiet till we knew more."

"No, I don't like that. You shoulda come to me right away, soon as Kayla approached you. Courtesy, if nothing else."

"C'mon, Captain. What was more likely? An ambush, or someone trying to waste our time? We would've felt pretty stupid wasting your time, too." Jarsdel crooked a thumb in the direction of the holding cells. "What'd you think about what he said? The rumors at Topsides that we weren't real cops. You hear anything like that?"

Oria scoffed, relaxing a little. "I'd give about as much weight to what comes out his mouth as what comes out the back end." He shook his head. "'Self-defense.' That's a good one."

19

IT's gonna kill you."

The two detectives were waiting in line at the ferry terminal, Morales leaning heavily on the railing.

"Tell him I missed the boat," said Jarsdel.

"Missed the boat, yeah. Wow, that's good. I'm sure that'll work. You know he wants us back in the station in, like, two hours, right?"

From where they stood, Jarsdel could see the enormous, rounded structure of the casino at the other end of the bay. He wondered if that was where the great lost temple of the Tongva had once dominated the coastline. His gaze wandered, lighting first on the Tuna Club, then the Yacht & Fish. Or maybe it had been there, where folks like Ellery Keating and Dell Pruitt now celebrated the high achievement of catching a fifty-pound tuna with a nine-ounce rod.

"I don't care," he said. "Tell Gavin whatever. Tell him Captain Oria needed me to help process the arrest warrants on the rest of the Lads. Tell him I'll be in this afternoon."

"You sure?" said Morales. "I got us Commodore Lounge tickets this time. Upgrade, baby."

"I'm sure."

A crew member came up the gangway and opened the gate.

He gestured for those in line for the Commodore Lounge to begin boarding.

Jarsdel extended his hand, but instead of his usual strong and steady shake, Morales pulled him into a half hug. Unsure how to respond, Jarsdel gave his partner's shoulders a couple gentle pats.

"Well," said Morales, breaking away. "That wasn't awkward or anything. See you when you're back overtown." He turned to go.

"Oscar."

Morales stopped and looked back at him.

"Maybe when I get back, we could watch *Chinatown*."

His partner grinned and gave him a thumbs-up.

Jarsdel turned and left the terminal, heading back to town, upstream against the current of sunburned tourists, their roller-board suitcases rumbling over the seams in the footpath.

He passed the Pavilion Hotel, where guests lounged on outdoor furniture and picked at the breakfast buffet, and he passed the Pleasure Pier, with its glass-bottom boats and bustling seafood shack. Children dug in the sand with bright plastic rakes and shovels. Seagulls wheeled overhead. A pelican dropped from among them, hitting the water and coming up a moment later with something silver slipping into its long beak. Seduced by a storefront poster of a cup of iced lemonade, he stopped into a place called Scoops and ordered a large. It was a thing of beauty, heaped well over the rim of the cup with sour-sweet snow, bits of real lemon flecked throughout, and he slowed down to savor it. He also didn't want to be spooning and slurping an icy dessert when he got to where he was going.

He passed Luau Larry's, which wouldn't open for another hour, and the Dew Drop Inn on Metropole Street, and finally onto Via Casino. A heavyset jogger chugged by him, taking wheezing, huffing breaths, and Jarsdel automatically stepped to the side to widen the distance between them. Since COVID, it was too easy to imagine that anyone might spray you with a life sentence of shredded lungs or myocarditis or even a toe tag in Ipgreve's morgue. A trio of Indian women draped in vibrant saris took a pause in their conversation to shield their faces as the man went by.

Jarsdel tested the gate in front of the Yacht & Fish. It was unlocked, so he stepped inside, retracing his route from the other day around the side of the building. He glanced up at the burgee, wondering again how that musket ball had struck Keating. He thought of the bruise or the welt that Ipgreve couldn't identify. What had caused it?

Larry "Dell" Pruitt was on the deck of *Sweet Caroline*, polishing the cleats. Sensing movement, he glanced up and saw Jarsdel approaching.

He slung the rag over his shoulder. "Heard you had quite the night."

"Yeah. Can I talk to you a minute?"

"You bet. Hang on." Pruitt went inside the cabin. A moment later, he called out, "Hey, you want a water?"

"No, thanks."

"Sure? No calories or sweetener or anything. Just sparkling water."

"I'm okay."

Pruitt emerged with a bottle of Pellegrino. He took a long drink, put his fist to his chest, and belched. "Sorry. What's up?"

"Well, first I wanted to give you my condolences."

"Condolences? About what?"

"Your bartender. Kayla."

"Oh, Jesus. Yeah, of course." Pruitt downed some more of the water. "Dry out here today." He scratched at the rash at his jawline. It looked to Jarsdel a little less angry than it had two days earlier. "Thought you and your partner left on the ferry," Pruitt added.

"I wanted to stick around till I cleared something up. You probably heard we got Boaz early this morning."

"Yup." Pruitt smiled, revealing a perfect set of gleaming white teeth. "Can't say I'll be too sorry about the concomitant loss in local color."

Concomitant, what Jarsdel's middle-school English teacher would have called a "five-dollar word." "Right. Anyway, I was curious about something he said—that Kayla heard a rumor at work that my partner and I weren't actual police officers."

"How d'you mean?"

"That we were hitmen working for some unnamed Mexican drug cartel."

Pruitt laughed. "Pretty terrific."

"Nothing like that on your radar?"

"You serious? No."

"Are you sure? He mentioned you being one of the people who was spreading that around."

Pruitt made a sour face. "And you believed him?"

"I'm not making accusations."

"Well good, because honestly, if that guy told me fire was hot, I'd double-check it for myself."

Jarsdel had thought as much. Who knew what bizarre game of telephone had resulted in Nilsen's garbled account in the station interview room. Still, Kayla had been certain enough of Jarsdel's and Morales's guilt that she'd been willing to set them up to die. That took a deeper than ordinary conviction. Even if she was as pathologically paranoid as Boaz Nilsen, she must still have put substantial trust in the source of the rumor to do what she did.

"Oh," said Pruitt, his expression clouding.

"What is it?"

"You know, Ken did say something about that."

"Captain Oria? What'd he say?"

Pruitt hesitated. "You, uh, you better come aboard. Just grab on to the...there you go." He led him into the cabin, which, like the few other cabins Jarsdel had seen, seemed so much bigger on the inside than the outside.

"I don't really know where to begin with this," said Pruitt, swinging himself up onto a barstool and taking another quaff of water. "Wanna have a seat?"

"No, thank you. What was it you were saying?"

"I didn't think it was a big deal at the time. But Ken said that you and your partner didn't seem genuine."

"Genuine?" It was news to Jarsdel.

"Uh-huh. That you didn't talk or act like cops. And he might've mentioned it at the table after your partner left that first night. I remember, yeah, I think Kayla overheard. From there, I could see how it would get to Boaz. They had kind of a thing."

Jarsdel frowned. The idea that he and Morales had been marked for death because Kayla snatched a few threads of gossip out of the air seemed awfully flimsy. And why would Oria make such a strange and unfounded statement in the first place?

Pruitt scratched at his rash, eyebrows raised expectantly.

"Okay," Jarsdel allowed. More dead ends. It looked like he'd stayed on the island for nothing. That would make his upcoming ass-chewing from Lieutenant Gavin all the more irritating. He scoured his mind for any other unanswered questions. Anything to redeem this boondoggle of an investigation.

"You mind if I ask you something else? It's a little out there, subject wise."

"Go 'head."

"The project you and Ms. Keating were collaborating on. Did you—"

"Project?"

"The Strand at Newport."

"The development—okay, yeah. Sorry, she and I were also discussing ways to broaden club membership, so maybe you could've meant that." Pruitt shook his head, chuckling. "Don't know why I thought you might've meant that, but anyway. Little scrambled this morning."

"What I was wondering," Jarsdel went on, "is while you were working together, did you happen to hear anything about an old diary?"

Pruitt blinked. "Diary?"

"We believe our shooting up in LA was connected to the disappearance of a journal." Jarsdel hesitated. "It's possible—I know this sounds weird—but it might describe the location of a cache of gold."

"Gold," Pruitt murmured. "First pirates and now we got buried treasure, huh?"

"So nothing like that?"

"You really need to ask?"

"I'm not suggesting the gold exists, just whether you picked up any rumors..."

Pruitt was shaking his head. "No treasure maps. No decoder ring, no X-ray specs."

"Okay," said Jarsdel, embarrassed. "I'm curious about one more thing, though."

"Oh boy. What's next? The Maltese Falcon? Death Star plans?"

"There a chance Ellery Keating could have gotten hold of your handgun?"

Pruitt's smile dried up.

"The .38 you reported stolen. Happened not long before the shooting in LA. Thing is, we know she didn't own a firearm, and we never recovered one from the scene. And it was a .38 that was used, we know that too. You can see why we'd think it could be the same weapon."

"No," said Pruitt. "Not possible. Natty Lads took the gun, and Ellery wouldn't have gone near them—certainly wouldn't buy a stolen firearm. I'm sure Boaz has it crammed away in his shack somewhere. Either that or he sold it to one of his asshole friends. I seriously doubt we'll ever see it again."

Jarsdel thought that over. "I don't want to pry into your business, but when's the last time you left Catalina?"

"When's the last time I left? Not since when I was robbed. My business trip overtown. Had to do with the development."

"You're sure?"

"Positive."

"What were the dates on that?"

"Man…" Pruitt's brow furrowed. "I dunno. Like the eighteenth, I think. The fifteenth to the eighteenth. Why's that important even a little?"

"And our guy in LA was shot a week later. Captain Oria's right. There has to be a connection." He regarded Pruitt with increased curiosity. "You were here in town that night."

"What night?"

"Captain Oria said you'd had too much to drink. That you'd left the bar early and gone back to your boat—to get some sleep, you told everyone. And no one saw you in town again until the next morning."

"Kinda personal." Pruitt wiped his mouth with the back of his hand. "Why're you asking all this?"

But Jarsdel couldn't stop himself, and Pruitt's mild disapproval wasn't nearly enough to make him back off. A picture was beginning to form in his mind—one still terribly out of focus but sharpening fast.

Pruitt out of town on business, gun stolen from boat. Natty Lads blamed. Gun now missing. Dean Burken shot in LA, presumably by Ellery Keating—after all, she had the glass in her shoe and a powerful motive: not to be publicly disgraced for pushing through Pruitt's land deal while acting as his silent partner. Because Burken was on his way out, and she couldn't protect him anymore. He was gonna bring the whole scheme tumbling down.

"Mister detective, sir?"

There was a closet on the starboard side, the door halfway open. Among the jackets and windbreakers hung Pruitt's wetsuit. Only it was different than the one in the pictures at Topsides. That had been monogrammed, Pruitt's initials printed in cursive above the left breast. This was new, all black. No monogram.

Where's the other wetsuit?

This thought quickly led to another.

Scuba gear. Why had Pruitt rented scuba gear? He had his own, all customized, right?. So if he had his own gear, why was he bitching about the rental equipment over drinks at Topsides?

"How'd you get that rash?" said Jarsdel.

Pruitt laughed, hopping down off his stool. "Gonna grab another water. Sure you don't want one?" He bent down to open a mini fridge, reached inside with both hands, and came out holding a Pellegrino and something concealed behind it. "No sweetener or anything," he said, then shot Jarsdel twice in the chest.

Jarsdel stumbled backward into the small galley area, arms flailing, and slammed his back against the countertop. His head rang against the bottom of the microwave, but he hardly felt it. There was a terrific pressure in his body, as if he were suddenly a thousand pounds and being compressed under his own weight. He made an effort to speak, to ask why, but no words came.

His attacker tried to fire again, aiming at Jarsdel's face, but the gun had jammed. Pruitt cursed and examined the slide, where a spent shell casing had become trapped.

"Unbelievable. This, by the way, is why I prefer revolvers." He set the gun down on the barstool and approached. "Hey. What do you think of that caliber?"

The detective opened his mouth, and a stream of blood poured out.

"That good, huh? Shit." He reached out of view, and Jarsdel heard the sound of a drawer being opened and closed. Pruitt's hand came back into sight gripping a steak knife—rounded at the tip but edged with scalloped, serrated teeth.

Jarsdel clawed clumsily at his sidearm. Pruitt grunted, amused, and kicked the hand away.

"You asshole. You have any idea how stupid this is? How pointless? I gave you everything on a silver tray, and you just kept pushing. Know what you are? You're that kid in school who reminds the teacher to give homework. And why exactly do you care so goddamn much about any of these people? Can you honestly tell me, right now, that you're willing to die for Dean Burken and Ellery Keating? And Kayla Meyrink, the one who set you up to die? The world will not miss them, I promise you."

He hefted the knife in his hand, then shook his head bitterly. "Jackass. And now I'm in this crazy position. I sincerely hope you're happy, now that you're sitting there with two bullets in you."

Jarsdel reached for his gun again, this time succeeding in disengaging the lock on the holster. Pruitt watched with curiosity, then squatted down in front of him.

"Really think I'm gonna let you pull that?" He leaned closer, moving the tip of the blade back and forth in front of Jarsdel's face. "What d'you think'll happen first, realistically?"

Jarsdel let his hand fall away from the gun.

"Good," said Pruitt. The amused curiosity was back in his eyes, joined by a fresh note of triumph. "Thought you were pretty clever the other night, huh? That little circumference trick. What an intellectual powerhouse. Really put me in my place." He sighed. "So here's what's gonna happen. In about two minutes, I'm gonna take us out to the open water, weight you down, and throw you overboard. You probably already know this, being a certified genius, but it's about a mile to the bottom. You can say hello to my long-lost Redhawk when you're down there. But just to be on the safe side..." He turned the knife in the dim light of the cabin. "Gotta cut the stomach. Gases from decomp fill it up like a balloon. Wouldn't want you popping up to greet the tourists as they crossed the channel."

He seized Jarsdel's hair and pressed the edge of the knife against his throat. The detective tried to fight, lifting his hands to grasp Pruitt's arm, but the other man just rapped his head against the wall until he stopped. Jarsdel began to fade from the world.

No, he thought. *It's isn't at all as I imagined. The feeling of ultimate rejection. Of being something contemptible, a stain to be scrubbed away.* What he felt was fury—deep and hot and hungry to fight.

"Well, I'm sorry about this." In a single swift motion, Pruitt swiped the blade along the side of Jarsdel's neck. The skin popped open, and blood began to flow. "Not deep enough," he said. "Gonna have to go a lot deeper if we wanna wrap this up. I think I actually might've hesitated a little. It's different from shooting. Just feels more personal. Leverage is funky too. Need a better angle. C'mere."

He wrapped his free hand around Jarsdel's tie and yanked, hard.

Pruitt was unprepared for the sudden absence of resistance. He'd allocated most of his upper body strength to pulling the detective from his sitting position—probably so he could more easily get to his neck. But like the man who picks up an empty suitcase he expects to be full, Pruitt was both surprised and confused. These emotions quickly gave way to alarm, however, as he lost his balance, shoes catching on the thick pile of the carpet. He caught himself, bracing an arm against a cabinet, and was already on the way back when Jarsdel drew his gun.

He shot from the hip, focusing all his remaining strength in the index finger of his right hand, snapping away at the trigger and sending as many rounds downrange as he could before the other man reached him.

The magazine was full—fifteen, plus one more in the chamber—and Jarsdel fired them all. Most of them missed. Pruitt was moving the whole time, and more than half the shots simply tore up the cabin, showering the room with sparks and wood chips and shards of plastic. But the rest found their mark. Pruitt's right knee vanished in a vermillion spray, and bullets slammed into his thigh, abdomen, and shoulder. The final round landed below his lip, knocking his jaw askew before taking most of the contents of his mouth and spraying them out the back of his head. His lifeless body collapsed onto the galley's small oval table.

In the soundlessness that followed, amid the smoke and the blood, Tully Jarsdel stared at Dell Pruitt's shattered form. And though the two bullets implanted in his own chest made it difficult, he offered the universe and anything that happened to be listening a wheezy, ragged laugh.

Pruitt's hand, frozen in death, still gripped Jarsdel's shitty clip-on tie.

PART III

SLOW FIRE

20

.

It was a strange thing to investigate your own murder.

An error on the first police report, completed by none other than Captain Ken Oria, stated that Jarsdel had been killed in the line of duty. Oria later explained he'd filled it out that way after an EMT loading the gravely wounded detective in the medevac helicopter had shouted, "We're losing him!" The captain's decision to prematurely report the death to Hollywood Station, along with Jarsdel's own subsequent—if brief—loss of sinus rhythm on the operating table, had compounded the mistake. After that, it had all taken on a life of its own, echoing from one agency to another and resulting in reams of paperwork marking the death of Marcus Tullius Jarsdel on July 8, 2021.

Jarsdel himself was initially unaware of his alleged passing, as it had been officially corrected by the time he regained consciousness sometime on the tenth. It was Morales who broke the news. He'd been sitting by Jarsdel's bedside and, having finished *Chain Saw Confidential*, was now on to *Awake in the Dark: The Best of Roger Ebert*.

"Told you there was gold," murmured Jarsdel.

Morales marked his place with the flap of the dust jacket, set the book down, and looked at him. "Gold?"

"Why else..." Jarsdel blinked, his eyes adjusting to the light. "Treasure?"

"Think you're still flyin' a little bit. How you feel?"

"Hmm."

"Yeah? Well, you look okay. 'Specially for a zombie."

"Zuh...zombie?"

Morales produced the previous day's edition of the *Times*. He pointed to an article below the fold.

"Glasses," said Jarsdel.

"I'll just read it. 'LAPD Detective Murdered.' That's the headline, then we got, 'Detective Marcus Jarsdel, of Hollywood Division's homicide table, has been killed in a deadly shootout that has rocked the peaceful seaside community of Avalon. The renowned investigator, known as the "Professor Detective" due to his previous life in academics, was conducting a joint investigation with the Sheriff's Department into the murder of Ellery Keating, a City of Orange philanthropist who was killed during a Fourth of July fireworks show.'

"He was a dedicated law enforcement officer," according to Lt. Bruce Gavin of Hollywood Station. "The department could've used a thousand more just like him. His untimely death is a tragedy for all Angelenos. And I've lost a friend."

"Stop," Jarsdel croaked. "Gonna throw up."

"Well," said Morales, "you'll be happy to know he's snapped out of it. They were gonna give you a posthumous Medal of Valor, but now that you're alive, Gavin convinced the chief to knock it down to the Police Medal of Heroism. Said it wasn't going above and beyond the call of duty to save your own life. Pretty good, huh?"

"Oscar. What about my parents? They know I'm okay?"

"You mean your dads? Yeah, don't worry. I got hold of them before some asshole told 'em you'd been killed. They only left, like, an hour ago. Went to Fred's for lunch, I think."

"I'm at Hollywood Pres?"

"Yeah. Think I'd be sitting here if you were in County? Not gonna deal with that kinda traffic."

Realization dawned. "So you know."

"Know what?"

"About my parents."

Morales cocked his head. "You mean, like, that you got two dads? Who cares? Dude. What d'you think this is, the mid-90s?"

"Yeah, but cops can be…"

Morales shook his head. "If anything, pretty much makes you untouchable. Who's ever gonna fire you? And I didn't even know you were half-Iranian. Half-Iranian with two gay dads? You'll be chief inside a decade." He laughed. "Oh, by the way. Thought you'd like to know we pulled the security footage from the quarantine room."

"Quarantine room?"

"At the Huntington. C'mon, man."

"Right, right. Of course."

"Yeah. Just wanted to see what we could see, especially since that Dr. Louro guy was being such a dick to you. Well, now we know why."

"Yeah?"

"Night of that big Memorial Day fundraiser. Dr. Louro and Lorraine Cinq-Mars. Both went down there for some full-contact collections management. Can't see much 'cause of the angle of the camera, but you got 'em coming through the door with his hand on her ass, then them leaving a few minutes later tucking in their clothes. Anyway, no wonder they didn't want us looking at the tape."

Jarsdel felt a stab of pain in his chest and groaned. Morales's demeanor changed, his jaw setting in the way it always did when he was angry. "Why'd that shitbag in Avalon try to kill you? What was the last thing you guys talked about?"

Jarsdel struggled to recall what had happened. Most of it was shrouded in fog. They'd been on the boat, Pruitt talking about his gun being stolen by the Natty Lads. And then Jarsdel had said something. Was it about the scuba gear? No—the rash.

He'd asked about the rash.

"Pruitt killed Dean Burken."

Morales smiled. "Okay, Dragonslayer. Let's hear it."

He was tired, but hearing Morales call him that gave him the energy he needed. "He pretends to be drunk on the evening of the twenty-fifth. Plenty of people saw his performance. Goes back to his boat, making sure to make as much noise as possible so everyone will remember. Soon as he's in the cabin...changes into a wetsuit, puts on his scuba gear, and gets in the water. Swims to some spot where he can get out unnoticed. Got a suitcase there waiting for him. Changes out of the wetsuit and into regular clothes. Packs all the gear into the suitcase, then grabs the ferry to Long Beach. Blends in with the rest of the tourists. Can you gimme some of that water?"

Morales got the cup off the nightstand, holding it for him so he could sip through the straw. When Jarsdel had enough, he gave a thumbs-up.

"How you know all this?" said Morales, replacing the cup.

"Couldn't have done it without you. You're the one read me that article in the *Catalina Islander*. Algae bloom that day. Some people get bad rashes. His was only around the edges of his face, exactly where the cowl of a wetsuit would stop. And he screwed up when he complained about the scuba rental place. Why would a guy who spearfishes all the time need to rent diving equipment? Because he left his on the mainland."

Morales nodded. "So when he got to Long Beach, then what?"

"Probably just took a cab to somewhere close to his house in Newport, paid cash, then once he was home, dumped all his stuff and drove to LA. Parked out of sight near Burken's house. Then he shot him."

"Why?"

"I don't know."

"Oh."

"I mean to say, he was looking for the diary. Ennis P. Smith's diary. But I don't know why. When it was just Keating I thought was involved, I assumed it was about a stash of gold somewhere."

"Right, Keating," said Morales. "What about all that stuff about the glass on her shoe?"

"She was there. After Pruitt couldn't find the diary, she must have driven over."

"Where's the murder weapon?"

"The .38? Bottom of the Catalina Channel. Pruitt reported it stolen just a couple days before the murder. Knew the Natty Lads would make convincing patsies, and that way he'd have a clean gun to work with. Anything went wrong, gun turned up somewhere, or even if the police did a search of gun owners, his would come up stolen."

Morales looked skeptical. "I still don't get it. This stuff fits, but no DA in their right mind would file charges. There's no proof. So why kill you?"

"The algae bloom. Once I was onto the rash, the circumstantial evidence would clinch it. CID would be able to find traces of the bloom on his scuba gear at his house on the mainland. He'd also of course have to explain how the gear even got there, considering he'd stated in front of witnesses that he hadn't left the island since his business trip. Remember that picture Oria took of him, the one with the sea bass hanging right there in Topsides, where he had on his monogrammed wetsuit? That was the twenty-fourth, just a day before the Burken murder. So again, how would that same wetsuit and all his customized equipment have made it to the mainland?"

Morales nodded at the cup of water. "You sound dry. Want some more?"

"Sure, thanks."

After Jarsdel rehydrated, Morales brought out his field interview book and skimmed his notes. "Okay, so let's move on to Keating. Pruitt killed her too, I guess? Used the musket ball to sic us on the Natty Lads?"

"Correct."

"How'd he do it? Couldn't be at Chimes Tower with a musket and standing on the deck of the Tuna Club at the same time."

"Simple."

"Don't say 'simple,' dude. You sound like an asshole."

"Sorry. I was thinking about it when I was on my way to talk to Pruitt. The distance, the wind, and that burgee in the way."

"The *what* in the way?"

"The yacht club flag. How unlikely it was that the shot had come from that far away. But what could the alternative be? After all, no GSR anywhere on the body, and a gun going off that close would've gotten everybody's attention. I was stuck, then I started thinking about that bruise on Keating's head. The one no one can seem to identify."

Morales grinned. "Really milkin' this shit right now."

"I'm trying to give you the foundation. The background. So you can see how I got there."

"Just spit it out."

"Remember the no-smoking rubber band? That little trick Oria was doing every time he got a craving? You mentioned you did it too, that night we were all drinking at Topsides. Can leave a mean welt, right? Now scale it up."

Morales blew out a gust of air. "Jesus. A slingshot? Telling me the murder weapon was a slingshot?"

"Slingbow, technically. Used it to catch flying fish off his boat. But yeah, a wrist rocket. Approximates the velocity of a handgun round. Eight hundred, even a thousand feet per second. More than enough power at close range."

"Ballsy move, doing it like that in front of everyone."

"Well, *behind* everyone, technically. They were watching the show, he sneaks up, and that's it. Made sure to load her up with barbiturates first, prevent her from moving suddenly or crying out if something went wrong. Run the labs on the bartender yet? I bet they'll come back the same."

"You'd be right about that," said Morales. "Kayla was loaded up good when she got thrown off that cliff. What was that whole thing about?"

Jarsdel's head began to throb, the scar above his right ear lighting up with hot, spasmodic life. He grimaced, closing his eyes.

"You all right?"

"Fine. What was the question?"

"Kayla."

"Right. Pruitt was the one who set us up that night. Told Kayla we weren't real cops. Knew she'd tell her boyfriend, who always had an inflated sense of his own importance. He was the only one in the world who'd believe cartel hitters would bother snuffing out his minuscule operation. Pruitt felt safer getting rid of Kayla, especially after you and I survived."

"You just got real pale," said Morales.

"Yeah. Maybe better rest."

"'Course." Morales got to his feet, then looked at his partner with something nearing affection. "Guy really did a number on you. That new scar on your neck, look kinda like Clint in *Hang 'Em High*."

"Hmm."

"Check us out, man. Both kinda messed up, huh?"

Jarsdel gave a noncommittal grunt.

"You thinkin' it's worth it?"

"What d'you mean, Oscar?"

"Actually," he said. "I don't know. Starting to sound like you." He headed for the door.

Jarsdel relaxed a little, thinking his partner had gone, when Morales spoke up again. "I still don't get it. All this over a book?"

"I'm barely here."

"What?"

"Never mind." Jarsdel exhaled. "Yeah. A book. Treasure book."

"Right, a treasure book," said Morales, his voice fading. "Let me know when you find it and we can retire."

Six weeks had passed since that day in the hospital. Now, on indefinite paid medical leave, Jarsdel spent most of his time searching for the reason four people were dead, three more faced charges for conspiracy and attempted murder, and he himself often felt as if he were drowning in the simple act of taking a breath.

He'd been shot with a .22. A beautiful grouping, from a marksmanship perspective. The first round had cleared the way, shattering his fourth rib just to the right of the sternum and lodging just outside the pleura. The second had perforated the lung, burrowing into the muscle a mere centimeter from his spine. The bullet had almost but not quite broken through the skin of his back, doming the skin like a blister. That one had been easy to remove—a simple incision and it was out. The other had required nearly eight hours of surgery to dig it free.

Morales had delivered everything related to the Burken case to Jarsdel's apartment at Park La Brea, and Jarsdel had transformed the den into the investigation's headquarters. Most of the time, he was on his own, but sometimes both detectives would pore over the documents together. In a few instances, Morales had even brought over a movie for them to watch when they were done. The first had been—of course—*Chinatown*.

The rest of his leave had been consumed with proving he was alive, a seemingly impossible process since there was no ultimate agency he had to convince. Instead, he had to address each incident on its own, submitting copies of his birth certificate, social security card, and passport. Ironically, most of his claims stalled when he couldn't produce a death certificate.

"You actually have to show us the death certificate so we can nullify it," said an official at the county clerk's office. "We obviously believe you that you're not deceased, but since none of this is based on an actual paperwork error, there's not a whole lot we can do." This left Jarsdel a latter-day Joseph K., listing from one drab, linoleum-tiled office to the next. He existed in a limbo of alto-sax hold music, online customer service chats, and stacks and stacks of forms. Researching the phenomenon, he was glad to learn he wasn't alone. The Uttar Pradesh Association of Dead People had been founded by a man in very similar circumstances, though his ordeal had lasted eighteen years. As there was no Los Angeles Association of Dead People, Jarsdel had been sorely tempted, more than once, to report the demise of Captain Ken Oria so he could have some company. He also thought it was only fair that Oria too could experience what it was like to live as a dead man.

Jarsdel checked the time—almost ten. Since Dad was finally well enough to be left on his own for a few hours, Baba had been freer to share his new skills as caregiver. He was supposed to come by soon with a load of groceries, and after that, he'd insist on vacuuming and doing the laundry. As it always did, his father's impending arrival filled Jarsdel with anxiety. If he didn't tidy up enough before the man arrived, he'd find himself on the receiving end of those chiding, thin-lipped glances Baba could be so generous with.

Shouldn't have given him a key card, Jarsdel thought. At least if his father still had to stop at the gate, he'd have a little more warning. He looked at the time again. That strident knock would come any second.

He hurried into the den, wondering why he'd waited till the last minute to clean up the Burken case materials, and began stacking papers and folders in neat but disorganized piles. He topped off the last tower of paperwork, already teetering, with the yellowed page from *The War of the Worlds* he'd found under Burken's rolltop. When the knock finally came, Jarsdel assumed a pose of artificial relaxation in his wingback chair. He picked up *This Was Hollywood* by Carla Valderrama, which Morales had given him to bolster his burgeoning film literacy. It was the best thing he'd read in years, and Jarsdel was forced to concede he might've sacrificed some real pleasure in his willful ignorance of cinema.

"Come in," he called.

Baba unlocked the door and came in carrying two bags from Whole Foods. Jarsdel began to stand, but his father flapped a hand at him. "Rest, rest." He headed straight to the kitchen and began to unpack. "Dad sends his love."

"How's he doing?"

"Not bad, not great. Wants you to come by when you're feeling up to it."

"I *am* feeling up to it. It's just an hour drive across town, not an Apollo mission."

"No, with the medication you're—"

"I'd Uber, Baba. It's really not that hard."

"We'll see."

Jarsdel rolled his eyes. Classic—Baba posed a problem, Jarsdel proposed a solution, and his father changed the subject.

After Baba finished with the groceries, he came into the den with two cups of tea and a dish of sugar cubes. The two men sucked on the cubes, filtering the hot tea through the pores. For a while, neither spoke, then Jarsdel decided it was finally time to clear the air.

"Baba."

"No."

"What do you mean, no?"

"No, as in I can tell you're about to say something serious or upsetting, and I'm not interested. Not today."

Under normal circumstances, Jarsdel would have followed his father's wishes. But he was frustrated by the lack of progress with Burken and Keating, and if he couldn't solve one riddle, the next in line would have to do.

"When I called you from Catalina, and I talked to you about Mrs. Rostami, you said some pretty intense things."

Baba crunched down on his sugar cube, then washed it back with a long sip of tea. He replaced the cup onto the saucer with enough force to chip the porcelain.

"Isn't it enough that I come to visit you and care for you, but now you—"

"Whoa, I *never* asked you to—"

"*Don't* interrupt me, Tully. That is one thing your adulthood does not grant you."

Jarsdel waited, but Baba had lost the thread of his complaint. They glared at each other for what seemed a very long time.

Finally, Jarsdel said, "Do you remember what my dissertation was on?"

Baba was taken aback. Apart from whatever he was concealing about his relationship to Mrs. Rostami, no subject was as loaded as his son's dead academic career. "Why're you bringing that up?"

"It was called 'Shock and Awe: Roman Art as a Tool of Colonial Expansion during the Early Principate.'"

Baba shrugged. "Okay, sure. I remember. Well-worn territory, but not totally exhausted."

"I spent a long time on that title, did you know that? Ran it by everyone I knew. Moved words around like Scrabble tiles, trying to get that perfect blend—originality and rigorousness of the research, generously seasoned with intellectual loftiness and scholarly disinterest to taste. September 20 to September 23, 2013."

"I don't follow."

"Those were the four days I obsessed about the title. The twentieth to the twenty-third, September 2013."

Baba regard him with naked confusion. "I'm mystified. What's this have to do with anything?"

"You asked me recently what the push was, what made me leave everything behind. It was those four days that changed everything. Exploded my world. I'm sitting there at my computer, and I finally get the title just right. Got the local news on, and they're talking about a homicide. A twelve-year-old girl had just been found in her uncle's crawl space. He'd kidnapped her, tortured her, and while he was sexually assaulting her, she started to hemorrhage. She bled to death, so he wrapped her up in a tarp and stuffed the body under the house."

Baba didn't say anything.

Jarsdel continued. "They'd just found her that day. Search-and-rescue dogs led the cops straight to the uncle's place. And then the news anchor says she was kidnapped on the twentieth. The twentieth to the twenty-third. Almost fell out of my chair. I thought about my life, and I thought about that girl, putting those two lives side by side over those last four days. What her experience had been and what mine had been. And I had to go into the bathroom and vomit."

Baba looked down at his hands and began kneading the flesh of his palm, as if trying to work out a cramp. He only did that when he was stalling for time. Jarsdel gave him the time. When he looked up, his eyes were like chips of ice. "Let me guess. You took her picture and put it over your desk and looked at it every day. And the picture was a gawky class portrait, and her innocent smile haunted you. Never would you forget this terrible crime, and eventually you made up your mind you could never be at peace until you'd fought for the side of goodness and justice."

"No," said Jarsdel. "There is no side of goodness and justice. How could there be? Where were they when that girl needed them?" He shook his head. "All I could think about was saving myself."

"I don't understand."

"I thought if I could become a policeman, I wouldn't feel so helpless. That maybe at least I could exist inside my own ordered construct. An enclave where the things I did mattered in a real physical sense. And then I wouldn't be so afraid. I wouldn't be so afraid of the void."

Baba worked the thumb of his right hand between the fingers of his left, massaging the pockets of skin with the sound of paper rubbing against paper. "The void," he said. "You believe there's any way out?"

"I really don't know, Baba." He put his hand over the spot where the bullets had plowed into him. "I've been looking."

His father nodded. "Yes. We're all looking. But I have you, Tully, and that helps."

"Helps?"

"Of course. Because there's no explanation for your courage. You didn't get it from me. You've probably guessed by now I was nowhere near that protest in Tehran, the one where they got Izad. How powerful it felt to stir my students' emotions, how gratifying to stoke the cause of righteousness. How impossibly frightening to follow through when it counted. That boy died in prison because of me."

The hardness in his eyes had melted away, and he looked at his son for the first time without anything between them. "I was born to talk. But not you. I gave the world a brave man." He mulled that over a moment, then said, "So perhaps I disagree with you. The side of goodness and justice does exist. But perhaps its defining characteristic is an ignorance of its own value."

He got up and strolled over to the papers and notebooks piled a few feet away. "Who was this one?"

Jarsdel, still reeling from his father's confession, was slow to comprehend. "What?"

Baba gestured at the casework.

"Oh. That's the curator-registrar I was telling you about. At the Huntington."

"I thought the case was closed. The same slimy bastard who shot you."

"Yes. But I still don't know why."

Baba noticed the page from *The War of the Worlds* in its plastic document folder. "May I?" Jarsdel nodded, and he picked it up, holding the paper to the light. "Looks old. Why's it here with the rest of these things?"

"It was next to the victim's wastebasket, right by his desk. I think he must've missed when he threw out the rest of pages. Figure the binding must have come apart or something."

"Why'd you save it?"

"We save just about everything."

Baba squinted. "'The storm burst upon us six years ago now. As Mars approached opposition, Lavelle of Java set the wires of the astronomical exchange palpitating with the amazing intelligence of a huge outbreak of incandescent gas upon the planet.' What is this?"

"Wells."

Baba replaced the folder and its meager contents atop the stack, the distaste plain on his features. "Science fiction," he said, as if he were passing sentence. "Wonderful this sort of thing survives when Melville's *The Isle of the Cross* crumbles to dust somewhere, lost to time."

"Wow, Baba."

His father smiled, then held out his arms. "Please."

Jarsdel stood and approached him. The two hadn't embraced in so long that Jarsdel expected the shape of Baba's body to feel unfamiliar against his own. But it didn't, not at all. They fit together just as easily as they always had.

"I love you, Tully. My gift to the world."

Jarsdel closed his eyes and willed the moment to last as long as it could. A man of forty feeling safe and at home in his father's arms. And it seemed also that the tighter they clung to each other, the more they let go. The accumulated weight of two lifetimes, dull and rust-caked, sharp-cornered and cold to the touch, peeled and fell away. He could feel it go.

Baba gave his shoulder a final squeeze of his hand, then stood back, wiping his eyes. Clearing his throat, he said, "I can't come tomorrow, but maybe the day after that." He turned to go.

Out of the corner of his eye, Jarsdel noticed the yellowed page from *The War of the Worlds*.

Slow fire, he thought, then cocked his head, as if listening for a faint voice.

"All right. See you, Tully," said Baba, opening the front door.

Crumbles to dust. This survives, but Melville crumbles to dust.

"Tully?"

Jarsdel smiled and looked at his father. "You're a genius."

Baba returned the smile. "You're just realizing this now?"

Dr. Ezra Louro watched as Jarsdel worked his way down the chromed wire shelving, index finger sweeping past the spines of the quarantined books as he scanned their titles.

"Do I get to know what you're looking for?" Louro asked.

Jarsdel glimpsed the word *war* and paused. No, *War and Peace*. A fine book, but not the one he wanted. He continued.

"Detective?"

"We watched the security footage, Dr. Louro." He glanced at the man to make sure his words landed. They did. Jarsdel went back to reading the spines. "Despite your assertion that it would be a waste of time."

"It was a slip in judgment."

"Probably. Should always wear masks and gloves in here, right? Basic protocol."

"There was alcohol involved and...you know, Lorraine, she..." He sighed, beaten. "Are you going to tell the board?" This was a moment he'd clearly been dreading, and now it was here.

Jarsdel's index finger came to a stop. *The War of the Worlds* by H. G. Wells. "Not unless your hermetically sealed tryst in some way resulted in the shooting death of Dean Burken. Which I don't think it did." He removed the book from the shelf, opened the cover, then quickly closed it again. "This is evidence. I'm taking it with me."

"You can't."

"Of course I can."

"No, I mean you literally can't. It hasn't been cleared."

Jarsdel, aching to lecture Louro on the misuse of "literally," instead began to head for the exit. "Call security," he said, waving at the camera as he passed beneath it. "They've got me dead to rights."

"You gonna tell me what the big deal is? I'm supposed to cook tonight." Morales checked the time on his phone. "You've got me for, like, thirty minutes, then I gotta run."

Jarsdel, who'd planned on enjoying this moment as much as possible, refused to be rushed. On the empty seat beside him—out of his partner's line of sight—lay the two props in his upcoming reveal. He brought out the first, the envelope containing the yellowed page, and pushed it across the breakfast table. Morales barely gave it a glance.

"So?"

"The first edition of *The War of the Worlds* was published in the UK in 1898. This is from an early U.S. edition, dime a dozen. Still old, though, 1901."

"Mind blown, dude."

"Look at the condition that page is in."

"Okay, it's yellow."

"Exactly. Slow fire." Now he brought out the second item, the book he'd retrieved from quarantine. "This is the actual book it came from. Don't open it yet. I'm gonna put them side by side. Notice a difference?"

"I don't wanna do the whole 'notice a difference' thing."

"Humor me," said Jarsdel. "I've so few pleasures these days."

Morales gave a heavy sigh, but he acquiesced, looking from the book to the page, then back again. "The edges." He looked up. "It's the edges, right?"

"Right. Look how clean the sheet is, then compare it to the ragged, crumbling edges of the pages in the book. This book"—he patted the cover—"is in bad shape. This page"—he pointed—"has nice, straight edges. Could've been cut yesterday, if not for the yellowed paper. And yet it's from the same book."

"You're sure?"

"Oh yes. You see, when we first found this in Burken's house, I assumed the binding had come apart on an old book of his, and he'd thrown away the pages. But that's not what happened. Look at the—"

"The size. It's way smaller."

Jarsdel smiled. "There you go. Isn't that more rewarding than if I just told you?"

"For sure. Wow, thanks for thinking of me. I'm confused, though. He took out this single page and cut the rough edges off?"

"No, but you're getting warmer. I'll give you a hint: the rest of that page is still in the book."

Morales thought about that for a long moment, then understanding lit up his features. "That fucker hollowed out the book, didn't he?"

"Open it."

Morales did. At least two-thirds of the pages had been carefully cut out at the inner margins, creating a cavity deep enough to hide a small object. In this case, that object was a compact, leather-bound volume tied with a cord.

It was the diary of Ennis P. Smith.

"Some old books were sewn, not glued, so the text was aligned center and the font kept relatively small. The outer margins were kept large so the bookbinder had plenty of room to work, also to protect the text from rats nibbling at the sides of the pages. That's why I thought the page we were looking at was intact. It wasn't until I thought about—"

Morales held up his hand. "Dude. Have you read this yet?"

"No, I was waiting for you."

"So you think we're gonna find a treasure map in this, huh?"

Jarsdel grinned. "Possible."

"How're we gonna do this? No offense, but I don't wanna cuddle up side by side over this little thing."

"You go first. I'm gonna pour myself some wine. Want some?"

"Long as you don't go on about its nose or its ears or whatever wine people talk about."

"Agreed." He got up and went into the kitchen, where he took a bottle of Mer Soleil from the waist-high wine cabinet. As he uncorked and decanted it, Morales untied the diary and began to read.

Jarsdel got down two Burgundy wineglasses and poured generously into each. He brought one over to Morales, who took a perfunctory sip and resumed reading. Jarsdel went back to the counter and picked up his own, cradling the bowl in the palm of his hand, letting the heat volatilize the aroma compounds. He swirled the wine for half a minute, then took a slow, pleasurable sip.

Delicious. He looked over at Morales to see if he was enjoying it as well, but his partner was absorbed in the diary. Jarsdel almost asked what he'd discovered, but the focused intensity on the man's face persuaded him to wait. He went into the living room, retrieved his copy of *This Was Hollywood* from the seat of his wingback chair, then sat across from Morales.

The two men read their books, the level of wine staying the same in Morales's glass but emptying—and refilling—in Jarsdel's. Twenty minutes passed, then thirty. After he finished his second full glass of wine, he glanced up to check on Morales.

To his surprise, his partner had already finished. The diary was closed, pushed back toward the center of the table. Morales sat with his hands clasped together; his eyes were strange and unfocused, staring out at nothing.

"Well?" said Jarsdel. "How much is it worth?"

Morales didn't answer, but his eyes cleared somewhat. He looked at Jarsdel as if coming out of a dream. "What?"

"The treasure."

His partner got to his feet. "Gotta go, man."

"Hey. What's going on? Don't you want your wine?"

Morales moved toward the door.

"Hey," Jarsdel repeated, standing up. "What's wrong? C'mon, we gonna be rich? What's it worth?"

Morales opened the door. He turned, and the look on his face stopped Jarsdel cold. "Worth? About three-quarters of a billion dollars."

He left without another word. Jarsdel closed the door and went back to the kitchen table. He picked up the book, turning it over in his hands. Three-quarters of a billion dollars? That seemed highly unlikely. Only a handful of strikes approached anything like that, and they took years to excavate and were major news. And why had Morales looked the way he had?

Annoyed that his evening had taken such an unexpected and unwelcome turn, he turned to the first page.

Smith's journal was an account of a growing dispute between a white settlement and a Tongva village near what would later become Newport Beach. After some cattle had gone missing, Smith and his men had organized a party and run down half a dozen Indians who'd been tending their crops. The massacre had been just one of hundreds of pedagogic murders committed in California during early statehood and part of the much larger, organized genocide. Settlers drove Indians to starvation, and when they stole food to survive, a few would be killed to "educate" the others not to steal.

According to Smith, the nearby Tongva were led by a chief called Huunut. But since whites had trouble pronouncing his name, they'd given him a new one—King Henry. As Smith explained, however, "If the Indian we call Henry is flattered by his royal title, he ranks among the world's great idiots. Being aware of his claim as sovereign over the land and its people to be equal to that of, as he put it, 'your great king in Washington,' we determined it might provide us some amusement if we encouraged the savage's lofty comparison. After a vote, we happily obliged him with the title and, just as the people of Paris crowned the delighted Quasimodo their Pope of Fools, so too did we honor Henry with his equally meaningful designation."

The killing of Henry's men had caused alarm among the settlers, who feared a retaliatory attack. They enlisted the help of John Pruitt, an agent with the Bureau of Indian Affairs, to act as intermediary. Pruitt had agreed and gathered the settlement's men together to confront Henry and offer terms.

Jarsdel turned to the final entry, dated May 15, 1854.

Dawn has broken, and my pen is my proof that I survived the night. I'm very tired, but I dare not rest until I put my account to paper, lest the mists of time and the natural fatiguing of memory conspire to rob posterity.

As we drew closer to the camp, Pruitt had us stop while he went up ahead. He called out as he approached, and I was surprised at the facility with which he spoke the Indian tongue. We saw movement, some stirrings at the entrances to the huts, as some of the savages emerged. A few of the men were armed, but I could see by the confused expressions on their faces that they had no advance knowledge of our visit.

The men formed a kind of delegation, moving toward where Pruitt had halted. Even from our location, shrouded in the darkness of the tree line, it was easy to pick Henry out from the rest. He was as tall as Pruitt had described him and looked even taller when wading among his stunted peoples.

Henry came forward without any sign of fear or caution, staring down the man on the horse as if no weapon on earth could harm him. The two men exchanged words, but even if distance had not muted their conversation, I still wouldn't have known what was said. Henry appeared pleased and gestured for the other to dismount and follow him into camp.

That was when the true purpose of our expedition was made clear and petty fiction dispensed with. I realized then that Pruitt had softened the details of his scheme, suspecting perhaps rightly that some might hesitate in committing to such a course. But now that we were all there, armed and ready, the leader of our expedition revealed his intention. Because instead of negotiating with the Indian, Pruitt drew his revolver and fired into Henry's back. And though no signal had been prearranged, the shot acted as a command to the rest of us. We charged, united in a single unspoken cause.

A great cry had gone up among the Indians at the

death of their leader, but the grief became panic at
the sudden appearance of horses and men and weapons.
We poured into the camp, matching the yelps and yowls
of the Indians with triumphal shouts. We stove in the
huts by hoof and by sword, but their appearance belied
their sturdiness, and we quickly turned to the torch.
Indians endeavoring to escape our onslaught by remaining in their hovels quickly found themselves most
anxious to depart. We did our best to prevent this,
beating them back into the flames and shooting the
runners. An elderly Digger, perhaps once a fearsome
warrior in his own right, decided it would be better
to die a hero's death and came at our lines with a
hatchet. Golden Bill happily obliged him, sending the
old Indian to his Happy Hunting Ground with a sword
thrust to the neck.

The killing continued without discrimination toward
age or sex. I myself put a bullet through the head of
a squaw who'd unadvisedly rushed up beside my horse
to plead mercy. When I saw that the small bundle she'd
been carrying was one of their papooses, I fired
another shot, providing such mercy as I could give.

Many of the Indians survived the initial attack,
but we pursued the rest into the fields and picked off
those who tried hiding in the nearby stream. The next
several hours, up until perhaps three in the morning,
were occupied with gathering up the dead in the center
of the small village, where Pruitt had converted the
largest of the burning huts into a makeshift funeral
pyre. We'd hauled a dozen onto the flames when Houston
Yates, just returning from one of the chases, let out
a terrible squall.

"Damned fools! Would you throw coin into the fire
too?"

He reminded us that our young state had recently passed a bounty of twenty-five cents for each Indian scalp and proceeded to demonstrate the best way to remove them. To a man, we set about the grisly work, stripping the heads clean and only then consigning the bodies to the inferno. It's true that not all had fully perished as we undertook this task, but if the scalping didn't finish them, the fire surely did.

All in all, I'd estimate we succeeded in stamping out at least a hundred fifty savages this morning, with not one of our number felling to an Indian weapon. Could there be better evidence of the righteousness of our cause?

I noted that John Pruitt did not shirk his duty, even in his elevated station as Indian Agent, but put in as much sweat as the rest of us. He took special care to ensure the death of King Henry, taking the scalp himself before helping swing the body atop its charring brethren.

His dedication to our efforts puzzled me, as he was an outsider with no immediate stake in the welfare of the settlement. When the moment was right, and there was a reprieve in our labor, I took him aside.

"Sir," I said, "this was a good and important deed, and I don't regret my part in it, but neither my father nor mother raised a fool. What's your interest in leading this charge?"

He attempted to evade the question, making reference to Manifest Destiny and our inevitable triumph over the Red Man. But I could see he hadn't expected my forthrightness. I pressed him again, and finally he capitulated. It had been critical, he said, to first protect King Henry's land from seizure by the state. If we carried out our business without securing title to the place, the government of California might lay claim to those thousands of acres upon which we then stood. He had accomplished this, he said, by acting as Henry's representative in a transaction with the federal government. The terms of the treaty were simple. The lands of Henry's people would remain theirs in perpetuity, protected from any and all encroachment, so long as a single member of his band lived.

I nodded, beginning to understand. "I suppose, then, there's some artful legal wording that transfers custodianship, should this batch of Diggers cease to exist?"

Pruitt was surprised at the celerity of my acumen and even offered me a little smile. Yes, he confirmed, such a codicil had been included. It stated that upon the unlikely event of their total demise, the Indians' land would be made available for purchase to qualified private parties. He lowered his voice to hardly more than a whisper. Anticipating the outcome of our excursion, he had already initiated the process of purchase. Should I be discreet, he'd be willing to offer me a portion of the lands at the same price he had paid.

I pretended to hesitate, so as not to appear overeager, and he mistook my shilly-shallying as misplaced sympathy for the dead. He reminded me that the Indian's time had passed and that if we had not seized the opportunity to relieve them of life and land, another white man would surely have done so. Our conversation continued at some length, and we settled on the terms with a handshake. I added a final point then, but it was such a small and inoffensive matter that he quickly agreed. It seems I now have the honor of striking the first official map of the region.

And while history will doubtless forget the personage of King Henry himself, I've decided to memorialize both the man and his vanishing race with a fitting designation. Thinking of the haughtiness with which he faced his death this morning, I hereby dub this portion of earth, "King Henry's Pride."

Jarsdel closed the diary.

Morales had been right. Three-quarters of a billion dollars, at the very least. If it came out that Dell Pruitt's family lands had come to him through a massacre, the development would have died. The public outcry alone would have done it, even if no related Indian tribes remained to cause Pruitt legal trouble.

He could imagine how it must have started. Dean Burken flipped through the diary when it arrived with the rest of the estate's items. He would've noticed the name Pruitt, and it would've been easy to confirm it was the same family by comparing Ennis Smith's map of Newport Beach—and King Henry's Pride—with the land currently owned by Pruitt Equities.

Knowing he was on his way out due to the harassment allegations and doubtlessly familiar with her approval of Pruitt's massive development deal, he'd approached Keating with his blackmail scheme. He'd squeeze them for all he could. If not, he'd reveal the diary and sink them both. In a panic, Keating had called Pruitt and told him the situation. After all, on top of a hundred fifty murders, one more must have seemed a reasonable price to pay.

But the diary hadn't been at Burken's house. Neither Pruitt nor Keating had been able to find it.

Okay, but why did Keating have to go?

Jarsdel didn't know for sure, but he could think of at least two reasons. One, she was simply a loose end. She knew Pruitt had committed murder, and that made him nervous. But there was also the possibility, in Pruitt's mind, that Keating actually *had* found the diary and might be planning her own blackmail to get a heftier return on her investment. Better all around for her to stop breathing.

Jarsdel replaced Smith's journal inside *The War of the Worlds*. It felt better that way, out of sight. Tomorrow he'd return it to the Huntington, this time to Margaret Rishkov. She'd make sure it got the rollout it deserved.

Steeped in blood. Where the thought came from, he didn't know. It didn't even seem to belong to him, to be his own. And yet how it pounded and echoed.

The soil, so steeped in blood.

EPILOGUE

Yaldā Night

S hab-e Yalda, the longest and darkest night of the year, when
the veil between the realms of good and evil is at its thinnest
and the forces of Ahriman—the master of illusion, falsehood,
and destruction—are at their greatest. You don't go to sleep on
Shab-e Yalda, lest you make yourself vulnerable to the malevolent
entities lurking at the periphery of our world. Instead, you gather
your friends and family together in solidarity, harvesting love and
warmth to beat back the terrors of the night, passing the hours by
reading Hafez and telling stories around heaps of pomegranates,
nuts, and watermelon. For many Persians, especially Zoroastrians,
the longest and darkest night of the year is one of purest joy.

Tully Jarsdel would have spent December 21 alone, just as he
had every December 21 since he'd joined the LAPD. But not this
year. Baba, encouraged by Nourangiz Rostami, had decided upon
a return to tradition. The Jarsdel household was once again alight
with candles, the air heady with the odors of saffron, jasmine, and
roses.

It was almost midnight, the food well eaten—encrusted plates
and cups of tea resting among gutted tureens of pudding and

platters of fruit. Mrs. Rostami sat on the couch, chatting with Dad, while Baba opened a fresh bottle of wine in the kitchen. Jarsdel leaned against the countertop, sipping at a glass of pinot. He and Rostami had been the only wine drinkers until about ten, when Dad and Baba had finally caved.

"So does she buy it?" said Jarsdel.

Baba knew what he meant. The cover story, explaining the two men living together in the grand Pasadena craftsman. Because his sister Tahmina wasn't feeling well enough to join them, Baba had originally suggested that Dad was going to pose as his nonexistent brother-in-law. But he quickly dismissed the idea. It would be far too easy to bungle such an elaborate and fragile deception. Besides, it felt dishonest. So with Dad's amused permission, he'd ultimately gone with the creakiest, most shopworn fiction of them all—roommates.

"No," said Baba. "But I think she's more progressive than she gives herself credit for. She was a little stiff about it at first, but look how relaxed she is now."

Jarsdel thought so too. Rostami looked radiantly happy.

He got down to his last sip of wine. "How's that bottle coming?"

"Cork broke in half."

"Let me." Jarsdel stepped in and finished uncorking. He wiped the cork dust off the rim of the bottle and gave both himself and his father a fresh pour.

"Last one," Baba promised. "And if your Dad asks for another, tell him we're out. He's still not supposed to have any of this. Don't know what I was thinking."

Laughter from the living room. Baba glanced over at his husband and Rostami, his expression inscrutable as usual.

Jarsdel put his hand on the man's arm. "You all right?"

"Fine. You read beautifully tonight. The Hafez. I don't know how you do it, with so little opportunity to speak Persian. Even have this weird Kerman Province accent. How do you have that?"

Jarsdel smiled. "I don't know."

"My father was from Kerman, so I know it well, but I don't have it. Why do you have it? Very strange. Just this way you have of pronouncing certain sounds. Mostly your *a*'s." He paused, considering. "I've decided I'm not going to tell her."

The change in subject was swift and caught Jarsdel off guard. "You're not?"

Baba shook his head. "I can't. It would be the most selfish thing I've ever done. Next to the first thing, I mean. My..." He took a breath, exhaled, gathered himself. "Anyway. It would be selfish. Knock down what little she has left to get her through her memories of that awful time. Me, this idea she has of me. If I take that away. If I take *that* too, then..."

Then her son died for nothing, Jarsdel thought. *But he* did *die for nothing.*

God, this soil, this earth, so steeped in blood.

For absolutely nothing.

Yes, but she didn't know that. Did she need to know? Would it balance some forgotten scale somewhere? Satisfy some obscure divine whim?

Jarsdel checked the time. Past midnight. Now the days would begin getting longer. For a while anyway. Then they'd get shorter again, the evenings creeping up earlier and earlier, slipping their chill into the afternoons and dimming the light.

Until the next longest, darkest night of the year.

WHAT WAITS FOR YOU

1

Tully Jarsdel hated the arm-wrestling table. Loathed, despised, and detested it. And not just because he'd already barked a shin on one of the 14-gauge steel legs, but because it sat right in the center of the break room, turning what had been a generally peaceful place to eat lunch into an aural hell of shouts, grunts, and whoops.

It was a squat thing, the size of a card table. A custom logo— stressed red typeface against a background of fractured concrete— read "Eat. Sleep. PULL," and in smaller print, "Hollywood Station Patrol." At each end was bolted a vinyl elbow rest and a knurled handle. The combatant would plant his arm on the rest, seize the handle with his free hand, and—making as much noise as possible—try wrenching his opponent's limb to one of the touch pads.

Will Haarmann, a patrol officer with rippling forearms and a flat, blandly handsome face, had brought the table in one day, and no one had objected. On the contrary, Lieutenant Gavin was the first to throw his support behind the idea. Maybe if there was enough interest, he announced at roll, Hollywood Division could put on a local championship and open it up to the public. It was just the sort of thing that could take off, become an annual event, even spread department-wide. Just imagine—the LAPD Arm-Wrestling Open, followed by a community-outreach barbecue. A spirited fund-raiser for the families of fallen officers. Over which he would of course preside.

But more importantly, according to the lieutenant, arm wrestling in the break room would foster a spirit of healthy competition and spur a boost in morale. Even Gavin, who put little stock in recent departmental trends like resilience training, sensitivity seminars, and whatever the chief meant by "organizational climate," recognized the importance of morale.

And morale at Hollywood Station was very low indeed.

After the third murder, Angelenos began repainting their houses. Bill and Joanne Lauterbach, the Rustads, and the Santiagos had all lived in white homes. Practically overnight, every professional painting company in Southern California—along with a robust showing of Craigslist amateurs—were booked two months out. Before long, anyone who could haul a ladder and a can of paint was desperately throwing color onto their walls. That lasted until July, when the killer hit the Verheugens in Eagle Rock. The Verheugens' house was blue. You could almost hear him saying—

Nope, not gonna be that easy to figure out.

Half a year had passed since he'd come to Los Angeles. That was the assumption, anyway—that he'd arrived from somewhere else. The idea that he'd emerged from among the city's own ranks was unpalatable. Even by the rock-bottom standards of Hollywood sensationalism, this guy was bad for business. The crimes were too foul, the victims too sympathetic. No, he must be an outsider. Better yet, a foreigner. Still better, a demon.

But in many ways the murders had only been the beginning. Whether it was a run of bad luck or divine retribution for the city's collective sins, no one knew. The only thing all could agree on was that what once had been home was now somehow alien, as if it were now subject to the logic of dreams. As if anything could happen.

———

There'd been an earthquake just before the Lauterbach murders—a fearsome shaker that ran for a dozen seconds, darkening the southland from Castaic to Mission Viejo. An aftershock tipped the Richter scale to 6.4; some living near the epicenter in Lancaster said it was like "a shout coming from the earth"—a furious, accusatory blast. Others compared it to the roar of a lion. One woman said it sounded like a word: *YOU*.

Following the discovery of the Lauterbachs, the Santa Ana winds—as if summoned by the fear and misery already beginning to settle on the city like a cowl—came sweeping in from the desert. They didn't come alone. Pathogenic fungi, freed from the soil by the quake, were borne aloft by the hot gusts, and thousands soon came down with valley fever. For most, the infection presented merely as a nuisance—a cough, headache, and rash. Others experienced a sickness more at home in medieval Europe than modern-day SoCal. Joint pain, meningitis, weeping abscesses, and lesions in the skull itself. By the time death came to those so afflicted, it was welcomed.

On the heels of the outbreak came the second murder, the one that would earn the killer his name. Like the Lauterbachs, the Rustads were a couple living alone, albeit two decades younger. Maja Rustad crafted art pieces from found objects and sold them online. Her husband, Steffen, had been in a New Wave band in Norway and found a niche teaching guitar to the kids of his Gen Xer fans out in LA.

The crime scene was in Highland Park, putting it in LAPD's Northeast Area and therefore under the jurisdiction of Central Bureau. Detectives Darla Mailander and Tom Claraty were dispatched from the Sixth Street headquarters. The extent of the carnage and antemortem brutality told them they were probably dealing with the same killer who'd struck in Los Feliz, but it wasn't until they checked the crawl space beneath the house that they knew for certain.

Mailander and Claraty wanted to hold back as much as they could from the press, but conceded to their captain that there was one detail in particular the citizens of Los Angeles needed to know.

A press conference was held the following day, and even the

hardest of the hardened crime reporters grew unusually quiet when Captain Cheng outlined the killer's modus operandi. Heather Malins of the *LA Weekly* later said it was during that conference that she devised the nickname, mostly because of the way her skin had popped with gooseflesh as the captain spoke...

The Eastside Creeper.

It was as close to perfect as such things went, and everyone thought so. Even the *Times*, which was usually first in dubbing the city's predators, thought Malins had captured the essence of the shadowy thing lurking among them. Not only did it describe the visceral reaction, the revulsion and terror people experienced when learning of his crimes, but it suggested the slyness of a crawling, climbing vine. By the time you noticed it, it was already coiled tightly in place.

The back row of chairs in the Hollywood Station conference room was empty, and Jarsdel picked the seat closest to the door so he could leave once it was over. A few turned their heads when he came in, regarded him with disinterest, and went back to chatting or checking emails. Just one offered him a smile—Kay Barnhardt, the only other detective in the department who'd been promoted straight from patrol to HH2, the new Hollywood Homicide.

What had originally been conceived as a stop-gap measure to address rising crime stats in West Bureau was now an established—if not wholly respected—investigative branch of the police force. The brainchild of Deputy Chief Cynthia Comsky, HH2 had seen a rocky start. Those who'd labored for years to make detective watched with gut-punched amazement as Jarsdel and Barnhardt swept past them. Virtually all the rank and file at Hollywood Station harbored some degree of resentment toward the rookie whiz kids. Even their own newly assigned partners, homicide veterans Oscar Morales and Abe Rutenberg, made no effort to hide their disgust at command's decision. Earning their respect, grudging as it was, had taken a very long time. Jarsdel nearly had to die at the hands of a murder suspect to convince Morales he wasn't just playing at being a cop.

Barnhardt stood and made her way along her row, excusing herself and pretending not to hear the annoyed sighs from those who had to move their feet. She was perhaps forty, though some long-ago sun damage had given her premature wrinkles and made her look a decade older. She had on wire-rimmed glasses, just as Jarsdel did, and kept her thick brown hair in a regulation ponytail. The sober gray suit she'd dressed in that day did her no favors—baggy in the arms and legs, but pulled taut across her oversized bosom. Jarsdel imagined her figure presented more than a few difficulties in a career like law enforcement. Female cops learned to deal with obscene commentary from criminals, but Barnhardt had had to endure the same from her own colleagues. At least two officers so far had been formally reprimanded for making double entendres in her presence.

"Hey," she said, sitting down.

"Hey."

"You're all by yourself. Mind if I join?"

"Please." Jarsdel liked Barnhardt. She'd been a clinical psychologist before she joined the force, and Jarsdel had tracked down a few of her published articles. One, on the pathology of vexatious litigants, impressed him with its originality and stringent scholarship. She was a good thinker, methodical and more than a little relentless. Suspects entered her interview room with the typically flat, steely affect of the career criminal, and often emerged broken, blubbering, and handcuffed.

"Where's your partner?" Barnhardt asked.

"Flu."

"Didn't he get his shot?"

"Yup. Got sick anyway. Isn't happy. What do you know about this?" Jarsdel gestured toward the front of the room, where a woman he hadn't seen before shuffled through some papers at a lectern. She was petite and attractive, with dark skin and East Indian features, her glossy black hair pulled back in a bun.

"Not a whole lot. But I do know *her*," said Barnhardt. "She's famous."

"Famous?"

"In my field, anyway. She's a behaviorist, teaches all over. President of the Pavlovian Society. Specializes in operant conditioning."

"Ah."

"You know what that is?"

He didn't. "I think so. Refresh my memory."

"You know, application of reward and punishment. There was some controversy a few years back about her methods, though no one could deny they worked. Measurably reduced violence in two prisons, while those in the control group stayed the same."

Jarsdel looked again at their guest speaker. Her most noticeable feature was her lips, which she'd painted a vibrant red. It seemed a strange choice, one that conflicted with her conservative charcoal skirt and blazer, but Jarsdel guessed it was some technique of covert influence. He grunted, wondering what the city had forked over for the benefits of her expertise.

"What's funny?"

"Bit pop psych, isn't it? Just seems like a bunch of woo-woo the department's throwing our way to make themselves feel better. We don't need a behaviorist. We need a thousand new sworn officers."

Barnhardt shrugged. "It's not all just theory. She's pretty brilliant. Designs security systems for missile silos."

Lieutenant Gavin entered and hurried past them to the front of the room. He'd undergone a transformation since Jarsdel's first year in HH2. Then, Gavin had been a surly, myopic blowhard, a candidate for central casting's no-nonsense police commander—if absent the wit and charisma such a role usually required. But at some point he'd gotten hold of Bill Bryson's *A Short History of Nearly Everything*, and now—unbelievably—Gavin seemed to consider himself an intellectual, even something of an amateur scientist. He kept spare copies of the book in his office, doling them out with sage authority to those he favored.

Most surprisingly, he'd taken down a photograph of himself posed with the governor, hanging in its place a framed eight-by-ten glossy of Max Planck. The bald, mustachioed physicist gazed morosely back at Gavin's puzzled visitors, most of whom assumed it was a picture of his great-grandfather. Anyone unfortunate enough to inquire was given a sour, disapproving look. "That's Max *Planck*," Gavin would say, and proceed with an error-riddled précis of energy quanta and blackbody radiation. The routine culminated with Planck's winning the Nobel Prize, an honor the lieutenant pronounced as the "noble" prize.

Whereas before Gavin had been obnoxious but predictable, he'd now entered the realm of insufferable pedantry, and he was growing bolder by the day. Physics textbooks—always conspicuously placed—had begun appearing in his office, along with grade-school science paraphernalia like Newton's cradles and Rubik's cubes. A NASA bumper sticker showed up on the break-room fridge one day:

JUST WHAT PART OF
$GxmxM/R=mxVesc2/2$
DON'T YOU UNDERSTAND?
IT'S ONLY ROCKET SCIENCE

The whole business infuriated Jarsdel because, for one, the man hadn't earned his pretensions. He was the worst sort of imposter, surrounding himself with the trappings of a culture that wasn't his own, as if those books and the bumper sticker and that ridiculous picture of Planck could compensate for what was plainly an average brain.

And he was getting away with it.

Jarsdel had picked up the first few murmurings, things like, "Gavin's no fool," or "Guy must be pretty smart." The most irritating had come from an attractive patrol officer who, upon leaving Gavin's office after a meeting, remarked, "Wow, did you see what he was reading? I didn't even understand the *title*." It wasn't so much her words but the awed delivery that made it sting.

Gavin shook hands with their guest speaker, then edged her out of the way. He spoke into a mic clamped to the side of the lectern. "Okay, folks—hey." Gavin flicked the mic with his finger, sending a percussive bolt through the speakers. Conversation quieted down. A few officers winced and rubbed their ears.

"Okay," Gavin repeated. "Thanks. Okay. We're gonna get started. As you know, we have a special presenter today, right? But what you may not know is that our presenter is Dr. Alisha Varma, president of the Pavlov Society. These are people who do all kinds of very complex, very deep research on pressing scientific concerns related to behavior. You know who Pavlov was?"

No, thought Jarsdel. *He's not really going to—*

"Ivan Pavlov was a doctor who discovered he could condition his dogs to salivate by ringing a bell. That's because every time he was about to feed them, he rang that bell, so even when he wasn't about to feed them and rang the bell anyway, the dogs still got excited. That's called *conditioning*. And that's what Dr. Varma does." He pointed at her without taking his eyes off the audience, as if challenging anyone to contradict him. A silence followed. Varma endured it with a frozen smile, reminding Jarsdel of a bride weathering a speech by the drunken best man.

"So that's what's going on," Gavin said with a nod. "Your department's provided you with the top, absolute top in her field. I expect your full attention, obviously. And your cooperation with anything Dr. Varma wants to move ahead with. Okay. Let's give her a round of applause."

Gavin backed away, clapping his hands, and waved at Varma to step forward. She adjusted the mic, glanced down at her notes, and looked out over the audience.

"Good morning." Jarsdel realized he'd been expecting the accent of a Maharashtrian Brahmin—the dusky, mellifluous, vaguely erotic offspring of the British raj and Indian aristocracy. Instead, he got the flat, CNN-standard timbre of Grosse Pointe, Michigan.

There were a few mumbled replies from her audience. Varma smiled at the anemic reception. "And that's about what I expected," she said. "I get much the same at every department I speak at. A few months ago I gave a seminar to An Garda Síochána cadets in Dublin, and I'm not embarrassed to say the ones that weren't asleep were playing *Jewel Quest* on their phones. At first, anyway. And I'll tell you something else. You don't need me."

A few heads that'd been bowed toward handheld screens glanced up, mildly curious. Most consultants didn't start off by asserting their own uselessness.

"What's going on in your city right now is painful. And as is the case with any painful experience, you can't conceive the end of it. It's especially upsetting considering last year marked nearly two decades of consecutive annual *drops* in homicide, down to 238—or 4.3 per 100,000. That's a record low. But since January you've already topped 250 homicides, with six months left to go before they hit the reset button on stats. If the trend continues, you're looking at numbers you haven't seen since '81. But I'm telling you right now, it's unlikely my ideas are going to be of any help at all."

Jarsdel scanned the room. Nearly everyone now had their attention on Dr. Varma.

"I say that because, mathematically speaking, Los Angeles has been following in step with the global decline in violent crime. These last few months, then, have been anomalous—a freak drift toward lawlessness spurred on by a cocktail of factors. Now we can speculate on what those factors may be and try to address them piecemeal, but we may never know exactly how it happened and, really, it's not even that important. What's important is recognizing what's happened as an anomaly, meaning that regardless of anything you or I do, odds are your numbers are going to stabilize, then return to an approximation of their previous downward trend.

Any system, whether it be simple or complex, tends to regress to its mean level of performance after an extraordinary event.

"Let's say the situation was flipped, and you'd only had—say—*ten* homicides so far this year, and instead of me standing in front of you, it's the chief of police. And he's telling you what a great job you've done. Now would you think it actually had anything to do with you? Probably not. And you'd probably be very skeptical such a pattern would continue. Complex systems generally don't change overnight, not for the better and not for the worse. In other words, things are going to get back to normal with or without my help."

Gavin looked uneasy. This didn't appear to be part of the script. His arm twitched, as if he wanted to raise his hand to ask a question, then stilled.

Varma shrugged. "Then again, history provides us with countless examples of the status quo being upturned—events that would've been considered unlikely or even impossible before they occurred, but which of course happened anyway. We try to assign some inevitability through hindsight, but that's a classic bias. So, yes. It could be as bad as it looks. It could be the city's been plunged into a terrible and unforeseen crisis. The point is, we don't know one way or the other. But what we can't afford is to take the chance that things will get better on their own. We simply can't."

Jarsdel looked at Gavin, who now nodded along with Varma's speech. Apparently it had once again found its moorings. Varma glanced at him, then looked back at her audience—left, center, right, center, left.

"I have the feeling you agree. Good. Let's get started."

READING GROUP GUIDE

1. Describe the emotional turmoil Jarsdel faces throughout the narrative. Is he able to overcome any of it by the end?

2. Discuss the dynamic between Jarsdel and Morales. Do they work well together?

3. Explain how Keating and Burken each used their roles at the museum for personal gain. Do you think one of them is worse than the other? Why?

4. Pruitt ends up being a perfect rival for Jarsdel. Outline their similarities and differences.

5. There are many kinds of crime in this book: the bloody massacre in 1854, Baba's cowardice, the senseless murders. Discuss the legacies they leave behind.

6. What was your first impression of the Natty Lads? Did your opinion change throughout the book?

7. Do you think Rostami deserves to know the true

circumstances around her son's death? Baba chooses not to tell her—would you make the same choice?

8. Jarsdel and Baba have a contentious relationship. Why do you think that is? Do you have a similar relationship with a parental figure?

9. Explain the terrible truth behind "King Henry's Pride." How is it tied to the journal and Pruitt Equities?

A CONVERSATION
WITH THE AUTHOR

Pulling Jarsdel out of LA, his home turf, was an interesting choice. Why did you choose Catalina Island as the new setting?

Catalina's very special to me. I do my best writing there, and when I was making the final push on *What Waits for You*, Anna watched the kids and just let me slug away at the manuscript by myself in Avalon. All I did was write and walk and stare out at the ocean, and I started to think how perfect a place it was to set a mystery novel. You've got the proximity to LA, so it's a plausible destination for Tully, and its geography as an island let me indulge a classic trope of the genre. You know—how did the killer do it if he was separated from the victim by water? And how's the isolation from the mainland going to affect the story and the characters? Mostly, though, I was captivated by Avalon's vibe and wanted to see if I could translate it to the page.

When the story opens, Jarsdel is grappling with what one might call an existential crisis. What made you decide to put him through that?

In listening to detectives talk about their job, you get an idea of how painful it can be when you've put so much into a case—all those countless investigative hours, sacrificing time with your loved ones, dealing with the aftermath of the violence—just to have it fall apart. It can make you feel angry and demoralized. I wanted to show that part of Tully's life and in so doing, start him off with a serious loss, which gives him a powerful motive to solve the new case.

The ever-growing stack of dusty cold case files Jarsdel finds himself tackling is disheartening. Was this something you came across in your research with law enforcement?

Yeah, and I don't think Tully's cut out for it. Too impatient, too easily frustrated. The folks I've spoken to who work cold cases are very clear-headed and surprisingly upbeat. They're also able to follow the trajectory of a case over years and years as they work on it, even when new ones come across their desks.

What books are on your bedside table right now?

The Secret History of Magic by Peter Lamont and Jim Steinmeyer, *How Magicians Think* by Joshua Jay, *The Scarlet Plague* by Jack London, and *Entangled Life: How Fungi Make Our Worlds, Change Our Minds & Shape Our Futures* by Merlin Sheldrake.

This story digs into the history of Iran and Jarsdel's family, and how that shapes his relationships with his Baba. What inspired you to write that subplot?

I wanted something that would echo the theme of the main story—that the past may sleep, but it never dies. No matter how long it's been dormant, it can snap awake at any moment and rock us to our foundations. Both Baba and the villain try to avoid the consequences of the past, and neither are successful.

Being a crime writer involves juggling many narrative threads at once. In your writing process, at what point do you know who the killer is?

I thrive under structure—without it, I'm a mess—so I plan all that stuff out in what screenwriters call a beat sheet before I start the first chapter. Outlines can fudge on the side of vagueness, but beat sheets demand the writer catalogue every discrete unit of action from start to finish. I also indicate, in bold, where clues are threaded in so that the mystery plays fair with the audience.

It seems that this story explores the aftermath of terrible things. What, for you, is the takeaway?

I believe the only way for us to make any real progress, both as individuals and as a people, is for there to be a true and honest reckoning with the horrors of history. This is a painful—even agonizing—process but one that's nevertheless essential in the advancement of human compassion and understanding. It's the avoidance of honest confrontation with the past, and the concomitant ignorance that results, that lies at the root of so much suffering. And the confrontation will come anyway, one way or another, so it's best to meet it with courage and open eyes.

ACKNOWLEDGMENTS

You'd be hard-pressed to find a more peaceful, relaxing, and irresistibly charming destination than Avalon. For their hospitality and kindness, I'm grateful to the managers and staff of the Catalina Island Company, the Zane Gray Pueblo Hotel, the Catalina Island Museum, the Avalon Public Library, and the Catalina Island Conservancy. And while Topsides, the Yacht & Fish, and the Dew Drop Inn don't exist, Scoops indeed does, and the author consumed many frozen lemonades while revising this book. It probably goes without saying, but there are no Natty Lads or anything like them on the island.

Due to COVID restrictions, I wasn't able to revisit the Huntington or meet with any of its personnel at the time of writing. Suffice it to say that not a single character appearing in these pages is based on a real person and that the sublime beauty of the grounds and the collection must be experienced to be believed. If you're ever within a hundred miles, give yourself the gift of a visit.

The brilliant Dr. Jonathan Gray returned once more to provide medical expertise, a generosity I abuse with shameless frequency. Police procedure in the manuscript was reviewed for accuracy by my wonderful technical advisor, Det. (Ret.) Richard Bengtson, while additional details were filled in by fellow Rotarian and dear friend,

Lt. Brian South of the Moraga Police Department. Contributing to my understanding of the Iranian émigré experience was Dominic Rains, who provided marvelous brushstrokes of detail.

The atrocities committed against First Nations people of California are documented with scholarly precision in *An American Genocide: The United States and the California Indian Catastrophe, 1846–1873*, by Benjamin Madley, and *When the Great Spirit Died: The Destruction of the California Indians 1850–1860*, by William B. Secrest. Both are excellent; both are heartbreaking. I also learned many new terrible and fascinating things about my state's early history from *Death in California* and *California Justice*, both by David Kulczyk. Further resources include *Catalina Island, A HarborTown History*, by Gayle Baker, *Wild Catalina Island: Natural Secrets and Ecological Triumphs*, by Frank J. Hein and Carlos de la Rosa, and *Chapman Piloting & Seamanship, 68th Edition*. Marine biology questions were answered by Adrienne Wallace, who graciously taught me about algae blooms and how they work.

I'm so very thankful to Poisoned Pen and Dominique Raccah for bringing Tully back for another adventure, and for the privilege of working with the most skilled and passionate folks in the business. These include my editorial duo, Anna Michels and Jenna Jankowski—whose contributions to this manuscript can't be overstated, senior production editor Jessica Thelander, art director Heather VenHuizen, and the marketing team of Molly Waxman, Shauneice Robinson, and Mandy Chahal. In addition to providing her always stellar copyediting services, Sabrina Baskey rescued me from a nasty continuity error.

Gratitude always to my agent, Eve Attermann at WME, along with Sian-Ashleigh Edwards, Sam Birmingham, and Haley Heidemann. Thanks also to my fabulous publicist, Traci Harper, and to the following for their support and encouragement: my wife, Anna; Murshida Conner; Andrew Schneider; Diane Frolov; David Chase; Sarah and Michael Berry; Carol Gray; Joyce T. Nakamoto; and the faculty and staff of the Saint Mary's MFA program—in particular Marilyn Abildskov, Lysley Tenorio, Krista Varela Posell, and Sara Mumolo.

There are so many others I'd like to recognize here—far more than I'm able—so please forgive me if your name does not appear.

Finally, dear reader, it all comes down to you. Thanks for letting me do what I love.

Joseph Schneider
Los Angeles, summer 2021

ABOUT THE AUTHOR

 Joseph Schneider lives with his wife and two children in California. His professional affiliations include the Magic Castle, the Imperial Society of Teachers of Dancing, and the Worshipful Company of Makers of Playing Cards.